STORM
OF
INK
AND
BLOOD

BOOKS BY NISHA J. TULI

THE NIGHTFIRE QUARTET
Heart of Night and Fire
Dance of Stars and Ashes

ARTEFACTS OF OURANOS
Trial of the Sun Queen
Rule of the Aurora King

CURSED CAPTORS
Wicked is the Reaper

To Wake a Kingdom

STORM
OF
INK
AND
BLOOD

NISHA J. TULI

SECOND SKY

Published by Second Sky in 2024

An imprint of Storyfire Ltd.
Carmelite House
50 Victoria Embankment
London EC4Y oDZ
United Kingdom

www.secondskybooks.com

Storyfire Ltd's authorised representative in the EEA is Hachette Ireland
8 Castlecourt Centre
Castleknock Road
Castleknock
Dublin 15 D15 YF6A
Ireland

ISBN: 978-1-83525-214-7
eBook ISBN: 978-1-83525-213-0

To everyone who felt they didn't have a voice but still used it to change the world.

CAST OF CHARACTERS

People you already know

Zarya Rai: Queen of our story and our hearts. The chosen one. Aazheri with six anchors and a prophecy inside a magical stone that's shaking up her life. Yasen's second-best friend.

Yasen Varghese: The one and only. Former commander and soldier in Daragaab's army. Enjoying his freedom from his old life. Emotional support companion and king of our hearts.

(Rabin)dranath Ravana: Zarya's destined magical servant who knows how to treat a woman right. Until he didn't, and now he's in the doghouse. It'll be interesting to see how he gets himself out.

Raja Abishek: King of Andhera, the most powerful Aazheri in Rahajhan, and Zarya's father. Rabin's mentor, which makes things, like, really complicated.

Aishayadiva (Asha) Madan: Zarya's mother, Row's lover, and former queen of Gi'ana. She's been missing for twenty years.

Rani Amrita: Queen of Daragaab. Now a tree and about to give birth. Don't think too much about the details. You don't want to know.

Vikram Ravana: Steward to Rani Amrita and brother to Rabin. About to become a father. Sort of.

Suvanna: Merdeva from the queendom of Matsya. Has water powers and could kick your ass. She's got a thing with Apsara, but she doesn't do commitment.

Apsara: Vidyadhara from the region of Vayuu with powerful ice and wind magic. Definitely does commitment.

Koura: A healer from the region of Svaasthy and powerful wielder of Niramaya—the magic of healing.

Aarav: Gave up his life for Zarya in the fight to save Rani Amrita.

Kindle: Agni from the region of Bhaavana, known for his fire magic and ability to alter emotions in others.

Professor Dhawan: The first villain in our tale. Betrayed everyone to get back into Abishek's good graces, but Zarya offed him. As she should have.

Gopal Ravana: The nawab of Daragaab, powerful rakshasa, father to Vikram and Rabin.

Jasmine Ravana: Third wife of Gopal Ravana, Vikram and Rabin's mother.

People you'll meet soon—skip if you don't want any spoilers

Ajay Chandra: One half of the Chandra twins and supporter of the resistance.

Rania Chandra: The other half of the Chandra twins and supporter of the resistance.

Farida: Vanshaj and girlfriend to Rania. Leader of the resistance.

Dishani Madan: Zarya's half-sister and oldest of the Madan siblings.

Kabir Madan: King consort and former husband to Asha.

Advika Madan: Zarya's half-sister.

Miraan Madan: Zarya's half-brother. Oldest brother. Advisor and right hand to his sister Dishani.

Talin Madan: Zarya's half-brother. Youngest of the Madans.

Vikas: Vanshaj member of the resistance.

Ekaja: Commander of Raja Abishek's army. The only female commander in Rahajhan.

Rahajhan: Name of the main continent, comprised of seven main regions: Daragaab, Svaasthy, Vayuu, Gi'ana, Andhera, Bhaavana, and Matsya.

Gi'ana: The queendom of knowledge and one of two regions that are home to the Aazheri. Located on the western shore bordering the Saaya.

Ishaan: Capital city of Gi'ana. Located inland, surrounded by forests and distant mountains.

Andhera: Northern kingdom and the second region known as the home of the Aazheri. Home of Raja Abishek.

Saaya: Unceded territory located between Gi'ana and Andhera. Uninhabitable and constantly under dispute between the two regions thanks to its abandoned diamond mines.

Daragaab: Queendom of earth magic, lies in the southeast corner of the continent and is bordered by the Dakhani Sea to the south and the Nila Hara Sea to the east.

Dharati: The capital city of Daragaab. Home to the Jai Palace.

Pathara Vala Mountains: Enormous mountain range in the northeast corner of the continent bordering Andhera and parts of Gi'ana.

Matsya: The underwater queendom of water magic. Lies in the depths of the Dakhani Sea.

Vayuu: The mountain kingdom of air and wind magic, residing high in the Pathara Vala Mountains.

Bhaavana: The kingdom of love and passion, known for fire magic. Located in the northwest quadrant of Rahajhan, east of Gi'ana.

Svaasthy: The queendom of spirit magic and Niramaya and the power of healing. A land of desert sands and residing on the southwestern shore.

Dakhani Sea: Southern ocean of Rahajhan.

Nila Hara Sea: Eastern ocean of Rahajhan.

Ranpur Island: Small island on the southern coast of Daragaab and Rahajhan.

Premyiv: City located on Ranpur Island.

Other Creatures and Magical Things

Aazheri: Mage-like beings who use anchors that represent each element to create magic: fire, earth, air, water, and spirit. There is a sixth anchor known as the darkness.

Vanshaj: The descendants of the Ashvin twins, relegated to positions of servitude and forbidden from using their magic by the application of a magical ring of tattooed stars around their necks.

Paramadhar: A magical servant destined for a specific Aazheri to help control and amplify their magic, protect them, and heal them.

Masatara: The name for the Aazheri portion of the paramadhar bond.

Bandhan: Official name of the binding that joins the masatara to the paramadhar.

Jadugara: Ancient sect of Aazheri hailing from Gi'ana. Responsible for applying the vanshaj star collars.

The Ashvin twins: Two powerful Aazheri brothers who used the darkness to bring misery upon Rahajhan and were banished away.

Chiranjivi: Powerful beings that represent each region of Rahajhan—kind of like the Avengers.

Vidyadhara: Winged beings from the region of Vayuu, capable of wind magic.

Merdeva: Beings of water magic who come from Matsya.

Agni: Beings of fire magic from Bhaavana.

Niramaya healers: Beings from Svaasthy who use spirit to heal.

Rakshasa: Blood-drinking beings who use earth magic. Some can shapeshift into animals.

Khada: Elite force of soldiers whose job is to guard the wall around Dharati against the blight.

Fairies: Colorful beings with various skin and hair tones and known for their beauty.

Peri: Miniature versions of fairies.

Bayangoma: Magical birds that live in secret groves and bestow knowledge on those who are worthy in exchange for a drop of blood willingly given.

Naga: Snakes that live in the swamp, white and gelatinous and without eyes.

Ajakava: Giant bronzed scorpions.

Nairrata: Demon army that once did the bidding of the Ashvin twins.

Kala-hamsa: Red-feathered birds of varying size that are birthed from marble-like eggs that can hatch in the middle of the sky.

Dakini: Bipedal demons with black hides, big teeth, and long claws.

ONE

Zarya wedged the palm-sized explosive between two wooden slats, pinching the wick to ensure it stood straight. Beams of silver moonlight filtered in through high, smudged windows, illuminating rows and rows of stoppered glass bottles filled with midnight-black ink.

More bottles covered tables and shelves in neat, orderly rows like soldiers standing at attention, while others were packed in padded wooden crates stacked against every wall of the seven-story warehouse.

She worked quickly on the third-level mezzanine, placing more explosives at strategic points. Below her giant vats of ink bubbled on the sprawling main floor, churning up a bitter odor tainted with the edges of something rotten and sinister.

The building housed Rahajhan's main supply of ink used to collar the vanshaj into servitude. Located within the Siahi District in the city of Ishaan, the capital of Gi'ana, it was both a forgotten and significant place.

Forgotten because so many things related to the vanshaj

were shoved into this dilapidated corner of the city to be cast aside where no one would be forced to look upon the injustice committed against an entire group of innocent people for a millennium.

Significant because without this building, control over the vanshaj would be in jeopardy, and with any luck, eradicated entirely.

Every day hundreds of men and women were forced to stand at the conveyor belts, filling tiny glass jars with shadowy ink and stoppering them with pieces of cork before carefully placing them in wooden crates to be shipped all over the continent.

Thin arms stirred the massive vats surrounded by torches sparking with black flames, which were said to be the source of the magic that infused the ink. The flames generated noxious fumes that left the workers dizzy and often disoriented, making their working conditions untenable.

The magical fire was a creation of the Jadugara, an ancient sect of Aazheri native to Gi'ana, and the architects of infusing the ink with the binding enchantment. They added insult to injury when every worker in this warehouse was vanshaj, forcing them to act as unwilling cogs in the machine keeping them bound within their chains.

A silhouette passed overhead, and Zarya caught the telltale silver flash of Yasen's hair reflecting in the dim light. He stopped, carefully placing a small explosive on a shelf before prowling along the walkway. They had only a few more minutes before the city watch would inevitably circle their way to this end of the warehouse on their nightly rounds.

At various points around the building, other members of the vanshaj resistance were placing tiny explosives at designated locations throughout the warehouse, including the ramparts overhead. They had to make this count. The goal: ensure it would take months before anyone could even think about resurrecting this place again.

Zarya descended a flight of stairs, crossed the floor, and nestled more explosives around the vats' bases until she had run through her entire supply. She then headed for a long shelf at the far end of the room, wedging more of the tiny bombs between the supports.

Her arm brushed a bottle, and it wobbled precariously, threatening to tip. Thanks to years of combat training, her lightning-quick reflexes snatched it mid-descent right before it smashed at her feet. As her fingers closed around the vessel, a strange tingling traveled up her arm and spread through her chest, kicking up her pulse. She stared at it, trying to parse out the peculiar sensation, when a noise drew her attention up. Yasen leaped down from a high platform, light on his feet, before he jogged down the stairs to where Zarya waited.

"All finished?" he asked in a low voice.

"Almost." She grabbed a crate sitting near her feet and began gently packing it with bottles. While Yasen waited for her to finish, he watched the shadows moving above before they also made their way to the main floor and then melted out of the exits.

"Hurry up," Yasen whispered.

Zarya nestled the last few bottles into the crate. "Okay, let's go."

"Hey!" came a deep male voice breaking through the silence. "Stop! What are you doing in here?"

Yasen and Zarya whipped around to find two members of the city watch wearing fitted black jackets set with large square pockets, black pants, and tall black boots, both with a talwar already gripped in their hands. Zarya looked left and right, noting the sinister glint of moonlight off their blades. They were cornered in an alcove, and their only exit was through the now-blocked path.

Yasen withdrew the blade at his hip, and though his posture remained casual, Zarya knew he was coiled to strike.

"We were just leaving," he said. "Nothing to see here."

The guard on the left bared his teeth. "In the name of the royal family, you are under arrest. It is forbidden to enter these walls without permission from the Jadugara."

"Oh?" Yasen asked. "Is that all you need? I know I have our letter somewhere."

He made a show of patting his pockets while Zarya scanned their surroundings for an escape route.

The guards advanced, and Yasen stretched out a protective arm as he shuffled Zarya back, crowding them against the shelves while she clutched the crate in her hands.

She *could* use magic, but she refused to abandon the bottles, nor did she want to draw any more attention to their presence. It was a miracle that more of the dozens of city watch circling the building hadn't also come to investigate.

A moment later, a shrill whistle mimicking a mynah's call sounded in a rhythmic pattern—two short blasts followed by a long one. That was the signal. Yasen's and Zarya's gazes met, understanding they were out of time. Other resistance members planned to light the wicks in a matter of seconds, but they wouldn't realize Zarya and Yasen were trapped inside.

The guards' foreheads furrowed in confusion, understandably wondering why a mynah would be anywhere in this area.

"Run," Yasen said, and without further warning, they barreled towards the guards, catching them by surprise. Yasen swung his blade, slashing across one guard's chest before he collapsed with a cry.

The other grabbed Zarya's arm as she passed, causing her to lose her grip on the crate. She screamed as it tumbled from her hands, the bottles shattering with a crash. Black ink spread across the concrete, soaking into the hem of her cloak.

Yasen swung a fist, connecting it with the guard's cheek and dropping him to the floor with a thud.

"No, no, no," Zarya repeated as she fell to her knees, sifting through the remnants while trying to avoid shards of broken glass.

"Zee! We have to go!" Yasen snapped as he grabbed her elbow.

Another shrill cry pierced the air, and a moment later, dozens of fireballs arced through the windows, catching the wicks. Yasen yanked on her arm again, hauling her to her feet.

"The ink!" she screamed.

"Leave it!" He tugged her towards the entrance. As they passed a worktable, she reached out to swipe two bottles with a soft clink, clutching them in her sweating palm.

They burst into the street, where flames were already licking at the windows. They'd designed the bombs to burn at a steady rate, giving everyone time to clear the area. They now had less than three minutes to find safety.

Spinning around to face the building, Zarya pulled on her fire anchor before a flame appeared hovering above her palm. She still had to finish her part. She blew on the flame as it soared through a third-floor window, catching on a wick.

Each tiny explosive had enough power to level a small house. Dozens of them working together would easily flatten this building.

Hopefully.

"It's done," she said.

"Then let's move," Yasen replied, scanning the street for any signs of the watch. "We're clear. Let's go."

They clasped hands and raced through the shadows, making their way towards the neighboring Rasoi District.

They'd been careful to contain the strength of the blast within the currently deserted Siahi District that emptied of life once the vanshaj finished their shifts for the day, minus the watch. She would feel no remorse for taking those lives. These men willingly chose their profession. In fact, most reveled in the power and prestige of the position, and now they would feel the consequences of their callous choices.

But their efforts would be tainted if they killed innocent bystanders in the process. Zarya hoped their calculations had been accurate. However, she couldn't help thinking that, truly, no one in this queendom was innocent—not as long as they continued to turn a blind eye to the vanshaj.

She will be the one to free them all.

The prophecy Zarya had heard in her mother's necklace all those months ago was a constant whisper filtering through her thoughts. Those words literally meant life or death. She'd made them a part of her, as though they'd also been inked into her skin with powerful, ancient magic.

Before abandoning the safety of the shadows, Zarya and Yasen removed their cloaks and tossed them into a large rubbish bin against the wall of a nearby building.

Underneath, Zarya wore an emerald-green salwar kameez embellished with silver beading, while Yasen wore a bright blue kurta and mustard-yellow pants. She hoped no one would notice the ink that had soaked through her cloak to stain her knees. Being careful to wipe their shoes dry of evidence, they linked their arms and rounded the corner, emerging into the light.

A bustling street stretched ahead of them, lined with three- and four-story buildings made of white stone and marble, gilded with ornate silver and gold window frames. They passed tall iron streetlamps molded with curling vines and flowers, all flickering with orange flames now that the sun had set.

Hopefully, they resembled an ordinary couple heading out to dine on one of the various patios that lined the street. They passed a busy establishment with tables covered in crisp white linen and topped with tall golden vases sprouting with delicate white feathers. Strings of lights gave everything a soft, merry glow.

Zarya and Yasen picked up their pace, attempting to put as much distance between them and the warehouse as possible. She cast one last look back before they lost themselves in a sea of a thousand faces.

A few seconds later, the explosion ripped through the night.

TWO

Zarya and Yasen stopped and turned around—partly because it would have been suspicious otherwise and partly to take in the aftermath. A cloud of dust and fire billowed across the sky, backdropped by Ishaan's screams of panic and surprise.

Their gazes met, and they allowed themselves a small, triumphant smile before they turned and continued walking, heads down and hands linked as if they were simply attempting to flee the chaos.

It wouldn't do to linger here for long. The royal soldiers would soon arrive and start asking questions. Zarya and Yasen hoped they'd blended in well enough for no one to remember they'd been anywhere nearby.

Zarya's heart pounded with adrenaline as they wound through progressively less crowded streets. After months of careful planning and plotting, they'd delivered a crushing blow to the queendom of Gi'ana and scored a much-needed victory for the rebellion.

Finally, they turned a corner towards the four-story haveli that had been their home for the past three months. They'd rented the top floor, and this was where their fellow resistance members would convene once it was safe.

Checking one last time to ensure no one had followed, Zarya and Yasen entered the building made of the same creamy white marble as most of Ishaan's homes and bounded up the spiral stairs. When they reached the top landing, they heard the low drone of their guests waiting inside.

Zarya opened the door and smiled at the sight of dozens of Aazheri and vanshaj filling their flat. It was generously sized, with an ample living space in the center, perfect for entertaining. To the right was a kitchen with white wooden cabinets and a small glass table where Zarya and Yasen ate their meals. On the opposite side were a series of doors leading to three separate bedrooms, and directly ahead was a wall of windows that opened onto a white stone balcony.

Some of their friends converged in the kitchen, bottles of beer and glasses of wine in their hands. Others lounged in the large sunken living room, propped up against thick cushions scattered on a bank of low divans and across the floor.

This was the vanshaj rebellion, known as the Rising Phoenix.

Ajay Chandra looked over with a wide grin as they entered. Short black hair framed a face made for royalty. Refined and elegant with a straight nose and high cheekbones, he looked fit for the cover of one of her romance novels. Dark brown eyes flecked with silver and filled with emotion regarded Zarya with admiration. Next to him stood his twin sister Rania, her same regal features sparkling with excitement.

They made up the second tier of the rebellion's leadership and were both powerful Aazheri who had been working for years to bring about freedom for the vanshaj with little success.

Until tonight.

Ajay raced over to where Zarya stood, wrapping his arms

around her, lifting her into a warm hug, and then placing her back on her feet before clapping Yasen on the back.

"We did it!" Ajay said. Rania hugged Zarya tightly as they all congratulated one another.

"Did you see it?" Zarya asked, accepting a glass of sparkling wine from a passerby. It was spectacular."

Ajay and Rania had also been amongst the dozen rebels inside the warehouse, setting the bombs and then waiting for the signal.

"A group of city watch nearly caught us," Ajay said, raising a glass. "But *they* are no longer our problem."

"Why are you covered in ink?" Rania asked, scrutinizing the knees of Zarya's pants and noting the discoloration staining her fingers.

"We ran into a little trouble," Yasen explained while the twins' eyebrows climbed up their foreheads.

"Everything was under control," Zarya said with a wave of her inky hand.

That wasn't entirely true, but they'd gotten lucky. She reached into her pocket. "But I only managed to swipe two bottles of ink."

Rania looked at them and then at Zarya, her eyebrows knitting. Neither sibling understood what Zarya planned to do, but they hadn't asked too many questions so far. Ever since she'd met Meera, the vanshaj soldier in Dharati, Zarya had wondered if her magic was connected to their tattoos or possibly the ink it was created with.

But the substance was highly regulated and controlled thanks to the Jadugara, and sabotaging the factory had been the perfect opportunity to get her hands on a few bottles.

She knew it was only a matter of time before Ajay and Rania began questioning her further, and she was worried about how they would react once they learned the truth.

"Really, we were fine," Zarya said to Ajay again. "It was a close call, but we knew this was dangerous."

"Don't worry," Yasen said, wrapping an arm around Zarya's shoulders. "I took care of those guards."

"I mean, he did," she said. "Even if he's not all that humble about it."

"Always here to save your ass, Zee."

She rolled her eyes as Ajay nodded and then turned to face the room, again raising his glass high as silence fell over the crowd.

"A toast," Ajay said, his voice proud and strong. "After years of disappointment, the Rising Phoenix has dealt a fatal blow to the kingdoms and queendoms of Rahajhan and their inhumane practice of enslaving the vanshaj. Without the continent's main source of ink, they will be prevented from branding babies barely out of their mothers' wombs for a very long time!"

A round of cheers and clinking glasses circled through the room as Zarya watched Rania embrace her girlfriend, Farida, whose ring of tattooed stars stood out in contrast to her brown skin.

The two had met four years earlier in a tavern where Farida had worked as a server. The women had struck up a conversation, and Rania claimed she'd fallen in love that very night. After months of visiting the tavern to be in her company, Rania offered to purchase Farida's servitude from the tavern owner for more than twice the going rate.

The twins' high-brow looks came by them honestly as the offspring of one of the wealthiest noble families in Gi'ana. The tavern owner couldn't say no, and Rania had effectively freed Farida from the insult of her servitude, but the collar of stars around her neck acted as an ever-constant reminder.

With Farida at the helm, the trio had begun to stir up a quiet resistance, eventually forming a council comprised of several vanshaj members. Significant decisions and necessary consultation went through them via Farida. The council preferred to remain anonymous for their safety, with their identities only known to Farida.

Rania and Farida also wished to wed, but the laws of Rahajhan forbade it.

The Chandras' parents had no idea what their children were getting up to or that they had initially funded large portions of the rebellion. But Ajay and Rania were cut off when they couldn't explain what they were doing with all that money. Their parents were sure they were dealing with something illegal, and they technically weren't far off the mark.

Just when the twins believed their cause was lost, a mysterious and very wealthy benefactor appeared at the most opportune moment. No one had any clue about who was sending the money, but it always arrived with a note stating it was to be used in aiding the vanshaj rebellion in whatever manner they saw fit.

After Ajay's toast, the conversation resumed as food was brought in from a restaurant owner who also supported their cause. They had friends throughout the city acting as ancillary members without 'official' ties to the resistance. Though it had been a small group at first, it was steadily growing as the months and years passed.

Great steaming platters of bright chicken makhani, bowls of sunny spiced saffron rice, and towers of buttery roti crowded the large kitchen table, the rich aromas filling the air.

The mood was high as plates were passed around, and the din rose with the excited chatter of a job well done.

Zarya took her glass of wine and walked outside to the wide balcony that wrapped around the apartment, surprised to find it empty. While she was pleased about the mission's success, her joy was somewhat dampened by the fact that, after all these months, she still hadn't found a way to contact her family—the Madan siblings—in the royal palace.

Only Yasen knew who her mother had been, and she wanted to keep it that way for now. The Madans were poorly regarded amongst the resistance due to their archaic laws and callous treatment of the vanshaj.

Zarya had clung to a vague hope that speaking with them wouldn't be this complicated, but after months of petitioning to see the carefully guarded royals, she was no closer than she'd been when she'd left Daragaab with Yasen. She was wary of revealing her origins without understanding what manner of welcome she might receive, and thus, her requests were lost in a sea of other citizens' needs and demands.

She wasn't sure what she'd say to them, anyway: *Hello, I'm your half-sister from our mother's prophecy, and I've been working to undermine you ever since I arrived in Ishaan?*

Zarya turned at the sound of someone approaching as Ajay came to stand next to her.

"It's quite a victory," he said, staring into the distance.

"You should all be very proud," she answered, and he turned to give her a soft smile.

"Have you made any progress on the tattoos? What do you need the ink for, exactly?"

She shook her head. For months, Zarya had considered how she might use her magic to break the enchantment bound inside the vanshaj tattoos, but so far, she had come up empty. Some deep-seated premonition told her the sixth anchor was the key.

No one else knew this secret, either—not even Yasen—but she *had* told the others that she felt something whenever she touched the markings.

She will be the one to free them all.

It had to be connected.

"I just have a... hunch," Zarya said. "If magic binds them, then magic can surely undo it."

He shook his head. "I know you've said that before, but

others have tried before—why do you think you'll succeed where so many have failed? I don't mean to doubt you—"

"No," Zarya said, interrupting him. "You're right to question me. I realize we haven't known one another long, but I'm asking you to entertain this mystery until I can give you a more sufficient answer. I don't want to get anyone's hopes up."

Ajay nodded, turning to look out over the city. "Very well."

She folded her arms as they watched a plume of black smoke hovering in the sky. His arm brushed against hers, and she stole a glance at his face, noting the carved lines of his rather pleasing profile.

She'd be lying if she hadn't considered their relationship beyond mere friendship. But they *were* friends, and she was still nursing a broken heart.

"I'll try some things with the ink first thing tomorrow," she said, "I want to speak with Farida again if she's willing."

"Sounds good," Ajay said. "I think I'll go home and get some sleep."

"You don't want to stay and celebrate?"

He shook his head. "I'm quite tired. This has all been very draining." He gestured vaguely out over Ishaan, where the glint of hundreds of shiny domed rooftops reflected in the moonlight.

Then he took her hand and leaned down to press his mouth to the back of it.

"Good night," he said before he disappeared through the doorway.

After he was gone, she sank to the floor, threading her legs through the railings. She liked the sensation of dangling over a precipice, the world spinning below her. Ishaan sat inland, far from the sea, and she missed the feel of the ocean breeze and watching the water stretch for miles, where she could imagine an entire universe waiting on the other side.

"So you blue-balled Ajay again, I see?"

Zarya turned and snorted. Yasen leaned against the doorway, his arms crossed and a dark grey eyebrow lifted.

"Shut up."

He sat down, allowing his long legs to dangle between the bars beside hers. "Come on. I think you'd look good together."

She sighed and pressed her forehead to a bar.

"Maybe. I just can't seem to let go..."

"I don't really get it," Yasen said. "You've been with other men. You seem to be enjoying yourself. Why *not* Ajay?"

"Those men don't *mean* anything. It's just fun. It's just sex. Until I have Rabin out of my system, it wouldn't be fair."

He nodded. "I think I get that. So why can't you let go?"

"I don't know. Part of me wants to hear him out and hopes that he didn't deceive me with ill intentions. But every time I think about it, I just remember how I was lied to my entire life. And he *knew* that, and he did it anyway. I thought he was a clean slate, but he was just like all of them. It's over, and that's for the best."

"But?" he asked, sensing the hesitation in her voice.

"I miss him so much. What I felt for him... I don't know; it's not like anything I can describe. I think about him all the time, and I'm not sure what to do."

Yasen nodded. "So, why are we here, then? Why are *you* here? Go and find him."

She ran her tongue over her top teeth as she stared ahead. "I don't know where he is. I fear he went back to Raja Abishek after I left Daragaab. I never got the sense that he wanted to remain in Dharati. And I'm not sure it's safe for me. How loyal is he really to my father?"

"Rabin wouldn't let anything happen to you. You know that."

She tipped her face towards him. "What makes you so sure he could stop him?"

Yasen shrugged, taking a sip of his drink, the ice clinking softly in his glass. "Can't you call up one of those dream things and talk to him?"

"If only it worked like that," Zarya said. "I've never known how to control them. And maybe that's also for the best. Maybe this ache inside me will go away with enough time and distance."

The truth was that Zarya had gone to sleep every night for the past three months, hoping to enter the dream forest. Every morning, she woke up more and more dejected, wondering if she'd ever see him again or if whatever the gods had once planned for Zarya and Rabin was no longer in their sights.

All those speculations about him being her paramadhar had clearly been pointless.

"Do you forgive him?" Yasen asked.

Zarya chewed on her bottom lip and thought hard about her answer. "I don't. I'm still angry. And though I owe him nothing, I also kind of want to see him and give him the chance to explain." She let out a huff of air. "Maybe things were easier when I lived in Row's cottage."

"Sure, except I'm pretty sure you would have killed both Row and Aarav by now," Yasen said with a smirk.

"You're probably right," Zarya replied, laughing.

She thought often about Aarav and the sacrifice he'd made. He'd left a hole in her heart she hadn't expected. As for Row, they wrote to each other often, and she filled him in on what they'd been doing since arriving in Gi'ana. While he warned her to be cautious, he also agreed with the cause they were fighting.

"So, what are you planning to do?" Yasen asked.

"I don't know," Zarya replied. "Pretend I'm okay and distract myself with everything else?"

Yasen's laugh was low and dark. "Oh, Zee, how you've grown since I rescued you from the swamp."

"You didn't rescue me. How dare you?"

He smiled, and she reached out, grabbing his hand and squeezing it.

Then they stared across the horizon as they both watched a plume of smoke curl gently against the starry night sky.

THREE

TWO MONTHS AGO

Kingdom of Andhera

The mountains of Andhera loomed in the distance as Rabin soared over the landscape, his chest tightening at the sight. Though he hadn't been away long, this place had become home when his own had rejected him so many years ago.

Banking left, his wings snapped against the frigid atmosphere, and he closed his eyes as a blast of wind slipped over his scales, savoring its fresh bite after the heat and humidity of Dharati. There were days when the stinging cold of the north made him wish for the warm, sandy beaches of the south, but there was also something purifying about the icy air freezing in his lungs.

When Andhera's sprawling castle—made of dark stone forged from the Pathara Vala mountains—came into view, he arrowed down, swooping over the high towers and the surrounding city. With his keen eyesight, he spied the sentries stationed on the ramparts, watching him with cautious looks. Even after all these years, very few were used to him. Shapeshifters were uncommon enough, but a dragon was something most of these northern people had only heard about in story books.

With a soft thump, his feet hit the stones of a tall tower, wide enough to accommodate his size, before he dissolved into black smoke, shifting back into his rakshasa form. He paused on the high platform, taking in his surroundings: the soaring mountains blanketed with snow and the miles of evergreens spreading in every direction. He inhaled a deep breath of clean air, welcoming the chill snaking down the back of his neck.

He wasn't properly dressed for this climate, and already the cold nipped at the tips of his ears and fingers. But it made him feel *something* at least. Turning on his heel, he strode towards the castle, entering through a door, and wound his way down the narrow staircase, planning to see Abishek first. The king of Andhera would expect an update on Rabin's activities in Daragaab.

After the events with the blight and Dhawan's betrayal, he'd remained in Dharati to offer whatever assistance he could to Vikram, but his brother wanted nothing to do with him. He'd made it clear Rabin was not welcome in the Jai Palace, and he could take the hint. Though Rabin's actions were the reason for their strained relationship, he hoped they could find a way to work past this somehow.

Rabin understood he'd condemned his brother to an unwelcome fate as the steward of Daragaab, but how could Vikram have expected him to remain in Dharati when he'd suffered so much at their father's hand? Gopal had never paid much attention to Vikram, but at least he hadn't beaten the shit out of him for half of his life. Rabin knew he had bridges to mend with his brother but also refused to feel guilty for choosing himself when he'd been given no alternative.

After Vikram had forbidden Rabin from going anywhere near Zarya, he realized it was time to put some distance between them lest he be tempted to snap his brother's neck.

Besides, the only person in Daragaab who cared about him was his mother. Though she also bore no love for her husband, she was at least comfortable enough and surrounded by friends. She didn't really need him, and Rabin had no place there. In this northern kingdom, he'd finally found somewhere to belong.

He entered a long hallway lined with thick scarlet rugs, the dark stone walls hung with intricate woven tapestries. A servant wearing a simple black sari passed him, bowing her head and staring at her feet as he passed. Here, they were all scared of him, too, but after a lifetime of being shamed for his nature, he was learning not to hide who he was any longer.

Stalking through the castle, he approached Abishek's wing and nodded to the sentries posted outside. They were a bit more accustomed to his presence, and Rabin was one of the few people in the king's circle permitted entry without question. The only other people on that list included Abishek's personal mystic, Kishore, and Ekaja, Abishek's army commander and Rabin's only real friend.

"He's in his workroom," a guard said, and Rabin nodded his thanks.

He entered another long hall lined with wooden paneling engraved with complex enamel art along its length, the bright colors directly contrasting the monotone palette of greys and whites of the snow-capped mountains surrounding them.

He knocked on the door with a sharp rap and waited.

"Enter," came a voice, and he swung the door open to reveal Abishek's enormous workroom, which served as part library and part refuge. The king was obsessed with knowledge and research, and the high walls were lined with shelves stuffed full of thousands of books, most of which he'd apparently read at some point.

A large window opened to a view of the mountains, and at the far end was a series of worktables covered in an array of glass vials and bottles, along with scales and a small cauldron where he conducted much of his experimentation. No one knew more about magic in Rahajhan—of every variety—than Raja Abishek.

"You've returned," he said from his workbench, where he was mixing ingredients into a bowl.

"Happy to be home," Rabin said and gave him a quick bow.

"You've been missed."

Rabin wasn't sure how to respond to that. Had anyone ever missed him before?

"Are you hungry?" Abishek asked with a wave. Next to him sat a large platter of food—roti and channa, along with a bowl of raita—and a pitcher of water floating with ice.

"I'm good, thank you," he said.

"Then have a seat. Tell me everything. Did you uncover who your mysterious dream woman is?"

Rabin pulled up a stool and sat across from the king. He folded his hands on the table and took a deep breath. "I did."

Abishek cocked his head, placing the instrument in his hand on the workbench and offering Rabin his full attention, perhaps sensing Rabin's inner conflict.

"And? Who is she?"

This is where Rabin hesitated. He'd told Zarya he wouldn't reveal her existence until she was ready, but he would need Abishek's help if there was any chance of convincing her to hear him out.

"You're keeping something from me?" Abishek asked. The question was pointed and a little cold. He wielded a firm grip on his inner circle and demanded obedience in everything. Of course, Abishek would read the truth in him, anyway.

The king had gifts and abilities Rabin couldn't even begin to comprehend, and given the king's expression, he didn't know how he'd ever planned to keep this secret in the first place. That had always been a fool's hope. A promise offered in a desperate attempt to regain Zarya's trust.

"I have many things to tell you," Rabin said, already wondering how he'd beg her forgiveness for this added transgression. "Of significance."

"Such as?" Abishek asked.

"The woman in my dreams was... *is*... your daughter."

A beat of surprised silence filled the room before Abishek shook his head. "My daughter? I don't understand."

Rabin opened his mouth and then closed it before sucking in another deep breath that did little to settle the churning in his gut. "I'm not sure I do, either, but she isn't only connected to me. A thread binds her to you as well."

"I don't have a daughter," Abishek replied, though his tone suggested he was open to being convinced otherwise.

Rabin peered at his mentor, studying his face for any hints of recognition or deception. Any signs the claims Row had made were the truth. Rabin trusted Abishek, but he would also never do anything to endanger Zarya. "You didn't know about her?"

Abishek blinked in confusion. "Of course I don't—please explain the meaning of this."

Rabin nodded and shared the details of Row's return to Dharati and his story about the queen of Gi'ana. Of what he'd done to protect Zarya by hiding her on the shore. When Rabin finished speaking, Abishek pondered in thoughtful silence for a long minute.

"This is..." He ran a hand over his head, brushing back dark hair that fell to his shoulders in soft waves. The finest lines bracketed his eyes and mouth, and he appeared like a mortal man in his early forties, though he'd lived through many turbulent centuries on this plane. "I'm speechless." He looked at Rabin, blinking heavily. "Tell me what else happened."

Rabin then recounted the events during his return to his homeland, including the confrontation with Vikram and his father and what Dhawan had done to try and earn his way back into Abishek's fold.

The king wrinkled his nose at the mention of the traitorous old Aazheri. "That little worm never had a chance. There was nothing he could do to earn my favor."

"Well, he's dead now, so it's no longer your concern."

"How?" Abishek asked as a wicked light entered his eyes. "I hope the cranky old shit received a suitably wretched ending."

Rabin arched a brow. "Your daughter killed him. A sword through the neck."

The king's face stretched into a pleased sort of smile. "Did she?"

Rabin nodded, and Abishek blinked heavily again before tilting his head, a softer smile turning up the corner of his mouth. "And what is Zarya like?"

Rabin hesitated before he continued. He hadn't only remained in Daragaab to help his brother—he had also hoped he could convince Zarya to hear him out. To understand that while he'd made a mistake in lying to her, he hadn't done so because he'd meant her harm. But she'd left, and Row refused to tell him where she'd gone, nor would he speak to Rabin at all other than to repeat he was not welcome before slamming the door in his face.

Of course, he'd guessed she'd fled to Gi'ana and had taken Yasen with her because he, too, had disappeared. And though he'd wanted to fly straight there, he was resisting the urge to unceremoniously barge into her life. It would do no good to force his presence on her. Zarya wasn't the type to be swayed until she was ready, which was why he had to *talk* to her.

"She's... absolutely ferocious," Rabin finally answered after a long pause.

Abishek smiled. "I would assume so of any daughter of mine." He leaned forward. "And her magic?"

"Powerful," Rabin said. "The charm you gave me to free her from the binding worked as well as we hoped."

"This binding that was supposedly placed by her mother? By Asha?"

"Yes."

"Because she believed I wanted to harm Zarya?" Abishek confirmed.

"Also yes."

Abishek sighed and ran a hand down his face, clearly frustrated by this knowledge.

When Row had shared the story of Zarya and her mother and her father, it had taken all Rabin's willpower not to jump in and counter Row's claims, including the absurd notion the king of Andhera would plot to steal his own daughter's magic. He had more than enough magic of his own.

"I see," Abishek said after Rabin finished explaining. "After all these years, the prophecy has finally been fulfilled." He shook his head. "And Row's infatuation with Asha prejudiced him against me. I cannot blame him for believing the words of the woman he loved, but I also cannot pretend it doesn't sting after all the years we spent together."

"It's a lie, then?" Rabin asked. He felt guilty for the question but also wanted to be sure. He wouldn't ever willingly put Zarya in danger. He'd meant everything he'd told her, even if it had come too late. Something he'd regret forever.

"Do you believe I'd harm my own child?" Abishek asked. "I'd only wish to know her. I don't know why her mother believed this of me, but it weighs on my heart." Abishek folded his hands and peered at Rabin. "I would never hurt her."

"Yes," he said. "Sorry. I just..."

"It's fine." He waved a hand. "You are right to always question things. Only fools believe whatever they're told."

"Right," Rabin said, his tense shoulders easing.

Abishek reached for his water and took a sip while Rabin allowed him to absorb the heaviness of these secrets.

"Something else weighs on your mind?" Abishek asked a moment later, ever perceptive of everyone and everything around him. "Where is she now?"

Rabin hesitated again, wondering how much to reveal. Should he explain his feelings for Zarya? That they'd quickly turned from fascination to so much more? That from the first moment he'd seen her, he'd felt something that made his entire body sing with the promise of their future? Could he hide this secret, either?

She had been a stranger when he'd first told Abishek about the woman walking in his dreams, but now... he wasn't sure how to explain what he felt. He doubted a father would want to hear about the nights of passion they'd shared. So Rabin decided to keep that aspect of their relationship to himself for now. Assuming it was possible to keep anything from Abishek for long. At least he would until he could convince Zarya to listen to him. But first, he had to find her and he'd need the king's help for that.

"I'm not sure," Rabin said. "We parted ways. I wasn't entirely forthright about my relationship with you, and when she found out, she believed I meant her harm, too."

"Because of what Row told her?"

Rabin nodded and rubbed his hands against his thighs in a nervous gesture. "Have you ever heard the term 'paramadhar'?" he asked, and Abishek's thick, dark eyebrows drew together.

"I have," he said. "But they are very rare." He paused for a split second before adding, "The dreams."

"Yes," Rabin said. "She was in possession of a notebook that once belonged to you. It talked about paramadhar, and she believed we might be connected."

"A notebook of mine?"

"Apparently, Row took it from Rani Aishayadiva, believing it to be hers."

The groove between Abishek's eyes deepened. "Did she mention anything else she'd found in it?"

"Only that the Jai Tree was the seal holding in the darkness. That was how we knew Dhawan had double-crossed us."

Again, Abishek appeared puzzled, but he gestured for Rabin to continue.

"I was wondering if there was some way to control the visions?" Rabin asked. "Could I summon her to the forest?"

Abishek scanned the many shelves filling the room. "I'm sure there's something that may help."

"I want to see her again," Rabin confessed. "I'd like to apologize for deceiving her, and if I can talk to her again, then maybe I can convince her to come to Andhera and meet you."

Abishek studied Rabin from head to toe, giving him a piercing look that made Rabin wonder if he already suspected the truth about his feelings for Zarya.

"I would like that very much," he said after a moment.

Rabin's fist clenched against the table, a twist of guilt burning in the back of his throat for deceiving his mentor.

"So you'll help me find her?"

"Of course, my son. Anything you need. Let's bring Zarya home."

FOUR

PRESENT DAY

City of Ishaan

The morning after the factory explosion, Zarya made her way towards the Chandras' flat. She inhaled the scent of smoke still hanging in the air like a reckoning. Flakes of ash drifted from the sky, settling gently on her clothes and hair. Wild theories were already circulating about what had caused the blast, but most understood it was the work of the Rising Phoenix.

Despite many rumors, the royal family had always claimed the resistance was a myth, doing everything they could to deny their existence. In secret, they'd tried to root them out, but the Phoenix had been careful, operating quietly in the background, slowly drumming up support. Yesterday, they'd finally stepped into the light, declaring their bloody intentions, but they all knew this act couldn't go unchallenged.

Ishaan awoke with the sun each morning except on Sundays, when everyone lingered inside their homes until noon, enjoying a slow, leisurely breakfast and time with their families. Since it was the middle of the week, the streets were already alive with activity. Horse-drawn carriages that resembled wide black lanterns bumped over the cobbles as mischievous children scattered out of their way.

Women dressed in elaborate saris adorned with strings of pearls, lace, and delicate netting strolled with their arms linked, making their way to one of the city's many fashionable tea houses that glittered with crystal chandeliers and served sparkling wine in wide-brimmed glasses. Shops were busy hawking every item one could conceive, from fruits and vegetables to trinkets and fabric.

Zarya crossed a square, passing a giant bronze astrolabe squatting in the center as an homage to Gi'ana's love of science and learning. Dozens of similar structures could be found throughout the city made from various materials like crystal, jade, and copper.

She then approached the building where the twins lived with Farida and wound up the staircase to where they occupied the entire fourth floor. When their parents had cut off their income, they'd allowed Ajay and Rania to remain in their flat, at least. She was pretty sure the Chandras hadn't worked a day in their lives, but Zarya wasn't really one to talk.

Rania opened the door and eyed Zarya from head to toe.

"Hi," Zarya said. "I'm here to see Farida."

Rania nodded and opened the door wider, allowing Zarya in. On more than one occasion, Rania had made it excruciatingly clear she didn't approve of Zarya's interest in Farida's tattoo, but Farida herself had no such qualms.

The Chandras' flat was notably more spacious than the one she occupied with Yasen. The large living room boasted ornately carved furniture upholstered in heavy jewel-toned velvet that matched the curtains hanging from the tall windows. Thick woven rugs covered wide honeyed wooden planks, and a fireplace sat at the far end of the room. There was even a layered crystal chandelier suspended over it.

Rania led her into the large kitchen, where Farida was boiling a pot of tea on the stove.

"Zarya," she said cheerfully. "What brings you here?"

Farida was a small woman, coming barely to Zarya's shoulder, with a round face and an easy smile. Her dark hair was usually pulled back in a neat bun, highlighting a pair of deep amber eyes and a scattered line of freckles bridging her nose. Today she wore a lemon-yellow salwar kameez complemented by a sky-blue dupatta.

"I was hoping to examine your tattoo again. If you're willing?"

Farida always grew quiet at the mention of the binding mark, but she nodded firmly. "Of course. Let's go into the living room. Can you finish this, Rania?"

"Sure," answered Rania, and Zarya followed Farida to sit down next to her on the sofa. She pulled the stolen bottles of ink out of her pocket and placed them on the table, noting the wary look in Farida's eyes. Zarya's fingers tingled at the contact, and she shook her hand out as Farida tracked her with a curious expression.

A moment later, Rania bustled out of the kitchen carrying a tray with a teapot and a few mugs. She placed them on the table and then backed up, giving them space but keeping an eye from the doorway.

"May I?" Zarya asked, reaching out to Farida. She nodded, and Zarya gently touched the woman's throat, tracing the line of stars, feeling a tug deep inside her chest. Her anchor flared to life, spinning in her chest as if waking to its call.

They'd done this before. Many times, in fact. And each time she did it, Zarya felt it. Just like she had when she'd touched Meera's tattoo in Dharati all those months ago. Just like that first moment when she was sure her magic was somehow connected to this marking. The problem was that she couldn't understand what any of it meant.

Farida had been her willing subject, allowing Zarya to carefully examine the stars while she sat patiently for Zarya, who kept her secrets close. She didn't want to use magic on Farida yet, worried about its effects, but this was also getting her nowhere. Sooner or later, she'd have to try, though Rania would flay her alive if she did anything to hurt Farida. And with good reason, of course.

Zarya continued to trace the lines of Farida's tattoo, closing her eyes as she sensed a swirl of magic move in her blood, her anchors glowing brightly. They flickered and pulsed in a pattern unique to this moment, but what did it mean?

She focused on her sixth anchor despite thousands of reservations. As much as she didn't want to admit it, she was sure it was the key to this puzzle. The darkness. She hadn't used it since the day she tried to help Amrita and had inadvertently hurt her. After that and Dhawan's little speech before she'd killed him, she'd sworn she'd never touch it again, but what if that was a promise she couldn't keep? Freeing Farida and the other vanshaj was so much more important than her fear.

Exhaling a frustrated huff, Zarya sat back while Farida reached for her chai and took a calm sip. She was unflappable, her back straight and her chin up, and nothing seemed to shake her.

"I'm sorry," Zarya said, trying to keep the dejection out of her voice.

"You have nothing to be sorry for," Farida said, "though I'm not sure I understand what you're trying to do."

Zarya caught sight of Rania watching the two of them with her brows pinched. While Farida's patience appeared infinite, Rania never allowed Zarya quite as much allowance for her failings. Or anyone's, for that matter.

Whether the women would still be prevented from marrying even if Zarya managed to remove the tattoo was a question yet to be answered. What made one vanshaj? The presence of the collar itself or their very essence? Did it matter? Surely, to some, it did. Even if it were gone, how would Farida be received by others?

There was also the question of what exactly Farida might be capable of once she was no longer bound, but the need to free her outweighed the worry of any potential consequences. It had to. This kind of evil couldn't remain unchecked. Farida deserved to be free, as did the thousands of other vanshaj living across Rahajhan.

"I don't really know, either," Zarya answered. She picked up a bottle of the ink as that same tingling traveled up her arm before unstopping it and sniffing the contents. The scent was crisp and dry, though she sensed the cloying hint of rot deep between its layers.

"Have you done anything with it?" Rania asked, sitting down next to Farida. "You still haven't explained why you needed it."

"Not yet," Zarya said. "And I promise to explain once I know *what* I'm doing. Do you have a bowl or something I could use? Something you're not attached to if it's ruined?"

"Sure," Rania said, retreating to the kitchen and returning a moment later with a small silver dish. "How about this?"

"Perfect," Zarya said, holding out her hand. She poured a small amount of ink into the well and sniffed again, detecting a pungent note that sent a shiver creeping down her spine.

She placed the dish on the table, once again shaking out her hand from the lingering effects of touching the bottle, and addressed Rania.

"What happens if you use your magic on it? Try some spirit."

Rania controlled all five anchors typical of powerful Aazheri and nodded before she pointed her hand towards it, a soft ribbon of yellow light curling out from her palm. Unlike Zarya, Rania and her brother manipulated their magic with their hands rather than their hearts. It was a subtle variation in how they manifested their power, meaning the results and control were slightly different.

Rania's light dipped into the small black pool, and they all watched as the ink started to glow, like it was lit from within. It flared bright for a moment before darkening again.

"Did you feel anything?" Zarya asked.

"It felt no different than filtering spirit into a glass of water or tea," she said. "I just heated it up a bit."

Zarya touched her finger to the ink, and sure enough, it was warm. She wiped it on her dark leggings before preparing for her turn next. She drew on her spirit anchor and sent a similar vein of soft light out from her fingertips. It curled over the ink, sliding against the surface.

CRASH

The ink blew apart, the metal bowl skidding off the table and slamming into a wall hard enough to crack the plaster. For several seconds, they all sat in silence, staring at one another, before Zarya stood up. She retrieved a towel from the kitchen and picked up the bowl before carrying it over to the sink. When she turned on the water, it hissed with steam, the entire thing now black and dented.

"What just happened?" Rania asked with narrowed eyes as she came up next to Zarya.

"I'm not sure," Zarya answered, though this further confirmed her suspicions about her forbidden magic. But as liberal as the Chandras were in their views, she worried her sixth anchor would stretch those limits. She imagined horror in their eyes if she revealed what she was.

"Why did your magic do that?" Farida asked, now standing on Zarya's other side, as she, too, stared at the ruined bowl.

"I'm not sure," Zarya repeated, but that wasn't really the truth. She looked up at Farida, and something exchanged between them. The woman's eyes narrowed before Zarya backed away, hoping to avoid too many questions.

"Well, at least that was something," she said, maybe a touch too brightly. She studied the tattoos on Farida's neck. Her earlier fears about using her magic on the woman had just tripled. If Zarya's magic elicited a similar reaction to the tattoo, she'd have to find a way to control it before trying anything on a living person. "I'll keep looking into this."

She slung her bag over her shoulder before stashing the ink bottles in a pocket. With only the two to work with, she'd have to be careful about how she went about this. She was still regretting the crate she'd lost, but that couldn't be helped now. Their raid had destroyed most of the supply in Gi'ana and Rahajhan, for that matter, minus whatever was stockpiled in the Taara Den, where they inked vanshaj infants straight from their mothers' wombs.

"Any time you need me again, let me know," Farida said. It was obvious how badly she wanted this for herself and for everyone else. She would endure anything to achieve that goal. But Zarya couldn't treat her like a specimen to be used and broken at her will. She would figure this out, but she would do it without hurting anyone.

"Thank you," Zarya said. "I'll see you later."

Then she pressed her hands together in front of her heart and exited the building, emerging into the busy streets of Ishaan. She ducked her head down, threading through the crowd as the smell of smoke still hung in the air, obscuring the sun and the clouds, leaving the sky a muddled wash of grey. Posters she hadn't noticed earlier hung at intervals affixed to lamp posts, offering rewards to anyone with information about the factory bombing.

Zarya allowed herself a small smile. They had done that. It had taken weeks and weeks of careful planning, but they'd all come together to deliver this crushing blow to the oppressive forces of Rahajhan. She scanned the paper, searching for clues on whether they had any leads, but it was only general information about the time and location, as if the blast hadn't been heard for miles.

The reward offered in exchange for information had Zarya stalling in her tracks. People would do terrible things for that kind of money. If the wrong person discovered what they were planning, their cover would be blown wide open.

But Farida, Ajay and Rania knew what they were doing—they'd been at this for years—and had everyone's best interests at heart. Thanks to their anonymous benefactor, they had more than enough money to carry out their activities, and Zarya had learned just how valuable that could be.

She proceeded with her head down, coming upon a street where a crowd gathered along the edges. A group of soldiers were busy clearing the road while people scrambled out of the way.

Unlike the city watch in their plain black uniforms, the royal soldiers of Gi'ana stood out in their violet-colored sherwanis with emerald-green sashes and red pants, almost like peacocks unfurling their feathers for a slice of attention. Their gleaming talwars hung at their hips, the sharpened edges flashing. They weren't afraid to use them at will, and their army was considered second only to Daragaab's, though she wondered if any of them agreed with that evaluation.

With people pressing in on all sides, Zarya elbowed her way through the crowd, hoping to find a way across the road towards her flat. She planned to find somewhere she could work with the ink in private.

She stretched onto her toes, attempting to see what the commotion was all about.

Up ahead, more guards preceded two massive elephants, decked out with ornate cloths across their backs and heads, covered in beading and small mirrors that reflected in the daylight despite the cover of smoke.

All this fanfare could mean only one thing.

At that realization, Zarya changed course, threading her way towards the street, now vying for a front-row seat, her mission with the ink temporarily forgotten.

A giant float rolled towards her, laden with marigolds, roses, and every flower one could conceive. The progression drew nearer, and Zarya watched with her eyes wide and her heart climbing up her throat. Her fingers tingled for an entirely different reason now.

She'd glimpsed them only a handful of times from a distance, but their presence never failed to make her stomach flip.

There they were.

The Madans.

The royal family of Gi'ana.

Her family.

FIVE

Zarya stood rooted to the spot as she watched the royal procession draw near. Musicians walked alongside the float, pouring out the strains of a medley, and it was clear this entire spectacle had been choreographed for a reason.

A distraction. The Rising Phoenix had gotten one up on the Madans, and they would not lose face by cowering behind the walls of their palace.

Dancers cartwheeled down the street while bare-chested men blew fire from their mouths. The crowd watched on and clapped with delight despite the ash raining from the sky.

Surrounding the float marched the fabled queensguard, decked out in pure white sherwanis trimmed with silver and bright red sashes crossing their chests. The elite branch of guards was charged with protecting the royal family, particularly their queen, and culled from only the very best soldiers in the continent.

The float came into Zarya's line of vision, and she felt something twist in her chest at the sight of the five people standing atop. She'd yet to see them this up close before, but she had learned enough from Row and her time spent in Ishaan to recognize the various members of the royal family.

The king consort, Kabir, stood at the front, waving to the crowds below. He looked about Row's age, closer to a middle-aged human, with wavy midnight hair and the slightest crinkle at the corners of his eyes.

He wasn't Zarya's father, and she had no blood connection to this man, but he *had* been married to her mother, and she wondered if he might have become her pseudo-father had things gone differently. What kind of man was he? He looked regal in his cream sherwani embroidered with gold, more gold adorning every finger on his hands.

Next to him stood the woman who occupied most of Zarya's focus. Dishani, her sister. Half-sister. The woman who waited in the wings for her crown. Her coronation had been announced weeks earlier, and finally, she would become Gi'ana's queen.

The laws of Ishaan included a statute of limitations that expired after twenty years in the event of a missing royal who was presumed dead but whose body was never found. Given Asha disappeared shortly after Zarya's birth, the timing lined up for Dishani to assume the mantle.

She was beautiful—her entire disposition dripping with confidence and the indefinable noble quality of someone raised in a life of privilege. The way she held herself. The exact angle of her nose held in the air. The careful way she waved to the people below and the calculated manner in which she turned her neck, slowly but not too slowly. She wore a sari of the deepest royal blue, covered with silver beading. In her hair was a piece of black netting pinned to the side of her perfect bun.

Dishani was absolutely breathtaking to behold. She *was* already a queen. There was no doubt this was her destiny and her purpose.

Suddenly, Zarya felt a rush of insecurity sweep into her bones. How could she ever present herself to these people? They were different than Amrita had been—she was humble and down to earth—but it was clear Princess Dishani wouldn't tolerate even a speck of dust on her shoes. The crowds cheered as she passed, while that practiced smile never wavered. Her dark eyes weren't exactly cold, but they lacked any kind of warmth. She was driven to do her duty and would do it with every fiber of her being.

The crowd dipped their heads as she passed, many murmuring soft words of benediction and prayer. Zarya continued to watch in wide-eyed fascination.

Finally, she turned her attention to the rest of her half-siblings.

The other woman she knew was Advika, the second youngest of the lot. Her round cheeks were dusted with pink blush, and her big green eyes were surrounded by thick lines of kohl. She wore a bright pink lehenga adorned with colorful beading and flowers woven into her hair. It was said she was the easygoing one between the sisters, more interested in parties and her numerous suitors than politics of state. Her warm smile clearly endeared her to the mooning crowd.

The two men were her brothers. She wasn't entirely sure which was which, but she guessed the one facing the side was Talin, the youngest. She'd heard he was considered a bit of a loose cannon, drinking, gambling, and enjoying the brothels that filled the Khushi District. He sat on a small divan, upholstered in red velvet, with one ankle crossed over a knee. His hair hung in loose, disheveled waves around his ears, and the opened buttons of his crisp white shirt showed off a sliver of warm brown chest.

He offered an insouciant smile to the crowd, not bothering to wave, just waggling his eyebrows as a greeting. The way everyone reacted to him made it obvious he was one of the royal favorites.

Finally, Zarya watched the last man, Miraan, her eldest brother and the second oldest of the Gi'ana siblings. It was said he was Dishani's right hand and her most trusted advisor. The way he radiated competence even from this distance made it easy to understand why.

He wore a tailored black sherwani absent of adornments, and his straight shoulder-length hair was neatly tied at his nape with a strip of black leather. Watching over the crowd with his posture straight and his hands behind his back, his thick eyebrows were drawn together in a tight *V*, his dark eyes assessing everything.

He seemed so serious, and she wondered what was going through his head. It was hard to separate her desire to know these people from the things they allowed to happen in their home.

"Zee!" She turned at the sound of her name to find Yasen shoving through the crowd. "I've been looking for you."

"And I've been right here," she said, practically hearing the roll of his eyes.

He fell silent as they watched the float pass, his eyes glued on Miraan.

"He's cute," Zarya remarked before she tipped her head and squinted. "In a severe kind of way."

The corners of Yasen's mouth pressed together, but he didn't respond. They continued watching until the procession had passed, trailed by a few more acrobats, elephants, more soldiers, and a smaller float with some fancily dressed people that Zarya assumed were lesser nobility. They elicited far fewer cheers and benedictions from the crowd, and she couldn't blame them.

The way they all sat there wrapped in their jewels, staring with mistrust at everyone on the street, made them look like a petulant bunch of children. Where the royal family knew how to engage the masses, these only repelled.

When everyone had finally passed, Yasen grabbed Zarya's arm and pulled her over.

"Come on," he said, dragging her through the crowds.

"What's going on?" she asked. "Why were you looking for me? Is everything okay?" She realized that Yasen hunting for her in the middle of the street might be a worrisome sign. "Has something happened?"

"Relax," he said with his usual exasperated air. "Wouldn't I tell you if something bad happened?"

"Honestly, I'm not sure," she replied, and he laughed.

"Good point. Don't worry, this is a good surprise."

"Okay," she said, still skeptical but willing to concede he probably was being truthful. As much as he liked to tease her, he also knew when to be serious—sometimes.

A short while later, they arrived at the doorway to their apartment.

"Well, this isn't very exciting," she remarked. "In case you've forgotten, I live here."

"You're so annoying," he said, and she laughed.

They ascended the stairs and Yasen threw open the door. Curiosity eating at her now, she stepped into their apartment, half expecting some wild animal Yasen had decided to purchase in the market to knock her down while he stood over her and told her that its teeth weren't *that* big.

"What?" she asked, scanning the empty apartment until she saw two familiar figures standing on the balcony.

"Apsara!" she said, throwing her arms around the winged woman before she pulled away and then faced Suvanna, whom she did *not* attempt to hug. "What are you both doing here?"

Apsara and Suvanna exchanged a glance, and then Apsara said, "We heard you could use some help."

"How?" Zarya asked, exchanging a worried glance with Yasen.

"Row," Apsara answered. "I was asking about you, and he

mentioned everything you've been up to. Fear not, your secrets are safe."

During her months in Dharati, Zarya had sensed the innate goodness of the Chiranjivi. They were noble and had never been corrupted by their unique power. Perhaps that was exactly why the gods had selected them in the first place.

"Then I'm so happy you're here! Did Yasen make you some tea?"

Suvanna arched an eyebrow and stared at him. "He neglected to get to that part."

"Would you like some tea?" Yasen asked in a deadpan voice.

"Love some," Suvanna replied, her expression stone cold.

"Very well."

Yasen spun around and made his way to the small kitchen in the corner of the room while the women settled at the table that served as their dining space.

"Where have you both been?" Zarya asked. "What have you been up to?"

"After I left Dharati, I returned home," Apsara said. "It had been far too long."

"Me as well," Suvanna said as Yasen placed some mugs on the table and then returned with a silver pot a few moments later.

"And how were things at home?" Zarya asked while she poured tea.

"Restless," Apsara said, her brows pinching together before she sipped her chai. "Word of vanshaj rebellions has reached even the highest mountain peaks and is filtering into every realm. I've been writing with Kindle, and it's the same in Bhaavana. He's been busy working with a small but growing rebellion hiding out near their borders. The time is coming for a change."

"What about you?" Zarya asked Suvanna, who shrugged.

"We don't have vanshaj in Matsya. They can't breathe underwater."

"Oh," Zarya said.

"But that is only circumstance. I have no doubt that if it were possible, they would also live amongst my people." Her stern expression suggested what she thought about that.

"When Row told us what you two have been up to, we knew we had to come immediately to help where we could," Apsara said before taking another sip of her tea.

"Row's not coming, is he?" Zarya asked. It wasn't that she didn't want to see him, but she wasn't eager to live under the careful scrutiny of a guardian again. She needed her space and freedom, and no matter what Row said, he would always watch out for her in a way no one else would.

Apsara chuckled. "He said to assure you that he's staying where he is unless you need his help. He's got his hands full in Dharati, regardless."

Zarya nodded. She knew from the letters they'd exchanged that riots in support of vanshaj freedom were also amassing in her former home. It seemed that a pinhole that had been leaking water for centuries was suddenly close to bursting. Like one card falling, it had taken just a few rumors spreading across the continent to start toppling them all.

"You'll need vetting before you can be allowed into the Phoenix," Yasen said, leaning against the counter with an ankle crossed over the other and his mug cradled in a hand.

"Understood. We're happy to offer whatever assurances we can," Apsara said solemnly before she looked out the window where clouds of smoke still hazed the sky. "Are you responsible for that?"

She looked back at Zarya and Yasen, and their silence confirmed the truth.

"Posters have been hung," Zarya said to him. "They're offering a lot of money to anyone with information."

Yasen nodded. "I noticed that. This all just got a lot more dangerous."

At that moment, a knock sounded at the apartment door. Three quick raps, followed by two slower ones with two beats between them. Zarya and Yasen exchanged a look.

"Well, I guess there's no time like the present," he said with a grin as he strode to the door and opened it.

The three women watched as he conversed with Ajay in a low voice for a moment. Then he stepped aside, and Ajay entered, his gaze wandering to Zarya before it settled on Apsara and Suvanna.

"Hello," he said with a small bow. "Yasen tells me you're friends of his."

"I'm Apsara. I hail from Vayuu," Apsara said, pressing her hands together in front of her heart with the tip of her head. Suvanna remained in her seat, her posture relaxed, and her arms crossed as she assessed Ajay. "And that is Suvanna of Matsya."

"Apsara and Suvanna were instrumental in helping us defeat the blight in Daragaab," Zarya said. "They can be trusted."

"You're sure of that?" Ajay said, his eyes narrowing. She knew he was only being cautious. So many lives hung in the balance if they made one wrong move.

"Absolutely," Apsara said. "We came here to help in whatever way we can. We are at your service and vow to keep any secrets you share. We also live to see the vanshaj freed."

Ajay considered them and then turned to Yasen and Zarya. "I came because I have bad news."

"What is it?" she asked.

"The explosion spooked the royal family. My palace informants report that harsher laws will soon be passed down for the vanshaj and anyone aiding them. They're mobilizing more patrols through the vanshaj district to root out possible resistance members. They're no longer pretending we don't exist."

"How much worse can the laws possibly be?" Yasen asked as they all shook their heads. No one knew or wanted to know the answer to that question.

Ajay addressed Suvanna and Apsara once again. "You understand what's at stake here?"

They both nodded.

"Absolutely."

Ajay dipped his chin. "Then you are welcome as far as I'm concerned. We could use as many powerful allies as possible. But first, you'll need to meet our leader."

LETTER

Dear Zarya,

Things in Dharati remain unsettled. We've completed most of the repairs since the attack, but everyone is still on edge. Rumors are surfacing about what caused the blight, and it's no longer a secret the darkness nearly found its way into Rahajhan. It's making everyone nervous, and it's only a matter of time before speculation spreads to the other realms.

Unrest is also stirring in the vanshaj quarter, and I can't help but feel like these events are connected. Whispers of rebellion are traveling across the continent, and the nobility are sleeping with one eye open.

Vikram is making decisions I cannot support and lashing out at everyone around him. Amrita has changed since you knew her. Or at least that's all that I can assume. Since only Vikram can speak with her, I must take him at his word when he conveys her wishes. She does not seem concerned about the citizens, and all those *dreams and plans she once spoke about appear to be forgotten.*

Koura returned to Dharati last month to monitor her pregnancy and confirmed the child is healthy, so at least we have that to be thankful for. To answer your question, she's growing inside a clear seed nestled in Amrita's womb much like a baby would inside a human mother, but instead, she is nourished by roots and sap rather than veins and blood. When the time is right, the child will be born when the seed splits open to welcome her into the world.

I wish I could bring more auspicious tidings, but it seems things are shifting more than we understand.

I hear Suvanna and Apsara have made their way to you and are sure to be useful in your endeavors, but I do urge you to be cautious, Zarya. These are ever more dangerous times, and I worry about you. Give my best to Yasen, and I hope you're both taking good care of each other.

It's quiet here without you.

Row

SIX

Once they'd set Apsara and Suvanna up in their guest bedroom, Zarya convinced Yasen to accompany her into the forests beyond the city, where she was hoping to explore her magic's strange reaction to the ink.

She also planned to tell him the truth about everything. She couldn't keep this secret festering inside her any longer and had to share it with *someone*. She only hoped he wouldn't look at her differently.

But he already knew more than anyone, including her dreams in the forest with Rabin and her reaction to Meera's tattoo in Dharati. He'd been the first witness to her magic, and he'd never let her down. She knew she could trust him with this.

A loud smack followed by a huff of annoyance drew her attention behind her. Yasen was frowning as he flicked his fingers. "What are we doing out here exactly?" he asked. "I'm being eaten alive by these fucking things." Another smack and another grunt signaled the untimely death of yet another mosquito.

Zarya waved a hand, forming a thin shield of air around them both, blocking out the tiny bloodsuckers.

"You couldn't have done that twenty minutes ago?" Yasen asked, stomping through the bushes. "I was dying."

She huffed out a laugh. Yes, she could have done that twenty minutes ago, but where would the fun have been in that?

"Poor Yas," Zarya said. "Such a tough life."

He snorted. "Tell me you at least brought something to drink."

"That I can do," she said, digging into the bag slung over her shoulder and pulling out a small silver flask. After tossing it to him, he opened it and then sighed.

"Much better."

They walked in silence for a little longer while Yasen nursed his drink.

"How much further are we going?" he asked.

"I'm not sure. We need just the right spot."

"Oh, thank you, very helpful," he grumbled, but she ignored him as they continued to push through the bushes. The smoke from the factory explosion was finally starting to clear, and the high moon offered just enough light through the tree cover. It wasn't a particularly dense forest, so Zarya wanted to be deep enough to properly shield them. After another few minutes, they came upon a small clearing with a large, flat rock in the center.

"This looks good," Zarya said, coming to a stop while Yasen collapsed on the stone with a dramatic flourish, as though she'd just asked him to climb a thousand-foot mountain and not take a stroll through a lovely forest on a pleasant night.

"Thank gods," he said. "I thought I was going to die."

"Aren't you a trained soldier?" she asked, and he grinned.

"Yes, but I hate exercise."

She laughed because she didn't believe that for a moment and then circled around the clearing, ensuring they couldn't see the glow of the city lights in any direction. Everything stood quiet, suggesting they were as alone as they could be without turning this into a multi-day excursion.

"Can you finally tell me what we're doing out here?" Yasen asked, sipping from the flask as he sat forward with his knees spread and his elbows on his thighs.

"Yes," she said, rummaging through her bag again and pulling out a bottle of ink, shivering as her fingers wrapped around the glass. "We are going to practice with this."

"We?"

"Well, I am, and you're going to watch."

"Lucky for me. Why?"

"Moral support," she said, and he cocked his head in a gesture that said *fair enough*.

She held the bottle up to the light, twisting it left and right to watch the swirls of iridescence churn like ribbons floating through water. "When I tried this the other day in Rania's apartment, things went a little awry."

"In what way?"

"I'll show you. Can you stand up?"

He rolled his eyes and made a rather impressive show of heaving himself off the rock before standing next to her. She pulled out a small bowl, placed it in the center of the stone, and added a few drops of ink.

"Okay, don't get too close," she warned.

"Why not?"

"You'll see."

Then she called up her magic, again pulling on her spirit anchor. A wispy ribbon of glowing light spread from her fingertips and touched the ink. Like last time, the ink exploded, spraying up as the dish flew off the rock, smacking into a tree with a thunk before it dropped into the grass with a hiss. Zarya exchanged a look with Yasen, whose entire forehead pleated with concern and confusion.

"What did you just do, Swamp Girl?"

Zarya pressed her lips together and approached the stone to find a black mark smudged across the surface.

"Zee?" Yasen asked, his voice unusually soft. "What aren't you telling me?"

She looked up at him. "So when Rania tried to do that... *that* didn't happen."

He tipped his head, waiting for her to continue.

"Her magic worked as expected and warmed it up."

Yasen approached and clasped her shoulder. "Is this related to whatever you've been hiding for the last few months?" he asked.

She blinked. Of course he'd noticed.

"You didn't think I'd pick up on the whole seeing that creepy army that no one else could? Or that Meera could see it, too?"

Zarya let out a long breath as he released his hold. "You didn't say anything."

"I was giving you space. It was obviously bothering you."

She gave him a tight smile. Yasen could pretend he didn't care and didn't like people, but he was good and kind. Even if he never wanted anyone to realize that.

"How much do you know about Aazheri magic?" she asked, holding up her hand as though the answers were written on her palm.

"Just the basics," he said. "Five elements. The more you have, the stronger you are."

"Right," she answered. "The five anchors. But did you know there was once a sixth?"

He settled onto the scorched rock and drew her down next to him.

"I've heard of it," he said, his expression giving nothing away. "I remember Koura talking about it. The brothers..." he said. "The Ashvin twins had it?"

"Right. And that's what they were supposedly protecting everyone from when they caged the vanshaj."

She gave him a significant look, waiting for him to sort the pieces she was offering up like shattered pieces of crystal.

"The Ashvins had a sixth anchor. And... the vanshaj did, too?" he asked slowly.

She shook her head. "The Ashvins did, and I'm not exactly sure what the vanshaj have yet. But I'm almost positive my magic is connected to this ink."

"Because..." he said slowly, circling his hand.

"Because I have six anchors." She grimaced as the words seared her tongue. Now that she'd said them out loud, they felt like they were floating on the wind for the world to judge and examine, never to be taken back.

Yasen's shoulders slumped. "Well... shit."

"I discovered it the night of the binding ceremony," she said. "When I killed the kala-hamsa, it exploded out of me along with my nightfire."

Yasen ran a hand down his face. "That's big, Zee."

"I know," she said, pressing her hand to her chest. "It's been sitting there like a lead brick, and everyone's so sure it can't be touched, but I can." She couldn't keep the fear and the loneliness out of her voice. Yasen's expression softened as he wrapped an arm around her shoulders and drew her closer. She circled her arms around his waist and pressed her cheek to his chest.

"And you were worried what everyone would say," he said as she nodded against him.

"The morning after the attack, I was planning to run away. I thought *this* was why Row had hidden me. That he knew and he'd locked me away so I could never hurt anyone. I thought I had to go somewhere where no one would find me."

He stroked the back of her head, allowing her the chance to confess all the worries she'd been carrying for months.

"But then Row showed up and told me the real reason,

which convinced me he didn't actually know what I was hiding. And when I learned that my nightfire killed the demons, I wanted to stay and help."

"I'm glad you did," he said, and her heart squeezed inside her chest.

She pulled away and leaned forward, bracing her elbows on her knees as she twisted her fingers together.

"And now what?" Yasen asked. "Why did we come out here?"

She looked over at him. "Because I have a theory."

Her gaze flicked to the charred copper bowl that lay in the dirt.

"You think you need to use your sixth anchor," he said, picking up on the train of her thoughts.

"I'm not entirely sure, but I'm wondering if I can manipulate the ink with it. However, I wanted to see what my other anchors did first."

"Makes sense," he said, standing up. "So let's try it."

She stared up at him. "This doesn't change anything?" she asked, and he frowned.

"Change what?"

"Us? You still want to be my friend?"

"What the hell are you talking about?"

"I'm tainted. I'm... a monster," she whispered.

His expression softened as he reached out a hand and pulled her up. "Maybe. But you're my monster, and nothing will ever change that, Zee."

Zarya's eyes stung. She'd been so worried, and of course, Yasen wouldn't judge her.

"Just don't cry."

She snorted a laugh and then picked up the half-empty bottle of ink.

"I don't have much to practice with," she said. "I really wish I hadn't dropped that crate."

He considered that. "I'm sure we can get more if we need it. The Jadugara must have some stockpiled in the Taara Den."

"They won't give us any."

He shrugged. "No. But we'll steal it again."

"Okay. Right," she said, some of the tension releasing from her shoulders. He always knew what to say to make her feel better.

"So try the other anchors." He bent down and retrieved the bowl, handing it to her. She poured some ink into the well and then centered it on the rock. They retreated into the shadows of the trees, using them for cover.

"Let's try fire," she said as she twisted out a tendril of orange magic. Delicately, she touched the surface and wasn't all that surprised when the ink flared, spurting up in a tall column of flames before sputtering out. They shared a look, and Zarya walked over to find a pile of ash in the bottom of the bowl.

"Well, I can't try that on Farida."

"No. Rania would gleefully pull out each of your toenails."

She gave him a rueful smile.

Zarya then cycled through the rest of her elements. Her water anchor vaporized the ink into mist, and air froze it solid. Her earth anchor caused the ink to transform into crumbling dirt, which at first seemed promising. Maybe she could use that to break apart the tattoos. But a moment later, it started to corrode the copper, burning a hole right through the metal until only a ring remained.

"None of these will work," she said grimly.

Zarya then tried a few combinations of elements, but each had the same end result: fire, explosions, or the production of corrosive substances, which she absolutely couldn't try on a living person.

Well into the second bottle of ink now, she poured the remainder into another bowl.

"This is the last of it," she said before placing it on the rock.

Then she closed her eyes, feeling for her sixth anchor. It had been months since she'd accessed it, but there it was, waiting for her. A little more muted but still glowing like melting silver. She heard Yasen moving around in the grass behind her and backed up with him.

From where she stood, she stared at the bowl in the center of the clearing, starlight reflecting off the ink's dark surface.

"We could try another night if you aren't ready," Yasen offered.

"No," she replied with her jaw clenched. "I need to figure this out."

She reached inside herself, feeling for the tendril of darkness, and slowly drew it out. This was the first time she'd ever called it up on its own, having previously used it only in combination with the others to create her strongest nightfire. The magic felt cool and slippery, like caressing satin ribbons. It had a certain kind of seductive beauty as it swirled across the clearing. At first, it appeared like a whisp of dark smoke, but it reflected the light with a million shades of muted color. It reminded her of the scales on Rabin's dragon. Like moonlight over an oil-slicked pond.

She twisted her fingers as the shadowy ribbon spiraled over the bowl, and then she held her breath as the tip touched the ink.

It didn't explode, and it didn't catch fire. It didn't dissolve into a toxic substance. She felt it dip into the liquid, and then she twisted her magic as the darkness stirred the ink, gently moving it around in the bowl. She shifted left to right, feeling how it responded to her magic. Without realizing it, she'd started moving, and the closer she got, the more control she had.

She pulled back and lifted her hand as a thin tendril of ink spiraled up from the surface. Drawing it higher, she formed a loop that curled through the air.

She fed in more magic, feeling every individual particle of

the ink, manipulating them, and shaping them into patterns that obeyed her silent commands. Slowly, she directed the ribbon back into the bowl, where it dissipated into a pool of ink once again.

She held still for a moment and then puffed out her cheeks before she looked at Yasen, who stood with his hands stuffed into his back pockets.

"Well, that was something," he said.

"Yeah," she replied.

Something indeed.

She just wasn't sure what yet.

SEVEN

Zarya lounged on the divan on the balcony of their apartment a few days later. The city was quiet—it was that peaceful hour between the late-night crowds stumbling home and the early risers stirring for the day. Ever since they'd left Dharati, she'd been having trouble sleeping and often found herself here, waking up with the dawn.

At night, she would toss and turn, craving the release of oblivion, not only to calm the constant churning of her mind and body but because she so badly wanted to connect to the dream forest.

It was ironic that the thing she needed most was the thing her body refused to give her. Did she need to be in a deep dreamlike state for it to work? Maybe she had to be asleep for a specific number of hours first?

Whatever combination of factors had brought Rabin to her previously had failed to manifest again. What if she were involuntarily blocking it in the depths of her hurt and betrayal? She didn't know why she wanted to see him—she was still furious that he'd lied to her—but she couldn't deny how much she craved him.

She let out a long sigh and tucked up her feet. The evening was warm, though a fresh breeze blew off the distant mountains. Next to her sat a cooling cup of tea infused with herbs intended to help her sleep, but it hadn't been much use. It did tingle through her blood, and she allowed herself to sink into the soothing sensation.

Also on the table was a romance book—ever since arriving in Ishaan, she'd been introduced to a shocking variety of novels with storylines and tendencies that were entirely new to her. When she couldn't sleep, she'd take solace between the covers, definitely not imagining Rabin's face and body as she learned about all the new ways one could indulge in... pleasure.

She flipped through the pages, skipping ahead to a smutty part, but not even that was working right now. With a sigh, she slapped it shut and took another long sip of tea. Her head tipped back, and she stretched out her neck, wishing she could ease this knot of tension lodged at the top of her spine.

"Couldn't sleep?" asked a voice, and Zarya looked up to find Apsara standing over her. She'd never seen the winged warrior so at ease in a soft white sleeveless shirt and a pair of shorts that showed off her toned brown legs.

"Couldn't sleep," Zarya confirmed.

"Mind if I join you?"

"Of course not."

Apsara sat down, adjusting her wings so she could get comfortable. She gestured to the pot on the side table.

"Got any more of that?"

Zarya filled up her half-empty mug and then passed it to Apsara. "Help yourself."

"So, how have you been?" she asked Zarya. "Row misses you. He doesn't say it, but I can tell from his messages that he wishes you were at home."

Zarya scrunched her nose. Of late, she'd felt guilty for leaving and refusing his company on her quest to Gi'ana. She was safe here—she hadn't truly felt threatened, but Row had always had a way of making everything seem solid and stable. In spite of everything that had happened at the cottage, she'd always felt protected.

"I'll be back soon," she said, but her words were unconvincing. She had no idea where her future might lead her. She wasn't sure what she wanted for her life but hoped the right path would eventually reveal itself.

"How about you?" Zarya asked. "How have you been? Why did you show up here with Suvanna?"

Apsara let out a dry huff. "It's not because we've been spending time together," she said. "If that's what you're wondering."

"I was wondering," she said. "I hoped."

"Why?" Apsara said.

Zarya shrugged. "You might say I've always been a bit of a romantic."

"I've always liked that about you."

"What?"

"Your ability to see the world with rose-colored glasses. Even with plenty of evidence to the contrary, I think you really believe the world is a good place."

"That makes me naive," Zarya said with a weary sigh. "So much of my life was shaped by books that always had a happy ending, so I guess I thought life worked that way, too. Even when I was at my most miserable, I never gave up on the idea that a happily ever after was waiting for me."

She held up the book sitting in her lap, and Apsara shook her head. "It doesn't make you naive. It's a wonderful thing to believe. I wish more people felt that way."

Zarya dropped the book again and smiled. "Thanks. I guess."

"And no, Suvanna and I haven't seen each other since we left Dharati. She decided we both had to come to Gi'ana when Row shared what you were doing." Apsara rolled her shoulders back. "Maybe I'm the naive one. Every time I think things will be different, I end up having my heart broken again."

"This time, too?"

She shrugged and sipped her drink. "Not yet, but it's always the same. Suvanna is happy to carry on with our physical relationship, but that's all she wants or needs. Or so she says."

"You don't believe that?" Zarya asked.

"It's hard not to wonder sometimes if that's really all it is or if it's just *me* she doesn't need those things from."

Zarya's heart twisted at the vulnerable look on Apsara's face.

"Which definitely makes *me* a fool," she said.

"No," Zarya said. "It's not foolish to hope that someone you admire and have feelings for might return them. It's never foolish to want the best for yourself and your life."

"See?" Apsara said. "There you go, making everything look nice again."

Zarya snorted. "You wouldn't say that if you'd lived with me at the cottage. I was a giant pain in the ass."

Apsara laughed, too. "That I *do* believe."

Zarya picked up a pillow and playfully swatted Apsara as they both continued chuckling.

"Here," Zarya said, holding out her book. "Try some light reading to help make you a believer, too."

Apsara eyed the novel, which depicted an embracing couple with their clothes nearly falling off while the wind tossed their hair.

"Trust me," Zarya said. "You'll never be the same."

Apsara took it and flipped through the pages.

"Okay, I'm game." Her mouth stretched into a yawn. "But I'm exhausted, and I only came out here because I needed some water, and you looked a bit lonely. You okay if I go back to bed?"

"Of course," Zarya said. "Have a good sleep. In the morning, we'll take you to meet Farida."

After Apsara went back inside, Zarya considered returning to her bed as well, but the evening was the perfect temperature, and her breath came easier when she sat out here.

The mountains stretched to one side, overlooking the rolling city of Ishaan, while miles of forest spread in the other direction. This view always felt like a reminder of how far she'd come in her life. From her quiet corner of the sea to this queendom on the very opposite end of the continent, she was still having trouble reconciling that after everything, she'd made it here.

She tugged the blanket off a nearby chair and wrapped it around her shoulders, lying down on the divan before she finally drifted off into a troubled sleep.

* * *

Rabin padded across his darkened bedroom towards the large windows that overlooked Andhera's snowy landscape. In his hand, he held the book he'd been studying for weeks. Abishek had plucked it from the recesses of his vast collection. Years ago, when paramadhar had been more common, new pairings were given a handbook outlining the role's various conditions, limits, and duties.

Rabin had read it cover to cover, learning the secrets of these ancient magical servants. The more he read, the surer he was that he belonged to Zarya. There was so much he could do. Help control her magic. Heal her. He'd never forget the moment he found her lying in the mud on the outskirts of Dharati and coaxed her back to life. Once they forged the connection between them, known as the Bandhan, he could save her from death itself. Once they both wore matching tattoos applied by a mystic, the Bandhan would be complete, and it would bind his life to hers.

If she died, then so would he.

But he'd already accepted this fate months ago. If he were being honest, maybe part of him had accepted it from the first moment he'd seen her. Who was he to refuse if the gods had seen fit to bestow him with this gift? There was no doubt there was something important about Zarya, and Rabin wanted to be a part of the future that awaited them both.

The book also warned against physical relationships between paramadhar and their destined Aazheri, known as a masatara, but as long as Zarya was willing, he didn't care about the rules. He'd always been good at breaking them, and this would be no exception. But first, he had to earn her forgiveness.

Abishek wanted to meet her. And what kind of father wouldn't want to meet his only child? It was a natural desire, and Rabin was determined to bring them together. They were the two most important people in his life, and he'd met them both through independent events. He'd become their only link, and he was sure part of *his* purpose was to bring them together.

He ignored the disquieting voice that reminded him of everything Row had claimed about his mentor. Abishek had put those lies to rest. Row's opinion of his king had been tainted by his love for Gi'ana's queen. He was an unreliable character witness, and Rabin had spent years with Abishek and trusted him.

He wasn't deluding himself that Abishek wasn't ambitious and ruthless when he needed to be, but he wouldn't harm his own daughter. There were limits to what everyone was capable of. The king had shown him too much kindness and understanding for Rabin to believe that.

He flipped to the chapter about mind walking. This is what he and Zarya had done in the dream forest without realizing it. And the good news was that one *could* control the process.

Sleep or unconsciousness wasn't required of either party, though it was often encouraged, as pulling someone from their surroundings and into the mind plane without warning could be risky.

They'd only be 'taken' from their normal surroundings for a few seconds—time moved differently in the mind plane—but even that could be dangerous under the wrong circumstances.

Rabin had waited months to find her in the dream forest, but he'd woken up disappointed every morning. Armed with his new knowledge, he'd take matters into his own hands.

Dressed for sleep, he wore only loose pants on his bottom half. He rubbed a hand against his bare stomach as he scanned the page again. A fire crackled in the hearth, casting orange shadows across his large bed chamber. He'd waited until late at night to try this, hoping to catch her in slumber.

Like much of Andhera's castle, his room was decorated in hues of black, with a giant black bed pushed against the wall and towering floor-to-ceiling black curtains. The tiles were covered in massive woven silk rugs pieced together with colorful threads.

He inhaled a deep breath and blew it out, fogging the tall windows that offered unobstructed views across the horizon. Moonlight gilded snowy peaks that sparkled in the distance, and the stars sat heavy in the sky like a million silver flames.

He closed his eyes and pictured the dream forest. Those tall trees and that deep violet sky. He pictured Zarya. Her brown eyes flecked with tiny points of green and the long fall of her thick, midnight hair. He imagined the luscious swell of her hips and her long legs, toned from hours of training. He licked his lips, remembering the taste of her in his mouth and her breathless noises when she'd come apart on his tongue.

That night on Ranpur Island had been a defining moment of his life. He summoned the vision of her panting under him, dark strands of hair strewn across the pillow as her nails had dug into his biceps while he'd fucked her mercilessly into the mattress. The way she'd felt coming around his cock, her tight wet pussy clenching against him, had been nothing short of transcendent. And the flavor that had filled his mouth when he'd bitten into her neck had been like drinking in golden nectar delivered by a divine hand.

It had been at that moment he'd known she was *it*.

He had to see her again. He had to explain himself.

The key to creating a mind plane was to empty one's thoughts of everything but her and their destination. This could be difficult for some, as the mind tended to wander, distracted by the mundane details of life, but Rabin had no trouble thinking only of Zarya. He'd already been doing it for months. It was nothing to fill his consciousness with images of only her.

He realized now he'd been the one to force the connection when Zarya had been suffering with her blocked magic. He'd felt her pain and her agony like a distant echo twisting in the back of his chest and sought out Abishek to convey his worries about the woman in his dreams who had still been a mystery to them both.

Thankfully, the king had immediately recognized the signs, offering him an enchantment that would break it. And then Rabin had spent days trying to join her, desperate to help, eventually opening the connection without understanding how. Now, he realized it had been his singular focus on finding her that had been the catalyst.

So he continued to imagine her and the forest, directing his mind inward as he felt his breath slow and his heart thrust against his ribs. It took only a minute before a warm breeze of air dusted the back of his neck, and he opened his eyes, exhaling a shocked breath.

He'd done it.

Above him, that violet sky sparkled with its dense blanket of stars. They felt so close it almost seemed like he could reach out and scoop up a handful to carry in his pocket. The leaves rustled softly, and the moon hung low, a bright glowing orb, the edges smearing into the night.

He stepped softly, wanting to keep his presence a secret for now as he waited. Not sure how long it would take, he concealed himself in the shadows, hoping against hope this would work.

After a few minutes of tense silence, he began to worry he'd done something wrong, but then a soft rustle drew his attention. Through the shadows, Zarya emerged, wearing a white sleeveless top and silk shorts. Her long hair hung in messy waves around her shoulders, and her brown skin glowed in the gilded moonlight. She was absolutely fucking breathtaking, and his heart stopped.

"Hello?" she called, her voice uncharacteristically tentative. She stepped lightly on her tiptoes towards the center of the clearing where they had met so many times. "Hello? Ra—"

She cut herself off with a shake of her head. Had she been about to call for him?

Rabin studied her, trying to assess her state of mind. Was she happy to return here? What would she say or do if he revealed himself?

Zarya stood in the center and turned around and around, studying the shadows. Was she looking for him? She remained planted in the center of the clearing as if she feared searching too deeply. What conflicting thoughts warred in her mind?

She blew out a breath and pushed her hair back, peering up at the sky and watching the stars for a long time. His admiring gaze traced over the lines of her profile and the arch of her neck that he'd dreamed of sinking his teeth into every night while he slept.

He wanted to suck on the swell of her breasts and bite her nipples peaking against the thin material of her top. His fist clenched as he thought of smoothing his hands over the curve of her stomach and her ass. He drank her in, his cock stiffening with wild desire, memorizing every detail as she continued to search the clearing.

He'd already decided he wouldn't reveal himself tonight. He'd only wanted to see if he could create the mind plane, *and* he wanted to see her. This was enough.

Now, he knew it was possible, but he'd try to bring her to Andhera next time. The book said creating any environment was possible with the right focus. He wanted to give this to her, encourage her to understand it, and release her fear of this place.

Next time, she'd see the other half of her home.

* * *

Zarya opened her eyes, blinking several times as her breath stuck in her chest.

The forest.

She'd returned. Finally. Everything had been as she remembered. The clearing and the trees, the vibrant violet sky. The stars that seemed to breathe with life. The tree he'd pressed her against that night he'd almost kissed her and then walked away, and the rock where he'd "apologized" for his behavior on his knees. Her cheeks warmed at the memory despite the fact she'd played it in her head at least a thousand times.

But the forest had been empty. She'd waited, staring in the direction where he usually appeared, her heart pounding as she tried to decide what she really wanted. She'd spent months missing him, but the idea of actually confronting him had suddenly felt like too much.

What would she say? What would *he* say? She'd imagined so many conversations they might have. Him telling her he'd manipulated her. Tricked her into feeling something for him. Him swearing he hadn't meant to lie to her.

But she shouldn't have worried herself over these questions because he hadn't been there at all. Was this it, then? No more connection? Had he ever been her paramadhar?

As she'd stood in that clearing, she'd considered calling for him, but something stopped her. She wasn't ready to see him. Not yet.

Despite the hole he'd carved out of her heart and the many nights she'd spent thinking of him, she wasn't.

When the sun began peeking over the rooftops of Ishaan, she sat up, rubbing her chest, and wondered if that empty space would ever close again.

EIGHT

"Can I buy you a drink?" asked a handsome Aazheri later that evening. He leaned against the bar where Zarya was sitting, debating on what to order. Somewhere in the crowd was Yasen, while Apsara and Suvanna sat at a nearby table, chatting and preparing to meet Farida.

This establishment was owned by a member of the Rising Phoenix and was ideal for clandestine conversations due to the constant noise at all hours of the day. The proprietor also had a number of secret back rooms useful for even more private conversations.

Zarya had spent the day holed up in her room, practicing her magic with the last of the ink tipped from the dregs of the bottle, though it hadn't been enough to do much. And now every drop was gone.

She had to get her hands on more, and soon.

Zarya eyed the man up and down. He appeared close to her age, though she knew that didn't mean much when it came to Aazheri. He had soft brown eyes and black hair that curled to the tops of his shoulders.

"Who's asking?" she said with a coy tip of her head.

She'd been enjoying her months in Gi'ana, exploring all the things she'd been missing during her sheltered upbringing, engaging in some harmless flirting, and having plenty of fun. Discovering she had this kind of power was a freedom of its own kind, and it allowed her to explore a new side of herself—one that could be anyone and anything.

"I'm Rahul," he said, taking the question as an invite to move closer. He hovered over the next seat as if asking for permission, and he was cute enough to pique her interest.

But after last night, the dream forest was weighing on her mind, throwing her off-kilter. She owed *nothing* to Rabin. Not her loyalty and certainly not her body. He'd *lied* to her. Betrayed her.

So she forced a welcoming smile and said, "I haven't decided what I want yet."

Finally, he sank down as he laughed softly and then ordered himself a drink from the bartender.

"And whatever she'd like," he added.

"Nothing for me right now," Zarya answered as she scanned the bar, finding Yasen with a male Aazheri deep in conversation. He, too, had been enjoying himself since their departure from Dharati and sometimes took off on his own to indulge in a game of cards at one of Ishaan's many gambling lairs where he might find his own handsome stranger. She knew he'd made a few friends, too, though she hadn't met any of them yet.

Once in a while, he'd come home with a smattering of cuts and bruises, but he'd be smiling and assure her everything was fine. He'd changed so much without the burden of Vikram's protection and Gopal Ravana's threats hanging over his head, and she loved watching him flourish.

Apsara and Suvanna were no longer talking, both staring pointedly away from each other as though they'd been arguing. It wasn't her business, and she knew she shouldn't pry, but she wanted to see her friends happy. Apsara had grown on her during those weeks in Dharati, and she had a good heart. She wasn't as sure about Suvanna, but there was a fierce right-eousness about her that was impossible to deny.

"Are you from Ishaan?" Rahul asked, bringing her attention back.

"Not originally," she answered.

He waited for her to elaborate, and when she didn't, he continued. "What do you do?"

People loved that question around here. Everyone's station and rank were determined by how they earned a living. The question always rubbed her the wrong way. It was as though people were constantly trying to differentiate themselves from the vanshaj by declaring they had a good job with good pay that they did by choice. It was an underlying thread that governed nearly every interaction in Ishaan.

"A little of this and that," she said, purposely being evasive. One couldn't be sure of who they could trust. She avoided bringing people back to her apartment for that reason. She didn't want anyone to know where she lived if anything went wrong, plus there might be revealing paperwork or other incrim-inating items scattered around the flat.

"I work at the university," he said, with a touch of pride in his voice.

"Oh?" she asked because that actually did interest her. She remembered when Yasen had first told her about Gi'ana's center of knowledge. The massive compound was an hour's ride from the city, nestled into the base of the mountains. Formed by dozens of golden domed buildings, it was surrounded by lush greenery and a high iron fence.

So far, she'd only had the chance to view it from a distance, but she'd constantly imagined enrolling in a few classes and roaming their libraries, absorbing every bit of information she could. She'd looked into admission, and it was a simple enough test that one had to take. She'd have to study but was sure she could manage it. There just hadn't been time since they'd arrived.

"What do you do there?" she asked.

"I teach science and math," he replied. "Both fascinating subjects."

He went on to describe some of his courses in more detail, and Zarya found herself enraptured by all of it. She swore she'd *find* the time to sit the exam soon.

The door to the bar swung open, and Zarya saw Farida enter with the Chandra siblings.

"Sorry," Zarya said, interrupting Rahul. "My friends are here. It was nice chatting with you."

Rahul's eyebrows pulled together in surprise, and she hoped he wouldn't cause a scene. "Sure," he said. "Can I take you out sometime?"

"Perhaps," she replied and smiled before heading towards the door.

"Where will I find you?" he called, and she spun around to shrug.

"Around," she said with a wave of her hand before turning to the Chandras.

"Hi," Zarya said, hugging Farida and Rania. "How are you?"

"We have news," Farida said, her eyes darting around the bar. They all headed towards the back of the room to their usual secluded booth.

"I do, too," Zarya said.

She gestured to Apsara and Suvanna. "And some people for you to meet."

Zarya knew Ajay would have already briefed the two women on their arrival.

Farida gave them both a warm smile while Rania eyed Suvanna and Apsara up and down as they approached. Though she always regarded newcomers with a healthy dose of suspicion, she was obviously impressed.

Apsara and Suvanna *were* impressive with those wings, blue hair, and the fact that they both radiated unflinching power and confidence. Zarya had grown somewhat used to it, but now she was seeing what Rania saw for the first time.

After introductions, she then went on to explain who they were and how they'd aided in defeating the blight in Dharati. While Zarya was talking, Yasen made his way over, sliding into the booth next to Ajay.

"While I'm honored you've chosen to aid our cause," Rania said, "we'll need some assurances that you will keep our secrets under any circumstances."

Suvanna's navy eyes flashed. "You dare question our honor," she hissed as she slammed her fist on the table, and Zarya had to admire the way Rania held her ground.

"Of course," Apsara said, playing the diplomat, placing a hand on Suvanna's wrist and giving her a pointed look. "We understand what's at stake and that we need to be careful. That *you* need to be careful. But we want to help." Apsara appealed to Farida, who quietly watched the exchange. "Please."

Everyone waited. While Ajay and Rania tended to be more vocal in their leadership, likely due to their upbringings, Farida presented a more contained front. Ultimately, additions to their inner circle were only made with her approval.

Farida asked Apsara and Suvanna a few more questions about their pasts and their roles in their realms. She also questioned the state of the rebellions in their homes, weighing each of their responses carefully.

When she was done, she folded her hands in her lap and dipped her chin. "It sounds like we could use some powerful allies such as yourselves," she said. "Welcome to the Rising Phoenix."

Apsara smiled as Rania leaned over the table and hissed,

"Should you betray us, then thousands of lives will be on your heads."

"Understood," Apsara said as Suvanna nodded her assent with her arms folded tightly.

With that done, Zarya turned to Farida. "What were you planning to share?"

She exchanged an uncomfortable look with Rania and Ajay. "We received news from the palace," she said. "They're ransacking vanshaj homes and are threatening the entire district if someone doesn't come forward with information about the Rising Phoenix. They've threatened imprisonment... and worse."

"What could be worse?" Yasen asked.

Farida inhaled a deep breath and then blew it out, her body trembling. "They're threatening to break apart families and banish them to the Saaya if no one talks."

"What?" Zarya sat up. "That's preposterous. That land is completely uninhabitable."

"I know," Rania said. "It's basically a death sentence. Rumors are suggesting they plan to secretly start mining diamonds and using vanshaj labor to do so. It's the perfect solution."

"Solution for what!" Zarya cried out in exasperation, recalling the Saaya was unceded territory between Gi'ana and Andhera, where hundreds of abandoned diamond mines lay untouched due to endless disputes over ownership. "What are they all so afraid of?"

Farida shook her head, the threat of tears lining her eyes, while Rania's thunderous expression could split mountains in half. If these laws passed, they might be separated forever.

"Who will do their grunt work here?" Suvanna asked with disdain in her voice. "Surely they dare not lift a single delicate finger."

"It's the influence of the Jadugara," Rania said, speaking of the Aazheri sect who were responsible for collaring the vanshaj. "They don't care if the whole city falls apart, so long as they maintain their power. They're monsters whispering in the ears of the royal family."

"We won't let this happen," Zarya said to Farida.

"How are we going to stop it? The Phoenix has been working for years and has made almost no progress. *Nothing* has changed," Farida said, her voice rising.

"That's actually what I wanted to talk to you all about," Zarya said. "You remember what happened with the ink when I touched it with my magic?"

"Yes?" Rania asked, and Ajay nodded. Zarya assumed his sister would have already filled him in on this too. The two shared everything.

"Well, I've been trying some things, and I might be circling closer to a solution."

"What kind of solution?" Ajay asked, his brows knitting together.

For months, he'd been extremely curious about her magic and her interest in the vanshaj tattoos. He hadn't outright asked why, but his growing suspicion was obvious. When they'd arrived in Gi'ana, it was clear the prophecy about her mother was common enough lore that had she revealed it, everything about her would be exposed.

"I managed to... control the ink," she said, her gaze sliding to Apsara and Suvanna. They both knew about her nightfire and though she hadn't asked them to keep it secret, they were perceptive enough to understand the need for discretion.

"How?" Farida asked, sitting forward, a mixture of disbelief and hope in her expression.

Zarya swallowed the nervous knot in her throat. "It's probably better if I show you."

"Then show us," Ajay said.

"I would, but there's a small problem."

"What?"

"Remember when I dropped the case in the warehouse?"

"You're all out of ink," Ajay said, immediately picking up on the issue.

"Right. To show you, I need more. I also need it to test if my theories are correct."

"And we blew it all up," Rania said.

"So, I'm wondering if you know where we might find another source."

"With the ink so heavily controlled, the only place to find more would be at the Jadugara's Imarat," Ajay said, and everyone's gazes met around the table.

"What's the Imarat?" Apsara asked, sensing the uptick in everyone's apprehension.

Ajay's mouth formed into a thin line. "It's where the Jadugara live. It's attached to the Taara Den, where pregnant mothers must convalesce near the end of their pregnancies so they can collar the babies the moment they're born."

The laws of Gi'ana required every vanshaj who fell pregnant to register with the Jadugara. Failure to do so came with harsh penalties, and many parents had tried to hide their children over the years, but few ever got away with it. The Jadugara's mandate also included hunting down anyone who might have escaped their collar and bringing them to swift justice. Or at least, what they considered their cruel brand of "justice."

"They haven't closed the den, so they must be using whatever they have left," Ajay added.

"What are the talks of rebuilding the factory?" Suvanna asked. "Surely, they're already underway."

Ajay shook his head. "We have a number of spies from the Rising Phoenix working inside the palace as servants, but so far, they haven't picked up on anything. Any conversations must be happening behind closed doors."

"So we should find that out, too."

"That's how we can help," Apsara said. "We can present ourselves as emissaries from our realms, which isn't untrue."

"Why will you say you're here?" Yasen asked.

"Do we need a specific reason?" Apsara said. "We can say we're here for a visit."

"You could use the upcoming coronation as your cover," Rania offered.

"Right," Apsara said. "It wouldn't be unusual for representatives from other realms to attend."

"Do you think they'd welcome you?" Ajay asked.

"Most kingdoms welcome members of the Chiranjivi unless they want to make enemies," Suvanna said with a sharp look.

"Okay, then. You'll get inside and see if you can learn anything about the rebuilding plans. In the meantime, we need to find a way into the Imarat."

Zarya looked at Yasen. "So, I guess we're planning another break-in."

Yasen held up his glass and tipped it in a toast. "Lucky for all of you, this is becoming my specialty."

NINE

Once again, Zarya stood in a dark alley with a hood obscuring her face. Perhaps she should examine how her life had found her in this particular situation with such frequency of late.

The Imarat was a massive, sprawling four-story compound in the heart of the bustling city that housed the members of the Jadugara. They occupied the top floors, each living in opulence, thanks to the funding and support they received from the nobility and the royal family.

The Taara Den was housed on the main floor, where pregnant women presented themselves in their third trimester. They remained here, sleeping in large dorm rooms on the second and third levels until they gave birth. Zarya had walked past it many times, hearing the cries of labor and the wails of the babies screaming at the sting of needles forced into their tiny necks. And even worse, the delirious, heartbreaking screams when a child failed to survive the hideous procedure.

Just the thought of it made her want to throw up. The callousness and disregard for human suffering were incomprehensible. Having lived sheltered from the world, she'd never been exposed to the way indifference could filter into the cracks of society, turning people into monsters who confidently walked through broad daylight.

"Does Daragaab have a place like this?" she asked Yasen, who stood next to her, similarly hooded and cloaked, looking up at the building. Shame burned at the back of her throat that she hadn't spent more time paying attention to the vanshaj while she'd lived in Dharati.

"No," he said, shaking his head. "A small group of Jadugara live in the city to place the markings and receive shipments of ink from Gi'ana, but things are less organized."

"Does that mean some of them get away without being marked?"

"Sometimes," he answered, leaving it at that.

A few lights glowed in the building, but mostly, it sat dark, its inhabitants asleep for the night. Normally, the Imarat was only loosely guarded by the city watch. The Jadugara feared no one. On one side, they lived in the back pockets of the wealthy, and on the other, they ruled by fear, whether you were vanshaj or not.

No one came near this place willingly, terrified of incurring the Jadugara's notice. While their authority technically gave them jurisdiction over the vanshaj, they also used their considerable magic on anyone who they believed had escaped the collar. Ajay suspected they liked to make an example of an innocent person now and then just to keep everyone afraid.

But after the factory explosion, the royals had apparently offered up some of their own soldiers, and now a line of them stood protecting the front entrance in their regal emerald sherwanis. If Zarya and Yasen were caught, the royal family would undoubtedly impose more threats, and who knew when they'd start acting on them? It might unravel the careful rope they'd been weaving. The Rising Phoenix had been at this for years with little success, and Zarya hoped she was close to offering, if not a solution, then at least some leverage.

"Let's go," Yasen said, peering up at the sky. "We'll try entering from the back."

Yasen and Zarya retreated into the shadows and made their way through the twisting corridors to arrive at the rear of the compound. The building was made of the same white stone as most of the city, carved with whorls and flowers. Gilded borders framed the windows, and small silver domes crowned various towers and sections of the roof. Bordered by a high iron fence, the grounds were an impeccable field of clipped green grass and flowering bushes.

Two bored men in uniform guarded the back door, looking like they would rather be anywhere else.

"Are they even awake?" Yasen whispered. "Some soldiers they are."

"They're just hired thugs," Zarya said, noting their somewhat threadbare clothing. But they also proved the royal soldiers standing out front were only a show of intimidation. The Jadugara were too confident. She hoped she could inflict a crack in that armor.

Yasen snorted. "You get what you pay for, I guess."

He peered up and then left and right down the alley. Everything remained quiet except for the usual sounds of the city. "Can you do something about them?" he asked.

Zarya nodded and then sent out two slim tendrils of air magic circling around their necks. Just enough to make them pass out but not to kill them, though she did kind of want to kill anyone who willingly supported this behavior. They'd get their chance for their revenge. But first, she had to get to the bottom of all this.

The two guards slumped against the wall, and quick as lightning, Yasen darted across the alley, catching each of them around a bicep and easing them gently to the ground. When Zarya gave him a quizzical look, he answered, "Don't worry, I wasn't concerned about them falling. I just didn't want their weapons to make any noise."

"Smart," she said, stepping over one of them.

"I'm not just a pretty face, Zee."

She snorted. "Sure you are."

He laughed as she bent down and peered through the keyhole. Using a bit more air magic, she felt inside the lock, probing the mechanism. After she was rewarded with a click, she continued through the opening, coming out the other side and finding the deadbolt before flipping it open.

The door creaked quietly as they entered a dark hallway before closing it softly behind them. Waiting, they listened for any sounds of life.

When all seemed quiet, they ventured down the hall and stopped when they came upon a branching corridor leading towards a brightly lit room. Zarya made out the din of low chatter and the clink of cutlery, plates, and glasses, indicating a kitchen already up preparing meals for the following day or perhaps tending to a few late-night cravings for the Imarat's residents.

Yasen pressed his finger to his lips, and they scooted past, slinking deeper into the shadows. The polished marble floors gleamed in the streetlights filtering through windows covered with gauzy curtains.

Their earlier reconnaissance had revealed the ink was kept in a cabinet in the front of the building that served as a sitting area. They proceeded down the hall, pausing occasionally to listen for sounds of anyone approaching. A creak from overhead had them pressing against the wall with their breath held. They listened as footsteps neared the top of the stairs before they continued past, receding into another part of the building.

"Let's move," Yasen whispered. "This place gives me the creeps."

Zarya nodded before they searched the sprawling main

floor to locate the front hall. Off to the left, they found a large living area filled with plush furniture, perfect for receiving guests.

At the back was a long glass-fronted cabinet that ran nearly the length of the wall. Even in the dimness of the room, Zarya could see the inky reflection of the bottles sitting in neat rows like trophies. She suspected they kept these out in the open as a constant reminder of their power.

"Jackpot," Yasen said, giving Zarya a triumphant look.

She nodded, and they prowled closer, still keeping one ear peeled, when she noticed the large padlock fastened to the front of the cabinet.

"It's locked," she whispered. "They didn't say anything about a lock."

Yasen picked it up, studying the heavy contraption before gently laying it down. "I wonder if they added it after we blew up the factory."

"Great," Zarya said, her gaze tracing the edges and lines of the cabinet, searching for another way inside.

"Can you use your magic to open it?" Yasen asked as he ran his fingers along the edges of the door, clearly having similar thoughts. There were no visible joints or weak spots, so the lock was the only option short of smashing the glass.

"I'll try," she said. As she had with the door, she spun out a thread of air and fed it into the keyhole. With her tongue wedged in the corner of her mouth, she rooted inside it, searching for a way to spring the mechanism.

"Zee, hurry up," Yasen said, his gaze flicking towards the doorway and back again.

"I'm trying," she snapped. "This is hard."

He grunted but said nothing as she continued to poke and prod. This lock was far more complex than the one guarding the back. Perhaps the factory explosion *had* rattled the Jadugara more than they were letting on.

As she worked, it took her a few moments to notice another sound filling the quiet room. Clinking. A soft chime, like beads tinkling in a breeze.

"What's that noise?" Yasen asked as their gazes drifted to the bottles that were now... vibrating. Zarya placed a hand on the cabinet while they shook harder, the ringing of glass growing louder.

"My magic," Zarya whispered in horror. There was so much ink here. Was it reacting to her mere *presence*? She curled her magic back, hoping to settle the bottles, but they continued to rattle, the sound swelling to fill every corner of the room.

"Zee, do something!" Yasen whisper-yelled. "Make them stop."

"I don't know how," she whispered back. "Wait, let me try—"

She inhaled a deep breath and allowed her sixth anchor loose. She had controlled the ink with it earlier, so maybe this would work.

It was then that several things happened at once.

Light filled the room, and a deep male voice shouted, "What are you doing?"

Zarya had just enough time to register the Jadugara's signature blood-red robes before she noticed the shaking bottles were now bouncing where they stood, the sound like a hailstorm of nails dropping onto crystal.

"Duck!" Yasen cried just as he threw himself on top of her, flattening them both to the floor as the cabinet shattered with a crash that made her eardrums ring. Black ink exploded everywhere, coating them from head to toe.

"Arrest them!" came the fevered cries as the entire building began to stir awake. They had to get out of here.

"Get up," Yasen said, "we have to run."

"But we didn't get anything," Zarya said as Yasen tugged on her arm. With her sixth anchor already at her fingertips, she cast out a puff of dark shadows that descended over the room, obscuring everything in darkness.

"Please tell me that was you," she heard Yasen say as she reached out for him, clasping his hand.

"Stay next to me," she said as she felt out for the direction of the cabinet, hoping against hope that something had survived. She moved towards the edge of the room and to the bottles that had been farthest away. "See if you can find any still intact."

She heard Yasen moving next to her as they ran their hands over the shelves. "Shit," Zarya hissed as she cut herself on a piece of glass. "Yas?"

"Got some," he said before she felt him grab her wrist and then push down on her head. They dropped to their knees as they listened to the panic of clashing weapons and thudding bodies. While Zarya's shadows continued to darken the atmosphere, they crawled along the wall until they found the exit.

"The door," Yasen said, yanking on her sleeve. "This way."

Keeping low to the ground where the shadows were thinner, they arrived at the front entrance. Yasen reached up to swing open the door, and then together, they tumbled outside.

"Get up!" Yasen shouted as they rolled down the front steps. Morning was arriving, and the sun was just starting to rise over the rooftops.

"Hey!" shouted one of the guards who spotted them. "Who are you?"

"Don't mind us. We're just leaving," Yasen said, leaping to his feet and tugging on Zarya's arm before they turned and ran for their lives.

TEN

"Wow, you two really made a fucking mess of that," Ajay said as he paced back and forth. They were all gathered in Yasen and Zarya's apartment several hours later. The pair were still covered in faded ink that had yet to wash away. It would take at least a few more baths before they'd get it out of their skin. The clothes they'd been wearing were completely ruined.

Zarya would have tossed them, anyway. After what happened, she realized how careful she would have to be using her magic around the ink. As it stood, she wouldn't attempt it until she'd scrubbed off every last drop.

"Oops?" Yasen said, his grin suggesting he was anything but sorry. After they'd absconded from the Imarat, they'd had to scrape off the soles of their shoes on the hard cobbles and avoid touching anything lest they leave a trail, pointing everyone in their direction like a bright, flashing light.

Ajay let out an exasperated huff, but it was hard to ever stay mad at Yasen.

"They've doubled their efforts to find out who's responsible for the bombing," he said. "They know these two incidents are connected."

"True," Farida said, "but they still don't understand the real reason for what happened last night. They'll assume we attempted to destroy the last of the stockpile."

Ajay sighed and ran a hand along the back of his neck.

"That doesn't make this situation any less precarious. Soon enough, they'll figure out who's responsible for this, and they *will* make someone pay."

"We knew the risks when we started this," Rania said, her jaw hardening. "If you want out, then just—"

"No," Ajay said. "You know that's not what I'm saying. I just don't want anyone to get hurt."

"People will get hurt, Ajay. That can't be helped," his sister said, and his mouth pressed into a flat line, clearly disliking that answer.

"Then we need to ensure that's as few people as possible."

"No one got hurt tonight," Zarya said. "Or at least no one on our side. Do you really care that we inflicted damage on the Jadugara?"

"No, of course not," Ajay said. "But if we sink to their level, then we're just as bad as all of them, aren't we?"

"I don't know about that," Zarya grumbled. "Sometimes, the means justify the ends. We're the ones in the right here."

Their gazes clashed. Sometimes, they argued. Sometimes, Ajay was too damn noble for his own good. He'd grown up surrounded by vanshaj servants and, like many young people, hadn't considered their situation in relation to his privilege. She knew he wrestled with that constant guilt, and it made him fight hard against every setback.

"Did you at least get what you went for?" Ajay asked, and Yasen strode over to pick up his stained jacket, pulling out three bottles of ink. Zarya sagged in relief.

"Well done," she said, reaching out. "I was worried I'd broken them all."

"About that," Ajay said, narrowing his gaze. "What exactly happened?"

Zarya knew the question was coming. It was becoming obvious that any thread of her magic, save her sixth anchor, caused the ink to react in volatile ways, and *something* in the ink was connected to dark magic and the legendary sixth anchor that had been supposedly locked away.

But already Zarya suspected it was a cover-up.

What if the sixth anchor had been used to *create* the ink? Which would mean she wasn't the only one with six anchors and they'd all been living a lie.

But she wasn't ready to confess all of that yet.

"My magic slipped," she said. "I'm still getting used to how it works."

While she hadn't revealed everything about her past to Farida and the Chandras, they did know she only had access to her magic recently. But her stories were wearing thin and starting to show holes; sooner or later, she'd have to come clean.

Ajay's gaze flickered with wariness. He'd been quick to offer his trust, but she was walking a precarious line. Zarya *did* have all of their best interests at heart and only wanted to help. She just needed to figure out the best way to reveal these secrets. It's not like she could just walk around claiming she was the heir to the queen, a member of the royal family, and, more importantly, the one foretold in the prophecy.

And they didn't even know about the second half of it yet.

She touched the turquoise stone hanging around her neck. She'd replayed her mother's message, locked inside, so many times that she knew every breath and cadence of her speech. It circled through her thoughts on a constant loop. She was sure the prophecy explained why her magic was connected to the ink and why she had to figure this out. She was destined to help the vanshaj break free of their chains, and she would die trying if she had to.

Before anyone could question her further, Zarya stood, gesturing to the ink. "I'm going to get some sleep and then practice some more with this tomorrow."

Farida stepped in her way and looked up at Zarya with a hopeful look in her eyes. "Do you really think you can do something with it?"

"I don't know," Zarya said. "But I want to try."

"How?" Rania asked, always the more suspicious of the pair, and Zarya let out a short sigh.

"Just trust me, okay? I'll tell you everything once I know for sure."

Rania swallowed, her throat bobbing, but whatever she saw in Zarya's face convinced her to let it lie for now.

She squeezed Farida's hand, hoping to offer some reassurance. "Just give me a few more days, and I'll come to see you."

Then Zarya headed for her room. She studied her ink-stained hands, wondering if she should have another shower, but she'd been awake since yesterday, and exhaustion weighed heavy on her shoulders.

She settled into her bed as her mind swirled with a million disparate thoughts.

She'd used her sixth anchor in a completely new way tonight, pulling out shadows to shield them from view. She held her hand up, flipping it over, studying her palm and then the back of it. She'd been so afraid of touching this power, but maybe that was foolish. This was her gift. She thought again about the prophecy. Her darkness might be the key to manipulating the ink, and how could it be wrong to use it for such an important purpose?

She flipped over to her side, her hand sliding under her pillow, where she'd stashed a dagger for safekeeping. Ever since leaving Dharati, she'd slept with one eye open, conscious of Row's warnings about her father, the king of Andhera.

With that sinister thought floating in her mind, she closed her eyes and attempted to drown in the bliss of sleep.

* * *

"Tell me about her nightfire?" Abishek asked from where he sat across from Rabin. They were dining in the king's massive domed solarium, surrounded by greenery, the windows revealing the night sky sparkling with stars overhead. Candles flickered on the table between them, the surface laden with every delicacy the kitchen could conjure.

Abishek had few indulgences—he was a man of restraint and modesty unless royal decorum required otherwise—but he did love to eat.

"It's mesmerizing," Rabin said. "Absolute raw power. She was having trouble controlling it after I arrived in Dharati, but I helped her through it thanks to your lessons about Aazheri magic."

Abishek nodded as he reached for his drink and took a long sip. "And after that?"

"During the battle, she used it against Rani Amrita, assuming it wouldn't harm her, but..."

Rabin trailed off, remembering the moment when Zarya realized her magic had affected the queen. "But it injured her."

Abishek's eyebrows drew together. "Nightfire hurt the queen?"

Rabin nodded and then leaned forward. "I have a theory."

"Do you?" the king asked, arching a dark eyebrow.

"She asked me questions about the darkness, wondering if it was evil."

"And?"

"And I explained what you taught me: that the darkness is only another form of magic. Only those who use it with nefarious intentions are evil."

"Good," Abishek said, nodding. "But why would she ask such things?"

Rabin shook his head. "I don't know. But she seemed... relieved by my answers."

"And what is it you believe?"

"Do you think it's possible she has the sixth anchor?"

Abishek let out a loud breath and sat back, running a hand down his face.

Rabin thought of the tattoo on his back. Six petals inside a flower, each representing the continent's magic, save one that sat empty until it could be freed from its seal. With his keen interest in magic, he'd reveled in Abishek's lessons over the years, absorbing his vast knowledge about every form of magic.

The Ashvins had used the darkness in a way that resulted in their banishment. Ever since, Aazheri magic had been considered tainted, but that was only prejudice.

The king had six anchors—a fact he'd confided only to Rabin, his army commander, Ekaja, and his personal mystic. It was another reason why he believed Row's claims were false.

But the seal kept others from reaching it, and Abishek's life's work centered on breaking down that barrier, hoping to restore full Aazheri power across the continent.

His theory was that anyone who could sense the presence of a wall pressing in on their magic also had six anchors, but a few rare Aazheri, like himself, could already access it due to some outlying factor he hadn't yet deciphered.

At Rabin's question, Abishek nodded. "It would make sense my child would have six anchors and that a gift so rare would belong to an Aazheri of such strength." Rabin watched as the king's eyes shone, the edges lined with a hint of emotion. The king wasn't generally a sentimental man, but he held those in his confidence close and cared deeply for them.

"My daughter," he said softly, drifting off before clearing his throat. "In my many years, I never imagined myself as a father, but knowing she has already achieved such greatness fills me with a pride I never expected..."

His gaze drifted towards the heavens, and Rabin allowed him a moment to collect himself. When the king was ready, he returned his gaze to Rabin.

"How have your experiments with the mind plane been progressing?"

"Very well," he answered with a dip of his chin. "I was able to conjure the forest."

"And she was there?" he asked, his eyes wide with interest.

"She was. I didn't speak to her, but it worked."

Abishek nodded, his pride in Rabin also evident. "When will you try again?"

"Soon. I'd like to show her this place." He cast out an arm to encompass their surroundings.

"That is a far more difficult bit of magic," Abishek said, and Rabin nodded.

"I think I can do it."

"I have no doubt, my son." He smiled at Rabin, and he felt his heart twist. A father of sorts. After so many years of craving someone who might be proud of him, this king had filled that raw, gaping void.

"Thank you for your faith in me," Rabin said, and Abishek dipped his chin.

"You make it easy." He leaned forward. "But don't wait too long. I am very eager to meet her."

"I understand," Rabin said. "I will not let you down."

ELEVEN

Once Zarya had scrubbed her skin until it was red and raw, until every last trace of the magic ink was purged, she headed through the city towards the forest. Her route through Ishaan took her past the royal palace.

Anytime she came this way, she couldn't help the way her feet would draw her closer.

The massive structure stood in vivid contrast to the white marble of Ishaan's architecture, made of sky-blue stone forged from a secret, enchanted cave inside the Pathara Vala Mountains. It would dull the magic of anyone within its walls, thus ensuring the royal family's protection during an invasion. Each immediate family member wore a special object that nullified the effects and, every so often, bestowed a charm on those they deemed loyal and worthy of the honor.

A wide central tower dominated the center of the palace, stretching into the clouds with tall windows ringing the perimeter, offering an unobstructed view of Gi'ana in every direction. Or at least, that's what Zarya had been told.

The rest of the palace boasted hundreds of arched windows, all framed in ornate silver, wrought into twists and curls. White marble doors inlaid with colorful stones admitted hundreds of people in and out of the courtyard at all hours of the day.

Zarya stopped at the gates and peered into the massive square, where a huge astronomical clock dominated one wall. It stood several stories high, and the polished gold, silver, and bronze gears and mechanisms reflected brightly in the sun.

In the distance hung a balcony at the front of the palace where the Madans often gathered to greet their subjects. It stood empty today, but Zarya noted the line snaking out of the main door. Three mornings a week, at least one member of the royal family would meet with the citizens in the throne room to hear their grievances. Vanshaj were not permitted, of course.

When Zarya first arrived, she'd tried joining the line, but the clerics managing the crowds demanded to know her business. When she couldn't answer their questions, she was turned away. As she learned more about the city and the Madans, she wasn't sure if her primary reason for coming to Gi'ana still made sense. These people of her heritage ran a queendom built on blood. Did she really want to know them better?

But a crackle charged the air today, signaling a shifting tide. Zarya was sure it was all a result of the explosion, the theft from the Jadugara, and the threat of new laws. The royals had been spooked and scared bullies tended to react in unpredictable ways.

They were running out of time, and Zarya had to do something fast.

She turned away and continued through the city, passing the walls into the forest beyond.

She found the same clearing where she'd brought Yasen a few nights ago and sat on the rock in the center, studying her surroundings. While this forest bore little resemblance to the dream forest, she couldn't help but be reminded of it. Despite her best efforts, Rabin continued to occupy her thoughts.

She sighed and rolled her neck, trying to quell a riot of

emotions. She had more important things to do right now. People were relying on her, and she couldn't let them down.

Opening up her bag, she pulled out a bottle of ink and a copper bowl, pouring out a few drops. She had to figure this out. Who knew where they'd find more ink? While they'd scored a victory in destroying most of what remained, the catch was that she only had this small amount left to work with. She *would* figure it out. She was meant for this. As much as she missed Row and Dharati and Amrita, she was more sure than ever that coming to Gi'ana had been the right choice. The fact she'd met Farida and the Chandras within the first few days of her arrival only confirmed it.

She was being led down the right path, but it was up to her to fit the pieces together and create the desired outcome.

She placed the bowl next to her and then turned to face it, one leg folded under her.

There was no point in bothering with her other five strains of magic. She'd already proven there was only one option here.

Closing her eyes, she felt for the spinning star in her heart, unfolding the sixth anchor from its place where it hid behind her fire anchor.

Maybe there wasn't any need to lock it away. Maybe this, too, was part of the plan. She remembered Rabin's confident words about magic being neither good nor evil; only the people controlling it could decide the spectrum of its morality. With that thought in mind, she let it snap free, locking it into place with her five other anchors. She considered the arrangement, appreciating the symmetry and the completeness of this picture.

This was the full extent of who she was. Right?

She pulled on the darkness and allowed it to filter out of her fingers, touching it to the surface. The ink responded instantly, rippling in the sway of her magic. She drew it up and pulled it into the air, directing it into a series of intricate, twisting patterns.

Then she let it settle back into the bowl and stared at it, contemplating her next step.

After pulling out a pen from her bag, she dipped the tip into the ink and scratched a string of random letters onto the surface of the rock. She then called up her sixth anchor and touched it to the ink, rooting around for weaknesses in its makeup. Her working theory was that she could possibly pull the ink apart or simply dissolve it from the skin.

She closed her eyes as her magic slid over the ink. Slowly and with careful concentration, she felt the individual molecules that made up the dye and, more importantly, the dark magic they contained. It was hard to describe the sensation, but it was akin to vibrations or a low resonance. It hummed gently, and she wondered if other forms of magic had a similar footprint or if this feeling was unique to her sixth anchor.

She filtered in another sliver of darkness, forcing the particles to vibrate with increasing vigor. This felt like the right direction. She continued making them quiver, feeling them lift and shift against one another. With another sliver of magic, she tried to slide it in between the tiny hairline spaces they were forming. It took a few tries to get the angle and position right—like threading the end of a fine needle—but then she felt it slip between and exhaled a small grunt. The sensation was awkward at first, like she'd tried to shove a square peg into a too-tight hole, but the molecules eventually adjusted to its presence, expanding to accommodate the intrusion.

She dug into it and tried to peel the pieces apart, teasing away the edge of a letter. Then, in fascination, she watched as it lifted away from the stone before dissolving in the air and scattering into nothing.

Zarya pulled her magic back, staring at the spot where the ink had been a moment ago. She wanted to jump up and squeal for joy. Had she just done it? Had she just broken the mark?

This wasn't the same as the vanshaj mark—this had just been written and not embedded into skin—but this had to be a start.

She tried again with the next letter, using the same combination of vibrations and sliding between each note of the ink's magic. It took her an hour to erase each of the letters, and by the time she was done, she was covered in sweat and panting heavily. A pain throbbed behind her eye from the strength of her concentration, but this was something.

She will be the one to free them all.

It had to mean *something*.

Over the next few days, Zarya returned to the clearing, attempting to lift the ink off various surfaces: wood, metal, and paper. The paper and wood proved harder to shift due to their porousness, where the ink embedded deeper.

This was closer to human skin, but it was still a far cry from the real thing, which was why she found herself standing in a butcher shop where she acquired several pieces of meat.

"Skin on," she said when she asked for a ham hock. The butcher gave her a quizzical look, but it wasn't such an unusual request. Was it?

She then repeated the process with the ink using bits of bone, flesh, and skin. The skin was the hardest, but she succeeded with each variation. Still, she was worried that this wasn't tattooed on but simply drawn.

At some point, she'd need a human test subject—one with a tattoo—and the very idea made her stomach twist with fear and worry and a sick sense of wrongness.

The other issue was that she was rapidly running out of ink, and there was no possible way to get more before the royal family began acting on their threats. So, she practiced every day, coming home exhausted and covered in sweat before she'd collapse on her bed into a dreamless sleep.

Upon her return home one rainy day, Yasen sat at her bedside, stroking her hair. "How'd it go today?" he asked, and she could only manage an exhausted grunt.

"You're killing yourself," he said. "I think you need to take a break."

"I'm so close," she said. "Just a few more days, and I think I'll have it."

"Zee," he said, a thread of reproach in his tone.

"I'm almost out of ink, anyway," she said. "Either I figure this out soon or not. Either way, I'm almost done."

"Okay," he said. "But be careful. You don't want to burn yourself out."

She sighed and rolled over onto her back, tucking her arm behind her. Yasen lay down next to her, their heads touching as they stared up at the ceiling.

"Are you planning to tell them?" Yasen asked her.

He didn't elaborate on what or who, but she knew that he was referring to Farida, the Chandras, and her sixth and forbidden strain of magic.

"I have a suspicion about the Jadugara," she said. "I think they must be lying about the sixth anchor, and they have it, too."

Yasen was quiet for a moment. "That would make sense."

"Why are they lying about it, though?" she asked. "Why pretend it's this secret thing when it's obvious more than a few people have it?"

"My guess would be power," Yasen said. "They want to keep it all to themselves."

"So they know," she said. "And the vanshaj must have the darkness, too. Like Meera, who also saw the ghost army."

"That would also make sense," he said.

"So, why weren't the members of the Jadugara also collared?"

"Another very good question," Yasen said.

"Do you think we should expose them for the liars they are?" she asked.

"That's an entire can of snakes, isn't it?"

She snorted a wry laugh. If what she was attempting wasn't bad enough, exposing the Jadugara as frauds might bring this queendom to its knees. She was trying to decide how she felt about that. This was technically her home. These were technically her people. But they'd been operating out of cruelty and malice for so long. How might things have been different if she'd grown up here? Would she also have turned a blind eye to everything?

"I guess one problem at a time," Zarya said, and she felt Yasen nod.

"So, what's next?"

"I keep trying until I'm confident enough."

"Enough for what?"

She twisted her head and looked at him. He met her gaze, open and trusting. She was so grateful she had him and that she could tell him anything without fear of judgment.

"To tell the Farida and the Chandras everything."

TWELVE

What Zarya hadn't been ready to confess to Yasen was that she intended to practice on herself with the last of the ink. Animal flesh and skin were only a substitute and no comparison to a living, breathing human being.

Once again, she found herself in the clearing with the last of her ink and her tools.

She started by drawing a five-pointed star on the back of her hand. She went through the motions, which required a little extra effort, but eventually, she managed to lift the ink off her skin. This was progress, and she was pleased, but this was her own magic. It didn't hurt her. Would it be the same for someone else?

She then pulled out a needle and dipped it into the ink. Bracing herself, she made a small line of dots along her forearm, wincing at the sharp sting. She had to see if embedded markings would react differently. When she'd tried it with the pigskin, it had held on tighter. She watched the blood well on the surface before the dye settled into her skin.

As she predicted, the ink was harder to lift, but after some effort, she managed to peel off the dots before they dispersed.

She had the technique down. She knew what to do, but was this enough?

She held up the last bottle of ink, studying the thin layer coating the bottom. This was it. She only had a few more chances before requiring an actual human for this task. She dipped her needle in the ink and then tattooed another line down her other arm. She would let this one sit for a few days before attempting to dissolve it.

A knot formed in her chest as she used up the last drops, tipping the bottle upside down until nothing came out.

When she was done, she sat on the rock, surveying the forest, when her gaze snagged on a dark patch of leaves in the distance.

Her neck prickling with an unwelcome sense of déjà vu, she stood and walked over, peering up at the branches waving softly in the breeze. Blinking hard, she stared up, willing the scene to change. Black leaves. Some of them fully transformed, and some only partially covered in a line of black rot.

She shook her head and stepped back as bile churned up the back of her throat. It *couldn't* be. She remembered this. The memory stood out in her mind as if it had only been yesterday when the forests around the seaside cottage had done the same.

The swamp. The rot. The *darkness*.

Amrita had forced it back, but they hadn't destroyed it. They weren't able to. Was it back? They were miles from the Jai Tree, but was the seal a physical thing? Or rather a representation?

She shouldn't keep this to herself, but the truth clogged in her chest, making it hard to breathe. *Row*. Was he okay? She should alert the royal family about this threat waiting on their door, but would they believe her? And in doing so, what would she reveal?

Swinging around, she spied more patches of rot scattered

through the trees. She wanted to run, but she also couldn't look away.

Forcing one foot in front of the other, she approached a tree dotted with black leaves and placed her hand on the rough bark of the trunk.

Suddenly, her surroundings went dark before flashes of things she had no memory of materialized in her vision. A dark, opulent palace nestled between soaring snow-capped mountains. Armies of demons wearing beaten metal armor marching over a ruined landscape. Flashes of star-flecked magic and clouds of black smoke. She heard screams and voices—two distinct male ones—speaking a language she didn't know. In her mind's eye, she saw a bearded man with fire in his eyes staring at her, ruin and war reflecting in their depths.

Zarya dropped to her knees, striking against hard pebbles, her breath coming in tight, ragged pants. She fell to her hands, her head sagging between her shoulders as it spun and spun, the world tilting on an axis. It took several long seconds before the images dissolved, leaving only the grass and flowers. She blinked several times before she pushed back onto her heels and scanned the forest as the black leaves continued waving overhead.

But there were more now. In fact, the trees surrounding her had all turned completely black. She looked at the tree she'd touched as her breath turned to mud.

A smoking handprint scarred the surface like a brand.

She studied her unmarked palms as she recalled the flashes of the bearded man with fire in his eyes, remembering the same face in her reflection before she'd left Dharati. She'd pushed it out of her mind. She thought she'd imagined it—or at least she'd convinced herself of that.

Stumbling to her feet on shaky legs, she stared around the forest, which had suddenly turned sinister, like it was concealing an entire world of devastating secrets in its heart.

What was happening? Who was the man with the burning eyes?

Surely, you've realized by now that you *are responsible for all of this? That the darkness lives in you?*

She shook her head, dislodging Dhawan's words from their hold in her mind. He'd been lying. Trying to manipulate her into following him.

She stumbled another step, clinging to a tree trunk before she snatched her hand away, holding it to her chest as a knot in her heart pulsed with life.

A flash of movement caught her eye, and she spun around. For several long seconds, she stared at the empty spot, *sure* she'd seen something made of scales and shadows. Sure it was something she'd seen before living on an abandoned shore surrounded by death and rot.

The darkness lives in you...

But what if Dhawan had been telling the truth?

LETTER

Dear Zarya,

I bring terrible news. Yesterday, there was a riot outside the palace. Vanshaj and their supporters stormed the gates, demanding an audience with the queen. Word of what is happening in Gi'ana is spreading, and it's giving them the confidence they need to fight back.

I joined the march and wrestled my way to the front, where Vikram waited. I tried to reason with him, but he refused, claiming Amrita had no desire to entertain these demands. I don't believe that. I have known Amrita long enough to be sure this is not what she would desire. Or at least the old Amrita would never have felt this way.

The crowd was angry, and things got out of hand. Vikram sent his soldiers into the streets, and fighting broke out. Many died on both sides, and it is a tragedy the likes of which I have never seen.

It seems Vikram is also taking his cues from Gi'ana, threatening all manner of punishments should some-

thing like this ever happen again. He's trying to keep the status quo, but we are on the cusp of change.

I hope that, whatever you're doing, you can all find a solution that doesn't result in more bloodshed for the vanshaj.

I also must continue to caution you against getting any nearer to the royal family. I understand why you went to Gi'ana, but now that you see what kind of rule they keep, you must understand they are dangerous. If they were to find out what you've been involved in, they would not hesitate to use it against you.

If you need me at all, please send word. The baby is doing well and should be born in a few months. Koura is confident she will be healthy and strong and loved very much despite Amrita's seeming changes.

Be careful. All of you.

Row

THIRTEEN

A few days later, Zarya sat in her bed, examining the dots she'd pierced into her skin. She tried not to think about what had happened in the forest, though she was failing miserably. Her dreams were plagued with the images she'd seen—screaming monsters and dying armies, fire and ash, and a vast wasteland of nothing.

She also tried not to think of Dhawan's words, but they wouldn't stay quiet.

Was the darkness... *following* her?

She needed to talk to someone. Maybe she could write to Row? The same thing couldn't be happening again. This had to be something else.

Shaking her head, she cast these thoughts aside for now, determined to focus on the ink tattooed on her arm. If she couldn't lift it, then she'd have to find another way to break the collars. If she could, then she'd have to confront the next step.

She started on the first dot, using the techniques she'd practiced.

A knock came at her door.

"Come in," she said, and Yasen swung it open.

"Morning," he said. "You were back late last night."

Zarya didn't look up from where she was concentrating on her arm.

"I was working," she said.

He made a sound of surprise. "What did you do?"

She looked at him and then her arm. "What I needed."

She pulled up another tattooed dot, and Yasen let out a low whistle. "You weren't kidding about making progress."

She blew out a breath. "I don't know what else I can do at this point. I've tried it on several materials, animal skin and flesh." She held up her arm. "And now my own skin."

She fell silent, and Yasen sank on the bed beside her. "But you don't know how it will affect a real live human who's been wearing the tattoo for years?"

"Exactly," she said.

"How did you know the tattoo wouldn't steal *your* magic?" he asked.

She shrugged. "I was hoping that just a few dots wouldn't hurt."

Yasen shook his head, exasperation crossing his face. "That was incredibly stupid."

"Probably," Zarya said, pushing the blanket off her legs and scooting off the bed. "I'm going to tell the Chandras."

"You are?"

"I want to try this on Farida, but she has a right to know what I'm attempting. It wouldn't be right to use the darkness on her without making her aware of what I am."

"I'm worried about how they'll react," Yasen said as Zarya dug into her closet for a light blue cotton salwar kameez. She walked into the bathroom to change.

"I am, too," she shouted from the other room. "But what choice do I have anymore? They already know something is weird about my magic."

"Yeah," Yasen said. "I hope... I hope they're who we think they are."

Dressed now, Zarya returned to the bedroom. "What do you mean by that?"

"I just think we put a lot of trust into people we'd never met until a few months ago. Once they know your secrets, there will be no putting them back."

Zarya snapped a silver bangle onto her wrist and tipped her head. "Aw, are you worried about me?"

Yasen glared. "Of course I am. I came along to keep an eye on you, remember?"

She smiled and patted his cheek. "And I'm so glad you did."

He snorted and then stood. "Okay, let's go then. I'm coming with you."

Zarya nodded and linked arms with Yasen.

They entered the street, pressing into the throng of bustling people. More posters plastered every surface, demanding information about the Rising Phoenix and its members. Updated versions included hazy illustrations of two people that Zarya presumed were meant to be her and Yasen. They stopped to scrutinize the drawings.

"Do they look like us?" she asked softly, and Yasen shook his head.

"Not really. But I don't know how they could have gotten a good enough look at us to compose a proper sketch. My hunch is they're just pretending they know more than they do to make it seem like they're in control."

"Hmm," Zarya said, hoping that was true. Yasen was right, and between the darkness, their hoods, and her shadows, it would have been impossible to see their faces, but they were dealing with powerful Aazheri, and she had no idea what they were truly capable of.

As if thinking about the Jadugara summoned their presence, a hushed murmur ran through the crowd a moment later. The sea of people was parting, clearing the busy boulevard to press along the sides. Zarya and Yasen had a clear view down the street towards a group of men wearing long blood-red robes with belts made of colorful fabric and embroidered with tiny mirrors and beads.

Everyone fell silent as the Jadugara approached. They eyed the crowd, most of them with thick dark beards, though a few had only a light layer of stubble covering their cheeks. What they all had in common was a straight set to their postures and an imperious tilt to their chins—like men born to privilege who had never had one of their ideas dismissed.

Their appearance set Zarya's hackles up. She didn't trust them, especially knowing what she did about the magical ink. They were all hiding something, and her plans included discovering what.

Alongside the men walked various vanshaj servants dressed in white, each holding swinging lit thuribles. The scent of sandalwood drifted into the air, mixing with the smells of the city—food, bodies, and horses. She felt Yasen reach for her wrist, his hand closing around it.

She looked up at him, and silently, they agreed to remain where they stood. Ducking away might draw more attention to themselves than hiding in plain sight. Everyone knew that when the Jadugara approached, you cleared out of the way quickly, and then you stood witness and waited for them to pass. No errand or appointment was considered as important as giving the Jadugara the honor they were due.

It was all such complete bullshit.

The Jadugara took their time as though they were strolling through a garden on a lazy Sunday afternoon. Except for the fact they were glaring at everyone as if trying to peer into the very marrow of the secrets they kept. They were working with the royal family on rooting out the members of the Rising

Phoenix, and Zarya had the distinct impression that if anyone were to come forward with information, the only reward they'd get would be the inside of an urn.

As they passed, an Aazheri near the front of the pack turned to look at Zarya. Their gazes met, and she held his stare, determined not to look away. These frauds wouldn't cow her. Maybe it was foolish, but something about the truths she knew made her bold. She noticed the way his eyes narrowed only a fraction, probably incensed that she hadn't immediately dropped her gaze to her feet.

She wondered how powerful they really were. Everything she'd read suggested her nightfire made her incredibly strong. Her mother had been notably powerful. Her father regarded as the most powerful Aazheri in Rahajhan, which made her wonder about his magic, too. Could she best any of these men? Probably not all together. But maybe one or two at a time.

"Zee," Yasen hissed. Zarya hadn't noticed the entire procession had stopped because the Jadugara were all staring at her now, studying her with disdain like she was a bug to be squished under their boots.

She blinked and slowly lowered her head, staring at her feet. It killed her to do it, but finding herself arrested for this minor infraction would serve no purpose. A hushed breath of silence pulsed through the street, and then, a moment later, the line stirred into motion.

Zarya stood with her eyes down, waiting for the chaos to settle before she looked up at Yasen.

"What was that about?" he asked. "Are you trying to get us killed?"

"I'm sorry," she said. "I just..."

She wasn't sure how to explain her feelings, and Yasen didn't force them out of her.

"It's okay," he said. "Just be more careful."

She nodded, and he tugged on her arm and winked.

"C'mon. Let's go tell Farida and the Chandras what a monster you are."

FOURTEEN

Zarya knocked on the door of the flat, attempting to tamp down her nervousness. Though she'd grown close to them over her months in Ishaan, she didn't really know how these rebellion members would react to everything she was about to reveal.

Ajay opened the door, and his face broke into a smile at the sight of her and Yasen.

"Good morning," he said. "What a nice surprise."

Zarya hoped that was true. Ajay pulled her into a hug, and she returned it, hoping he wouldn't look at her differently when today was over. She respected him and valued his friendship very much.

"Morning," Zarya said as he led them into the kitchen, where Farida was making parathas at the stove.

"Sorry," Zarya said. "We didn't mean to interrupt your breakfast."

"No problem," Farida said. "There's plenty. Have a seat."

"Is Rania here?" Zarya asked. "I have something to tell you all."

"Sure," Ajay said. "She's just getting ready and should be out soon. Is everything okay?"

Zarya and Yasen each slid into an empty seat.

"Yes. No. Honestly, it'll be better just to tell you when she gets here."

"Okay," Ajay said, taking the chair next to her, his expression brimming with curiosity and a touch of concern. "Masala tea?"

"Yes, please," Yasen said, and Zarya nodded. Farida hummed at the stove as she flipped over a paratha and then slid it on a plate before placing it in front of Yasen.

"Eat up," she said.

"Did you see the new posters?" Zarya asked Ajay as she sipped her tea.

"I did, but I don't think they actually have any idea what you two look like based on those drawings. I suspect the Jadugara and royal family are just making it seem like they have more information than they do."

"That's what we figured, too," Zarya said.

"They were preening their way down the street this morning," Yasen said. "We passed them on the way here."

Ajay shook his head. "A bunch of posturing cowards. They don't know what to do with themselves now that someone is finally standing up to them."

Zarya hoped they hadn't overplayed their hand. Cornered, frightened men tended to act out in erratic ways that could mean more trouble than any of them bargained for.

"Have you heard from your friends?" Ajay asked. "How are they doing in the palace?"

Yasen nodded. "I received a message this morning. Suvanna and Apsara have been invited to stay with the royal family and are doing what they can to find out more about the rebuilding of the ink factory and the proposed raids of the vanshaj district. It may take them some time to get close to those conversations."

"Let's hope the royal family's ego means they aren't guarding their tongues too closely," Ajay answered.

He spoke of the royal family with such disdain that Yasen's gaze flicked to hers. While she completely agreed with Ajay's opinion on the Madans and the criticism of their policies, it still twisted a deep hurt inside her chest. Her feelings for them were complicated. She knew that simply sharing the same blood didn't obligate her in any way, but a family was something she'd craved for so long.

"Let's hope," Zarya said, again sipping her tea as Farida placed a fresh paratha from the pan in front of her. "Thank you."

"Morning," came a cheerful voice as Rania appeared. "Zarya. Yasen. To what do we owe the pleasure of your company this morning?"

"Zarya has something to tell us," Ajay said.

"Oh?" Rania asked as she settled into a seat. "What is it?"

Zarya took a deep breath and willed herself to be brave.

"You know how I've been working with the ink?" she said, and Rania and Ajay both nodded. Zarya could see Farida had paused her cooking and was also listening.

"Yes," Ajay said. "What about it?"

"I think it'll be easiest to show you. Farida—I want you to watch this most of all because... well, you'll see."

Zarya held up her arm, showing them the remaining dots as she performed the series of maneuvers she'd been practicing for days. Using the thread of her darkness anchor, she pulled apart the ink and forced it to dissipate in the air. She kept her eyes on her arm, avoiding the inevitable looks on their faces when they realized what she was doing.

When the mark was gone, she revealed her blank skin and finally gathered her courage to meet their eyes.

Farida was staring at her with a mixture of hope and awe, while Rania and Ajay both looked like they'd seen a ghost emerge from the middle of the kitchen table.

"What was that?" Ajay said, his voice cracking. "Why is your magic made of shadows?"

Zarya wrinkled her nose. "So, I haven't been entirely... forthright about who I am."

"I should say so," Rania said, her gaze narrowing in suspicion. "Who are you?"

She looked to Yasen for a bit of courage, and he gave her a smile and nodded. "It'll be okay," he said.

"You know?" Ajay said, and Yasen frowned.

"Zarya's my second-best friend. Of course I know."

"What? Second best?" Farida asked, and Zarya rolled her eyes.

"Never mind him. It's just a joke."

"What's going on?" Ajay asked.

"There's no easy way to say this... but I have a sixth anchor."

At that, the blood drained from all of their faces. Rania's eyes rolled, darting about the room as though seeking an escape. She grabbed Farida's hand, clutching it to her chest as if to shield her from Zarya's very presence.

"What? That's impossible," Rania said, her voice raw.

"Apparently, it's not," Zarya said. "And there's more."

"What could possibly be more than that?" Ajay asked.

"You might want to sit down for this," Yasen said as every eye turned to him.

"We're already sitting," Rania said, clearly not amused by his attempt at levity.

"Right. But like, really... sit." Yasen pressed his hands down as though he were pushing air while everyone stared like he'd lost his mind.

"Okay," he said. "Not the time and place. Got it."

Zarya sighed and turned back to the others.

"You've heard of the prophecy bestowed on Rani Aishayadiva?" she asked. Though she'd become so familiar with the words, voicing this out loud felt ludicrous.

"Of course," Rania said.

Zarya took in a deep breath and plowed ahead. "She was my mother." She stopped, letting that sink in as their expressions slackened with shock. "And I have nightfire and the prophecy is about me."

They all sat in silence for several long seconds, absorbing that information.

"That is impossible," Rania said.

"You keep using that word," Yasen said. "But you seem unclear on its meaning."

Rania shot him a death glare, and he clamped his lips and mimed locking them shut.

"I know it sounds impossible," Zarya said, "but it's true. I used it to help battle the blight and I have six anchors. The darkness exists, and I have it."

A thick silence hung around the table, and Zarya gave them all another moment to process her words.

"So there's more," she added after another few seconds.

Rania threw up her hands. "What else?"

"I think Farida might have it, too."

She winced as Farida's eyes went wide.

"Or you might not. I don't think all vanshaj have it, but some of you definitely do."

"I... what?" Ajay asked. "The vanshaj have the sixth anchor?"

"Think about it," Zarya said. "The Ashvins had it. The vanshaj are their very distant ancestors, but that power didn't just go away."

"But it did," Rania said. "It was locked away. No one can access it."

"Or that's what they want you to think."

"What is *that* supposed to mean?" Ajay asked.

"The ink has the darkness, too. It's how it's made." She held up her arm, showing them another dot, and then performed the same trick, forcing it to dissolve.

"But that would mean..."

"The Jadugara have it, as well."

Ajay made a sort of part sigh, part wheeze as his frame bowed inward like his entire worldview had collapsed along with the skeleton keeping him upright.

"You're sure about this?" he asked.

She lifted her hands in a gesture of helplessness. "Pretty sure."

"Those scheming, lying bastards." Ajay stood up from the table, pacing back and forth as he ran his hands through his hair. "They've been duping us? Lying to us? Deceiving us for a thousand years?"

His voice was rising with each word, every syllable like a cannon blast through plaster.

"How?!" he said. "How have they gotten away with this?"

"Ajay," Farida said, her voice calmer. "This isn't helping."

His shoulders sagged, and his teeth clenched as he pushed out a long puff of air through his nose, attempting to calm himself.

"This is... impossible."

The room collapsed into silence, everyone retreating into the turbulence of their thoughts. Zarya waited for them to digest the news, each with something to lose and something to gain with this knowledge. She knew it would shape their entire futures.

She'd been around enough Aazheri the last three months to know that not only did they believe the darkness banished and untouchable, they hung their hats on this truth. It was their immutable proof that their magic was pure, good, and untainted.

Zarya didn't understand how none of them had seen it. How had they kept lying to themselves for so long? How had this well-crafted deception prevented them from realizing what was right in front of their faces all this time?

Did they really not understand the vanshaj were Aazheri, too?

She folded her hands on the table. "When we were in Dharati, I saw a demon army that no one else could see. It stood in the blight—they looked almost like ghosts." Zarya shared a look with Yasen, remembering the night they'd been assigned to watch-tower duty.

"What are you saying?" Ajay asked.

"I didn't know what it was at the time, but I think I saw the nairrata."

At that, Ajay's frown grew deep enough to fill an ocean. "As in the Ashvin's *army*?"

She licked her lips, nervousness piling up in her chest. "It preceded a demon attack, almost like it was a warning. Only, I don't think they were trying to warn us so much as they were leading the demons in. We had one of our worst battles that night against the ajakava."

No one said anything as Zarya continued. "I found out shortly after that someone else had seen the army. It wasn't only me."

"Who?" Farida asked.

"Her name is Meera, and she's a soldier in the queen's army." Zarya paused, knowing she was about to tip the scales yet again. "She is vanshaj."

As expected, those words landed between them all with a heavy thump.

"Vanshaj," Farida said as she wrapped a hand around her throat, her fingers brushing her collar of stars.

"Yes," Zarya said. "She said that sometimes she felt it." She gestured towards the tattoo. "That sometimes it seemed to be calling to her."

Rania reached over and took Farida's hand as if seeking confirmation. Farida shook her head.

"I haven't felt anything like that."

Rania's expression crumbled with disappointment and worry.

"I don't know if that matters," Zarya said as she searched their faces. "Do you all really not see it?"

"See what?" Ajay asked, and Zarya blew out a breath.

"You, who stand here as some of the vanshaj's most passionate allies, have all been brainwashed into missing the entire point."

"Zarya..." Yasen said with a warning. She knew she was treading a dangerous line, but how could they all be so blind?

"The vanshaj are Aazheri, just like you and me."

"The vanshaj have no magic," Rania said immediately.

"No," Zarya interrupted. "You've all been told that for so long that you've somehow internalized it as the truth, but they *do*. What they have are those tattoos that stop them from using it. I'm not sure how you all forgot that along the way."

Once again, everyone went silent.

"They were the descendants of two of the most powerful Aazheri ever to live. Tell me, what happened to their magic?"

"They bred with humans, and it eventually died out," Ajay said. "The markings have become only a precaution."

"But not all of them," Zarya said. "Not all of them lost it."

"So, what are you saying?" Farida said. "If I don't feel it, can you help me?"

"I think I can. It's the ink's magic I'm working with."

Farida rolled her lips inward, exchanging a glance with Rania.

"I'm telling you this because I haven't practiced on a person before. I haven't practiced on someone with the tattoo—someone who's had it for years and years. I've worked with paper, wood, animal skin, and, as you saw, my own arm. So I don't know what will happen if I try with you."

Zarya leaned forward. "And I'm telling you all of this because to even attempt it, I will have to use my sixth anchor—magic that has been forbidden for a thousand years. Magic that many claim is tainted and evil."

"Is it?" Farida asked softly.

Zarya rolled her neck. "I don't know." She paused. "I don't believe so. It didn't change me. It didn't make me someone else. All it did was offer me a different sort of power. It seems to work as both an amplifier to my other forms of magic, like my night-fire, as well as being valuable on its own."

At that, Zarya lifted a hand and sent shadows from her fingertips, directing them to surround her. They wouldn't be able to see her anymore, but she could see them watching her with a mixture of horror and tepid fascination. She pulled the shadows away, allowing them to retreat before she sat at the table looking at them, praying they weren't about to turn on her.

They all traded cautious glances around the room before once again focusing on her.

"Gods," Ajay whispered after another long moment. "This changes everything."

FIFTEEN

"You could say that," Zarya said, nodding at Ajay before she turned back to Farida. "I'm telling you all of this so you can decide. I don't know if it will hurt you. I have no idea what it will do to you, but if you let me try, I might be able to remove the collar."

Farida's mouth opened and then closed as she clutched her throat again.

"I want it gone," she said.

"I know you do. And I want to do this for you, but you must understand the risks."

"Could she die?" Rania asked. "I won't allow this."

"I've just told you I don't know," Zarya said. "I won't know the effects until I try on someone else."

"You will not use her as an experiment!" Rania shouted, her fist pounding the table so hard it rattled the plates and cups.

"If it's not me, then it has to be someone else," Farida said, her gaze turning hard as she faced Rania. "She's run out of ink. This is the only way forward."

Zarya clutched her necklace and inhaled a fortifying breath.

"There's another thing I have to share that might provide some assurance that this is the right path."

"What?" Rania asked, her dark eyes flashing.

"You know of my mother's prophecy, but there was more to it than anyone understands."

Zarya released the necklace and channeled a thread of spirit into the stone before her mother's voice floated into the air.

If you're hearing this, then you've found a way to unlock your magic. I knew one day it would happen, but I tried to protect you for as long as I could.

Your father will come for you. Whether it's soon or many years from now, he will find you. The day the oracle foretold your coming was a death sentence for both of us.

I don't have much time, but no one else knows everything the prophecy said. The oracle chose it for my ears alone. Only I know it in its entirety, and now you will, too.

> *To the queen of the west, an heir shall rise.*
> *Gifted of fire to tame the night skies.*
> *For the people caged by the stars after the fall,*
> *She will be the one to free them all.*

Zarya. Know that I loved you. That I always will. That I had no choice.

When her mother's voice fell silent, she looked around the room, taking in the depth of everyone's renewed shock.

"She will be the one who frees them all?" Farida asked in a quiet voice, looking at Zarya with an entirely new expression on her face. "*You* will be the one to free the people caged by the stars?"

Zarya shook her head. "I've listened to it a thousand times trying to understand its meaning, but what else could it be?"

Farida opened her mouth and then closed it, her eyes filling with unshed tears.

"How do we know this is the truth?" Rania asked. "How do we know you aren't lying to us? This necklace could be enchanted to tell us anything."

"You saw my magic," Zarya said. "*Why* would I be lying about this?"

"Rania," Ajay chastised, but she waved him off.

"I need proof."

"I don't have anything but this," she said. "The stories my guardian told me. He was the queen's lover and helped protect me from my father."

"Who is your *father*?" Ajay asked.

The way he asked the question told Zarya he already had surmised it wasn't Kabir, the king consort.

"My father is... Raja Abishek."

Rania hissed. "No. These are lies."

"Zarya," Ajay said. "Please explain."

She then went on to tell them everything, and when she was done, she was met with more stunned silence.

"You can't do this," Rania said a moment later. "It's too dangerous."

"Rania," Farida said, laying her hand on her arm. "Please, let me think."

"You can't possibly be considering this!"

"Why wouldn't I?" Farida asked. "I don't want to live like this anymore."

"But at least you're alive!"

"This isn't a life," Farida said. "Always wondering when the hammer will fall. Always under someone else's thumb. Being vanshaj is more dangerous now than it's ever been."

"But..."

"I understand why you're worried," Farida said. "But Zarya is right. We knew she was working on something related to the tattoos, and it makes sense for me to be the first. Who else would it be? We can't ask some innocent person. Besides, we'll want to keep this information within this room for now."

"What about the council?" Zarya asked. "Do you want to discuss this with them first?"

Farida shook her head. "This is my body and my choice. If we're successful, then I will take this to them."

"And if we're not?"

Farida pressed her mouth together before answering, "Rania and Ajay know how to reach them in the case of an emergency."

Zarya said nothing as she watched Farida. Several emotions cycled over the woman's face—fear, worry, hope, confusion—until they finally landed on determined acceptance.

"I will do it," Farida said after another moment.

"Farida," Rania implored, but Farida waved her off.

"I have made my decision. Do not presume to control me, too, Rania." She said the words pointedly, and they seemed to kick the wind from Rania's stomach.

"I'm sorry," she said, and Farida shook her head.

"It's fine. I understand your fear, but I trust that Zarya will do everything in her power to keep me safe. And if there's any chance that this might work, then I have to take it."

She turned to face Zarya, her shoulders back and her chin high.

"I'm ready. Do whatever you need."

Zarya nodded, suddenly feeling her stomach twist. She'd been mostly confident on her way over, but now that she was faced with the real thing, that conviction faltered. She had no choice but to push through it.

"You're sure?" Zarya asked, and Farida nodded.

"I don't think I've ever been more sure of anything in my life."

"Okay," Zarya said. "Let's move over here."

She gestured to the open living room, indicating Farida should sit on one of the chairs.

"Will it hurt?" Farida asked.

"I don't know," she answered truthfully. "It doesn't when I try it on myself, but..."

She trailed off, and their gazes met, silent understanding moving between them.

"Nothing could hurt worse than this," she said, touching the tattoo. "I want to be free. I don't care about magic, but I'm tired of having my entire life defined by something completely out of my control and by a fantasy concocted a thousand years ago."

"I understand," Zarya said, sitting down across from her.

Yasen, Ajay, and Rania hovered in the kitchen, watching the two of them, and her nerves twisted even tighter. Rania's expression had turned hard as diamonds, and Zarya knew she'd never forgive her if she hurt Farida.

"Okay," Zarya said. "Please try to sit as still as possible." She rubbed her sweating palms on her thighs. "I'm nervous," she admitted, and Farida gave her a patient smile.

"I trust you."

Hoping that faith wasn't misplaced, Zarya went inside herself before she pulled on the thread of her sixth anchor.

The room was silent as Zarya sent out a tendril of shadow. Farida's eyes widened, perhaps reconsidering her decision before it gently wrapped around her throat. Her mouth opened, and her back straightened, and she sat completely still, not even blinking as Zarya's eyes drifted shut.

She spent a few minutes using her magic to trace the markings. She stroked the edges, seeking the tiny particles that formed to make the whole. She felt their vibration. She wanted to take her time with this. One wrong move and... she didn't want to consider the consequences.

Zarya opened her eyes to find everyone watching her, completely frozen. She forced a grim smile and then sent out a second tendril of magic. She used the first to start the vibrations, forcing the molecules to move and shift. Farida reached for her throat before she stopped herself.

"What is it?" Rania demanded. "Does it hurt?"

"No," Farida said. "But I feel it."

Zarya nodded. She wasn't sure if that was a good sign or not, but she was here now, and the only way through was forward. She continued making the particles dance and then used the other ribbon, forcing it between the layers and spreading them further. Slowly, they pulled apart. It was harder than it had been before—they offered more resistance than her earlier experiments, but she thought it might be working.

She continued feeding magic through the ink as sweat beaded on her brow. Then she let out a huffed grunt as the first star fell apart. She watched in fascination as it dissolved off Farida's skin and dissipated into the air like a curling ribbon of destiny.

Rania cried out, tears already coating her face as she dropped to her knees and wrapped her arms around Farida's waist.

"What happened?" Farida asked, clapping her hand over her neck. "I felt... it sort of burned for a moment, and then it stopped."

"She did it," Ajay said, a mixture of respect and awe in his voice. "Zarya, you *did* it."

"Get her a mirror," Zarya said, and Ajay produced a hand-held one from a drawer. He passed it to Farida, who lifted it up and gasped, covering her mouth as she noted the missing star while she turned her head left and right.

"You really did it," she said, a tear sliding down her cheek and echoing Ajay. "I can't believe it."

"Do you feel anything?" Zarya asked.

"Not really," Farida said, stretching her neck and examining it in the mirror as she touched the blank spot gently with a fingertip. A bit of redness marked her skin, but otherwise, she seemed unharmed. "I truly can't believe it." More tears filled her eyes, tracks running down her cheeks.

"Well, I'm not done yet," Zarya said. "Do you think you can sit for the others?"

"Yes, gods, yes. I'll sit here for a hundred years if that's what it takes."

"Okay, then let's keep going."

Zarya resumed the process, slowly peeling off the stars one by one. Each one resisted more and more, forcing her to use more and more magic. So far, Farida appeared unaffected. She continued feeding in magic bit by bit, peeling away the tattoos. She was about halfway done when she urged in another pulse of magic, and then it slipped.

Zarya cried out as the power crested, slamming into Farida's neck, seething through the ink, burning off the stars in rapid succession like trees toppling in the forest. The whole thing took less than a second, and that's when Farida screamed and passed out.

SIXTEEN

"Farida!" Rania shouted, running over. "What did you do!"

"I'm sorry," Zarya said, falling to Farida's side. "I lost control."

"You lost control?!" Rania snapped. "You said you'd protect her!"

"I'm so sorry," Zarya said. "It was an accident."

Yasen was already kneeling on Farida's other side, checking her pulse.

"Rania, she's alive. I think it just knocked her out." Yasen gestured to Ajay, and they lifted Farida to the long divan and carefully laid her down.

"But for how long!" Rania asked, her voice rising. "What's wrong with her? Is she okay?"

Zarya crawled over to Farida, examining her neck. Where she'd slowly removed the stars, there was nothing but brown skin with a hint of red, but on the other side, where she'd lost control, the skin was charred black. Zarya's stomach cramped with guilt, and she willed herself not to pass out.

Yasen dropped down behind her with a bowl of warm water and a cloth, and he started cleaning the wound.

"Why is she burned?" Rania asked. "What did you do?"

"I don't know," Zarya said, her throat raw with the press of tears.

"It appears to be a standard burn," Yasen said. "I think it will heal over without any issues."

"You think?!" Rania asked. "You think!"

"Rania, calm down," Ajay said, placing his hands on his sister's shoulders. She shook them off.

"Don't tell me to calm down. We let this woman into our lives, and she's been lying to us this whole time. She just used dark magic on the love of my life and practically killed her. Don't fucking tell me to calm down!"

Rania screamed so loud that Zarya's ears rang, and her neck flushed with awkward heat from the shame and hurt of being spoken about this way. Yes, she hadn't been entirely forthright with them at the beginning, but couldn't they understand why that was the case? They would have shunned her instantly if she'd started with the truth.

"Rania, you're being really unfair right now," Yasen said, and she whirled on him.

"Don't you dare! You're also a stranger. You came here with *her*. Of course you would defend her. Why should I trust either of you?"

Yasen's mouth pressed together, his dark eyes flashing with anger before he resumed his attention on Farida. "If we can get her to a proper healer, then I think she'll be fine." He placed his fingers against her throat, feeling for her pulse. "Her heartbeat is strong."

"I'll send for Rishi," Ajay said. "He'll come right away."

He looked around the room. At Zarya, who sat in her chair, with her hands clasped between her knees and her head down. At Yasen, kneeling next to Farida, doing everything he could to help. At Rania, who stood in the corner, with her arms wrapped around her midsection as though she couldn't bring herself to get too close to Farida.

"Will you be all right if I leave you here for a minute?" he asked, directing the question at his sister.

She returned it with a glare and then dipped her chin. "Yes," she said. "Please hurry."

Ajay looked at Zarya. He opened his mouth as though he was about to say something else and then shook his head.

"I'll be right back."

After the door closed behind him, everyone waited in a discomfort that felt physical. Like it was a blanket of iron slowly crushing their organs. Zarya chanced a glance at Rania to find her glaring like she was trying to melt her into the floor.

Zarya turned away and scrubbed her eyes with her palm, whisking away a guilty tear. She'd only wanted to help. But she'd slipped, and she'd messed up. What would she do now? The only way to get better was to keep practicing, but she couldn't risk hurting anyone else. The success of the Rising Phoenix counted on this. She was sure of it.

The moment seemed to stretch into forever, the tick of a clock on the wall so loud it sliced through every strained second.

Yasen settled back, leaning against the sofa, his knees propped up and his wrists draping over them. He shared a look with Zarya.

"It's okay," he mouthed, and she pressed her lips into a thin line, willing herself not to break down.

Rania paced the length of the room, muttering to herself and occasionally throwing dark looks at Zarya and Yasen. Eventually, she stormed over to a cabinet against the far wall and pulled out a bottle of liquor. She poured herself a healthy glass and then tossed the entire thing back before she returned to Farida, resting a hand on her forehead. She sank onto the sofa and leaned forward, whispering something to the other woman that Zarya couldn't hear.

They all waited like that, stewing in uncomfortableness.

After what felt like a hundred years, the door to the flat finally swung open, and Ajay appeared with Rishi in tow. He hailed from Svaasthy and was gifted with Niramaya healing magic. After meeting Ajay at a university function, he'd joined the resistance and was often called upon to tend minor injuries.

Both men took in the scene, and Rishi's eyes shifted to Ajay, clearly picking up on the tension sagging between them.

"What do we have here?" he asked, his voice warm. He always reminded Zarya a bit of Koura, whose calm nature draped a soothing blanket over every room he entered. Maybe this was a key trait in being a Niramaya healer.

He approached Farida, and both Rania and Yasen scooted out of the way as he placed one knee on the floor.

Rania started pacing again, and Ajay went to speak with her in soft, hushed tones, but it was clear barbs edged all of Rania's replies.

Zarya felt herself folding inward. She wished she could take it back. She wished she could melt into the floor.

Rishi examined Farida, and after a few minutes, he stood up and wiped a hand across his forehead. "There doesn't appear to be any permanent damage, though I can't really determine what's wrong with her, either. Can you tell me more about what happened?"

Everyone's eyes met across the room. Now what?

"Rishi," Ajay said. "What we tell you cannot leave this room. It has to do with the resistance efforts."

"You know I'd never say anything," he replied, pressing a hand to his heart.

Ajay took a deep breath, his gaze sliding to Zarya.

"Do you want to tell him?" he asked. "Or should I?"

She inhaled a sharp breath. She was grateful he was considering her feelings in this, but could she get these words out again?

"I'll tell him," she said. With her knees pressing against her clasped hands, she recounted everything she'd already shared. Keeping her secrets was secondary to helping Farida.

Rishi's expression remained impassive during her explanation. Mostly. She could see the slight widening of his eyes a few times. He wasn't Aazheri, and the impact of knowing about the sixth anchor probably meant less to him, but he knew enough to understand its significance.

"I see," he said after she was done. "This is... well, to be honest, I'm not sure what it is. I have no idea how to treat a magical ailment such as this."

Rania glared at Zarya again, and she felt herself wither even further.

"I'm sorry," she whispered again. "I was only trying to help."

Rania scoffed, and Zarya felt it like a knife through the heart.

"I will have to seek further assistance," Rishi said. "For now, she's stable and breathing, and with any luck, she'll wake up on her own. But I'll need to consult some literature to see if I can find anything about curing her."

He turned to Rania and bowed with his hands pressed in front of his chest. "I'm sorry, but it's the best I can do for now."

"Thank you," Ajay said. "We appreciate it."

"Of course," Rishi said. "I'll come and check on her this evening, and I'll let you know immediately if I come across anything."

With another quick bow, he departed, leaving everyone to stew in their awkwardness once again.

"I don't want her here," Rania said, her lips pressing into a thin line.

"Rania," Ajay said.

"What? Just because you've got the hots for her doesn't mean I have to tolerate her presence."

Ajay's cheeks turned pink, and Zarya, who thought things couldn't be *more* awkward a moment ago, realized they had entered a new level of hell.

"I'm not—" Ajay said.

"No," Rania said. "She showed up here and is meddling in shit that isn't her business."

"It is my business!" Zarya snapped back, her nerves finally breaking. "I'm supposed to be here!"

"You're not even *from* here," Rania answered. "You think because you claim to carry our dead queen's blood in your veins, you have a right to any of this?"

Zarya's nostrils flared in rage.

"The prophecy says this is my destiny! And I will remain here to help as long as there is breath left in my body!"

Rania glared at Zarya, her mouth pressed into a line so tight it was a wonder she could breathe. Then, before Rania could say anything else to hurt her, Zarya turned and stormed out the door.

SEVENTEEN

Zarya marched through the streets, weaving through the crowds, consumed with guilt and regret and anger. Yasen caught up but said nothing as he kept pace with her furious strides.

"How dare she?" Zarya spat, the words bursting out of her. "How dare she speak to me like that? I was trying to help. I warned them. I said I would do my best!"

"She's worried about Farida," he said. "But you're right; you didn't deserve any of that."

Zarya stopped and faced him, her gaze lingering in the direction they'd just come. The surging crowds enveloped them in the pulse and noise of the city.

"The things she said to me—"

Tears built in her eyes, and Yasen shook his head as he blew out a breath. "I don't think she really meant any of it."

"Don't you? Or were those things she's been thinking all along and now felt free to say?"

Yasen closed his eyes and opened them. "I'm not sure."

"I fucked up," Zarya said. "I let my magic slip, but..."

"I know that, Zee. Give her some time to calm down."

"What if Farida doesn't wake up, Yas? Then what? I'm sure this is what I'm supposed to be doing, but it seems like I'm getting everything wrong."

He tipped his head and considered her. "What if that's not what those words meant?"

"What else could they mean?" she asked. "Who else is 'caged by the stars'?"

He pulled a face. "Yeah," he admitted. "It does seem pretty clear."

She turned and kept walking while he followed at her side.

"Did they say anything after I left?"

He shrugged. "Not much. I think you shocked them into silence."

Zarya huffed. "I bet that was a first for Rania."

"Sorry, Zee," he said. "That was hard to listen to."

"Thanks for trying to stick up for me."

"Hey, what are second-best friends for?"

Zarya found herself caving to a reluctant smile.

"Is there anything I can do?" he asked.

"Let's train," she answered. "It's been too long, and I need to burn off some energy."

With a nod, he took her hand, and they shoved through the afternoon rush, finding themselves on the rooftop of their apartment building. They'd discovered early on that no one ever came up here, and it was the perfect place to spar. With the sun beating down, they fought with their blades clashing. Zarya wasn't in the mood to talk, so she lost herself in the sway and the cadence of the fight.

When they finally stopped, the sun was setting, and they were both covered in sweat.

"Thank you," she said, wiping her forehead with the back of her hand. "I needed that."

"You really did," Yasen said. "Woo, you are rusty."

She snorted. "Shut up."

He grinned, and they sank down against the perimeter wall, their knees up and their shoulders pressed together.

"Feeling any better?" he asked.

"Not really. Do you think they'll let me check on Farida tomorrow?"

"Maybe I should go and assess the mood first," he said.

She picked at her bottom lip as she stared ahead. The sky was turning shades of pink and orange, and the stars were beginning to sparkle overhead.

"What are you thinking about?" he asked.

"I need to try again," she said. "But I'll need a volunteer, and after what happened with Farida..."

"We'll figure out something. I'm sure someone is willing, given the right price."

She rubbed a hand over her eyes. "That hardly seems ethical."

"We're fighting evil, Zee. Sometimes, you must do things you're not proud of and cross lines you might not normally consider."

"Maybe." She leaned down, resting her head on his shoulder, and wrapped a hand around his bicep. He placed his hand over hers, and they sat together quietly watching the stars.

She blinked and then sucked in a startled breath.

The scene around her had changed. She was somewhere else. Somewhere inside her dreams, but it wasn't the forest.

This was something new.

She sat against a dark stone wall inside a large and opulent room. The floors were covered with ornate woven rugs threaded with gold. A fireplace roared along one side, and a giant black bed stood at another. It was massive. The other walls were covered in stuffed, dark wooden bookshelves.

But none of that mattered.

The only presence in this room that counted for anything waited in the center, watching her.

Rabin.

Dressed in leather armor with two swords strapped to his back, his eyes glittered like he was peering right into the middle of her soul.

She swallowed the knot swelling up her throat, trying to find her breath somewhere at her feet. The sight shocked her in ways she hadn't expected. She wasn't entirely ready for this. After all these months of wondering if she'd ever see him again, now he stood there, watching her expectantly like he hadn't torn apart her life.

She studied him back, allowing the silence to shift and bend between them as she picked through several layers of emotion, experiencing a vast range of feelings, but mostly rage and betrayal. What she *felt* was the moment her heart had cracked when she'd begged him to tell her that Dhawan had been lying. What she *felt* was the way it had shattered into pieces when he couldn't deny it.

These emotions she expected. But what she didn't expect was a traitorous flare of sensation that veered a bit too close to... relief.

Pushing against the wall, she slowly stood, keeping her eyes on him. Around the room, large arched windows filtered in muted grey light. Tearing her gaze away, she glanced outside, shocked to see mountains and snow so close it felt like she could touch them. She'd never seen snow on the ground before. Her entire body went numb at the sight, premonition already signifying where she was.

"What's going on?" she demanded, whipping around to face him. "What is this?"

"You're in Andhera," he said, confirming what she'd already suspected.

Andhera.

Turning away again, she gazed out the window at the arctic landscape and the massive range of jagged mountains spreading across the horizon. She placed her hand against the cold window and felt a deep twist in her chest.

Andhera.

The other half of herself. A place she hadn't known she belonged to until Row had been forced to reveal it all.

The harsh and unforgiving landscape held a sort of clean, cold beauty that made her breath catch. It was so different from the shore and forests where she'd grown up with its icy, windswept mountains and foggy grey sky.

The weak sun filtered in pale light that she was sure would feel like nothing on her skin. She considered the bare trees with their spindly arms and the lush, green pines as the wind tore through their branches.

Gathering herself, she again turned to face Rabin, who stood with a hand gripped around the strap crossing his chest.

"What am I doing here? Why aren't we in the forest?"

"I've been reading up on paramadhar," he said. "I've learned how to control the visions."

What. Shit why hadn't she thought of that? She'd been too busy wallowing in the way he'd betrayed her, but this would have been a much better use of her time. If nothing, so she wouldn't be prey to his mercy or his call.

The corner of her mouth curled up in a snarl, rage creeping to the surface. Who did he think he was?

"So you dragged me here? Against my will? What about the other night? Was that you, too?"

"It was." The words were said simply. He wasn't sorry. He wasn't anything but confident.

"So, why didn't you show yourself?" she asked, crossing her arms.

"I wasn't sure if you were ready to see me, but I had to see you."

Zarya narrowed her eyes. "You had no right to do that."

He shrugged a shoulder. The insouciant gesture made her

want to walk over there and wrap her hands around his neck. Except he'd probably like that. "You already hate me. What difference does it make?"

A growl built in her throat. "Because you lied to me. Remember that? I told you I didn't want to see you."

His hand tightened, tendons standing out on the surface, reminding her of the raw power contained within his massive frame. "I was planning to tell you everything, Zarya."

"When? Before or after you delivered me to my father?"

His jaw clenched, his dark eyes flashing. "I was never planning to do that."

She huffed. "You treated me like the plague for weeks. Then you turned around and wouldn't stop pursuing me until I fucked you, all while you pretended to be someone else."

He took a step forward, his shoulders curving towards her. "Why do you think I resisted you so hard?" he asked through clenched teeth. "That night, when I walked away from you, I was *trying* to do the honorable thing."

She scoffed and shook her head. "So much for that."

A muscle feathered in his clenched jaw. "Zarya. I swear to you that I had no idea who you were."

She pressed herself against the window. "I don't believe you."

He spread his hands. "What was I supposed to say? Hey, no one really knows where I've been, but surprise, I was with your father, who apparently has been hunting you since before you were born?"

"Yes," she said. "Yes, that's exactly what you should have done."

He took another step towards her, his dark eyes burning, his chest rumbling with a deep sound reminiscent of a wild animal.

"And then what? You would have told everyone. You would never have trusted me."

"You don't know what I would have done," she hissed. "And you *proved* that I didn't have any reason to trust you."

The growl in his throat vibrated in the air between them. She tried to read the truth in his words. Was he being sincere? Or were these just more lies?

She *wanted* to believe him, but she'd already fallen for his silver tongue once. It was obvious he was very good at hiding things.

"Why did you bring me here?" she asked, looking around the room, her gaze landing on the door as a hard pellet wedged between her ribs. Was her father there somewhere on the other side?

"Is this real?" she asked. "Where exactly are we?"

"It's not real," he said. "It's a pocket dimension between worlds. One of us created the forest, and I created this."

"I didn't create the forest."

"You may have done so without realizing. I'm not sure which of us it was. From what I've read, it was likely me. The paramadhar seeks out their masatara. They cannot help but be drawn to them."

"Masatara?"

"I'm your paramadhar and you are my masatara."

Zarya studied him, turning that over in her head. *Masatara.* Another shiver climbed over her scalp. They were connected no matter what he'd done. No matter how hard she fought.

"Why did you make this?" she asked, waving her hand in a circle.

"Because I wanted you to see where I was."

Andhera. He was in Andhera. "So, you ran straight back to my father."

"This is where I feel safe, Zarya."

Her indignation wavered at the thread of rawness in his voice. He'd told her all the horrible things his own father had done. She knew why he couldn't stay in Dharati. Where else was he supposed to go?

"Again, I ask, why did you bring me here?"

"I was hoping we could talk."

"I don't want to talk to you."

But was that true? Was she the one lying now?

"Zarya, please—"

"No!" She stood straighter, taking a step towards him. "I didn't consent to being dragged here."

As she passed a desk covered with books and papers, her attention snagged on a golden dagger, the hilt inlaid with violet jewels. She grabbed it and pointed it at him. "I want to go home."

"Where is home?" he asked. "Where are you?"

She shook her head. "Oh no. We're *not* doing this again. Why? So you can show up unannounced and tear my life apart one more time? I'm happy. I have a purpose. I'm where I'm supposed to be."

But was any of *that* true anymore? The mistake she'd made with Farida was unforgivable. What if she never woke up? What if this wasn't really her purpose, and she was involving herself in things that weren't hers to meddle with, just as Rania had claimed?

"I'm glad you're happy," he said. "I want you to be happy, but I want you to be happy with *me* at your side."

Zarya took a step closer, holding the dagger in front of her. "You betrayed me."

"I didn't. I wouldn't."

"But you did!" she shouted.

"I meant you no harm. Give me another chance. Let me prove it to you."

His voice was so full of passion that she felt the dagger drop an inch.

She stared at him, tracing the hard lines of his face. The

sharp angle of his jaw and the arch of his thick eyebrows. Her gaze drifted lower, over his wide shoulders and broad chest. The narrow taper of his waist and his strong thighs encased in supple leather. She looked at his hands hanging loosely at his sides, but she saw the way his fingers twitched as if he was an inch away from destroying everything around him with the pent-up energy boiling under his skin.

It would be so easy to give into everything she craved.

But he'd been very convincing last time, too.

She hoisted the dagger higher, pointing it at him.

"I want to leave," she said.

"Fight me for it," he said, and he had to be joking. Not *this* again. "Prove to me you hate me as much as you claim."

"I do hate you," she hissed.

His mouth twisted into a smug smile. "Then you should have nothing to fear, Spitfire."

She gripped the dagger so tight it shook in her hand. "Do *not* call me that. You have no right." The words tore out of her, and she did her best not to show how much they affected her. He'd hurt her so deeply she felt like she was bleeding out on the floor, exposing herself for the world to witness her pain.

He reached behind his head and pulled out both swords from his back.

"Catch," he said, launching one of them in her direction. Taken by surprise, she nearly missed, snatching it out of the air before it clattered to the floor. The hilt had been crafted to look like the mouth of a dragon with lapis lazuli eyes, and the honed steel blade was engraved with curls of fire. It was stunning.

"They were a gift from your father," he said, and she nearly dropped it like it had burned her palm.

"Is this supposed to be funny?" she demanded. "Why are you doing this?"

"Because you and I are destined." Again, he said it with

such unwavering conviction that it was impossible to argue. Almost.

"The paramadhar is not a romantic partner," she said. "You are my *servant*." She hurled the words at him, hoping they stung. "You would be bound to me. Destined to die when I die. You'd never have a life that's yours. I would rule you in every way."

The corner of his mouth twisted up in a cold smile, his dark, golden-flecked eyes chipped from the heart of a bottomless underground pit.

"I don't care," he snarled. "I'll have you however you want."

Anger boiled in her blood. He was so fucking sure of himself. She wanted to wipe that cocky smile off his face.

"I don't want you," she said, trying to infuse her voice with an arctic chill to rival the wind howling across the tundra. Her feelings weren't quite so clear-cut, but she knew if she gave him an inch, he'd take it all. Her heart. Her body. Her spirit. And she wasn't sure if she was strong enough to take them back again.

"Show me how much you despise me, Zarya."

Without warning, he crossed the room in three long strides and lifted his sword, swinging down. She had no choice but to block the attack at the last second, the air ringing with their clashing blades.

"I'm keeping the dagger," she said, noting he held no other weapons.

"I would expect nothing less," he said, spinning around and arcing his sword overhead. Again, she blocked it at the last second, almost stumbling from the force. His face stretched into a feral smile, one of a self-assured predator.

That pissed her off, and she launched into the fight. This time, he was the one who stumbled as she swung with all of her strength and precision.

She regretted training so hard with Yasen this afternoon

because even in this dream she could feel the effects, her muscles and joints protesting due to her lack of training over the last few months. But she would die before she let Rabin have the upper hand.

Pushing aside her weariness, she fought with fury as they moved around the study, using the furniture to get in each other's way. She swung, and he ducked as her sword bit into a bookshelf, her blade sinking into the wood. She wrenched on it, hoping it would ruin this stupid sword from her *father*.

She spun around and faced him, crowding him against the desk. He bent nearly backward before he flipped over, landing on top in a crouch. Fuck, that was impressive. He hopped back, dropping to the other side as she followed him around before they circled each other, keeping the desk between them. He leaped over the back of a chair, and she kicked it away, shoving it against the wall.

"You seem a little tired," he said. "Where is that fire, Zarya?"

"Fuck you," she said. "Are you trying to kill me? Fight harder, Commander. Because I'm going to kill *you*."

She launched again, and their blades became a whirl as they fought. She was thankful she was at least wearing her training leathers after falling asleep next to Yasen, but she was tiring quickly.

Rabin advanced, and he wasn't going easy on her anymore. Could they kill each other in this alternate dimension?

She tripped over the edge of a rug, landing on the large divan in the center of the room. Before she could scramble off, Rabin pounced on top, his knees landing on either side of her hips and his weight pinning her to the cushions. He wrenched the dagger from her hand and then pressed it to her throat hard enough to draw blood.

"Didn't think you'd go down so easy, Spitfire," he hissed, his dark eyes flashing with bursts of fiery gold.

"Get off me!" she bit out, struggling against his bulk. Fuck, why was he so heavy?

She continued thrashing, then went entirely still as her body reacted in ways she was trying to ignore. Why did fighting with him always bring out that needy quiver between her thighs? This was so annoying.

She noticed the way his pupils spread, his nose flaring as her lips parted before she licked the bottom one. She hated that she wanted to kiss him. That she wanted him to kiss her. That kissing was only the first of many things on her mind. *Why* did she have to be drawn to him?

She sucked in a sharp breath, and his eyes dipped to her breasts before they zeroed in on her mouth. His grip on her wrist loosened as she slid her hand out and reached up, touching her fingertips to his lower lip.

He opened his mouth and nipped at them, sending a straight shot of desire below her navel. Her hand wandered lower, smoothing down the column of his throat, the prick of his stubble tickling her skin. He leaned forward, and she felt the evidence of his thick cock pressing against her stomach, causing another inconvenient flare of heat to climb up the back of her neck.

Oh, but this was almost too easy.

She moved lightning quick, grabbing him between the legs and twisting as she flipped him over so he landed on the floor with a thud. She fell on top of him, yanking the dagger from his hand, pressing it to his throat, and baring her teeth. His eyes swirled with anger, his jaw turning hard.

"I could kill you right now," she hissed.

"Then do it," he bit out. There was no fear in his eyes. Either he truly believed she wouldn't, or he didn't care. "End it. Without you, I am nothing."

Her heart stuttered and tripped over itself at that impassioned declaration, but she tried to ignore it.

"Let me go," she snarled.

"We aren't done," he said before the world blinked out.

Suddenly, she was back in Ishaan, sitting on the rooftop, leaning against Yasen, who slept with his head tipped back and his mouth hanging open.

Zarya sighed and rubbed a hand down her face, cycling through every emotion under the sun. Anger. Betrayal. The desire that was still pounding between her thighs. Fuck.

Paramadhar. *Masatara.*

It was time to find a library.

EIGHTEEN

Farida remained unconscious a week later, stable but frustratingly asleep. Zarya didn't dare go anywhere near their flat, but Yasen played the role of her knight in shining armor and carried reports of her condition back. Rishi was carefully monitoring her, using his Niramaya magic to keep her body healthy while she remained in a suspended state.

In amongst her worry about Farida, Zarya couldn't stop thinking about Rabin. So far, she hadn't found any more information about paramadhar despite combing the libraries and bookstores on the high street of Ishaan. She assumed she needed a more academic library, not the type where people went for stories of adventure and romance—of course, she'd picked up a few of those, too.

This was powerful and ancient magic and wouldn't be found in a common shop. Rabin probably had access to all kinds of rare texts in the king's palace, which put Zarya at a distinct disadvantage.

She was wondering if there was a way to access the university library when Yasen banged open the door.

"Zee," he said. "I've got someone who wants to meet you."

"Who?" she asked.

"Just come."

She knew there was no point in arguing. He wouldn't tell her, and her trust issues with him no longer applied.

"Fine," she said. She needed a break from this apartment, anyway. Along with her frustrations about Rabin, she was also stumped on how to proceed next with freeing the vanshaj from their collars. There was no point in practicing on herself or any other objects, even if she had any ink left. But she couldn't risk harming someone else. She'd done enough damage with Farida. So, what was she missing?

She threw on some clothing and followed Yasen into the street. New posters had been pasted over the previous ones, offering larger rewards for the capture of any active members of the Rising Phoenix.

They still depicted Zarya and Yasen's not-all-that-accurate likenesses, and she said a silent thank you for that. Few trusted the Jadugara in Gi'ana, but that amount of gold was bound to make anyone think about switching allegiances. They couldn't risk being nearly caught again.

"How are you doing?" Yasen asked as they wove through the busy streets.

Zarya shrugged. "Why?"

"You've been especially quiet lately. Is it just the Farida thing?"

Zarya wrinkled her nose. She hadn't told Yasen about Rabin yet, only because she wasn't sure how to describe her feelings. She'd been so angry when she saw him, but she also felt lighter than she had in months.

Yes, he'd hurt her, but a part of her understood that while she could logically try to fight her feelings, she couldn't deny what her heart craved. They'd grown close so quickly, and it was impossible to ignore their intense connection. One couldn't just turn off their emotions like that. Especially not Zarya.

"I had one of my dreams," she confessed, and Yasen raised an eyebrow.

"I'm surprised you're so subdued about it."

"What is that supposed to mean?"

"Nothing," he said quickly, and she glared.

"I was so angry when I saw him. But we weren't in the forest this time."

"Where were you?"

"He brought me to Andhera. He said he'd been reading up on paramadhar and had learned how to control the visions."

They continued to weave through the crowd, breaking through a line and emerging into a quieter street.

She opened her mouth, and Yasen raised a hand. "And you need a bookstore."

She snorted. "Am I that predictable?"

"You are," he said, and she pulled a wry face.

"I've already tried that. I haven't been able to find anything, and I'm annoyed I didn't think of it first."

"Fair," he said. "So, what happened?"

"We fought?"

"Fought?"

"Like with weapons. He threw me a sword, and we nearly killed each other."

Yasen smirked. "Killed or kissed?"

"You think you're so smart, don't you?" she asked with a glare.

"Listen, that sounds hot."

Zarya huffed out a laugh. "I mean... it kind of was." She bit the corner of her lip. "But I'm still so mad at him."

"Understandable. But love and hate are intimately tied emotions, Zee."

She gave Yasen a rueful smile, conceding his point.

Rabin seemed so certain that he hadn't betrayed her and had never intended to tell her father until she was ready. But what did that mean? Why would she ever be ready to meet the man who wanted to steal her magic? Was *that* the truth? What if Row had been wrong?

Everything she'd heard during her months in Gi'ana didn't paint the king of Andhera as anything but a monster and a murderer. She could go her entire life never meeting him. And yet, some deep knot in the bottom of her heart wondered what the man who'd sired her was like. It was impossible to disregard her curiosity about him completely.

They continued walking, and Yasen turned them down a narrow alley into the vanshaj district. Here, the buildings stood shoulder to shoulder, so tightly they were practically leaning against one another. It was quiet here, away from the bustle of the market and high street. Yasen knocked on a door in a pattern that was clearly meant to be a secret code.

"What is this?" she asked, narrowing her eyes with suspicion. "Where are we?"

"You'll see," he said.

A shuffle came from the other side of the door, and they waited for a few seconds before it popped open. There stood a young man with a ring of stars tattooed around his neck.

Yasen reached out and shook his hand. "Here's my friend I told you about." He gestured to Zarya. "Zee, meet Vikas."

"Hello?" Zarya said.

Vikas stared at Zarya, his gaze traveling over her with wariness. He was about Zarya's age with short, dark hair that fell in waves over his eyes. He was a good head taller than her and wore a simple blue kurta over his narrow frame.

"She's Aazheri?" he asked. Vanshaj were understandably mistrustful of Aazheri as a general rule.

"She is," Yasen replied, "but as I said, she wants to help you."

"Why would she want to help us?"

"Excuse me," Zarya interjected. "*She* is standing right here.

If you have questions, please feel free to address them to her directly."

Yasen rolled his eyes. "Can we come in? We shouldn't talk about this out here."

Vikas gave Zarya one more skeptical look and then dipped his chin.

"Very well," he said and then stepped aside.

They entered a small front room furnished with a table pushed into the corner where three more young vanshaj men sat. In front of them were stacks of cards and piles of small round chips.

"Boys!" Yasen said in greeting, and it was obvious they all knew and loved him from their enthusiastic hellos.

"Yas," Zarya asked, "what is going on?"

"These fine gentlemen are friends of mine. We play cards, and I beat them every time."

"Excuse me, but you haven't won a round in weeks," said another man at the table, and they all laughed heartily.

Zarya frowned.

"You come here to play cards?" she asked, and Yasen nodded before he dropped onto the threadbare divan in the corner and kicked his feet up on the table. He was obviously very comfortable here.

"Sometimes. Vikas saved my ass at a gambling den when someone tried to cheat me, and things got out of hand."

Zarya folded her arms and stared down at him. "Out of hand?"

"Turned out the sneaky bastard had three massive thugs working for him, and they were less than pleased when I broke their boss's nose. So Vikas jumped in, and we took care of them."

He held out a fist, and Vikas bumped his against it.

"Dhruv tries to scam everyone," Vikas said. "But we taught him a lesson that night."

They grinned at one another.

"Okay," Zarya said, rubbing a hand across her face and catching the wary looks from the other men around the table. "And what are we doing here now?"

"I've told Vikas and the others that you can remove their collars," he said casually as if Zarya wasn't about to strangle him.

"You did *what*?"

He peered at her. "I'm pretty sure you just heard me."

"You can't just go around blabbing that to people!"

"We won't tell anyone," Vikas said solemnly. "We would never."

His expression was so serious that Zarya felt her shoulders release. Of course they wouldn't tell anyone. They'd wind up in even more trouble than she ever could.

"They want to volunteer," Yasen said.

"What?" Zarya asked, whipping around to face him.

"Are you having trouble with your hearing, Zee?" Yasen asked.

"No." She shook her head. "They can't do that."

"Why not? Don't you need someone to practice on?"

Zarya pressed her mouth together in a tight line. "Yes, of course, but it's not safe. What if the same thing happens to..." She broke off.

"They all know about what happened last time," Yasen said, and Zarya sighed and pinched the bridge of her nose.

"Was that the best idea, Yas?" she asked through clenched teeth.

"You can trust them."

He was so earnest that Zarya *did* trust he hadn't gone around blabbing without considering the consequences, but this was still dangerous.

"They know everything. What you can do. What's in the

ink, and what we did with the supply. They also want to step up to volunteer."

"No," Zarya said. "I can't. What if something happens?"

"Please," Vikas said, interrupting their argument. "I understand the risks. We all do. And we stand here willing to accept them. If you truly possess this gift, it's a small price for the benefit of my people."

She stared at him as she read the solemn emotion in his dark eyes.

"This isn't a life, anyway," he added, echoing Farida's sentiments. "Please. I need you to figure this out."

Zarya's heart twisted at the hurt and sadness in his voice.

"I don't know about this," she said, but he wasn't wrong. There was no other way for her to learn without using vanshaj to practice. She'd been thinking about what happened with Farida, trying to recall every sensation and emotion. She was almost sure she had pinpointed the moment her control had slipped and had considered several options to ensure it never happened again.

"We're willing," Vikas said. "We all are. Please let us do this."

Zarya considered him for another moment before her shoulders dropped.

"I don't like this," she said, but the resignation in her voice was apparent.

"I'll go first," Vikas said. Zarya exchanged a look with Yasen, who had been sitting quietly watching their exchange. He dipped his head, the corner of his mouth tipping up.

"You can do this, Zee," he said, and she offered him a small smile.

"Okay, sit down," Zarya said, pointing to one of the empty chairs. "Over here."

There wasn't much space in the tiny house, but she directed him away from the others to give them a bit of room. She stared at Vikas, her heart pounding in her throat. She couldn't remember the last time she'd been so nervous. What if she hurt him? What if he also wouldn't wake up?

"It's okay," Vikas said, sensing her hesitation. "I want this. If I die, tell everyone what I did."

Great, did he have to mention dying?

"We'll throw you a fucking parade," Yasen said, and everyone laughed except Zarya. She swallowed the prickly knot in her throat and faced Vikas.

Once again, she repeated the same process, sending out the dark shadows of her sixth anchor, teasing and testing them against the ink. She felt that now-familiar sensation of the different particles moving and vibrating. She added another string of magic and peeled off the first star. Vikas sat still, not even blinking and barely breathing, as she slowly worked her way around his throat.

She'd become too excited with Farida and tried to do too much. She needed to maintain this methodical pace and take a break if she felt herself losing control.

When she was halfway through, she pulled her magic back, breathing heavily.

"Is everything all right?" Vikas asked.

"Yes, I just need a moment. Can I get some water?"

Someone at the table jumped up and retrieved a glass. She gulped it back and then wiped the sweat running down her temple.

"Let's keep going," she said after a moment. "Are you okay? Does it hurt?"

"It mostly feels tingly," Vikas said, and Zarya nodded.

"Okay, good."

They continued as she repeated the process she had done so many times. It was beginning to feel like an extension of herself, but she had to remain vigilant.

Slowly, she peeled each star away, watching the ink

dissolve. She could sense the tension in the room and everyone's wide-eyed wonder as they stood witness to this impossible and potentially momentous sight.

And then she did it. The final star fell apart before a bright line flashed around his neck in a ring of fire before it burned away completely. Vikas gasped, clutching at his throat as he bent over.

"Let me see," Zarya said, dropping to her knees. "Are you okay?"

Vikas nodded and then slowly sat up.

Zarya stared at him.

A band of reddened skin marked his throat.

But he was fine, and the tattoo was gone.

NINETEEN

"What happened?" Vikas asked, carefully probing the skin around his neck.

"Do you have a mirror?" she asked. Again, someone jumped up from the table, retrieved one from a drawer, and handed it over.

Zarya held it up for Vikas, and he stared at himself, still touching his throat.

"Does it hurt?" she asked, and he slowly shook his head.

"It burned a little bit, but I'm fine."

He examined his reflection for several long, quiet moments, twisting his head left and right. Zarya held her breath, waiting for his reaction.

Then tears filled his eyes and spilled down his cheeks.

"You did it," he sobbed, falling to his knees and clutching the mirror to his chest. "It's gone. It's really gone. I didn't really believe it could actually be done."

The other men seated around the table rushed over, circling Vikas and wrapping their arms around each other in a huddle as they wept. Zarya backed up, giving them space.

She looked at Yasen, who was giving her a proud smile. He

walked over and draped an arm around her shoulders, drawing her close and planting a kiss on top of her head. "Well done, Swamp Girl. I knew you could do it."

Zarya felt her own eyes fill with tears. She couldn't even begin to imagine what Vikas and his friends must be feeling right now. After they all spent a few minutes celebrating, they pulled away from each other.

"How do you feel?" Zarya asked Vikas, crouching down in front of him. "Any different?"

Vikas shook his head. "I'm not sure."

"Do you feel a presence?" she asked, flattening a hand to her chest. "It might be in your heart or your mind. Something that feels... alive?"

She tried to describe the sensation when she also sensed her magic for the first time. Was it a coincidence that Zarya had also once been blocked from accessing hers too?

Vikas rubbed the top of his head and then his chest.

"Something here," he said.

"Hold out your hand," Zarya said, recalling Rabin's instructions in the forest. "The fire anchor is the most common. Think of directing that thing in your chest here." She pointed to the center of his palm.

Vikas stared up at Zarya, worry crossing his expression. "What if I can't do this?"

"You can," she said. "This is what you've been waiting for. You *can* do this."

He nodded and then pressed his mouth together in determination.

She watched as he focused on the spot in the middle of his hand.

His brows scrunched together as he concentrated, and then it happened.

A tiny flame ignited above his palm. He was so surprised he

leaped back, knocking into the chair behind him before toppling over.

"Are you okay?" Zarya cried, but he wasn't hurt. He was laughing. He was lying on his back, clutching his stomach, tears streaming down his face as he laughed and laughed, the sound filling every corner of the room.

"I did it," he cried through his tears. "I did it!"

She smiled and laughed with him, feeling all the weighted sides and angles of what she'd just done. The lightness of this accomplishment and the heaviness of everything this could mean.

Had any vanshaj in history ever been freed from their collar? Had they just accomplished the unimaginable?

What repercussions might follow now?

Zarya touched the necklace around her neck, thinking of her mother's words. This was what she'd come here to do, and she would die trying to fulfill this promise. She didn't care what it took.

After another minute, Vikas sat up and stared at her, his mouth open as if waiting for further instruction.

"One more time," she said, and he did it again, concentrating before a flame burst above his hand.

"Me next!" another of the men said.

"What's your name?" Zarya asked.

"I'm Suni," he said, and she pointed to the chair.

"Have a seat then."

Over the next few days, Zarya freed them one by one. She discovered that the process required careful precision and was also draining on her magic. She could only manage about one per day. But she returned with Yasen multiple times until she sat in front of the final one. A soft-spoken man named Ashok.

She started again, taking her time to carefully peel away the collar as everyone watched. She was already feeling more comfortable with the process, though she didn't dare go any faster.

She freed Ashok from the tattoo with that same blaze of fire before it melted away, leaving smooth brown skin. They cheered as he lifted his arms overhead and once again took to celebrating. Though she'd tried to hone her technique, the process wasn't getting any faster, and it was nightfall by the time they finished each day.

It was a step on a winding and precarious path because thousands of vanshaj lived in Gi'ana, let alone the entire continent. At this rate, she'd never live long enough to free them all. Or they'd be caught long before that happened.

But this was a start.

Once she had broken all their collars, Zarya worked with them to discover who had magic and helped summon their anchors. Suni had no magic but didn't seem to care at all. He reveled in his freedom, touching his neck constantly while watching his friends work with their new gifts.

Yasen left to buy food and returned a short while later, laden with samosas, papri chat, and mounds of jalebi that he set on the floor where they all sat cross-legged, passing dishes around the circle.

Zarya helped them tap into their other anchors as they ate. As far as they could tell, Charun only had a fire anchor, and Ashok had both a fire and water anchor. He practically vibrated with excitement as he drew up a drop of water from a glass, pulling it to the ceiling before releasing it in a tiny burst.

She loved watching how encouraging they were with each other, and every win, big or small, was celebrated with equal enthusiasm.

Vikas had more anchors. She helped him discover and recognize each one in turn.

Fire. Water. Earth. Air. Spirit.

Their gazes met, and she sensed he wanted to say something but wasn't sure how.

"What is it?"

"I feel something else," he said, rubbing his chest.

Her breath caught. Could it be? Had she been right all along?

"It might be the sixth anchor," she said, and his eyes widened.

"But it is forbidden," he whispered, and she nodded.

"So they say. But remember that I have it, too."

He expelled a breath, his shoulders caving in. "You don't seem like a monster."

"Only before I've had my tea in the morning," she joked, which earned her a rueful smile.

She decided now wasn't the moment to bring up what had happened in the forest the other day. Nor the fact that she might have caused the blight in Dharati. She saw those fiery eyes and those horrible visions in her mind's eye again and again. What if she *was* a monster?

She explained her theories about the Jadugara and what she'd learned about the ink and its magic. When she stopped speaking, she was met with stunned silence, edged with a bitter taste of betrayal.

Vikas nodded with his jaw hard. "They've been lying to us. Not that I should be surprised by that."

"I'm quite sure they have," Zarya said. "They've tried to villainize all of you for something they're hiding and using to their advantage."

"Why?" Suni asked.

She shook her head. "I'm not entirely sure other than the obvious desire for power and status."

Their expressions all turned to anger and confusion, and she exchanged an uncertain glance with Yasen. Zarya might still not have much experience with the world, but she wasn't too naive to understand the consequences of the thread they were slowly unraveling. She had no intention of keeping the Jadugara's secrets, but rumors such as this would catch like wildfire, taking so many people down with them, and they had to be careful.

"If I have it, then could I help, too?" Vikas asked, already connecting the dots.

"That's what I'm hoping," she said as the seeds of an idea started to plant themselves in her head.

What if she didn't have to do this alone? What if she was only the catalyst, and her *purpose* was to discover what was possible? What if the vanshaj could free themselves with the sixth anchor? She envisioned an entire network of freed Aazheri, all of them helping one another. Eventually, it would have to be enough to make a difference.

Zarya looked over at Yasen, again touching her necklace.

This was her destiny. This was her fate. And it was calling.

For the first time since she'd escaped the seaside cottage, she had a clear sense of the direction she was heading.

Looking around the room at these men who'd spent their entire lives punished for something they had never done, she felt her resolve harden into shards of unbreakable iron. Sharp and jagged and deadly.

She would free them all if it was the last thing she did.

She would free them all even if it cost her everything.

LETTER

Dear Zarya,

I'm glad to hear of the rebellion's progress, but I'm pleading with you to be careful. If this news gets out, all your lives will be forfeit. The Madans do not take kindly to being undermined. But I must know how such miracles have been accomplished. What kind of magic is this? I did some digging regarding your questions, but I have never heard of someone breaking the collar in all my years.

I'm planning to request access to the Royal Library's restricted section to see if I can find out more for you. It's something I should have done a long time ago, but Vikram remains displeased with me, and I don't like my chances. I'll also look for a book on paramadhar as you requested.

I spoke with Koura about your friend's condition, and he didn't have any answers to offer without seeing her in person. He promised to write to the healer you mentioned—they are acquaintances—to see if he can offer any guidance.

Amrita is healthy, and the baby is doing well. I'm including a sketch of the seed since you asked. It's really quite beautiful, though my artwork certainly is not. I do wish you were here. I think she could use a friend.

Take care of yourself. Give my regards to Yasen.

Row

TWENTY

After they left Vikas and the others to continue practicing their magic, Zarya and Yasen headed for the Chandras' flat.

"Do you think they'll burn the whole house down?" Yasen asked skeptically, peering over his shoulder. There had already been a few near misses with a pillow, the edge of the rug, and Suni's hair, but they all understood the importance of discretion.

If anyone were to discover their collars were gone, there was no telling what the consequences would be. If this had truly never happened, there would be no precedent, but given the way the royals had been behaving of late, Zarya had no doubt the punishments would be severe.

"They'll be fine," she said, following Yasen's stare as a flare of bright orange light illuminated the window. "I managed, didn't I?"

"Yeah, but I think that was sheer luck."

Zarya huffed out a snort. "I'm flattered by your faith in me."

Yasen grinned, and they continued their walk through the busy evening streets packed with people heading home from dinner or the theater.

Zarya's stomach twisted with nerves at the thought of seeing Rania. She was going to slam the door in her face. But Zarya needed to share what she'd accomplished this week, whether Rania wanted to listen or not. Ajay, at least, would speak with her.

A short while later, they found themselves standing at the door of the Chandras' flat. Yasen waited for her to gather her courage as she willed herself to knock.

With her fist poised, she looked at him, and he smiled.

"It'll be okay," he said.

"Will it?"

He winced. "Eventually."

She blew out a breath and then rapped three times. It took a few seconds before the door popped open. Unfortunately, it was Rania. Zarya had really been hoping Ajay would answer.

"What are you doing here?" Rania hissed, her eyes narrowing. "You are not welcome."

She tried to close the door, but Zarya blocked it with her foot, one hand pressed against the surface.

"Please. I wondered how Farida was doing, and I have something to tell you."

"Get out!" Rania snapped, obviously just as angry as ever. Zarya pressed her lips together before she caught sight of Ajay coming out of the kitchen, probably to see what all the commotion was about.

"I did it!" Zarya shouted over Rania's head. "I did it!"

"Rania!" Ajay said, striding over. "Let her speak."

Rania bristled at the command but then fell silent.

"I did it," Zarya repeated. "I freed four vanshaj from their collars."

"You were practicing on others!" Rania screeched, already done with holding her tongue. "Have you no scruples? You think their lives are worth nothing?"

"They volunteered!" Zarya countered. "They understood the risks!"

"And that makes it okay?" Rania spit back.

"No! But what else was I supposed to do? I needed to try on *someone*!"

"Come in," Ajay said, giving his sister a look. "We should speak with her, Rania."

"I have nothing to say to her!"

"Really? Because you've said quite a lot already," Ajay said, a tense edge to his tone.

Rania's nostrils flared. "You're taking her side?"

"I'm not taking anyone's side, but it was obvious what happened with Farida was an accident, and Zarya is sorry. Yelling at her every time she opens her mouth isn't helping anything. Did you hear her? She just told us that she found a way to *free* the vanshaj, and all you can do is think about yourself!"

Ajay's voice rose with each sentence, and it was apparent these were words he'd been holding in for a while.

Rania stepped back, her mouth opening and her hand pressing against her chest. She was clearly as surprised by his outburst as the rest of them.

"Ajay," she said, her voice small.

He sighed and rubbed his face. "I'm worried about Farida, too, but this is getting us nowhere. She would not want us fighting like this."

At that, the wind dipped out of Rania's sails, and her body caved inward as her shoulders hunched. Zarya wasn't sure what to make of any of this, but she was grateful that Ajay had stood up for her. She understood why Rania was so angry, but he was also right. This *wasn't* getting them anywhere.

"Zarya," Ajay said, turning back to her and Yasen. "Please come in and tell us what happened."

Rania's eyes flashed, but she said nothing as Zarya entered and followed Ajay into the living room.

She spent a few minutes explaining what she had done with Vikas and the others, describing the process, knowing that as Aazheri, the Chandras would have some understanding of what she meant, even without a sixth anchor.

"One of them had no magic," she said, "and two of them had some."

"And the last?" Ajay asked.

"He... is like me," Zarya said.

Vikas confirmed all her suspicions that someone had been trying to contain the darkness. It had never really been banished. It had always been there, accessible to at least a few.

"The vanshaj have the sixth anchor," Ajay said, shaking his head, his face turning pale.

"It makes sense, doesn't it," Zarya said, and Ajay rubbed his chin before he paced away, muttering something to himself.

"It does," he said, turning to face her. "It actually all makes complete sense and clarifies so many things."

"I think I can teach Vikas to break the collars as well," Zarya said. "I think if we can find more vanshaj with the sixth anchor, then we could start freeing them all."

"That sounds dangerous," Ajay said.

"It might be," she agreed, "but isn't this what we've been working for? And I can't do it all alone. The process takes time. It took me days to free all four, and it's draining my magic. We need help."

Ajay shook his head as his eyes turned glassy with the threat of tears.

"I've always..." He stopped and inhaled a deep breath, gathering himself. "I was raised to fear this power. To shun and vilify it, and it's been under our noses all this time. We all pretend we're so noble and *pure*. I was told to reject it, but now

I feel like..." He stopped again. "I feel like a failure that I can't help, too."

Zarya walked over and laid a hand on his arm.

"You've done so much for this cause. You both have," Zarya said, including Rania, feeling generous now that she wasn't yelling at her. "You have no control over the magic you possess. There are still so many other ways to help. Freeing the vanshaj from their collars is only one step in a much larger plan."

Ajay nodded, though she could tell she hadn't convinced him yet.

"What we do need is someone to work on creating fake collars while we figure out our next steps," she said. "It was very obvious after we removed their markings, and someone is bound to notice. They'll wear scarves or clothing to cover their necks, but that will only conceal them for so long."

Rania nodded tersely. "This is good news," she said.

It wasn't forgiveness, but the slightest softness entered Rania's eyes.

"We also need a private spot where we can operate without detection. Somewhere we can direct people to have their collars removed."

Rania looked at her brother. "This is how we can help, then," she said. "And it is what Farida would want. We'll get in touch with the council to seek their approval, but I'm confident they would support this."

Ajay nodded as the siblings shared a secret exchange.

Rania then looked at Zarya. "They may want to meet with you first," she said, and Zarya nodded.

"Of course. Whatever you need."

"Then we'll find somewhere safe," Ajay said. He took Zarya's hand and pressed it to his heart. "And thank the gods that they've sent you to us."

TWENTY-ONE

Zarya tossed and turned in her bed that night, worrying about all the things that could go wrong. The risk of discovery was at the top of her worries. What would happen if the Jadugara uncovered what they were doing? What if the royal family found out?

Not only would they lash out with even more severe consequences, but there was also a good chance Zarya's identity would be revealed, and she couldn't begin to understand the repercussions of that.

As she flipped from side to side, her mind kept wandering back to Rabin. She still hadn't found time to uncover more about paramadhar and loathed that he currently had the upper hand. Tomorrow, she would add that to the top of her to-do list. While she was helping everyone else, she could help herself, too.

She continued to toss and turn, eventually caving to a troubled sleep, when a blast of cold wind pulled her eyes open.

She probably shouldn't have been surprised when she found herself in the middle of a forest clearing. But it wasn't the same forest where they'd met before. This one was darker, the sky a deep green, though there were just as many stars. She was surrounded by pine trees and snow dusting the ground and the rocks that formed the perimeter. In the distance loomed a range of soaring white-capped mountains.

Pulling herself up to stand, her toes dug into a thick fur rug cushioning her feet. Wearing only leggings and a sleeveless tunic, she rubbed her arms while she shivered. Rabin stood at the other end, dressed in leather with a thick fur cloak tossed over his shoulders. He looked like some kind of warrior god, staring down at her. This time, he wore only one of his dragon swords belted at his hip.

She said nothing as she stared at him, the wind whipping strands of hair across her face. He approached, sliding the cloak off his shoulders and holding it out. "May I?" he asked, and though she considered refusing, she was also fucking freezing.

She nodded, and he stepped closer, wrapping the cloak around her. It was warm from his body, and she did her best not to notice the way it smelled like him. She'd dreamed of that scent of midnight forests and smoky earth every night for months while trying to drown him out of her thoughts, but it was no use. It had never been any use.

"No sword for me this time?" she asked, her teeth chattering, before he arched an eyebrow.

"I was hoping we could talk instead," he said.

Clutching the cloak tight to her shoulders, she scanned him from head to toe. "I have nothing to say to you."

His mouth firmed into a hard line, revealing the depth of his frustrations, but he had brought all of this upon himself.

"Why did you bring me here?" she asked. "You don't have to be asleep for this to work anymore?"

She gestured to his clothing, and he shook his head.

"No, once you understand how to enter the mind plane, you can do it anywhere and anytime. Honestly, I'm surprised you haven't figured this out yet."

Zarya narrowed her eyes. "I've been busy."

"Doing what?" he asked.

"That is none of your business."

He rubbed his chin as he slowly circled around her. She resisted the urge to follow his path and wiggled her toes where she stood, the tips beginning to freeze.

"You won't tell me where you are?" He looped around to stand before her again.

"Why? So you can sweep into my life and fuck everything up?"

He stepped closer, leaving only a small space between them, forcing her to tip her head back. "Is that what I did?"

She exhaled a sharp breath, remembering that moment he'd appeared in Dharati and her entire world had tilted on its axis. "You know it is."

Another step had him towering over her, making it feel like she was being consumed. "Or did I help free you, Zarya? Would anyone else have been able to release your magic?"

"How did you do that?" she asked. "Not even Row understood it."

The corner of his mouth crooked up. "Your father is powerful. You have no idea what things he's capable of."

That answer churned a sour line up the back of her throat.

"*He* helped you?"

"I couldn't have done that on my own."

"So you *did* know who I was?"

"No," he said. "I didn't know. I told him about the dreams, but he had no way of knowing who you were. I went to him for a favor, and he granted it."

"Why?"

"Because he trusts me. Because I have been loyal to him."

Zarya swallowed. "Why?"

Rabin's fierce expression masked a hint of sadness. "He has never asked me to hide what I am. He has taught me to embrace my dragon and my magic. To discover things I never imagined myself capable of."

Zarya narrowed her eyes at that somewhat cryptic statement.

"That's it?" she asked.

He frowned, and she regretted the insensitive question. After everything he'd revealed about his father, she knew what that kind of acceptance must have meant to him.

"That's it," he said after a brief pause.

Zarya sighed. "So, where are we now?"

"In a forest at the northern border of Andhera. I thought you might be more comfortable here."

"What about our old forest?" she asked. "At least it was warm."

"I want you to see it. Its cold beauty and its magnificence. I want you to stop turning your back on the place that could be your home if you'd let it."

Zarya shook her head. "I don't want that."

"Why? Because of the lies you were told? Aren't you done believing Row? Why do you put so much stock into the things he says? He deceived you for your entire life."

Zarya opened her mouth to reply and then closed it. Did he have a point?

"Why do you care what I think?"

"Because I want you here with me." He said the words so matter-of-factly that she believed them with her whole self. There was no artifice in his expression or his words. She understood *he* believed his truth. But was that truth the best thing for her?

"You swear you didn't know?" she asked, studying him carefully. She'd spent months determined not to believe him, but he was right, and she wasn't always the best judge of what was real.

"I didn't know," he said, and for the first time, the seeds of doubt reluctantly filtered into the cracks of her resolve. "I saw the most beautiful woman I'd ever seen walking in my dreams, and I had to find her. When I realized who you were, I could only think this was destiny, Zarya. I never meant to lie to you. You have to see this was fated from the very start."

"I don't know," she answered, and then he stepped closer so there was no space left between them. He placed a finger under her chin and tipped her face up so their mouths were only inches apart, yet it felt like an ocean tossing them onto separate shores.

"Zarya," he said, his voice rough and full of passion. "Please let me in. I've been miserable these months without you. I need you, and you need me. Let me protect you."

Zarya scrunched her nose with uncertainty. "You want to be my paramadhar?"

"Why wouldn't I want that?"

"Because." She waved a hand and then immediately snatched it under his cloak. It was freezing out here. "You're basically my servant. If I die, then so do you."

He tipped his head and arched a brow as if to ask what the problem was.

"You don't think that's a little messed up?" she asked.

"It's an honor to be chosen," he said so seriously that she thought for a moment he had to be pulling her leg. But there was only sincerity in his expression.

"What if we aren't anything more than that?" she asked. "What if I don't want to pursue anything physical or romantic between us?"

"Then I will fulfill my duty with honor."

Zarya frowned. "Really? Why would you do that?"

His mouth opened, and he shook his head as though he didn't understand her questions. "Because," he said. "We will be more."

She almost laughed at his bottomless arrogance. The truth

was he was probably right, and her defenses were already crumbling. How much longer would it be before she gave in?

"You want to bind yourself to me forever in the hopes I'll change my mind about us?" she asked, still skeptical.

The corner of his mouth teased up. "You will change your mind about us. And when you do, it will be like the heavens exploding."

"Gods, you are so full of yourself, you know that?"

His smile stretched a little further, and the sight was so rare it did something weird to her heart. "So I've been told."

"What if I don't change it?"

"Nothing changes for me," he answered without hesitation.

"I still don't understand."

"You will," he said before he took her hand and slipped his arm around her waist. The touch sent heat flooding through her body as she leaned into his warmth. She stared up at him, his face so close to hers she could feel his breath as it fogged in soft white puffs.

Was he about to kiss her? Did she want that? She did. She knew she shouldn't but... fuck, if she didn't absolutely want his mouth on hers.

He then wrapped a hand across her nape and drew her closer, burying his nose into the crown of her head before he pulled back and took her hand, flipping it over and pressing his lips to her palm.

The act sent a bolt of sensation straight to her stomach, her knees turning to mush. How could such a benign touch elicit such a reaction? She'd thought so many times of the way his hands and mouth had felt. The way he'd tasted her and bitten her and fucked her. That night on Ranpur Island lived at the forefront of her many vivid fantasies.

His mouth lingered on her skin for another second before he pulled it away. He leaned down to speak in her ear, his lips brushing the shell, causing her entire body to flush with heat and want.

"Good night, Zarya. I will see you again soon."

* * *

Rabin blinked as he returned to the warmth of his room inside the castle. He'd done it again.

He stared out the window at the moonlit tundra, imagining the spot far in the distance where they'd met. He wasn't sure why that had felt like the right spot, but when he saw how she'd looked at him, he knew it had been the perfect choice.

"Went to see your girlfriend?" came a familiar voice. He spun around to find Ekaja sitting at his desk under the far window, her feet kicked up and her hands folded over her stomach.

She had been Abishek's army commander for decades, and Rabin had bonded with her over tales of their conquests and their never-ending fascination with battle strategy. She was a powerful Aazheri with five anchors and had a mind for war that many would envy.

Rabin arched a brow and began stripping out of his leather and furs. "Shouldn't you be with *yours*, not lurking around my bedroom?"

She shrugged as she picked her nails with a dagger. "We're taking a break. I'm into cock this week."

Rabin smirked and pulled his leather tunic over his head, leaving him in a thin cotton shirt. "Yes, I was with her."

Ekaja must have sensed the despondency in his voice because she pursed her lips into a mock pout.

"Did she blue-ball you again?"

Despite himself, Rabin huffed out something that might have resembled a laugh.

"You really know how to make me feel three inches tall,

Kaj," he said as he stripped out of his pants and retrieved the softer pair that he used for sleep.

"If I don't, who will?"

"And you do it with astonishing proficiency," he grumbled as he dropped onto the divan in front of the fireplace. A pot of tea had been set out, and he poured a cup to warm himself from the forest's lingering chill.

Ekaja swung her feet down and strode over, dropping into an armchair. She wore her training leathers—her standard uniform when she wasn't in her armor. As the only female commander in Rahajhan and the first in the history of Andhera, she refused to let anyone forget who she was. Her long dark hair was pulled back into a high braided ponytail, showing off the strong planes and angles of her face.

Rabin didn't know how anyone could meet her and think she was anything but an apex predator, but men were idiots when it came to fierce women.

"She's still angry with you," Ekaja said.

"Yep," Rabin said, sipping his tea. "But... I think she might finally believe me. I saw something in her face."

He shook his head and rubbed a hand over his mouth. He was so tied up about Zarya, and it was everything he could do to focus.

"What did you do? Glare at her until she conceded?"

Rabin rolled his eyes. "I do have some ability to converse, thank you."

"Could have fooled me," Ekaja said, snatching a piece of burfi from the tray on the table. "So, what next?"

"I'm not sure. I think I'll give her some space. I'm sure it's eating her alive that I've learned how to control the mind plane and she hasn't yet. It will only be a matter of time before she does, and then maybe she will reach out."

Ekaja whistled. "This girl is eating you up."

Rabin stretched and rubbed his side. His dragon tattoo

always seemed to pulse whenever he was in Zarya's presence. Abishek had encouraged him to get it years ago in an effort to leave behind his history and embrace who he was. It was a reminder. A bridge leading him away from a past he'd left behind.

The added bonus was that it was infused with magic that helped him control his transformations, meaning he could endure longer periods without that itch to change crawling under his skin. But now it ached with phantom pain as though it, too, missed Zarya.

"She's convinced the king wants to hurt her," he said.

"And you're sure he doesn't?"

Rabin's gaze flicked to Ekaja. "You think he would? You've known him longer."

She took a sip of her tea. "If you're asking if I think he's capable of it, then you know the answer to that. As to whether what you were told is true in this specific case, then I'm not sure."

Rabin groaned and sat back as Ekaja barked out a laugh.

"You know what kind of man he can be," she said. "He didn't get where he was by being anything less than ruthless. He's done many questionable things in the name of his power, Rabin."

"I know," he said. "But he had reasons for all of it. He wouldn't hurt his own child."

She nodded. "She's powerful and has strong magic. I do believe that would be of interest to him."

"But not in the way Row claimed," Rabin said.

"If you say so," she answered. She was skeptical, and Rabin understood why. But Abishek had taken Rabin under his wing and shown him the kindness that no one else in his life ever had. He was a king and was far from innocent, but being the ruler of a great nation meant blood on your hands. Rabin understood this.

Besides, it was too great a coincidence that both father and daughter had come into his life through such different circumstances. It had to mean this was the right course.

"I do," Rabin said. "I believe him."

"Then you have no reason not to trust him."

He looked up, his jaw hardening. "I would never let anyone harm her."

Ekaja nodded. "I'm beginning to understand that." She paused. "And you're sure about this whole paramadhar and masatara thing? You're sure you want to bind your life to this woman?"

He clasped his hands and peered at his friend. He hadn't had many in his life, and he cherished Ekaja's companionship more than she could ever know.

"I've never been so sure about anything."

She tipped up a smile. "I'm sure you'll wear her down. I mean, look at us. I couldn't stand you when you arrived all cocky and arrogant, but you wormed your way into my pitch-black heart."

Rabin snorted and sipped his tea as he stared into the crackling fire, her words ringing in his ears. He thought of Zarya and her fierce expression and the hurt in her eyes. He'd caused that with his foolishness and his cowardice. If he'd just been brave enough to admit the truth, then perhaps they could have avoided all of this.

He swore he'd never lie to her again and he *would* find some way to make amends.

All he could hope was that, eventually, she would forgive him.

That or he would die trying.

TWENTY-TWO

It had been two weeks since the encounter with Rabin in the forest, and Zarya's mind was occupied with three things.

The first, of course, was him. She wasn't too stubborn to admit that.

The second was studying the paramadhar and masatara bond, trying to puzzle out a method for controlling the visions. Row had come through for her and sent a dusty old book that had once served as a handbook for paramadhar that he'd found in the Jai Palace library.

The third was the underground operation they'd set up to free the vanshaj from their collars, and that's where she found herself today.

"Where should this go?" Vikas asked, holding a large crate filled with bottles of black ink. Regular black ink, not the magical kind.

When Zarya had explained her idea, he'd leaped at the chance to help. After swearing an oath using a promise spell to keep their identities secret, they'd met with the vanshaj council. Vikas explained what Zarya had done, and she shared her vision for breaking the collars.

When they were finished, the council agreed to their plans to set up an operation using the money from the rebellion's unknown benefactor. With Farida still unconscious, Vikas was temporarily promoted to take up her position as liaison between the council and the Rising Phoenix. All decisions would go through him first and then voted on when necessary by its members. For now, they'd keep knowledge of the operation within their closest and most trusted ranks until they might need help from their larger circle.

At first, Vikas seemed uncertain about his new role, but he was taking to it beautifully, and Zarya loved watching him find his confidence. He'd come up with the name Operation Starbreak, and that was how they were all referring to it now.

"Over here," Zarya said, gesturing for Vikas to follow.

The Rising Phoenix had purchased this sprawling manor in one of the city's most affluent neighborhoods to act as their headquarters. It was a short walk from the vanshaj district if you cut through Ishaan's twisting maze of alleys. They all had decided it was best to hide in plain sight.

A spacious salon at the front of the house would act as the main center of the operation. Chairs lined one wall, serving as a waiting area, while the remaining space had been divided into sections with sets of chairs facing one another. For now, it would only be Zarya and Vikas, but they shared a vision of filling this entire room with freed Aazheri helping to break the collars.

Leading off the salon was a dining room with a sliding door, and Zarya hauled one open. "I thought we could get some cots placed in here in case anyone needs to recover," she suggested. "Though hopefully, everything goes as smoothly as it did with you and your friends."

Every window was hung with thick curtains that Rania had installed the week before to keep prying eyes out. The house was situated far back from the street, and the entire property was bordered by a high fence and plenty of green space filled with dense plants, shrubs, and flowers. It helped obscure the manor from the passersby, and the private back lane provided the perfect spot for people and deliveries to move in and out.

Still, they all agreed they would limit traffic during the day and use the cover of night as much as possible.

"Once they've recovered, they'll come in here to have new tattoos drawn on," Zarya said, crossing into the hall into a large study. "We'll get some chairs and rolling carts."

They'd opted to use semi-permanent ink that would resist coming off as long as they were careful to keep it dry. Ajay had also tapped into his connections, searching for artists who might be open to recruitment within their network.

"This is incredible," Vikas said as he deposited the box on a table and opened it before they started pulling out the contents, lining up bottles of ink in neat rows. "I can't wait to get started."

Zarya smiled as they quietly surveyed their surroundings.

"How is your family doing?" Zarya asked. Vikas lived with his parents and his younger brother in the vanshaj district. She knew they were worried about his involvement with the Phoenix and, despite all evidence to the contrary, refused to believe his collar was gone and that he had magic.

"Not great," he said. "My parents are scared. I understand it, but I wish they'd have a bit more faith in me."

She nodded. "Give it time. This is all new to everyone."

He blew out a breath and placed his hands on his hips. "I know this is all necessary, but I admit that I'm scared, too."

"It would be strange if you weren't," she answered. "I'm terrified all the time—I just do my best not to let it show."

He turned to give her a small smile. "Then we can both pretend."

The sound of the back door opening drew their attention, along with the sound of voices Zarya recognized.

"Come and meet some people who are actually very brave,"

Zarya joked, and Vikas nodded before he followed her into the kitchen, where they found Suvanna and Apsara with Yasen. Behind them came Ajay.

"We brought lunch," Apsara said, holding up a bag before she began unpacking foil-wrapped parathas and small tubs of raita. Everyone circled around the large island as Suvanna deposited a large carafe of fresh coffee, and Zarya went in search of mugs.

She also introduced Vikas to Suvanna and Apsara, who became completely tongue-tied at their presence and couldn't stop staring. Who could blame him? Sitting here in this ordinary kitchen, they were both too ethereal and otherworldly for this place.

"How are things at the palace?" Yasen asked them. "How were you received?"

"With open arms," Suvanna replied as she pulled up a stool. "They're obsessed with magic and were very keen to discuss what we're both capable of."

"Are they?" Zarya asked.

"Well, the princess is," Apsara said. "Dishani."

Zarya always felt a weird tug in her chest every time she heard her sister's name. She wanted to know so many things about her.

"How are you feeling?" Apsara asked Vikas. "After the removal?"

Vikas shrugged and accepted a plate of food from Zarya. "I feel different."

"Good different?" Apsara asked.

"Yeah," he said with a smile. "The best. Like I'm as light as air."

"And your magic?"

"I'm learning," he said. "Zarya is helping me."

"I don't have a lot of experience, either," Zarya said. "But I'm trying."

"I'll work with you," Ajay said. "I'm not as strong as either of you, but I graduated top of my class at the university and know some techniques to help with your control."

Zarya tried to discern any hint of envy or irritation in his words but, thankfully, detected none. That wasn't the sort of man Ajay was, anyway.

"What else have you learned in the palace?" Ajay asked, turning to Suvanna and Apsara.

"Dishani and Prince Miraan have been meeting regularly with the Jadugara," Apsara said. "They're all very cozy."

"Do you know why?" Ajay asked.

Apsara nodded. "They aren't making a secret of it. They're working on plans to rebuild the ink factory and, of course, looking for ways to prevent further sabotage."

"They'll be increasing security," Yasen said. "It'll be impossible to get inside again. We had the advantage of surprise last time and their confidence that no one would ever confront them."

"Now they know that isn't true," Ajay said.

"Exactly," Yasen said. "If we want to thwart their plans, then we have to find other ways."

Zarya waved a hand, indicating the manor house where they were all gathered. "Well, this is the start."

"It is," Ajay answered. "What else?"

"They're trying desperately to root out members of the Rising Phoenix," Suvanna said. "They're gearing up for random searches throughout the vanshaj district. They've been holding back for some reason, but it's clear how antsy the princess has become."

"Is there anything you two can do?" Ajay asked.

"I'm not sure," Apsara said. "While we've been welcomed as guests, we'll have to be careful. It is not our place, and they may grow suspicious if we attempt to interfere."

That was met with silence as everyone stewed in their thoughts.

"I wish there was something we could do to affect their rebuilding plans," Ajay said.

"Like what?" Zarya asked.

"I'm not sure yet," he said. "But there must be something."

"In the meantime, let us show you how we have everything set up," Vikas said.

He walked them through the house, pointing out the different rooms and areas.

"As we free more people, I'm hoping some can be conscripted to help us," Zarya said. "It'll be a slow process at first, but the vision is for this whole house to be full soon enough."

Ajay stood in the foyer, staring up at the stairs leading to three more floors.

"It's incredible," he said softly. "I never thought we'd get this far."

"It's going to be glorious," Zarya said, following everyone's appreciative gazes.

This would be exceedingly dangerous.

The hardest thing they might ever do.

But also, the most important.

And, gods, how she hoped *everyone* would get their happy ending.

TWENTY-THREE

A week later, they all took a night off from Operation Starbreak. Yasen and Vikas, along with his friends whom Zarya had also helped free, had been assisting with clean-up and hauling in furniture and supplies. They were finally ready to begin receiving vanshaj.

Yasen and the others had decided to enjoy a few rounds of cards at the gambling den where they met while Zarya took the opportunity to finally curl up with the book Row had sent about paramadhar.

It had been almost a month since she'd last seen Rabin, and it bothered her more than she wanted to admit. Maybe she'd finally convinced him to keep his distance, and she hated when the thought caused a wave of disappointment.

Or maybe he was just waiting for her.

The book claimed she would need to enter the mind plane, and the easiest way to do so was to think of a place and imagine it as clearly as possible. It helped if it was somewhere that was important or had made her feel joy.

For some reason, the ballroom at the Ravana estate, where

she'd danced all night long, had been the first place to pop into her mind.

She put the book down and imagined the resplendent room —the golden chandeliers, the marble floors, the walls covered in ornate green silk. Everything had been so new and wondrous that night. She could still hear the music and the laughter as people danced, twirling in circles.

It had been one of the most magical moments of her life, and it was his home. She wondered what Rabin would think. Did he have any happy memories of the place where he experienced so much pain?

The book said you could also create almost anything, including clothing and objects, explaining how Rabin had conjured the rug to protect her feet from the snow.

She imagined herself in a light but beautifully decorated lehenga, the silver beading sparkling in her mind. And then she pictured herself stepping from this room into the mind plane. Since she was the masatara, her paramadhar couldn't refuse the summons. She could, however, refuse his if she chose, though that also required practice. It was harder to do when she was asleep, and so far, it was clear he'd used that fact to his advantage.

But it was late and she *did* hope she wasn't pulling him from a precarious situation.

Standing with her hands balled into fists, she imagined every detail, trying to recall the smells and every sound. There was a shift, like a bend in the atmosphere, and when she opened her eyes, she found herself standing in the empty ballroom of the Ravanas' home.

The soft music she'd fabricated played from some unknown source, and Rabin stood at the end of the room with his back facing her. There were no shadows where he could hide tonight. She'd selected his attire to coordinate with hers, opting for a sherwani of the deepest midnight blue embroidered with silver threads over the collar and wrists.

She waited as he slowly turned around, his eyebrow already arched.

He looked down at himself and then at her. "I see you've been doing some reading."

Zarya said nothing, simply returning an imperious look of her own.

"Why here?" he asked as he scanned the room.

"I don't know. It just came to me."

He pressed his mouth together. "I had some happy times in this room," he said softly.

"I'm glad. And I'm sorry. I worried that it would be painful, but it was the first place I thought of."

The corner of his mouth teased up. "I also brought you to your father's home. Perhaps this is only fair."

"That wasn't—"

He lifted a hand. "I know that. I'm glad you've been to this house. This was once my home, despite the memories. Vikram and I were friends once."

He uttered the last statement with such sadness, and it was clear how much he regretted their troubled relationship.

"Do you want to dance?" he asked, sweeping his hands over himself. "It seems a shame not to ask."

"Sure," Zarya said. She wasn't positive that's what she'd intended by choosing this place, but they *were* dressed up with music playing, and it was the next logical thing to do.

He walked towards her, his boots clicking against the marble. Zarya waited with her breath tight in her throat, trying not to be overwhelmed by his presence without much success. How could she ever feel anything less than ensnared by that dark, burning gaze?

When he was but a distant thought present only in her mind, she could pretend she wasn't completely helpless under his spell, but witnessing him in the flesh, it was impossible to ignore.

He reached out his hand, and she looked at it for a moment.

"Do you remember the first time we ever spoke?" she asked.

"Of course."

"Why do you think we met inside that egg of all places?" she asked, referring to the deadly shower of falling orbs when she'd broken her arm while picnicking with Vikram.

He shook his head. "I'm not sure if that's where we were exactly, but I think whatever magic lived inside triggered our connection."

"What do you mean?"

"Perhaps you haven't read that far yet," he said. "The connection needs a powerful activation to wake up, and we know there was strong magic in those orbs. That's one reason why it's so rare."

"But we met before that," she said. "Sort of."

"Apparently, we *could* enter the mind plane at any point, but we couldn't actually speak with one another until the link was initiated."

Zarya took a step and then laid her hand on his. "I see."

"Do you?" he asked. "Do you understand why this is destiny?"

She blew out a breath. "Let's just dance."

Without warning, he tugged her towards him, pressing her body to his. Then he wrapped an arm around her, his large hand splaying against her back. She shivered at his touch, a spark lighting up her skin. She didn't want to react to him this way, but she was slowly learning that either she had to find a way to forgive and eventually trust him, or she might be miserable for the rest of her life.

He began to twirl them across the floor, just like the night they'd danced in the forest. They moved like smoke, in tune with one another. There was no doubt something connected them.

"Are you still angry with me?" he asked.

"Yes," she answered immediately, and he nodded.

"But you called me here."

"I did."

"Why?" He tipped his head in curiosity. "Did you miss me?"

She narrowed her eyes. "I didn't. I just wanted to see how this thing worked."

His answering chuckle was low and dark, clearly reading her lie.

"And now that you've practiced?" he asked.

"Then..." she started to say that that would be it, and he would never see her again, but that wasn't the truth. Now that she understood how to do this, she'd be more tempted than ever to reach out. Maybe the only thing keeping her away had been her inability to find him.

"Zarya," he said. "Please. Stop this." He tightened his hold and brought her closer. "Talk to me. Let me show you I meant no harm."

"How will you do that? I won't come to Andhera."

"Then meet with me. Let me see you in person. I don't want to exist only in this space. This is not real."

"Isn't it?" she asked, though she knew what he meant. The visions were vivid and almost solid, but something distant kept them from becoming true reality. Like a layer of almost translucent glass coating everything and allowing light through but preventing it from touching what was underneath.

"You know it's not," he said, and she nodded.

"Where are you?" he asked.

"Will you come for me?"

"Yes," he said. "I'll fly across a thousand miles to find you."

"I'm in Ishaan," she said, the words slipping out of her

mouth. She wasn't sure if she'd meant to reveal this, but there it was. Again. His eyes gleamed with satisfaction.

"So close."

"What now?" she asked.

"Wait for me," he said, echoing the same words he'd said that night before he'd dropped into her life and changed everything. "I'm coming."

And then the scene disappeared, and Zarya opened her eyes, sitting alone in her apartment.

Wait for me.

A breathless shiver of anticipation climbed over her scalp and spread through her limbs, warming her from the inside out.

He was coming.

* * *

Rabin returned to Abishek's study where Zarya had pulled him from moments earlier. He stood by the fire where he'd been conversing with the king. He blinked as the world returned to focus.

Looking down at himself, he was almost surprised to find he was back in his regular black clothing.

"What happened?" Abishek asked. "You stopped talking."

"For how long?"

"Only a moment, but your eyes grew distant." The king sat forward. "Did you see her?"

"Yes," Rabin said with a small half-smile as he propped his elbow up on the mantle. "She learned how to call me."

"And why did she call you tonight?"

Rabin laughed to himself. "She said she just wanted to see how it worked."

"But?" Abishek asked.

"But... I'm sure that's partly true, but I also think she

wanted to see me." He looked at the king. "She told me she's in Ishaan."

The king leaned back, folding his hands over his stomach. "And what is she doing there?"

"If I know Zarya, it's because she wants to meet her family." Rabin's gaze shifted to Abishek, who watched him carefully.

"Did you get the sense she had done so?"

Rabin shook his head. "I don't know. We never discussed it."

Abishek studied Rabin for a moment. "I see. And? Now, what will you do?"

Rabin stood straighter. "I would like to go and see her."

The king nodded. "Then you should do that."

Rabin pushed himself from his spot by the fire and dropped into the plush armchair next to Abishek. "There's something I need to tell you," he added, deciding it was time to come clean. "I haven't been entirely forthright with you about Zarya."

His brows rose in a question. "Yes?"

"My feelings for your daughter are not only that of the paramadhar bond."

He fell silent, allowing his words to sink in. Several emotions crossed the king's face that he couldn't interpret. Would he be angry or welcome this?

"I see," Abishek finally said. "And does she reciprocate these... feelings?"

Rabin shook his head. "I think she did, but then..."

"She thought you betrayed her."

"Exactly."

Abishek crossed a leg over the other and reclined in his seat. "Many years ago, paramadhar were far more common, and those who ventured into physical or romantic relationships typically went on to regret it."

Rabin clenched his hands as he leaned forward, propping his elbows on his thighs, drinking in every word. "Why? The handbook cautioned against it, but it doesn't really explain the reason."

Abishek blew out a breath and picked up the drink on the side table. "Should you choose to perform the Bandhan, you will both be connected by powerful magic. You'll be privy to your masatara's deepest emotions. Any feelings beyond those of a platonic nature can make the bond feel... too intense. It grows stronger over time and often becomes all-consuming. There was more than one paramadhar through history who lost themselves to the passions that ate away at their spirits. Only those of the strongest mind can resist falling prey to its hold. I must caution against this."

Rabin nodded. "I suppose that makes sense." His hand curled into a fist. "But Zarya and I are different."

"Are you sure?" Abishek asked. "Some masatara abused the relationship, bidding their paramadhar commit unspeakable acts in their name. They were so overcome with their desires that they were helpless to resist. I believe it's that very reason the gods withdrew this particular magic, and very few pairs have been seen since."

Rabin knew his mentor wasn't trying to be difficult, but Abishek never took anything at face value. He always asked questions and attempted to poke holes, seeking the truth in everything.

"I'm sure," Rabin said after a moment. "I believe this was also destined. Why else would the gods have returned this magic to us?"

The king sighed. "I still believe it would be a mistake. It can be easy to confuse the connection with your masatara as being more than it is."

"I'm not confusing anything," Rabin snapped. "I know what I feel."

The king blinked at the sharp tone in Rabin's voice. He wasn't used to being questioned. "Then you will suppress it. I know you believe you are strong but you remain weak in spirit."

Rabin felt gut-punched by those words. He knew it was true. When he'd met Abishek, he'd been a broken man, worth less than nothing. Abishek had helped draw him out of his shell and given him the strength to recover, but he still had so far to go. He didn't deserve someone like Zarya, anyway. What had he been thinking?

"You'll see I'm right," Abishek said. "Go and find her, but do not give in to these desires. Perhaps when you're ready, we can discuss it again, but for now, I forbid this and order you to break off all romantic involvement with my daughter."

Rabin stared at the fire for several long seconds before looking up.

"Shall I go to her, then?"

Abishek smiled and folded his hands. "Of course. Bring her home, and then everything will be as it was always meant."

TWENTY-FOUR

Over the next few days, Zarya threw herself into her work, trying to push thoughts of Rabin out of her head.

Wait for me. I'm coming.

One night, after Vikas had returned home to his family, Zarya had slept in one of the upstairs bedrooms along with Yasen, as they'd lain awake talking much too late. She'd told him about her latest encounters with Rabin, and he was also having trouble understanding why he was so determined to be bound to her.

But Operation Starbreak was ready, and she had bigger things to focus on. As she walked about the rooms, admiring how her vision had come to life, she prayed they could find someone willing to trust them. She understood that most vanshaj weren't about to let some Aazheri they didn't know perform magic on them willingly.

When the house sat empty day after day, she tried to cultivate patience. This would take time. Unfortunately, that wasn't really a luxury they had.

Construction had begun on the new factory, and the royal family must have dug deep into their coffers because the site was swarming with hundreds of workers and guards at all hours of the day. The Jadugara also kept vigil outside, accusing anyone who passed of having ties to the resistance.

If they started producing ink again, then all of this would be for nothing.

They just had to be faster.

Ready for some lunch, she found Yasen in the kitchen, preparing food. Thunder boomed overhead, shaking the entire house. She pulled up a stool and settled into it.

"Hungry?" he asked, pushing over a plate with samosas and tamarind chutney.

"Starving." She helped herself, sinking her teeth into the flaky pastry, realizing just how hungry she'd been.

A moment later, Vikas banged into the house through the back door, shaking water from his hair and clothing. The rain was coming down heavier now, fat drops splattering against the windows.

"Any luck today?" she asked hopefully.

He'd been busy with his friends in the vanshaj quarter, attempting to recruit people to their operation.

"The usual," he answered as he shook off another shower of raindrops and then slumped onto a stool. "A few will listen for a short while, but most of them are too afraid to hear anything I have to say. I thought I was finally getting through to my father..." He trailed off and shook his head. "But not yet."

Zarya nodded and poured him some chai. "We'll think of a way. Maybe the council has some ideas."

"Maybe," he said, though his tone wasn't all that hopeful.

She gave him a sad smile as another clap of thunder rattled the windows.

"They're saying this storm is going to last for days," Yasen said, peering up at the grey sky. "That might keep people away."

Zarya let out a tense breath. "Hopefully, this weather slows the work on the factory down, too."

Yasen gave her and Vikas a grim look. "Even if people were willing to come, how many do you think you could free before they're finished? Once they start up ink production again..."

She shook her head. "I don't know. I haven't been able to practice since Vikas and his friends, and that took me days. Maybe I'll become faster with time, but I also can't risk rushing anything. If we could recruit a few extra people, then more, but even when we free them, and they have a sixth anchor, they also have to learn the process."

"I've had a thought," Vikas said.

"Hmm?" she asked, taking a sip while its warmth helped to loosen some of the stress in her bones.

"Do you think the Jadugara know a more effective way to break the collars? Maybe a different method for using the sixth anchor?"

Zarya wrinkled her nose. "I'd considered that, but how would we ever find that out?"

"Maybe they keep it written down somewhere?"

She cocked her head. "Maybe, but I have a feeling this kind of information would either be closely guarded or passed orally for fear of discovery."

"So we get someone to talk," Vikas said.

"How on earth could we do that without raising their suspicions?"

"Kidnapping and torture," Yasen said very matter-of-factly, and Zarya gave him an incredulous look.

"What? You don't feel bad for these liars?"

"No, but..."

"Just say the word," Yasen answered, and she huffed.

"I wonder if Suvanna or Apsara could do something," Vikas said.

"What about the rest of the Chiranjivi? Would they come?" Yasen asked.

"That would be nice," Zarya said. "We could use all the help we can get right now."

"What if you asked Row?"

This, too, she'd considered so many times. She hadn't told him everything about her magic yet, but of all the people around her, Row was one person she *knew* she could trust. She'd also planned to ask him about the strange incident in the forest a few weeks ago, but she'd been too scared to commit those words to writing.

"Don't you think he'd want to know?" Yasen continued.

She remembered a story Apsara had told during Zarya's first days in Dharati. Row claimed he could feel a wall if he tried to reach for the darkness with his magic. What if he could access it, too, and only some people were cut off? Ajay and Rania had never mentioned it before.

"I'll send him another letter," she said as a jagged streak of lightning flashed across the sky.

"This is a hell of a storm," Yasen said, and she nodded, rubbing the back of her neck. Something charged crackled in the air, sending the hairs on her arms standing up.

Wait for me. I'm coming.

Yasen sat down to eat, and they all fell into silence as they chewed, listening to the sounds of the rain. She pulled the paramadhar handbook out of her bag and flipped it open on the counter. Another chapter discussed using the mind plane to form a temporary bridge as a safer way to communicate without fully entering it. With the right practice, she could summon him into the space between worlds and dreams, but he couldn't do the same. It was another unbalanced aspect of the pairing.

She did as the book suggested, closing her eyes and searching for the spot where the link lived in her brain. She felt a bit guilty about even trying this, but she was also too curious not to explore the possibilities.

She would never do anything he didn't want. She'd already

made that vow to herself. No matter how angry she still was with him, that didn't give her the right to control him in any way.

She tried to relax as she attempted to sense the connection. It was like stumbling through the dark blindfolded. She really had no idea what she was looking for, though she was sure she would know when she found it.

For several long minutes, she probed the caverns of her mind, delving into its layers—her memories and thoughts—the things warring in her head. All she saw was black, though— just the insides of her eyelids, and she was feeling ridiculous. This couldn't be right. How could someone see their own mind?

"What are you doing?" came Yasen's voice, and her eyes snapped open. "You're making the weirdest face, like you're struggling to go to the bathroom."

She laughed and threw a napkin at him. "Shut up."

"I can brew you some special tea to help with that?" he asked, and she snorted.

"I'm fine. I'm doing a thing."

"A thing?"

"Magic thing."

He made a wry face. "Then far be it from me to interrupt the mystical act of constipation."

"You're such an ass," she said, and he grinned. She stood up and nodded at him and Vikas.

"I'm going upstairs."

She headed for the bedroom where she slept when their work kept them at the house late at night, closing the door behind her as she stared out the window. Rivulets of water ran down the glass as the sky thundered, drenching the world below. She pressed her hand against the surface and closed her eyes again, resuming the process, sifting through her thoughts until suddenly, there she saw it. Or maybe it was more of a feeling, but it was *there*, something glowing and silvery, buried deep, deep.

Zarya.

The voice in her head made her eyes fly open, and she jumped back. She stared at the window, catching the watery outline of her reflection. Did she really hear that? Or had that been her imagination?

She tried again, pressing her hand to the glass. It helped ground her and gave her something to focus on.

She repeated the process, seeking that spot. Edges of light teased her vision, and then she caught the flare of silver again.

She imagined herself touching it, scooping it up in her hands like water as his deep voice filled her head.

Zarya. I'm coming.

TWENTY-FIVE

Zarya snatched her hand away from the window as though it might sever their connection, but he was *inside* her head.

He was near. She looked out across the churning grey sky. He was coming. *Now?*

She closed her eyes and cast her thoughts out. She wasn't sure what she was doing, but this felt right.

Rabin?

Zarya. The answer was so full of raw emotion that her knees melted out from under her as she sank to the floor. *I'm coming.*

Where are you?

Not far from the walls of Ishaan.

That made her eyes fly open again as she stumbled towards the window, gripping the frame so hard her knuckles turned white.

Can you see me?

She stared intently at the sky, where the falling rain obscured the horizon. And then she saw it—the smallest flare of iridescent light against the gloom. It might have been invisible if the sun was shining.

Meet me beyond the walls.

Her breath caught, but her feet were already moving. She found the long cloak she'd tossed on a chair a few days ago and stuffed her arms into the sleeves before she flung open the door.

"Zee?" Yasen asked as she thundered down the staircase, catching the alarm on her face. "What's wrong?"

"Rabin," she said, cramming her feet into her boots.

"What about him?"

Doubt colored his voice as she laced them up furiously.

"He's coming."

"What?"

She brushed past him and towards the back door.

"Zee! Where are you going?"

She whirled around and grabbed Yasen's wrist. "He came for me, Yas. I have to see him."

"You're sure about this?"

"No, not really. But I owe it to myself to hear him out."

Yasen gripped her hand. "Just be careful."

She nodded. "I'm always careful, Yas." Then she pushed away, thumping down the hallway.

"I'll be back!" she called to Vikas, who was busy in the waiting room.

She didn't want to hear his reply as she ran out into the alley and circled her way around to the street.

Despite the weather, people were about, carrying fabric rain shields over their heads as they moved about their day. Zarya again searched the sky for the glow that signaled his approach—it had grown now, a black dot forming at the center. He was getting closer.

She started running, weaving through the people, some of whom called after her as she brushed past. The rain fell, soaking her hair and clothing. She felt nothing but an intense desire burning through her blood.

She stopped when she reached the city walls, pressing her hand to her chest and finding that spot expanding in the distance. She ran, her feet pounding along the road until she veered onto a stretch of grassy plain.

"Rabin!" she called into the rain, her voice torn away by the wind. She watched as he dropped through the sky, his majestic wings slowly flapping.

Then he dove, pulling up inches from the ground as he careened along the surface. Just as he was about to hit, he dissolved into a puff of black smoke before he shifted into the man who'd haunted her dreams for months.

She ran towards him, flinging herself into his arms as he swung her around. He was warm and solid, and that haze that always existed in their dream world was gone, and she *felt* him. The emotion she'd been keeping tethered inside her heart leaked between her ribs as she sobbed against him. He placed her on her feet and then framed her head with his hands as he leaned in and kissed her.

They stood in the rain, their hair and clothing sticking to them as they kissed, and she let every hurt and anger fade away at that moment. She'd forgotten how good he smelled and the way he tasted. She'd imagined kissing him so many times, but nothing could live up to the feel of his mouth and the warmth of his body.

He pulled away and touched her face, sweeping away a tear mingling with the rain.

"Zarya, will you come with me?"

"Where?"

"Somewhere I've always wanted to take you."

She found herself nodding as he backed up.

"You'll have to ride with me." Then he returned to his dragon form and crouched low so she could scramble onto his back. She'd been terrified the last time she had done this, but fear wouldn't stop her now. Once she was safely seated, she used a bubble of air to protect herself from the frigid rain and wind, and then Rabin launched himself into the sky.

Zarya looked over her shoulder as Ishaan quickly receded in the distance, wondering where Rabin was taking her and worried about leaving everyone behind. But she wouldn't be gone long. Operation Starbreak was ready, but with no one coming to see them, there wasn't much to do at the moment.

They streaked across the world, the ground beneath them blurring into nothing as her stomach leaped into her throat.

It took hours as she watched the landscape change, moving from the mountains and forests of Gi'ana to the desert sands of Svaasthy and then, in the distance, a brilliant patch of green. Zarya's breath caught, and she wondered if her eyes were deceiving her. Was it Daragaab? Was he taking her home?

They neared the border while Zarya watched that blue ocean in the distance that she'd missed so much. Despite her magic, her hands and legs were numb from the cold and aching from clinging to Rabin's slick scales. She could barely hold on any longer. Just when she was sure she might topple off from exhaustion, Rabin pitched down, heading for the surface.

She clung tighter with the last of her strength until they dove into the trees, and Rabin settled onto the earth. As soon as his feet touched the ground, she slid off, very nearly on the verge of fainting. She felt a woosh of air and then a pair of arms catching her before she fell.

"Zarya," came a rough voice as he lifted her up. "We're almost there."

Then she felt him walking as they moved out of the rain. The warmth of his body and his arms roused her enough to open her eyes. They traveled through a forest with the tallest, lushest trees she'd ever seen. This was no ordinary place.

Tiny peri skipped through the air everywhere she looked, many of them carrying miniature balls of colorful light. They bounced through the leaves that were each rendered to look almost like lace. She recognized some of the plants—they'd been the same wondrous variety she'd admired at the Ravana estate.

While studying the shining branches dangling with crystals, she clung to Rabin as she continued to shake, her teeth chattering.

"This is..." she trailed off, completely at a loss for words. "What is this?"

"This is my refuge," Rabin said. "Somewhere that belongs only to me."

He walked a few more steps. "Do you think you can stand?"

She nodded. The humid air had thawed out her limbs enough that she felt a bit steadier. He gently set her on her feet and turned her around. She gaped at the house that stood before her. She'd never seen anything like it. Rendered from shimmering silver, it was layered with so many vines and flowers that it was hard to make out what was man-made and what was Rabin's brand of organic magic.

"This is the home I built many years ago before I left Dharati," Rabin said, taking her hand. "It was my sanctuary of escape when I needed to be alone."

He tugged her further while she attempted to absorb the magnitude of their surroundings. This was easily the most magical place she'd ever seen.

"You *made* all of this?" she asked with a touch of breathless wonder.

"I did." There was no pride in his voice—it held the same awe as hers, as though he also couldn't believe he was capable of such miracles.

"You created the forests around your family's home, too." Zarya pointed to a small bud that resembled a paper lantern. "I remember thinking it was far too magical to be anything your father had created."

Rabin let out a soft, derisive laugh. "He hated them. Thought it was a complete waste of my time."

"I'm glad they survived."

"He had no choice," Rabin said, plucking a leaf off a tree

before a new one immediately grew in its place. "Anything he cuts down just grows back. It drives him insane that he can't undo it."

She snorted a laugh and grinned.

"Come on," Rabin said, scooping her up into his arms again. "I want to show you the rest."

She could have argued with this possessive hold, but her legs were still numb from the ride across the continent, and she liked how warm he was. Not just warm, but solid. Substantial, like a mountain protecting her with the inevitability of its shadow.

They approached the front entrance, and she could see it was no ordinary door but rather a series of overlapping leaves and vines. They melted away when they passed under the archway before entering a foyer that was part home and part forest.

Marble floors gave way to green grass, and a wide staircase curved off to their right. Instead of a wall at the far end, a large opening framed the entrance to what looked like a massive garden.

"My lord," came a soft voice, and Zarya turned her head to find a young woman wearing a green sari who pressed her hands in front of her heart. "Welcome home."

Rabin nodded. "Sarika. I'll be staying for a few days. This is Zarya."

He gestured to her with his chin, and then she felt a bit silly cradled in his arms. As if reading her mind, he tightened his hold. "Please send up some dry clothes and food for us," he said. "We are not to be disturbed for anything else."

Then he spun around and swooped Zarya up the stairs.

TWENTY-SIX

She looped her arms around his neck as Rabin took her down a long hallway towards a set of doors made of the same organic material. They seemed to sense his presence, the leaves and vines creaking open as they approached.

They entered a large bedroom to find a roaring fire in a hearth. The carpet was of the softest moonstone grey, as was the wood of the bedframe, the silk on the walls, and all the sheets. Rabin carried her to the divan in front of the fire and set her down.

"You can have a warm shower," he said. "When you're done, you can eat, and then we'll talk."

She nodded as he entered a room off the side before she heard the rush of water.

"It's all ready for you," he said after he returned, bending down and placing a finger under her chin. "I'm so glad you're here. You have no idea how many times I've dreamed of this moment, Spitfire."

Her voice stuck in her throat as she nodded. She hadn't been prepared for how emotional she'd feel being in his presence again. He stirred up so many conflicting thoughts and desires. He'd given her both the highest highs and lowest lows of her life.

He leaned in and placed a soft kiss on her forehead.

"Take your time," he said, his voice rough. Then he stood, his gaze lingering on her for a moment longer before he left the room.

Zarya waited a few seconds before she pushed herself up. She was exhausted but wanted to rid herself of these muddy, wet clothes. Making her way towards the bathroom, she stripped down and then stepped into the shower, luxuriating in the heat of the water.

The tiles were made of the same moonstone material, and everything shimmered softly like it had been sprinkled with stardust.

The air felt soft and light, like a soothing caress. Was that magic? Or something else?

She cleaned up before wrapping herself in a large fluffy towel and padding into the bedroom to find a long satin night-gown lying on the bed, also in the same soft grey. After she dressed she found the food left on the table on the far side of the room.

She should be hungry—she couldn't remember the last time she'd eaten—but she also couldn't keep her eyes open.

She took a small nibble of bread and then went to lie down, feeling her eyelids grow heavy before she curled up and drifted off to sleep.

When her eyes opened again, she had no idea how long she'd been out, but it had grown darker outside, suggesting at least a few hours had passed. She sat up and looked across the room to the balcony at the far end before noticing a folded piece of paper on the nightstand. She picked it up and opened it.

Zarya. I came to see you but wanted to let you sleep.
I'll return when you awake.

-R

She stared at his neat scribbles as her heart fluttered like an overwhelmed butterfly before shaking her head. Why was she being such an idiot about a piece of paper?

But then she pressed her mouth to it, imagining she could inhale his scent, proving she really was a complete fool. New food had been delivered, including some sliced fruit and yogurt. She fixed herself a plate and chewed a few bites before wandering outside to investigate her surroundings.

As she approached the balcony, her eyes widened. She was inside an open-air greenhouse enclosed by the walls of the house. A glowing pool sat in the middle of the space, flourishing with a ring of greenery. Flowers and bushes and trees grew everywhere, and amongst them were hundreds of flying peri, their translucent wings shimmering gently against the dark night.

It offered such a stark contrast to the serious man she knew, but this felt like witnessing a secret glimpse into a whimsical layer of his heart.

Propping her elbows on the railing, she leaned forward to take it all in, inhaling the scent of blossoms and savoring a warm breeze that gently caressed her bare skin. She could have stood there for hours.

After several minutes, she became aware of a presence in the room, and she stiffened, knowing it could only be one person. She'd been wanting to see him for months, and she'd been the one to summon him, but now, she was overcome by... everything.

Rabin came up beside her, and once again, she forgot how to breathe in his presence. He wore a pair of soft pants in moonstone grey, his top half bare. Her memories had done a good job of recalling his sheer perfection, but standing next to him in the flesh, she was nearly knocked sideways.

"How are you feeling?" he asked softly, and she nodded.

"Much better."

He tipped his chin and also leaned on the railing, staring out into the forest.

"This is unbelievable," Zarya said. "You made all this, too?"

"I did." He paused and then, a moment later, added, "It brings me peace."

He said those last words with such rawness in his voice that it felt like he'd just offered up a tender slice of his soul.

"I missed you," she said, not sure why she was admitting that, but something about his openness made her want to be honest. His head dropped as he blew out a long breath.

"Zarya, you have no idea what it's been like without you. I thought you hated me, and I thought I might never see you again."

"You broke my trust," she said, but it was no longer an accusation. Just a statement of fact.

"I know I did. I messed up. I've messed up so many times when it comes to you, but I've never been very good at relationships. I've lived a long time, but when I'm around you, I feel like I'm brand new at everything."

He pulled her towards him with a strong arm wrapped around her waist. She loved the way they fit together—her curves meeting the hard planes of his chest and thighs.

"I just need you to give me one more chance. I will do anything to make this up to you."

She nodded. She'd already forgiven him once and lived to regret it.

Except that she didn't. Not really.

Allowing him in that night might have led to the current state of her broken heart, but it also ranked as one of the most intense and life-altering experiences of her life. She wouldn't have given that up for anything.

Even if he had told her the truth, would it have changed things between them? Even if she'd known, would she have ever felt anything different? No matter her feelings, he was still her paramadhar and, therefore, a piece of her life. Nothing would change that.

"I want to believe you and to trust you," she said. "More than you can possibly know. You opened my eyes to the world. You make me feel things I've only dreamed about."

He tipped his head, the corner of his mouth crooking up. "You mean things like you read in your naughty books?"

She snorted a laugh. "Sort of like that." But then she shook her head. "But this is real life, not a story. And sometimes love and relationships are imperfect. I know that. I want to let you in. I want us to explore what we started in Dharati."

He traced the curve of her jaw with his finger. "I want that too."

She smiled, and he moved closer, dipping his head so their mouths were inches apart. "I want to kiss you," he said with a low, rough voice, and she nodded. Then he softly pressed his mouth to hers.

As his tongue probed the seam of her lips, she opened them, welcoming him in. They kissed languidly, their tongues sliding and their hands clutching at one another. This was so decadent. So *luscious*. She moaned softly as he dragged her in closer, spinning her so her back was against the railing.

His leg shoved between her thighs, pressing against her core, and she groaned as she writhed her hips against him. "Gods, I've missed the taste of you," he said. "The pure exquisite sound of that moan."

"Rabin," she breathed as he captured her mouth again, his body pressing flat against hers. She was sure they had things to discuss, but all she wanted was to answer this craving she'd been drowning in for months.

His hands grasped her hips as he drove his thigh harder against her, creating a delicious point of friction that had her hips squirming. She lost herself in the sensation, reveling in the feel of his leg against that sensitive spot that ached to be touched.

He leaned down, sucking the curve of her neck before he pulled up, bracing his hands on the railing and looking down at her.

"I want you," he said. "Right now."

She nodded, placing her hand on his chest. "You should know... there were others."

His eyes narrowed, his pupils darkening. "How many?"

"Does it matter?"

Again, he glared before offering up one of those wicked smiles. "That's perfectly fine."

"Is it?"

"Yes. Now you'll know I'm the best you'll ever have."

She couldn't help but laugh. "I'm glad to see you're just as full of yourself."

That earned her another grin. "It's just the truth, Spitfire." He paused. "There was no one else for me."

Though it wasn't fair to expect it, something tight loosened in Zarya's chest at those words.

"There will never be anyone else for me."

"How can you be so sure of that?" she asked.

"Because I am."

The answer was simple, unvarnished and raw, brimming with the force of his conviction.

"Because of the paramadhar bond?"

He shook his head. "No. That's not what the bond is about. What you and I have is something else."

She smiled. She did like the sound of that.

"Just trust me," he said. "There's no possibility this thing I feel for you could be anything but destiny, no matter what *anyone* might say."

She wondered if she detected a tinge of bitterness in that statement, but that also made no sense.

"I'm trying."

"I know. And I am grateful for that."

"Okay," she whispered, and he pushed himself up as he stared down her length. She could feel that look *everywhere*. Then he leaned over and brushed his mouth against her ear.

"Every fiber of my soul wants to take you to that bed and fuck you until you can't walk straight," he whispered. Her nipples tightened as heat flooded between her thighs at the wild desire in his voice. "But I think we should take things slow. I have things to explain to you first."

He pulled away, and she tried to quell her disappointment. But he was right. Jumping into bed was the last thing she needed, even if that was what she wanted.

He tucked a lock of hair behind her ear. "But if you'll allow it, I'd like to sleep next to you tonight?"

She nodded. "Of course."

He dipped his chin and then scooped her into his arms before carrying her back inside and falling into the bed.

And for the first time in months, Zarya finally slept.

TWENTY-SEVEN

The next day, Rabin toured Zarya around his house, proudly showing off every room and nook bursting with greenery. His entire home was like an enchanted fairy tale. The only thing it was missing was the princess. It even had the dragon, she mused to herself as they traipsed through a patch of small shrubs where the leaves were all shaped like little hearts.

Soft white petals fell from the trees, settling on their hair and clothing. She spun around, remembering when Rabin had dumped flowers on her head after she'd taunted him.

"Do you like it?" he asked, almost as if he were nervous about her answer.

She nodded. "It's the most magical place I've ever been."

"This place means so much to me. I'd love for it to mean something to you, too."

Her heart twisted at his expression, their gazes holding for several long seconds.

Or maybe the princess wasn't missing after all.

They continued walking the worn paths as butterflies and peri fluttered past. Even the sunlight felt different here, as if they'd stepped into another world where every edge had been smoothed down into something silken and gentle. Zarya inhaled a deep breath of fresh air, noting that even the breeze smelled almost like vanilla and cinnamon.

Rabin walked ahead as she studied his broad back and muscled shoulders. His thick, veined arms were exposed by his sleeveless kurta, and she admired those big hands she had desperately wanted all over her last night. But he'd been right when he said they needed to talk first.

They were currently talking about everything but the discussion they should be having, but she welcomed it. Just being in his presence eased so many disquieting thoughts racing through her mind.

Zarya caught sight of an archway made of greenery and wandered towards it. Beyond, she found a round clearing bordered by thousands of glossy white blossoms. She didn't recognize what they were, only that they smelled like heaven. She crossed the clearing and reached out to pluck a bloom to tuck into her hair.

As her fingers met the vibrant green leaves, her vision blurred. Flashes burst across her mind. The same ones she'd seen before—fires burning, demons marching, a man's face reflected in glass—and she stumbled back, gasping as black rot crept over the flowers, leaving a dark patch of dead, smoldering petals.

Frantically, she scanned the clearing as if an explanation might present itself. What was happening? She needed to tell someone, but who? A bead of sweat dripped into her eyelashes, and she blinked it away, inhaling a deep breath to settle her shaky limbs.

Backing up, she attempted to put distance between her and this damning evidence of everything that was wrong with her. But she already knew this thing would follow her no matter where she went. Rabin had promised her the darkness wasn't anything to be feared, but what if he was wrong?

"Zarya!" She turned at the sound of her name with a gasp. "Where did you go?"

She looked back at the flowers and the patch of black. She couldn't let him see this. She couldn't let *anyone* see this. She turned, planning to flee, when he appeared in the archway. His gaze snagged immediately on what she'd done.

"What's going on?" he asked. "What happened?"

She opened her mouth and then closed it before running a hand down her face. "I have some things to share with you, too," she said.

He blinked before he scanned the blackened flowers and leaves for another moment.

Then he held out his hand, and she took it before he drew her towards him. He said nothing as they stared at one another, their mouths only inches apart.

"You can tell me anything," he said in a low voice that sank into the marrow of her bones. "*Anything.*"

She nodded, but her throat was too tight to answer.

"Do you want to return to the house?" he asked, brushing a tendril of hair back from her forehead. "You look pale."

He swept his knuckles along her cheek, and she nodded again, grateful he wasn't forcing the answers out of her yet. But she would have to tell him soon and hope for what, exactly? He was determined to be with her, but would he feel differently once he knew everything? And would that break her heart all over again?

"Yes. Please."

He took her hand as they retreated in the direction they'd come. As they rounded the corner past a row of hedges, she turned to cast one more worried look back at what she had done.

. . .

Once Rabin returned her to her room, she decided to lie down for a nap. Yesterday's flight from Ishaan had taken more out of her than she'd realized, and the soothing atmosphere in this house invited long hours of luxurious sleep.

While she drifted off, she rehearsed the story she'd tell Rabin about what he'd just witnessed, but nothing sounded right.

Eventually, her mind settled, and when she awoke a few hours later, she found another note:

Have dinner with me. It's time we talked. Ring the bell when you're ready, and Sarika will retrieve you. Wear the dress if you're so inclined. It would bring me great pleasure.

-R

She couldn't help smiling as she tucked this note away with the first one. She slid out of bed to find the dress he'd mentioned. It hung on a hook on the wall, and she crossed the room to caress the fabric. Made of moonstone grey silk, it might have been the softest thing she'd ever felt.

After a shower, she pulled it off the hanger and wrapped it around her, tying it off at the waist. The delicate fabric swirled around her ankles, and the style left her legs exposed when she walked. It felt like wearing a cloud.

She applied some light makeup from the supplies in the bathroom and tied her hair up in a high ponytail, leaving a few soft tendrils to frame her face. There was little point in denying that she wanted to look nice for him. After a final check, she pulled on the cord by the door and heard a muted chime ring through the house.

She opened the door and waited until Sarika, wearing a bright orange sari, appeared a moment later. She bowed with her hands pressed to her heart.

"You look beautiful, my lady."

"Thank you," she said. "Thank you for the dress. I assume this was your doing."

Sarika's answering smile was sly. "Oh no. He picked that out for you."

She laughed, running her fingers along the silk neckline. "Really?"

"Really. He's always had an eye for beautiful things."

Zarya nodded, conceding this house was proof of that.

"Follow me. He's waiting." Her eyes sparkled as she gestured Zarya down the hall and through the manor. Zarya noted Sarika was human and not vanshaj. She'd yet to come across a single noble in Rahajhan who didn't use vanshaj servants.

"How long have you worked here?" Zarya asked.

"For as long as I can remember," she said. "My mother and grandmother were also employed by our lord."

"Where are they now?"

"Enjoying their retirement. Did he show you the village?"

"No," she said. "What village?"

"It's about a five-minute walk north of here. It's where I live with the rest of the house staff and our families."

"What's it like?" Zarya asked, feeling like she was uncovering yet another layer of what made Rabin tick.

"It's beautiful and peaceful, much like this place. He built it as well." Sarika stopped and gestured. "Here we are."

They stood in front of a set of grey wooden doors inlaid with silver markings. Sarika opened the left one and then stepped aside.

Zarya followed her in and paused. She was now standing inside a space that looked like a ballroom with a smooth marble floor, except for the racks and racks of gleaming weapons lining every wall. Chandeliers dripped from the ceiling, and tall arched windows looked out upon the surrounding forest.

In the center of the room was a small covered table with

candles, silver plates, and crystal glasses. Rabin stood next to a chair, one hand gripped on the back and his posture relaxed.

"Hi," he said with a tip of his head. He wore loose black pants and a shirt that draped open, showing off his tattoos and the stacked muscles of his chest. "I'm honored you decided to join me."

"Well, I already came all this way," she said, trying to make it sound like a joke, but it came out more like a breathless confession. "We're having dinner in your training area?"

"I thought you might appreciate it."

"You neglected to show me this during our tour today," she answered as she scanned the room, admiring the gleam of dozens of well-crafted swords and daggers.

"I wanted it to be a surprise."

She stopped in front of the table and looked down before meeting his gaze. "Then consider me surprised."

He smiled and pulled out a chair, gesturing for her to take a seat. "Sarika, we'll have dinner now."

She nodded as Rabin poured Zarya a glass of sparkling wine. As she took a sip, Sarika returned with a line of servants in tow, pushing silver carts covered in dishes of food.

Zarya spied all of her favorites—chicken and fish swimming in creamy spiced sauces—along with fluffy naan and every sweet she could imagine, each one as precise and perfect as a jewel.

"I hope you're hungry," Rabin said as Sarika and the others bowed and scurried from the room.

"Starving," she said as Rabin grabbed her plate and began piling it up.

"How are you feeling?" he asked as he filled his own and then peered at her. "About being here? With me."

She pressed her mouth together, unsure of how to answer. This place was a dream, but their relationship remained a question mark.

"Be honest," he said.

Finally, she replied, "Conflicted."

"About?"

"All of this... you."

She saw the hurt flash across his face and shook her head.

"I'm sorry. I won't deny that I have feelings for you, but I'm still..."

"I broke your trust. You have every right to be wary."

She clutched her napkin under the table. "I *want* to trust you. I really do."

He sighed and sat up, rubbing a hand down his face. "Can I share what has happened since I left Dharati?"

She also sat straighter in her seat, ready for everything. She hoped.

"Yes. I'd like to hear it."

"After Row refused to confirm your whereabouts and my brother refused to speak with me, I returned to Andhera. To your father."

Zarya felt a sharp tug in her chest at those words.

"That's when I told him about you, and he was shocked to learn of your existence."

"You told him about me," she said. "You said you wouldn't until I was ready."

"I'm sorry. He knew about the dreams and that I'd gone to look for you. I had to explain who you were and what transpired in Dharati. He sensed I was keeping something from him and pulled the truth out of me."

She nodded, supposing it made little difference at this point. With Rabin's connection to the king, it would have come out soon enough anyway.

"Zarya, he doesn't want to hurt you. He just wants to know you."

She considered those words, recognizing the sincerity in them. "What about Row's fears?"

Rabin reached over and took her hand, squeezing his fingers around hers.

"I asked him about all of it. Those two have a history. I'm not saying that Row doesn't believe those things, but your mother planted them in his head. She and Abishek ended on bad terms, and she believed things about him that weren't true. I won't pretend he is perfect and that he hasn't made unpopular choices as a king. That is the lot of a ruler, but he had sound reasons for all of it."

Zarya reached up and clutched her necklace. She wished more than anything she could talk to the woman who'd owned this. It was only Abishek's word against hers, and Asha wasn't here to defend herself.

She opened her mouth and then closed it.

"I believe you didn't purposely betray me," she said, watching Rabin's shoulders drop with relief. "But you still should have told me before I had to find it out from Dhawan. You have no idea how much that hurt. I'm not ready to forgive you for that."

"I'm so sorry," he answered. "I regret it more than you can possibly know. I had every intention of telling you, but things spun out of control."

She thought back to their conversation on Ranpur Island during their hasty flight back to Dharati. He'd tried to tell her *something*, but they'd been interrupted before he could continue. She puffed out a breath, wondering if perhaps she'd been too hard on him.

"Regardless, I still have many reservations about the man who is my biological father."

Rabin nodded. "I understand that, but can you consider that what I'm saying is possible? I'm sure your mother didn't mean to cause you any trouble, either, and we all believe the truth with our own sense of perception, but I've known Abishek for years now, and I don't believe he would do those things."

"Row once told me he was intent on saving the Aazheri line and that he couldn't support his decisions."

Rabin nodded. "The first part is true, and that is part of why he is so interested in magic and why he pushes limits."

"What does that mean?"

"You've heard of the sixth anchor?" he asked, and suddenly Zarya's throat went dry.

"I have," she croaked out.

"He believes it is the key to restoring Aazheri power, and Row never agreed with his plans to break through the seal keeping it locked away. That's partly why they fought and why he left."

With that knowledge, her mind spun with a thousand burgeoning questions.

"And has he done it?" she asked, focusing on the most important one first. "Does he have a sixth anchor?"

"He does," Rabin said. "He has it and wants to offer others the chance. He has a theory that should he break the seal, then more would be able to access it."

Zarya's entire worldview shifted at that moment. Abishek also had the darkness. She remembered Suvanna's declaration once upon a time that the king of Andhera was the one trying to free it. Had she been right all along?

"But the darkness is evil," she said.

"It's not. It's just power, Zarya."

He seemed so sure of that, but look at what she'd done to Rabin's flowers this morning.

Another thought occurred to her then.

What if... *Abishek* knew what the visions meant? Could he give her the answers that no one else dared? Maybe he was the one person who could help her. Who wouldn't judge this thing living inside of her.

She nodded and turned away, taking a sip of her wine as she

stared out the window, contemplating a whole new set of possibilities.

"Come with me," he said. "He wants to meet you."

"No." The word left her mouth immediately. "No. I'm not ready for that."

"Zarya—"

She held up a hand. "I'm not saying never."

She swallowed hard, realizing the things she'd been so sure of less than a day ago were already shifting into something else.

"I'm saying... not yet."

TWENTY-EIGHT

Rabin nodded, sensing a small victory with that response. It wasn't a flat-out no anymore.

"Why do you care so much about my father and I reconciling?" Zarya asked. "Does he mean so much to you?"

He blew out a breath and took a long sip of his drink before placing it on the table. Abishek's demands that he break things off with Zarya cycled through his thoughts. During the flight to Gi'ana, he'd weighed and considered them from every side, but the moment he saw Zarya, he knew resistance would be futile.

He'd never defied his mentor's wishes before, and he hoped Abishek would forgive him for this offense. The king was simply being protective, and Rabin understood it and even appreciated it, but he couldn't let her go.

"Shall I tell you how we met?" he asked her.

"Yes. Please."

He inhaled a deep breath and prepared to relive this ache buried in the meat of his past. "I already told you how much my father hated me and the thing I am," he said, and she nodded, fire brimming in her dark eyes.

He recalled the moment when she'd first noticed that awful, jagged scar on his back. She'd vowed vengeance for him, and that might have been the moment when he'd fallen in love with her. He hated anyone's pity, but he never saw that when she looked at him. What he saw was anger and rage, and he liked that. Anger and rage were emotions he understood, emotions he could work with.

"About twenty years ago, I'd returned home after a skirmish against Gi'ana," he said. "Though our territory was well established after the Khetara Wars over a hundred years ago, we still experienced an occasional bit of blowback. We headed out to mount a counterattack against a piece of land they were attempting to take for themselves.

"It wasn't far from here, in fact. They destroyed a sacred fairy grove of enchanted trees that grew only in that specific spot. Their leaves were known for their healing properties, and the flowers could be used for dozens of powerful tinctures. They salted the earth so that nothing could ever grow there again. I don't know if they truly understood what they'd done, only hoping to deliver a crushing blow to Daragaab. The result was heartbreaking."

Zarya's eyes grew wide as he spoke.

"So we invaded one of their most hallowed libraries," he said. "We honor the earth and its abundance, while Gi'ana cares about knowledge. So we hit them where it hurts and came away with some of the most valuable magical texts in Rahajhan as our spoils."

"The Jai Palace library," Zarya said, already picking up on the thread of his tale. "The restricted section? That's what's in there?"

"Yes," he said. "They were stored there under lock and key and a bit of complicated magic."

She blinked and nodded. "And then what?"

"When I returned home, my presence went entirely unacknowledged, but..."

He trailed off, and Zarya reached out a hand and laid it on his arm. He shivered at the warmth of her touch.

"But I learned that he had abused my mother in my absence. A guest had been praising my victories at the dinner table, and he couldn't bear to hear it, so he sought her out and struck her just for being my mother."

"Fuck, I hate that asshole," she whispered, which almost made him want to smile.

"I let my temper get the best of me, and we argued. I returned the blow with a punch to his jaw, but I should have known better. It was rash and impulsive, and I had no power there. I was surrounded by *his* guards in *his* house, and I didn't get far.

"I was tossed into a cell and left to starve for weeks. The only time they came to see me was to beat me black and blue before they'd leave me lying in a heap of shattered bones."

Zarya gasped, her face growing pale.

"They claimed no one knew where I was, and everyone had assumed I'd left. I didn't know if it was true at the time, but I've since learned they believed it. So I decided that was my chance to, in fact, leave once and for all."

Rabin stopped speaking and gathered the pieces of himself, trying to push past the hurt and anger that had consumed him through those days. He was growing and healing, but there were moments when he still retreated into the darkness of those moments. When it felt like there was no way out.

"It took every ounce of my strength, and I don't know how I accomplished it, but desperation makes us do desperate things. I managed to force a transformation as they entered my cell, causing our surroundings to crumble due to my size. I fried them all to ash, and then I burst out and flew myself to freedom.

"My limbs ached, and my wings hurt so much that I didn't

get far at first. I had to rest every few miles, but I was determined to get as far away from Daragaab as possible. I was so weak and broken, and finally, I came to a stop at the base of the mountains along the border of Andhera. Near death, I had given up, and I lay in the cold and waited for it to take me away."

Zarya squeezed his hand tighter and tighter as he spoke. "And?" she asked on a breathless whisper.

"And Abishek found me. His scouts noticed me lying on the ice, and before I knew it, I was surrounded by his people. I was too weak and hungry to turn back, so they hauled food out, dragging it across the mountains until I was strong enough to shift into my rakshasa form. Then they brought me to the palace where I spent weeks healing from my injuries."

He stopped again, looking away from the distant spot where he'd been staring to meet Zarya's gaze.

"When I woke up, Abishek was there, and I didn't disgust him. He was fascinated, and he was the first person in my life who encouraged me to appreciate my gifts. He gave me the courage to finally embrace who I was. So you see, I owe him my life."

He watched a thousand emotions cross Zarya's face as his thumb swept over the back of her hand.

"I'm so sorry that happened," she answered. "And I'm glad that he was there to help you." She shook her head as she let go of his arm and leaned back. "Perhaps... I've misjudged things."

"You had no way of knowing," he said. "You only had the information offered to you."

She nodded, casting her gaze towards the window, to the same place he'd just been looking, seeking north as though she could see over the miles separating them from her father.

"There's something else you should know," he said. Though he'd considered keeping this to himself, he'd also learned his lesson and wouldn't make the same mistakes with her again.

"What is it?"

"Before I left, your father suggested I break things off with you in terms of a romantic relationship."

Zarya blinked with confusion. "Why?"

He ran through all of Abishek's reasons, leaving out the part where the king had called him weak in spirit. The comment had hurt, and he wasn't sure he could be that vulnerable in front of anyone.

"I think in his own way, it's because he cares about both of us," he said. "And I confess I did think about not sharing this just yet only because I didn't want you to choose me out of spite, but I promised there would be no more secrets between us."

She snorted a dry laugh. "That does sound like something I might do."

He offered her a small smile as he waited for her reaction.

"Thank you for telling me," she said. "But he doesn't make those choices for me. No one does."

"I feel the same," he answered. "He's being protective as is his way, but nothing would keep me from you if you'll have me."

She blew out a long breath and ran her fingers through her ponytail. She was quiet for a moment before she said, "I need to talk to Row before I consider a visit to Andhera."

Rabin dipped his chin.

"I understand that. Whatever you need."

* * *

Zarya gave him a soft smile before she looked out the window one more time. Rabin's story about the Andheran king sounded nothing like the monster she'd expected. But surely even the worst people could be good from time to time.

"Yasen told me a story he'd heard," she said. "About Abishek killing vanshaj. Many of them."

"More lies, Zarya. I've been there for twenty years. I would have seen it if something like that was going on."

"But why?"

"Fear. Abishek has always been powerful. Anyone he might call a 'friend' is only out of political necessity, and he can be difficult. He tends to make a lot of enemies who stir up rumors to discredit him. The nobles of Andhera despise the fact they can't control him. They see how much power and influence the nobility hold in other realms, and it makes them act out in petty ways. But he isn't evil."

She could understand that to an extent. Being unlikable didn't equate to being bad.

"You don't use vanshaj in your household," she said.

His eyebrows pinched together. "I don't."

"Why not?"

"Why do you ask?"

"I'd like to know," she said, flipping her fork over and over in a nervous gesture. Rabin had shared what he'd been up to all these months, and soon, he'd expect her to reciprocate. Could she trust him with the secrets of the Rising Phoenix?

"Why should I want to use people who have no choice or say in the matter? It's... inhumane."

She studied him for a long second, realizing how aligned they were in so many ways.

He reached for a silver dish on the cart next to him a moment later. "Dessert?"

"Sure," she said as they settled into easy conversation about less harrowing topics. When they were done, Zarya sat back and rubbed her stomach.

"I'm so full I could burst," she declared.

He leaned forward and planted an elbow on the table. "Maybe we should indulge in a little exercise to work it off?"

The innuendo was obvious, and she narrowed her eyes. "You said we were taking things slow."

"Maybe I changed my mind." His mouth stretched into a cat-like grin.

"Well, I haven't," she said, though that was kind of a lie. Still, she could make him work for it at least a *little* more.

He shrugged. "Then how about a duel?"

He swept out an arm, taking in the weapons surrounding them.

"Another duel? Is *that* why you brought me here?"

He offered another lift of his shoulder. "It does always seem to bring out a certain fire in you."

She felt her cheeks heat at the suggestion, but he was absolutely right.

"I'm wearing a dress," she said.

"So take it off."

She arched a brow at him. "Nice try."

He chuckled. "Fine. I'll make you a deal. You can choose what I wear."

Zarya tipped her head. "Anything?"

"Anything." His eyes gleamed with challenge.

"Take off the shirt," she said, and without hesitation, he pulled it over his head and dropped it on the floor.

"Like what you see?" he asked with a cocky smile, sitting back and spreading his legs as he ran his palms over his powerful thighs. Yes, of course, she did. The man was all abs and chest and shoulders. He was absolutely breathtaking. If he asked, she'd probably willingly fall to her knees and run her tongue along every chiseled groove of his stomach. Maybe even if he didn't.

She shrugged. "You're all right."

He laughed softly again. "Is that all? What about my pants?" He snapped his waistband as she narrowed her eyes.

"You keep those on," she ordered. "I was just trying to even the field."

"Then what are we waiting for?"

He jumped up from his chair and retrieved two polished swords from a nearby rack. "Catch."

He tossed her one, and she caught it by the hilt as he spun around and approached with his shoulders curved like a panther stalking prey. Zarya kicked off her shoes and gathered her skirt in one hand as she readied her stance.

He grinned before they circled, sizing one another up.

"Ready to lose again?" Zarya taunted, and Rabin grinned.

"You lost the first time," he said, reminding her of the garden when he'd read the passages from her book.

"I was only pretending to give up," she said.

"And in the mind plane?" Rabin asked. "Who won there?"

"You know very well I was the one on top."

She almost winced, realizing how that sounded.

"I have no issues with that," he said, and then he swung.

But Zarya was ready. She blocked his sword with hers, the sound echoing in the large room. She countered, bringing her blade down as he knocked it aside. Zarya danced on her toes with a grin as their swords met again. Neither was taking this entirely seriously, so Zarya chose to test him and feinted before she swiped out and nicked his bare shoulder.

A tiny trickle of blood oozed down the swell of his bicep, forcing the mood in the room to shift. He stared down at it and then at her, challenge burning in his gaze.

"Is that how it's going to be, Spitfire?"

She smirked. "This was your idea."

He gave her no warning as he lunged, bringing his sword down. She blocked it at the last second before they became a whirl of movement, parrying back and forth as they maneuvered around the massive ballroom.

He thrust, and she slid left, barely avoiding the attack before she spun and struck out, catching the side of his blade with a clang. She was growing warm now, sweat trickling between her breasts. That line of blood down his arm seemed to taunt her with a sense of danger and intrigue. Why did fighting him always awaken such violent desire?

She couldn't help but admire how he moved as his muscles bunched and shifted. Normally, hidden beneath his armor, he was like watching poetry in motion. She was so absorbed in ogling him that a sharp slice of pain a moment later shocked her out of her reverie. She looked down to see he'd cut her thigh, a thin line of crimson cresting against the surface.

"You bastard," she hissed, and then, with a roar, they clashed, circling around the room as their blades moved so fast they became a blur. Rabin lunged and circled her blade, knocking it from her hand. It went flying with a clatter, and before she could recover, he snagged her around her waist and placed a dagger at her throat.

"Where did you get a dagger?" she snapped with a sharp intake of breath.

"Should've told me to take off my pants."

She huffed as his arm tightened around her. She wasn't afraid. She was almost certain he wasn't planning to slit her throat. In fact, finding herself trapped in his arms and helpless like this made her thighs clench as heat rushed through her limbs.

"You love drawing my blood," he cooed in a low voice.

She struggled against him. "Kind of."

He brushed his nose against the shell of her ear and whispered into her skin, "I like it, too."

Her breath grew tight as his hand slid across her stomach. He walked her back until he collapsed onto a bench against the wall, taking her down with him, tucking her between his spread legs with the dagger's blade still biting her skin.

"If I pressed a little harder. Drew more blood. Would that turn you on, Spitfire?"

"I... no..."

He laughed low and dark. "I think you're lying."

Then she felt the knife's sharp pressure and a warm trickle slide down her neck. With his free hand, he swiped up the drop and then sucked it off the tip of his finger. Her stomach swooped as a pulse throbbed between her thighs.

She'd definitely been lying.

"Every part of you tastes like heaven," he growled as he pulled her tighter towards him, where she felt the hard evidence of his cock against her ass. Then his hand returned to her stomach. "Do you still want to take things slow?"

"That was also your idea," she said as his hand slid lower, coming to a stop just above the slit in her skirt.

"Never listen to me," he murmured as his fingers dipped under the fabric. Almost involuntarily, her legs widened in invitation. He rumbled in approval as his fingers brushed the aching wet spot over her underwear.

She whimpered as he delivered light touches that were already driving her mad. "Rabin," she snarled, and he chuckled against her ear as he did another sweep that made her legs tremble in response.

She was consciously aware of the knife still pressed against her throat but decided she liked it there. Something about feeling like his prey did scandalous things to her insides.

He then reached under her knee and hooked her leg over his thigh, spreading her wide.

"How's this, Spitfire?" he asked as his fingers danced along the inside of her thigh. She couldn't quite form syllables into words, a sharp exhale of breath sticking in her throat. Slowly, his hand worked up the inside of her leg, once again finding the thin fabric covering her aching center.

He lifted a hand and she watched in fascination as his fingers swirled with black smoke before they morphed into a set of sharp dragon claws. Her eyes widened. She had no idea he could do that. Then, in a flash of movement, he shredded her underwear before his fingers returned to normal once again.

"Oh my gods," she breathed, unable to contain herself. A cool breeze brushed against her wetness, and then, finally, his finger slid along the crease before he circled her clit with a thick finger.

"Fucking dripping for me," he murmured.

She huffed out a breathless laugh as she felt the edge of the blade bite into her skin. He seemed to realize it because he asked, "Do you want me to take it away?"

"No." The word slipped out, and she could practically feel his approval.

"That's my girl."

He then pushed his finger inside of her as she gasped, her head tipping against him as he used his thumb to circle her clit while he pumped in and out. She felt him add a second finger, the sensation stretching and filling her as he curled them in, eliciting a whimper as she felt her release already climbing.

She clung to his thigh, her fingers digging into hard muscle as he continued pumping into her, driving his fingers deep before he circled her clit with her own release, as her stomach tightened and her fingertips tingled.

"Hold still," he whispered. "You don't want to cut yourself."

She moaned as he continued, his motions becoming rougher. Her hips writhed as her eyes fluttered before he tossed the dagger away and fisted his hand into the back of her hair, tilting her head back to expose her throat before his teeth sank into her flesh.

She cried out as her orgasm ripped up her spine, flipping her inside out. She moaned as the wave crested over and over as he continued touching her, and that magical sensation of his bite filtered into every drop of her blood.

When she finally stopped shuddering, he pulled out his fingers and his teeth, licking her neck and lapping up a warm trickle of blood.

Then she looked up at him, into his dark stare, alive with those shimmering golden flecks.

"That was..."

She stopped because she had no idea how to describe any of that.

"Good," he said with a feral smile. "Because I haven't even started yet."

TWENTY-NINE

Rabin scooped Zarya into his arms. She looked radiant, her cheeks flushed, and her eyes glazed over with lust. He buried his nose into the curve of her neck, inhaling deeply. She smelled like fire and shadows and blood. The taste of her was the sweetest, most decadent flavor, and he'd known from the moment he'd touched her that he'd never get enough.

He ignored Abishek's chastising voice in his head. He'd given a direct order, but Rabin was too wrapped in her to pay it any heed. If she would have him, then no one would keep them apart.

They made their way through the manor, the hallways quiet, just the way he preferred at this time of night. By now, the staff would be comfortable in their own homes. He didn't need tending at all hours of the day and enjoyed the solitude after the sun set.

This also allowed him to enjoy every inch of Zarya in complete privacy.

"Where are we going?" she asked as he veered down a hall leading away from the bedroom they'd shared last night.

"Someplace special," he said. He'd rarely felt the urge to

smile in his life, but around her, he couldn't seem to contain it. He loved the way she looked at him with wonder, those bright eyes brimming with curiosity.

He swept them down the wide staircase to the main floor and then towards a wall made of vines. As they approached, they began to move, slithering over one another to create an opening and revealing the enchanted garden at the center of the house.

"This is so beautiful," Zarya breathed as he set her on her feet. The smell of a thousand blossoms filled the air, mingling with the fresh, sweet scent of the tiny ponds dotting the space.

"Come," he said, taking her hand and dragging her down a path covered with soft moss. Dragonflies, fireflies, and butterflies swooped around them, along with the hundreds of peri who made these trees their home.

When Gi'ana had destroyed the fairy grove all those years ago, they'd also destroyed the peris' only natural habitat. With the seeds he was able to scrounge from the salted earth, he rebuilt this magnificent grove to rival the one they'd lost where the peri could thrive safely forever.

They entered a clearing bordered by high hedges scattered with a rainbow of flowers. In the center sat a large wooden platform surrounded by curtains of sheer white fabric. On it was a massive bed draped in white sheets and a mountain of silver pillows.

Zarya came to a stop, her hand pressing to her chest. She looked up at the sky and the stars visible overhead. He'd left it open to the elements so the birds and peri could come and go as they pleased. The natural rain also helped keep everything nourished.

"This is... I don't have words for any of this," she said as he drew her up the steps of the platform and tipped a smile. "You should understand how rare that is."

Rabin laughed as he drew her towards him, wrapping his

arms around her waist. Laughter wasn't something he was used to, either, but it was easy when he was with her.

"I love your words," he said. "Every single one of them."

She snorted a laugh and looked around them, her eyes wide with wonder. He still had to earn back her trust, but she was giving him this chance to start proving himself.

She turned to him, and their gazes met before he leaned down and kissed her. Their tongues slicked together as she melted against him. He pulled her tighter, wishing he could just keep her here forever. His cock throbbed painfully as she pressed against him. He wanted to consume her. *Be* consumed, but he was already drowning.

He felt for the tie of her dress and tugged as the fabric slipped apart. He kept waiting for her to stop him. For her to realize she was far too good for him. For rightfully never forgiving him for the lies he'd told.

She pulled away and looked up at him, stepping back and opening her dress before letting it slide off her shoulders into a puddle at her feet. He stared at her, taking in every line of her body.

The curves of her strong thighs and arms. Her perfect rounded breasts. The gentle slope of her toned stomach and those planes of muscle running down each side. She was a warrior from head to toe, forged in the acrimony of her loneliness. A lesser person might have broken under the weight of all she'd been through, but it had only made her stronger. It had turned her into this flame that sparked against the darkest night. A star exploding across the heavens.

"Are you just planning to stare at me all night," she asked as his eyes dragged up to her face with a smirk before he once again perused her from head to toe, his gaze lingering on the space between her thighs as his mouth watered for a taste. He wondered how wet she was. How it would feel entering her tight pussy as it swallowed his cock.

"I guess I have to do everything around here," she joked as she sauntered over and reached for the laces of his pants. He snatched her wrist and then dragged her towards him with an arm around her waist, crushing her breasts to his chest.

"I'm the one in charge here, Spitfire," he growled, causing her lips to part on a small gasp.

"Then prove it," she whispered.

Snaking a hand up the back of her head, he tipped it back and devoured her mouth, tasting the wine she'd been drinking and the sweetness of her breath. She was addicting. He became a helpless heap of nothing in her arms. Her willing servant, falling to his knees with a single look.

She rubbed against him, seeking the friction of his cock pressing against her cunt.

"Take it out," he ordered, and her lips parted as she licked her lips and nodded, truly at a loss for words this time. Her fingers danced along the waist of his pants, gently scraping the muscle and tracing the dip of his hips before her slender fingers slipped lower.

She peered up through her lashes before reaching down to wrap her hand around his cock. "That's it," he urged, his entire body reacting to the cool contrast of her skin. "Just like that." She squeezed him with the perfect amount of pressure as he continued encouraging her efforts. Faster. Slower. Tighter. He grew harder and harder under her touch, his stomach pushing in and out with the force of his gasping breaths.

Again, he slipped his hand up the back of her head and grabbed her hair, pulling her face up. "I want to fuck this pretty mouth."

Her eyes brightened, her cheeks flushing. "Okay," she breathed as he smirked, pushing her to her knees. She fell before him as he dragged a finger over her jaw. Then he grabbed her chin and tipped her face up.

Taking his cock in his hand, he pumped its length as she

licked her lips, watching him with a curious and open expression.

"You want this?" he asked. "You want to suck on it?"

"Yes," she whispered, and he smiled as he brought her closer, pressing the tip against her mouth. She opened for him, and he allowed just an inch to slip against her warm, wet tongue. He groaned, calling on every ounce of willpower not to drive himself to the hilt.

He pulled out, and Zarya watched him with a raw light burning in her gaze. Fuck, she was so beautiful. So utterly perfect. He rotated his hips, pushing in further as he shuddered, and then pulled out before doing it again.

"Are you okay?" he asked, and she nodded, her mouth too full to speak.

"You're such a good girl taking my cock so well. Ready for more?"

Again she nodded before he began fucking her mouth, thrusting in and out, feeling himself slide down her throat as she clung to his hips, her fingernails biting into his flesh. He wanted her to mark him. Claim him. Declare to the world that he belonged to her.

It didn't take long before he felt himself thickening, every vein pulsing and throbbing. Then he came with a guttural moan that rocked through every fiber of his body. "Swallow it all," he ordered, and she did as he demanded before he slid out with a pop.

With his hand still gripped in her hair, he dropped down and kissed her, his tongue thrusting into her mouth. He groaned, their tongues meeting in a wash of teeth and lips and heat. Then he lifted her up, wrapping her legs around his hips, his hands firmly gripping her ass.

He carried her across the room and tossed her on the bed before shoving off his pants and placing a knee on the mattress.

"Ready to be filled up, Spitfire?" he asked as he crawled

over her like a tiger stalking a mouse across an open plain. There was nowhere she could run or hide.

"Yes," she gasped as he ran a hand up her smooth thigh and along the side of her ribs before he cupped a round breast in his hand. She writhed as he leaned down to suck on her nipple, flicking the tip with his tongue before he bit down.

"Rabin," she moaned as her head tipped back and her back arched off the mattress. His hand slid between her legs, where he found her so fucking wet and ready. Then he kissed her again as he circled her clit, reveling in the desperate sounds she made. He leaned forward and dragged his cock along the seam of her pussy.

Pressing into her entrance, he took his time, going slowly, so slowly, torturing himself as he worked his way into her tightness. A rumble built in his chest as her heat climbed over his shoulders and down his limbs, seeking out every cold, dead corner of his spirit and filling them with warm light. Her slickness made every hair on his body react.

"Fuck," he whispered against her lips. "How could you think this is anything but destiny, Zarya?"

She couldn't seem to answer as he pulled out and thrust into her with force, her back curving as she cried out. "This is the only cock you'll ever touch again. Do you understand?"

He thrust once more, and she nodded. "Yes, oh fuck!" she cried out as he circled her clit with his thumb, driving into her with abandon as their flesh slapped and their breaths tangled in the charged air between them.

She clawed at his back and shoulders. "More," she said. "More."

He answered her pleas, driving into her and hooking a knee under her leg before he lifted it up so he could sink so deep he'd never find a way out.

"Zarya," he grumbled as he thrust again, and then she cried out as he felt her walls tighten around him, drawing him in, making his vision blur in a wash of white. He churned into her until he felt himself tense, and then he came with a moan that shuddered straight through the marrow of his bones.

He leaned down to kiss her deeply, trying to convey the message he couldn't put into words yet. He would never fear whatever lay ahead as long as she stood by his side.

He was hers, body and soul, no matter what happened next.

THIRTY

Zarya slowly blinked awake to the soft chirp of birds, the rush of a breeze through the leaves, and the soothing trickle of water. Wrapped in Rabin's arms, she stared at the translucent white curtains and the leaves beyond, recalling every vivid moment of the previous night.

Take things slowly, indeed.

Maybe it had been foolish to jump into bed with him again so quickly, but when she thought about the way he had worshiped her body, she was having trouble feeling bad about her choices. Especially as she snuggled down in the soft white sheets, luxuriating in the feel of Rabin's warm breath dusting the back of her neck.

She'd just lie here forever if she could, but she couldn't ignore the fact that she'd just hightailed it out of Ishaan two days ago. She'd sent a note to Yasen explaining that she was fine and that she'd be back soon, but her responsibilities weighed on her conscience.

Rabin shifted, and she turned around to find him awake with a soft smile on his face.

"Morning, Spitfire."

"Morning," she said, returning his smile.

His hand landed on her hip, sliding over the curve and down her thigh.

"Hungry?" he asked, and she nodded.

"I'd kill for some tea."

"Your wish is my command."

He slid out of the bed and flipped open the curtain before descending the steps. She watched as he held out a hand, and a moment later, a tiny colorful bird landed on his palm. He brought it to his mouth and whispered something before it flew off, swooping towards the house.

When he returned, Zarya stared at him.

"What?" he asked.

"Who *are* you?" she asked, and his expression turned sheepish in a way that made him look almost boyish.

"I'm here to make all your wishes come true."

She grinned as he slid back under the covers before cupping a hand behind her head and drawing her in for a languid kiss.

A few minutes later, they pulled apart at the sound of a chipper "Hello!"

"Breakfast has arrived," he said. Zarya spotted Sarika through the curtain, her eyes down as Rabin tugged on a pair of soft pants from a drawer next to him. With his back to her, she noted the jagged 'freak' scar carved into his skin, her fingers digging into the blankets at the grim reminder of everything he'd endured.

She heard him thank Sarika, and then he returned with a tray that he placed on a table in the corner.

"Do you have something for me to wear?" she asked, gesturing to his pants.

"No. You're forbidden from wearing clothing in my presence for the rest of your life."

She rolled her eyes and scooted out of bed. He watched her hungrily as she tugged open the same drawer to find a mound of soft grey fabric. She pulled on a light kurta that fell to her knees and smelled exactly like him.

"There," she said, folding her arms.

He cocked his head and raked her from head to toe. "Actually, seeing you in my clothes is almost as hot as having you naked," he purred, and she nearly grew lightheaded from the falling pit in her stomach.

"Can we eat?" she asked, shaking it off. He gestured towards the table before pulling out a chair. She settled into it and helped herself to an array of fruit and a giant mug of tea.

"Tell me about what you've been doing all these months?" Rabin asked. "Other than fucking other men who I'll now have to hunt down and kill."

Zarya smirked and took a sip of her drink. "That's pretty much it. Just all day, all night, every day. Seems a shame you'll have to wipe out such a large portion of the population."

A growl rumbled in his chest, and Zarya laughed before she rolled her eyes.

"Yasen and I have been exploring the city. Making new friends."

She stopped and wondered how much more she should reveal. Could she tell him about what she'd been doing with the vanshaj? What would he say? She also had a part to play if they were ever to trust one another.

"But?" he asked, picking up on her hesitation.

"We've made some specific friends." She picked at the tablecloth, suddenly nervous.

"What *kind* of friends?"

She looked up at him. "Yasen and I joined the Rising Phoenix."

He held still for a moment and then blinked. "I thought they were only a rumor."

"You did?"

"That's what they claim in Andhera."

She shook her head. "No. It's real. That's just what they want everyone to think."

"They?"

"The royal family." Her gaze met his.

"As in *your* family?"

"Yes. I've seen them in the streets of Gi'ana, but I haven't spoken with any of them yet." Heat rose to her cheeks, wondering why it was so difficult to admit that. She'd dreamed of this family her entire life, but she was *ashamed* of them. It would take some time to reconcile that.

He nodded. "And what else?"

"We blew up the Jadugara's ink factory."

He exhaled a sharp breath. "That was you? We heard the reports, but that was incredibly dangerous."

"I know," she said. "But necessary."

"They're planning to rebuild it," he answered.

"They've already started, and we're planning to stop them again."

When he met her gaze, she couldn't interpret what she read behind his eyes.

"What else?" he asked, and this is where she hesitated. He'd insisted more than once that he didn't believe the darkness was evil, but something stuck in her throat every time she tried to summon the damning words to the surface.

"I found a way to break the star collars," she said.

His eyebrows arched at that. "You *broke* them?"

She twisted her fingers together and winced. "A few."

"This has something to do with what happened in my forest?" he asked, studying her carefully.

"Yes. I think? Maybe." She looked down at her hands, now folded in her lap before he wrapped his fingers around her wrist. She looked up to meet his dark gaze.

"You can tell me anything."

So she did, expelling the words in a rush. Once she started, she wanted it out as fast as possible. The only thing she kept to herself was the full truth about her terrifying visions. She wasn't ready to share them with anyone yet.

After she finished, she stared at him and watched as he blinked, his head tipping with curiosity, but she read no judgment in his eyes.

"You were afraid of what I would say," he said.

"Of course."

"Tell me what else," he said.

"The vanshaj have magic."

Rabin blinked. "Of course they do. That's the whole point, isn't it?"

"People seem to keep forgetting that."

He nodded and leaned forward, folding his big hands on the table. "What kind of magic do they have?"

"Aazheri magic, of course."

He blew out a long breath. "Zarya, this will result in chaos."

"I know that, but you have to see this is right." She gestured towards the house. "You don't keep vanshaj in your household. You *know*."

His shoulders hunched as he peered up at her. "Yes. I do know. But it's one thing to refuse to keep vanshaj against their will, but it's another to *free* them from their chains."

"Why is it any different?" she demanded. "This isn't right."

"You're correct," he said. "But the world is not so black and white."

"I know that."

"They'll kill you if they catch you. Your friends. Your family. Row. Yasen. Anyone who's important to you."

She set her jaw and lifted her chin, her gaze challenging. "I know that, too. Which is why you must decide if you actually want to be with me."

"Zarya, I can take care of myself."

She shook her head. "I'm meant to do this. I was meant to join the Rising Phoenix, and I'm sure I'm on the right path."

He paused and looked down before looking back up.

"And I should get back," she said.

"Back?" he asked. "To Ishaan?"

"You could come with me. If you wanted."

He blew out a breath. "I want to be wherever you are, Zarya."

"Really? Now that you know what I am?"

He grabbed her wrist and tugged her onto his lap.

"Zarya, I meant what I said that I will go where you go. And I don't just mean that physically." He picked up the pendant that lay against her collarbone, rolling it between his fingers. "I will go anywhere destiny takes us."

She studied his face. She sensed his sincerity, but a tiny part of her still hesitated to trust him completely. What if he was still keeping things from her? What if he was wrong about Abishek? He spoke of the king with such reverence that she wondered if Rabin saw the man as clearly as he should.

Was she ready to forgive him for lying to her, regardless of his intentions? Lying for good reasons was still lying, no matter how you spun it. If she examined her emotions closely, she was afraid of being made a fool of again. People already thought her naive and inexperienced about the world, and the last thing she needed was another chance to prove them all right.

What if all of this was the same act as last time? She didn't believe it in her gut, but her logical mind was urging her to be cautious.

He said nothing as she stared at him, thinking of the story he'd told her last night. Of how Raja Abishek had rescued him from the cruelty of his own father. Then another thought occurred to her as she recalled the conversation with Vikas and his query on whether someone might know a more efficient way to break the collars.

"The Jadugara..." she said. He blinked at the abrupt shift in topic.

"What about them?"

"The books you pillaged from Ishaan—could they have belonged to them?"

He shook his head. "Very likely many of them did. Why?"

She offered him a rueful smile. "You're sure you're ready to go where I go?"

His hand tightened on her hip. "Absolutely."

"Then how about helping me break into the Jai Palace library?"

THIRTY-ONE

They arrived in Dharati under the cover of night.

It hadn't taken much convincing—Rabin was proving true to his word about following wherever she went—his only reservations were about her safety, but after a bit of coercing, he'd agreed but only if she listened to his orders.

She'd consented but also had no intention of doing so if it didn't suit her goals.

She had to take this risk if something in that library could help with Operation Starbreak. After transforming into his dragon, he flew them over the trees, keeping them as low as possible.

From her perch on his back, Zarya surveyed the distance and the effects of the blight still evident across the landscape. It would probably take many years for the rot to grow over and a healthy forest to reclaim the land. She thought of the forests outside Ishaan and wondered if Daragaab would ever get that chance.

How close to the surface was the darkness sitting, waiting to return? The burden of this secret was growing heavier and heavier. She needed to do something about it, but fear and worry left her paralyzed with indecision.

Instead, she focused on what she could do—namely helping the vanshaj and continuing her work. Despite everything that happened with the blight, their cause was still more important than the darkness and its distant threats.

They landed softly in a clearing, far enough from Dharati's walls to escape notice of the sentries. Row had mentioned in his letters that the Khada had been reduced in numbers, with only a handful remaining on watch.

Once Rabin shifted into his rakshasa form, they picked their way through the trees and towards the walls of the city, heading for the concealed opening the vetalas had used when they'd snatched Amrita from the peri anada. They hoped no one had thought to block it during all the resulting chaos, and they exchanged a relieved glance to find the way clear.

"Behind me," Rabin said, drawing his sword from his back. Zarya rolled her eyes but let him go first, reasoning that if some horrible creature ate him, she wouldn't have to decide whether to officially forgive him or not.

They entered the dark tunnel, and he cast out a glow of his coppery light. After looking over his shoulder, they plunged into the darkness, feeling their way along the path until they reached the door at the end. Rabin pressed on the latch, but it held firm.

"It's locked," he said, looking up as though he could see through the layers of wood and stone over their heads.

"You think the house is still abandoned?" Zarya asked, realizing that while it had been in ruins months ago, that had been right after the kala-hamsa attack. With the restoration efforts, it was more than likely that the owners had repaired the house and returned.

"Move," Zarya said, putting her arm in front of Rabin and squeezing past. She bent down to peer at the lock, feeding out a thread of spirit magic and rooting around inside the mechanism.

With her tongue between her teeth, she probed the metal until she was rewarded with a soft click.

"Ah," she said with a smile before easing the door open. They exited into the basement, which had been tidied up since their last visit. Dust no longer clung to every surface, and the charred bits of wood and debris had been cleared away, suggesting someone definitely lived here again.

They looked up at the ceiling and then at one another.

"It's late," Rabin said. "Everyone is probably asleep."

"Let's hope," Zarya said as she placed a gentle foot at the bottom of the stairs, and they slowly made their way up.

They paused at the top, listening for any of the home's inhabitants.

"Can you hear anything?" she asked Rabin, who shook his head.

"Nothing. Let's just do this quickly."

Zarya slowly opened the door and then slid out, entering the dark main level.

"Come on," she whispered, tiptoeing across the space and towards the front entrance. The floor was silent, free of creaks as they made their way across. When Zarya reached the exit, she stretched for the doorknob like it was her salvation and turned.

"Hey!" came a voice, and they both spun around to find an elderly man in his nightclothes holding a glass of water. "Who are you?"

"Sorry," Zarya said as she flung out a hand, conjuring a cloud of black fog. The man began calling for help. "Let's get out of here," she whispered to Rabin as they searched blindly for the handle. The man began shouting louder, probably rousing the entire neighborhood.

"Zarya," Rabin said in a low voice.

"This way!" she said, grabbing his hand. They hit the door, stumbling outside. "Move!" She slammed it behind him, leaving her shadows on the other side. Thankfully, the street was empty, and Zarya hoped her magic wouldn't cause any lasting damage to the house or its residents.

"Come," Rabin said, taking her hand and dragging her into a dark alley. They navigated their way through the streets, moving towards the center of the city until they came upon Row's haveli.

"That magic back there," Rabin said as they huddled against the walls. "Was that... it? The darkness?"

She nodded. "You've never seen the king use it?"

"I haven't. Though he shares many things with me, he's very private about that."

Their gazes met, and Zarya nodded. "Do you feel differently now that you've seen it?"

The corner of his mouth crooked up, his eyes sparkling. "Not at all. It looked dangerous and powerful, and I didn't think you could be any sexier, but..." He shook his head and ran a hand down his face. "I'm looking forward to the next time I get you alone."

In spite of herself, Zarya snorted. "You have a death wish, Commander."

He shrugged and ran the tip of his tongue over one of his sharp canines. "You love it."

She rolled her eyes and then stared up at Row's haveli and the darkened windows. He was more than likely asleep.

"You think this is a good idea?" Rabin asked.

"It's fine. He won't tell anyone we're here."

Rabin passed a skeptical eye over the building. "Are you sure?"

"Of course. He's my father." She paused and gave Rabin a look. "My real father who raised me, no matter what our blood says."

"I would never argue with that, Zarya, but he lied to you, too."

She pressed her mouth together, thinking about how far they'd come. "We talked it out. I've forgiven him."

Rabin dipped his chin. "Good. I'm not the only one who wants what's best for you."

She narrowed her eyes and then huffed before gesturing towards the house. "Let's go."

They entered through the back terrace, where Zarya had often sat during her short time in Dharati. She still had her key, so she let them in through the sliding doors into the quiet living room.

"Row?" she called, hoping to wake him up without startling him too much. "It's me!"

It didn't take long for them to hear movement upstairs. A light turned on, and Row appeared in the doorway, dressed in his nightclothes, his long hair unbraided and spilling over his shoulders.

"Zarya? What are you doing here?" His gaze moved to Rabin before it darkened. This was the scary version of Row she knew so well. "And why is *he* with you? Is everything okay?"

Zarya raised a hand at the thunder in his expression. "I'm okay. I promise. He's with me because... well, we're discussing things."

"But Zarya—"

"I'll tell you everything. I promise," she said. "I'm sorry if we scared you, but we couldn't let anyone know we were in the city."

"Why not?" he asked, coming closer, his brow now furrowed with concern.

"We're here to break into the restricted section of the palace library."

There was a beat of silence as Row absorbed those words.

"Zarya," he said, his voice already low with warning. "Why? Do you have any idea what trouble you'll be in if you're discovered?"

"I know," Zarya said. "That's why I'm hoping you'll help us?"

Her voice pitched up at the end as she took in the cavernous groove between Row's eyebrows. He huffed out a breath, his suspicious gaze sliding back to Rabin before turning and heading for the doorway.

"Then come and tell me everything."

They followed him into the kitchen while Row hunted through the cupboards.

"I have a feeling I'm going to need a drink."

"Ha," Zarya said as she pulled up a chair and dropped into a seat. Though she'd only lived here a few months, this place felt like returning to a warm hug.

Row produced a few glasses along with a bottle of something dark and strong. He set it on the table and then sat down. He and Zarya looked over at Rabin, who hovered in the doorway.

"Come on," Zarya said, kicking a chair out. "Don't be shy."

That earned her a glare as he stalked forward and settled into a seat.

"Before we get into why you want to break into the library, I have to ask," Row said, clasping his hands together. "What are you two doing together? He lied to you, Zarya."

"Remember when we suspected he was my paramadhar?"

"Of course."

"He figured out how to enter our mind plane." She thumbed at Rabin. "And now he won't leave me alone."

"Zarya," Row said, his eyes darkening on Rabin. "If you need help—"

"It's fine," she said. "I agreed to meet with him in person, and he's explained some things."

Row's eyebrows drew together. "But the king—"

"Doesn't want anything from her," Rabin said, cutting him off. "I know what you believe, but none of it is true."

Row stared at Rabin for several long seconds before he said, "I'll need more than that."

Rabin went on to tell Row everything he'd revealed to Zarya, and when he was done, he fell quiet.

"I see," Row said before he turned to Zarya. "You believe all of this?"

Zarya's eyes darted to Rabin, her shoulders tightening.

"I want to," she whispered as doubt crossed Row's face, rattling the fragile certainty she'd been building loose from its moorings.

"I understand that," he said. "But—" He shook his head and ran a hand down his face before reaching for the bottle between them and pouring out three stiff shots.

"We can talk more about this later. Tell me what you're doing here, then."

Zarya nodded and drew in a deep breath, sharing the entire harrowing tale with Row.

When she was done, he stared at her as if he was seeing her for the very first time.

"Six anchors. You have six anchors and *you* broke the collars?"

"I'm sorry I didn't tell you sooner, but I was afraid."

"Six," Row breathed again before he picked up his glass and took a long, slow pull. "And the vanshaj, too."

"It was actually a relief to find out I wasn't the only one," she said softly.

Row huffed out a breath, his shoulders dropping. "It creates your nightfire, too?"

"Not entirely, but I do think they're connected. I can create the magic without it, but using my sixth anchor makes it stronger. Much stronger." She paused as she spun the glass in her hand, idly staring at the wet ring it left on the table. "That day the blight tried to consume the city, I used it. I wouldn't have been able to stop it otherwise."

She looked at Rabin. "And you held my hand, and that helped, too. I think that must have been our bond."

He nodded. "I felt something that day, too," he said, and Zarya blinked. "You were so relieved when I told you it wasn't evil."

"Excuse me?" Row interjected. "You said *what*?"

Rabin glared at Row and then turned back to Zarya. "It isn't," he repeated. "The only issue here is people's prejudice."

Row ground his teeth, his jaw hardening, clearly disagreeing with that assessment. After a moment, he tore his gaze from Rabin and returned his attention to Zarya. "Tell me what else you've learned."

She then went on to explain her theory about the Jadugara and their lies about the sixth anchor. When she was done, Row couldn't have appeared more stunned. "It's been here all this time."

"Can you feel it? You said once your power felt like it was brushing against a wall. Do you think that you might have it, too?"

"Me?" Row said, shaking his head. "No... I..."

He stopped and looked at her, several thoughts crossing his expression as though he was coming out of a fog. "Still, none of this explains why you're here."

"I'm struggling," she said. "The process is difficult and dangerous and, most frustratingly, very slow."

"And?"

"And I'm hoping that one of those mysterious books in the palace library might have some information."

Row pursed his lips together, his gaze flicking to Rabin. "And you know the library contains a large number of rare texts stolen from Ishaan decades ago?"

"Exactly," Zarya said. "I can't get anywhere near the Jadugara, but if luck is on our side, then maybe something in that library can help."

Row folded his hands and blew out a long breath. "I believe in this cause with all of my heart, Zarya, but I don't want you to get hurt."

"This isn't about me," she said. "You know that."

She stared at him. He *knew*. He'd heard the prophecy in her mother's stone. And he understood she couldn't ignore that, even if she wanted to.

"Fine," he said, though it was clear he wasn't thrilled about it.

"Really?" she asked.

He cocked his head in a gesture that seemed to say he might not like it, but it didn't appear that he had much choice.

Zarya shared a look with Rabin. "So, how do we access it?"

"You'll need to find another way in. I can help create a distraction, but only strong rakshasa magic can open those gates."

"You mean the magic of the most powerful rakshasa in Rahajhan?" Zarya asked, gesturing to Rabin, who lifted an eyebrow.

Row gave Rabin a narrow-eyed look. "You trust him to help you?"

She sighed and threw up her hands. "I suppose I do."

That earned her a glare from Rabin, which she chose to ignore. He might have sweet-talked her the last two days, but she was trying to think with her head and not the unreliable emotions of her heart.

"Okay," Row said. "I'll pay a visit to the palace tomorrow and see what our best course of action might be, but I want it going on record that I don't like any of this."

Zarya cocked her head and wrinkled her nose. "Noted."

Row blew out an exasperated sigh and took a long pull of his drink, muttering something under his breath that sounded distinctly like "nothing but trouble."

THIRTY-TWO

Despite his reservations about their plan, Row held true to his word the next day. He intended to scout out the best opportunity to break into the library and ask Koura for help. He'd also been aiding in the vanshaj cause for years, petitioning his own kingdom to amend its inhumane laws.

That left Zarya and Rabin trapped inside the house for hours with nothing to do as she paced the living room with every curtain drawn. Rabin watched her with that intense gaze that always did its best to unsettle her.

She'd made him sleep in Aarav's old room last night. Though he didn't remark on it, she could tell he wasn't happy about his banishment.

Row had continued tossing him dirty looks and then giving *her* quizzical looks that suggested she was making a huge mistake.

And maybe Row was right. His conviction that Rabin was bad news shook the trust he'd been building. Once they'd emerged from the spell of his enchanted garden and that magical house, she was thinking more clearly. Yes, she'd given herself physically to Rabin, but she still couldn't be one hundred percent sure she could trust him. Or that she forgave him at all.

"I'm bored," Zarya said, stopping at the end of the room and pacing to the other side. "I wish we could go out." She'd been dreaming of Rupi's gulab jamuns since leaving Dharati and could practically taste the sticky syrup coating her tongue.

She wrinkled her nose as she peered through a crack in the curtains before she spun around and dropped onto the divan. She hated sitting around doing nothing.

Rabin lounged in a chair in the corner. He was wearing a kurta with his sleeves rolled up, displaying the length of his impressive forearms. Mesmerized, she watched the tendons flex in a way that was bordering on erotic. Gods, what was wrong with her?

He leaned forward and clasped his hands with his elbows on his knees.

"I have some ideas of how we could pass the time."

He arched an eyebrow, his gaze traveling over her and his meaning clear. Without waiting for an answer, he stood and strode across the room, falling to a knee and bracing his hands on the divan on either side of her hips.

"Stop it," she said, picking up a pillow and covering herself, though there wasn't much force in it. As much as she was trying to keep a clear head, it was impossible to deny what her heart and her body wanted.

"Fine," he said, standing up and turning around when she called out.

"Wait." He stopped and peered over a broad shoulder. "What... did you have in mind?"

She winced as the words left her mouth and clung tighter to the pillow like it might shield her from the consequences of her questionable decisions.

A smug smile tugged on the corner of his mouth as he spun around and resumed his position with one knee on the floor. He pulled gently on the pillow's corner, and after a moment of hesitation, she released it before he tossed it to the side.

He placed his large hands on her hips before sliding them up, his thumbs sweeping over her center and his fingers climbing under her shirt, caressing the bare skin of her stomach, before they curled over her waistband and gave it a gentle tug.

She sucked in a sharp breath as he wedged his big body between her legs, pressing his hard stomach against her already pulsing center. His hands traveled down over her hips and thighs, his thumbs digging into the tendons where they met.

"I can't stop thinking about this pussy," he said as his thumbs drifted inward, massaging her just beyond the spot where she craved his touch. "And how much I want to have it bouncing on my cock again."

Zarya knew she should stop this. Right? But she'd already given herself over to him, so what was one more time?

"Would that help pass the time, Spitfire?"

"It might," she whispered as he hooked his fingers into the waist of her underwear and her leggings more firmly and then *yanked*. She lifted her hips to allow him to drag the fabric down her legs before tossing it to the side.

"On your knees," he ordered. "Turn around."

She blinked and then did as he asked, turning over to brace her hands on the back of the divan. She looked over her shoulder as he stood behind her and smoothed a hand over her ass. A moment later, his thumb swept through her wet core, pulling a moan from the center of her chest.

She watched him drop down before he replaced his finger with his mouth while he tasted her from behind. With one hand wrapped around her leg, he used the other to circle her clit as his tongue drove into her, causing her arms and legs to tremble while she whimpered.

She felt his growl vibrate through her pussy as he feasted like a dying man. Like he hadn't already done this over and over just two nights ago. A moment later, he pulled away and stood, undoing the laces of his pants. She watched as he shoved them down and took himself in his hand, stroking his thick erection. She couldn't take her eyes off it as she licked her lips.

"You love this cock, don't you, pretty girl?" he asked. "You can be as angry as you want, but you're dying for me to stretch you open."

Taking in his smug expression, she scowled.

"Don't worry. I won't tell anyone," he taunted as he grabbed her hips and then thrust into her without warning. "It can be our little secret." She gasped, her back arching as he hit every sensitive spot. A riot of tingling sensations filtered to her toes and fingers as he stroked in and out, driving into her with abandon.

"Fuck," he moaned. "*Fuck*, you're so tight and perfect."

She didn't want to admit how perfect he felt, too. She'd now been with enough men to know that while sex could be pleasurable, nothing else had ever felt like *this*.

Being with Rabin was about so much more than the physical coming together of their bodies. It was like the stars aligning and the oceans' pull, drowning them together in the most exquisite bliss.

She clung to the back of the divan, her knuckles turning white as she pressed herself against him, the slap of flesh and their moans and sighs filling the room.

It took her a moment to register the sound of other voices. Voices that should *not* be here right now.

Then a door slamming and footsteps.

"Shit!" Zarya said. "Row's back. Get off me!"

She swatted Rabin from behind. "Stop it!"

Zarya clambered over the back of the divan, folding into a ball on the floor, her arms wrapped around her midsection. She willed herself to peer over the edge, and just as Rabin was tucking himself back into his pants, Row and Koura rounded the corner.

"Great news, we—"

Row stopped, his eyes widening as they jumped between Zarya and Rabin. There was no conceivable way they couldn't figure out exactly what they'd interrupted. Zarya's head felt like it was about to explode with mortification as Row's gaze continued darting between them, at a loss for words for once in his life. He cleared his throat and shook his head.

"We'll just... meet you in the kitchen."

Then he turned around, bumping into Koura in his haste. Koura stepped aside and smirked. He winked and gave them both a wide smile before he turned to follow Row.

When they were gone, Zarya sank to the floor on her knees, covering her head with her arms. "Oh my gods. Please let this carpet swallow me up whole. I can never look at either of them again."

She heard Rabin chuckle and looked up to find him peering over the divan, dangling her leggings and underwear from a finger.

"Would you like these?"

She glared, snatching her clothes before she sat up and tugged them on.

"Oh my gods. Oh my gods," she continued whispering to herself, wishing she would melt into a puddle and ooze out the door.

Rabin sat with his arm on the back of the divan, looking like he didn't have a care in the world.

"It's not that bad," he said, and she glared again.

"Not that bad? Row just walked in on us having *sex*! He heard me..." She rubbed a hand down her face. "*How* can I ever look at him again?"

"You are a grown woman, and surely he knows you've had sex."

She finished yanking on her leggings with a flourish. "*That* is not the point."

Then, she sucked in a deep breath and stared at the doorway where Koura and Row had been standing a moment earlier.

She threw her shoulders back and strode towards the exit before she looked back at Rabin, who couldn't seem to contain his amusement. Maybe she'd just pretend like nothing had happened.

Gods, how could *anyone* pretend nothing had happened?

She cleared her throat and shook out her hair. "Let's get this over with," she said before she marched out of the room.

* * *

Rabin watched Zarya retreat into the kitchen, unable to control his smile and refusing to feel ashamed for what was a perfectly natural thing to do. He tugged on the crotch of his pants, lamenting the fact that he hadn't had the chance to finish, or more importantly, the chance to finish Zarya. He'd be sure to correct that later.

Low voices from the kitchen forced him up from his seat. Row was hardly his biggest fan, and this wouldn't help matters. But Zarya's guardian would have to accept that he was a part of her life.

He sauntered into the kitchen, where he found her seated with Row and Koura. They all glared at him as he pulled up a chair and dropped into it. He shrugged it off. This was the sort of treatment he was familiar with.

He noticed Zarya's cheeks turn red again as she cleared her throat and then started to speak in an unnaturally high voice. She couldn't deny it had been exciting having sex somewhere they might get caught. Rabin vowed to get her to admit it, and maybe they could try that again.

"As I was wondering, when do you think would be a good time to access the library?" Zarya asked.

Row's gaze slid to Rabin and back to her. "Tomorrow night. There's a big party in the ballroom, and everyone should be distracted. The keepers guard the library at night and will be stationed at the gates as usual, so you won't be able to enter that way."

"So, how do we get in?" Zarya asked.

"From the roof," Row answered, and Rabin sat forward with his hands clasped, nodding in agreement. "There's an access point from above—a grate that you'll need to unlock, but that shouldn't be a problem with your magic. You can climb down, and I'll ensure the keepers are occupied while you search."

"We won't be able to take anything from the restricted section," Rabin said. "The books are spelled to sound an alarm if they're removed without permission."

"I know of an enchantment you can use to copy down whatever you find," Row said.

"What exactly are you looking for?" Koura asked Zarya.

Rabin had always liked Koura's calm, steady presence. He was one of the few people he admired. He watched as Zarya confirmed with Row.

"Koura knows everything you told me," Row said. "He will keep your secrets."

Zarya lifted her hands in a question. "Anything that can help us break the magic of the collars faster," she answered. "Or anything else that can help us stand up to the Jadugara. Maybe something that can expose them for the frauds they are."

"I'll be attending the party," Koura said. "I was asked to perform a magic demonstration, and it will serve as an added distraction."

"What time?" Rabin asked.

"Around midnight."

"Then we should be on the roof by eleven thirty," he said.

"I still have my concerns," Row said, and Zarya nodded.

"I know, but we have to try. We're running out of time in Ishaan, and it won't be much longer before the situation grows unstable here, too. We're not doing this just for Gi'ana but all of Rahajhan."

Row blew out a resigned breath. "Very well."

"Okay, great," she said, pushing herself up from the table. While she seemed to have gotten over her initial embarrassment, the incident was clearly still on her mind. A fact Rabin confirmed when her gaze darted to him and then flicked away, her cheeks flushing again.

"I'm going to shower, then," she declared and headed up the stairs.

Once she was gone, Koura also stood up from the table.

"Good luck," he said, reaching out to shake Row's hand and then Rabin's. "If there's anything else I can do to help, please let me know."

"Of course," Row said. "Thank you."

When he was also gone, Row focused his stony attention on Rabin.

"What is your intention here?" he asked, his voice tense.

"To help Zarya."

Row stood from the table, pressing his hands to the surface. "You lied to her once."

"And I've explained everything."

"And you've told Abishek about her?" Row asked, his jaw turning hard.

Rabin rolled his neck with a crack. He understood Row's reservations, but he wondered how long he'd have to spend proving himself. "He does not want anything except to meet her."

Row let out a breath, his mouth pressing together. "How can you be sure of that?"

"Because I am. I would never let anything happen to her."

Row flattened his hands against the table, his shoulders spreading wide. "I hope that you're right."

"I am," Rabin replied with confidence.

"And she says you are her paramadhar."

"Yes."

"You intend to fulfill this role?"

Rabin dipped his chin. "Absolutely."

"You will be sworn to protect her at all costs, then," Row said, a challenge in his tone. "You understand that."

Rabin kept his posture loose as he sat back in his chair. "I am aware of what this means, and I am prepared for all of it."

Row's jaw ticked. "You know that a physical relationship between you and your masatara is frowned upon."

Rabin shrugged. "I am aware." He was *more* than aware at this point, but he still couldn't find it in himself to care.

He stared at Row unblinking, refusing to back down or be made to feel this was wrong. Abishek would get over it, and as long as Zarya was willing, there was no reason for them to stay apart. Zarya was still on her guard, but he sensed she was softening.

Row dipped his chin slightly. "Do you know where to find a mystic to administer the Bandhan?"

"I was actually hoping you'd know someone," Rabin answered as Row's eyebrows drew together. If Zarya wouldn't travel to Andhera until she was ready, then Abishek's mystic was currently out of the question. "I don't know of any mystics in Daragaab."

"No," Row said. "But there is one in Ishaan."

"Perfect," Rabin answered. "I know Zarya is eager to return to her work there."

"And you'll be going with her? Not returning to Andhera?"

Rabin nodded. Eventually, he would return to Andhera with Zarya—once he could convince her to come—but for now, he would follow where she went.

Row watched Rabin, his dark gaze assessing him from head to toe.

"She may not be my daughter by blood, but I love her like one. Understand that I let it go last time, but I see that you are intertwined in more important ways than my distaste for you allows," Row said, leaning forward. "But if you hurt her again, I *will* kill you."

Rabin acknowledged the absolute conviction in his eyes. He placed his fist across his chest in a show of respect for Zarya and the man who'd raised her, no matter their feelings for one another.

"Understood."

THIRTY-THREE

A few hours later, Zarya and Rabin found themselves on the roof of the Jai Palace, keeping as low as possible. They'd dressed in dark clothing with hoods covering their heads, leaving only their eyes visible.

The city was still awake, music and the sounds of chatter drifting up from the plazas surrounding the building. Zarya hadn't realized how much she'd been missing Dharati since she'd left.

Their current vantage point offered a view of the boulevard stretching away from the palace. Zarya thought of the rift that once ran through it and, of course, the moment Rabin came along to fix it in his arrogant way. The memory made her smile. Sure, she'd been frustrated at the time, but it had also been a part of a delicious push and pull that made being around him all the more thrilling. He kept her on her toes, and she suspected that would always be the case.

Nothing about him was predictable and Zarya had always craved a more unpredictable life.

"Come on," he whispered. "This way."

He turned and began climbing over the roof like he'd been

born inside these nooks and crannies. She followed behind as he expertly maneuvered the towers and edges, leaping across the gaps with the grace of an acrobat and then waiting for her to catch up. She had to admit it was helpful having Daragaab's former army commander on her side. He knew this place like the back of his hand.

Along with their deep hoods, they had weapons strapped to their backs and hips should they encounter trouble. Zarya prayed they could get in and out without being noticed. She wasn't sure what to expect if Vikram got wind of their presence, but it seemed unlikely he'd just let her walk out of there with a book from the super-secret section of the library.

The interior of the palace formed a giant square with gardens and fountains in the center. They could see into the ballroom on the far side through the tall, wide windows. Music drifted on the night, loud enough to help disguise their movements. Guards were stationed at various points around the garden, several of them obscured by the trees and shrubs.

Lying flat on an angled stretch of rooftop, they watched dozens of guests mingling together. Zarya's gaze wandered past the palace towards the front courtyard and the leaves of the Jai Tree blowing gently in the breeze.

"You're sure we can't go and see Amrita?" she asked for the hundredth time since they'd cooked up this plan.

Rabin turned to look at her, his expression firm. "We've been over this. She's heavily guarded. Even if Vik isn't with her, he would never leave her unattended, especially in her condition."

Zarya huffed out an annoyed breath. She knew he was right, but that didn't stop her from wanting to see her friend. Logically, if they did get her alone, Zarya wouldn't even be able to speak with her, but she could at least let Amrita know she was thinking of her.

Her attention wandered back to the ballroom and the

milling guests. She spied Gopal Ravana chatting with a glass of wine in his hand. Rabin had noticed him, too, his gaze fixed on his father and a muscle feathering in his jaw.

"That day I caught you with him in the garden," Zarya said, referring to the morning they'd left for Ranpur Island and the Bayangoma Grove. "Who did he threaten?"

Rabin blinked, exhaling a short breath. "You."

She shook her head. "What is his problem with me?"

Slowly, Rabin turned to look at her. "Apparently, he fancied your mother. They met many years ago, but she rejected him."

She arched an eyebrow. Surely, Gopal Ravana wasn't *that* fragile. But, of course, he was. "And I look just like her."

Rabin's gaze drifted over her face. "Evidently."

"Well, at least she had some sense in her choice of lovers."

Rabin huffed. "I wanted to rip out his heart and crush it in my hands."

His voice was so full of bone-shivering menace that Zarya tipped her head and said, "That's sweet."

His gaze swung to her with an incredulous look before the tension in his shoulders eased and he shook his head with a soft chuckle. "Thank you," he said. "For always understanding what I need."

Her breath hitched when a flash of bright golden light drew their attention back to the party. Koura's demonstration had commenced, and every eye in the room was now focused on his extraordinary display of magic.

"That's our signal," Rabin said, pushing himself up before Zarya followed.

They approached a grate carved into the roof, and she peered into it, seeing nothing but darkness below. She sent out a tendril of spirit, working on the lock. No one had raised the alarm when they'd entered the city as far as they could tell, and she hoped the residents of the house assumed they'd just seen a ghost or perhaps an inexperienced thief.

She tinkered with the lock for a few minutes—it had obviously been constructed with a complicated mechanism designed to prevent tampering, but she persevered until she heard the click. She was becoming rather good at this.

Rabin then wrapped his big hands around the bars and heaved. The grate was incredibly heavy, and the tendons in his neck pulled as Zarya moved to the other side and helped shove it up. With a loud squeak, it lifted and then dropped at his feet with a thud.

They froze, scanning their surroundings for any signs of trouble. The party carried on uninterrupted, and the guards remained stationed at their posts. They both let out a breath.

"Let's go," Rabin said, and she watched as he channeled a thick green vine made of magic and directed it down the hole. "I'll go first and make sure everything is clear."

She nearly protested that she didn't need him protecting her but stopped. First, there was no point wasting time arguing about this, and second, if Rabin planned to become her paramadhar, then this would be his job. His literal existence. She'd have to get used to it.

"Fine, hurry up," she said impatiently, and he gave her a smug smile before he descended through the dark opening. She leaned over the hole as he disappeared into the shadows. A few seconds later, he tugged the vine, indicating it was safe to follow.

Zarya shimmied down, hand over hand, until she felt a pair of warm hands around her waist.

"Got you," Rabin whispered, his breath tickling her ear and making her shiver.

While she was mortified about being caught by Row and Koura, she also couldn't stop thinking about how they'd been interrupted. Last night, after they'd again retired to separate beds, she'd fallen asleep to the image of this man as she brought herself some relief from the constant needy ache below her navel.

Sometimes, she couldn't shake the feeling that one way or another, he would become the death of her.

Once they were on the ground, Rabin drew out a flare of copper light to help illuminate their way. They were inside a large duct that was just tall enough for Zarya to stand, though Rabin had to stoop his head.

He took her hand, and they slowly picked their way down the vent, trying to stay as light on their feet as possible. Soon, they reached a branch in the tunnel with narrower vents leading off in several directions.

"Which way?" she asked.

"The library is down here," Rabin said, releasing her grip and dropping on his hands and knees. Zarya crawled behind him as they navigated a path through the tight network.

Along the way, they passed several more grates that opened into various rooms and hallways of the palace, pausing before each one before hurrying past.

Finally, they reached another grate, and Rabin stopped.

"Here," he said as he pushed against the metal. It gave easily, and thanks to his lightning reflexes, he caught it before it tumbled to the floor and alerted the entire palace.

"Shit," he hissed as he clung to the grate. "That was close." He dragged it up through the opening and then gently placed it inside the vent.

"Ready for another climb?" he asked softly, and Zarya nodded. She cast out a thread of air to help muffle any noise as they descended into the library.

Rabin conjured another climbing vine and descended first before Zarya followed. A moment later, she found herself standing on the floor directly in front of the locked gate and the restricted section where she'd been denied entry.

At the other end of the long hall, she could see the backs of the keepers, both facing Row where all three were engaged in an enthusiastic discussion.

Zarya filtered out a puff of her dark magic, obscuring them in shadows as Rabin approached the gate and laid a hand on a bar. He closed his eyes, and a moment later, green light glowed under his palm, spreading out along the surface, transforming the iron into thick, ropey vines before they dragged open like curtains to allow them inside.

Once they passed through, the vines swung closed before the gate melted into iron again. Zarya didn't have time to marvel at the wonder of his magic as they exchanged a quick glance and then went in opposite directions. They'd agreed they were looking for anything about the vanshaj, dark magic, or the Jadugara. There were so many books, and Zarya couldn't even begin to imagine the magnitude of the secrets they contained.

She illuminated the spines with the tiniest flare of light, searching through the titles. Randomly, she tried a few books, perusing their contents, but found nothing that seemed right.

It felt like it was taking forever as they hunted through the shelves, checking on one another and shaking their heads.

But then she noticed it. A whisper buzzing in her ear. She'd heard the same thing when she'd stood before the gates last time. She'd nearly forgotten until this moment, but now that same chorus of indistinct voices sent a ripple of premonition racing down her spine.

She spun around, following the sound as it wove through the stacks, coalescing into a specific spot. Something was guiding her or perhaps calling to her. Finally, she noticed a book titled *Age of Shadows: History of the Vanshaj* and eagerly slipped it from the shelf. She flipped it open, scanning a few pages. This was exactly what they'd come for.

Before leaving tonight, Row had shown her how to use her spirit and earth magic to enchant a notebook to act as a copying device. Pulling it out of her pocket, she dropped to her knees, pressing the pages against the book, and counted to ten, waiting for the words to imprint onto the blank page. Once she was done, she flipped to the next and repeated the process.

Rabin sank into a crouch before her, and she glanced up.

"I think this is what we need," she whispered. "Search this area for anything similar."

With a firm nod, he jumped up and began combing through the nearest shelf. Zarya continued copying *Age of Shadows*, counting to ten under her breath as sweat gathered on her temples and under her collar. She tugged off her hood to get some air.

While Rabin continued searching, she moved as quickly as she could. Counting to ten and then flipping to the next page. Slowly, she worked her way through and was about a third done when someone called from a distance.

"Hey!"

Zarya looked up, peering past the bars, her nerves twisting with fear.

"We need to go," Rabin said. "Now."

"I'm not done yet," she said, desperation in her voice. They couldn't leave yet. They'd never get another chance like this again.

"Zarya, they're coming."

More shouts drew their attention outside as Zarya flipped to another page, pressing a blank sheet against it. "1... 2... 3..."

"In here!" another voice shouted. "The library. They're in here!"

That had both Zarya and Rabin looking at the gate and then each other.

"Shit," Zarya said. She still had half the book to go.

"We're leaving," Rabin said, grabbing her by the arm and hauling her to her feet. He picked up the book and shoved it back into its slot.

"Argh!" Zarya let out a sound of frustration as Rabin

dragged her through the gate and towards the dangling vine. She stuffed her notebook back into her pocket with another glance over her shoulder, wishing they had more time.

"We can't linger here, Spitfire." He pushed her in front of the vine. "Climb."

Zarya grabbed the rope, her gaze finding the book she desperately longed to take. They already knew someone had broken in, what difference would it make to steal it now?

"Open it again!" she begged, slipping past Rabin. "Let me grab it."

"Zarya! Leave it!" he said as she backed up towards the gate.

"Stop! I command you to stop!" came another voice Zarya knew all too well. She halted in her tracks, turning to face Vikram. Armed to the teeth and wearing a royal blue kurta, he stood at the end of the hall with a dozen soldiers flanking him. The air around them stilled as Zarya sucked in a breath.

Vikram took a step towards them, his posture stiff and his jaw hard, freezing Zarya and Rabin in place like a pair of cornered rabbits.

"What in the name of the gods are you both doing here?" he snarled.

* * *

Rabin stared at his brother, his rib cage tightening against his lungs. This was the last thing he'd wanted. Getting caught here like a couple of criminals inside Vik's palace. This would hardly be a step in mending their crumbled bridges.

He watched as Vikram's furious gaze skipped between him and Zarya. Vikram assumed several things in that look, some of which were definitely true and caused his mouth to harden into a straight line.

Zarya's worried glance fell on Rabin before it pinged around the room, searching for a way out. Rabin stood right beneath the vine and their rope to safety, but Zarya was too far away. He was about to lunge for her and shove her up when Vikram took another step.

"Don't bother," he said. "Every exit is guarded, and you will not escape. Did you think you could sneak into Dharati without my noticing? I have eyes and ears everywhere. And you didn't even make your entrance subtle. Did you take me for a fool?"

Rabin rolled his neck. It was obvious his little brother had learned a thing or two in the years since he'd been gone.

"What are you doing here with him?" Vikram asked Zarya. Rabin didn't miss the wounded flicker that passed over his expression. "Didn't he lie to you? Didn't you tell him to leave you alone? How can you trust him after what he's done?"

Zarya gave Rabin an uncertain look that pinched the space behind his heart. She *didn't* fully trust him. She was desperately attempting to keep him at arm's length, and maybe a better man would accept that and let her walk away. But Rabin had never pretended to be anything other than entirely focused on what he wanted. He'd broken her trust but was trying to do everything to earn it back. He would never give up.

"I..." Zarya said before her mouth snapped shut.

"What are you stealing from the queen's library?" Vikram demanded.

She shook her head. "Nothing. We just..."

"The truth or you'll both be thrown into my dungeons."

Zarya's worried gaze again met Rabin's while he considered their options. He had to get her out of this. He didn't care for his own safety, but hers was his only priority. Even if she fought against it, that was his job until he drew his final breath.

"What is the meaning of this?" came another voice as Row burst through the line of soldiers. "Zarya? What are you doing in Dharati?"

Rabin tensed, wondering if Row had double-crossed them. But Row's gaze flicked to Rabin with the slightest hint of acknowledgment. His shoulders eased as he realized Row was only playing along. After the way he'd threatened Rabin earlier, he was sure that even if Row wasn't on *his* side, he would always be on Zarya's.

"We just wanted to check things out," Zarya said. "No one would ever allow me in here."

She widened her eyes, playing the fool, and Rabin nearly exhaled a snort. How did she manage to constantly break through the tight hold he'd always kept on himself?

He resumed assessing their possible exits. He could transform into his dragon, but the space was tight, and he worried about hurting Zarya and even Row, as she did seem rather fond of him.

"With him?" Vikram asked, gesturing abruptly at Rabin, and Zarya rolled her eyes.

"He won't leave me alone, will he? So, I thought I'd use him to help get me in. He knows this place really well."

Vikram's angry gaze moved to Rabin. "And, of course, you'd jump at the first chance to betray me again. I *told* you to stay away from her."

"Excuse me?" Zarya asked. "You did *what*?"

Rabin pressed his mouth together as his gaze met Row's. They had to get out of this library *now*. Then he could shift and fly Zarya to safety.

"I'll handle this," Row said, throwing his shoulders back. "Zarya is under my charge."

"You'll do no such thing," Vikram answered with a glare. "They broke into my palace, and I want to know why. Why is it you can't stay away, big brother? Why can't you take the hint that your presence isn't welcomed or desired here?"

"Vik," Rabin said, having no idea how to appease him, but his brother held up a hand.

"Save it. You'll come with me for questioning."

He then gestured to the line of his guards, who filtered out to surround them. Maybe Vikram was still a bigger fool than Rabin had given him credit for because Zarya, Row, and Rabin could easily deal with these foot soldiers with a mere snap of their fingers. Maybe he was relying on the dregs of Rabin's loyalty to cooperate, but his allegiance lay with Zarya first.

His gaze met hers as he tried to convey that he had a plan and to go along with the guards for now.

She seemed to understand as she blinked, her chin dipping slightly.

"If you come quietly, then I won't make this worse," Vikram added.

Rabin and Zarya nodded as they followed the soldiers through the library. When they exited the room, they came upon the keepers who'd been guarding the entrance.

They spun around, taking in the sight of Zarya and Rabin.

"Intruders?" one of them gasped, his pallor turning pale. "In our sacred library?"

The second one then narrowed his eyes as they fell on Row.

Rabin saw it all happen in an instant, never more thankful that he knew every room and passageway of this palace. It might have been years since he'd walked its halls, but it felt like it had been only yesterday.

"*He* was trying to distract us," accused the keeper, pointing to Row.

Rabin watched as Vikram came to a halt and turned to glare at Row. "Is this true?"

"Run," Rabin growled before Row could answer, and all three of them shoved through the barricade of soldiers, catching them off guard. "This way!"

They bolted left down the hallway, their boots echoing in the silent corridor. It took less than a second for the shouts and footsteps of Vikram and his guards to follow as Rabin, Zarya, and Row careened around corners, their soles sliding and squeaking on the smooth marble.

Rabin pumped his arms, tempering his pace just enough so Zarya could keep up on her shorter legs. He checked back to see they were already widening the distance. Vikram led the charge, rage and anger burning in his eyes.

Rabin felt the sharp sting of an arrow graze his arm, but he ignored it, checking over his shoulder for Zarya, ensuring she was close.

"Where are we going?" she shouted as they entered a large room with a domed glass ceiling. This is where he'd planned to lead them. It was the perfect escape route.

"Stay near the wall and then jump when I'm ready!" he shouted.

He didn't wait to see if they understood as he ran for the center, black smoke dissolving around him as his body gave in to the transformation. For several long seconds, he felt himself suspended inside the nothingness of his magic, his limbs and torso and head becoming an amorphous collection of bones and sinew before he felt the telltale crackle that signaled the final seconds before he stood in the center of the room on all fours, his body stretching to the height of the ceiling.

He turned his massive, scaled head towards Zarya and Row, huffing out a breath as a signal. They looked at one another and then ran as he lowered his back, allowing them to scramble on.

A moment later, Vikram and the soldiers poured into the room, belting out commands to stand down. If Rabin could laugh in this form, he would have. There was no stopping him now.

"Arrows! Stop him!" screamed Vikram. "Fire! Fire at will!"

Rabin felt the sting of dozens more arrows scrape his thick hide, but the effect was about as useful as tossing a handful of toothpicks at an elephant.

Rabin extended his wings, knocking over the statues circling the room. The tips speared through the windows, glass exploding in a shower of glittering shards. Vikram began shouting louder as Rabin drew his wings in closer and blasted out a stream of pure blue fire towards the line of stumbling guards.

Then he flapped. Once. Twice. Three times before he launched into the air and crashed through the glass ceiling with a mighty roar.

THIRTY-FOUR

Rabin soared over the palace, circling the sky as Zarya and Row clung to his back. Screams floated up from below as the city ground to a stop at the sight of the monster flying overhead. The people of Dharati were largely ignorant of his form—that night he'd saved Zarya from the kala-hamsa was one of the few times he'd transformed within the city walls, and he knew the initial sight was always a little overwhelming.

He banked left, looping around the palace, reminding Vikram and his father, wherever the bastard was at that moment, they could never touch him up here. No matter how much they might hate him, in the sky, he was free. In the sky, he was home.

"Rabin!" Zarya screamed. "Get Koura!"

Rabin spied the healer weaving through the trees, trying to find an open spot where Rabin could pick him up. They couldn't risk stopping or spending even a moment on the ground. Daragaab's army was, no doubt, already headed this way.

Rabin dove, swooping towards Koura and brushing the

ground. He snatched Koura in his talons before lunging into the air again.

Then, just for good measure, he took another wide circle around Dharati, threw his head back, and roared before pointing west and towards Gi'ana.

* * *

Zarya clung to Rabin as he banked left and then right through the air. Once they cleared the sight of Daragaab, Rabin landed so Koura could climb onto his back. After they were all seated again and as comfortable as someone could be in this position, they took off, flying towards Ishaan and the next battle that awaited them.

Zarya thought of the notebook in her pocket, despairing she hadn't been able to copy the entire text and hoping what she had was enough. If they hadn't discovered anything new, they would have stoked Vikram's ire, and this entire mission would have been for nothing. Now he would be even angrier, and they could never return to Daragaab for help. She only wished she could have seen Amrita again.

She peered over her shoulder at Row and Koura, who both sat low, clinging to Rabin. *This* certainly wasn't what she had planned, but neither could remain in Daragaab, and she was responsible for that. So as much as she hadn't wanted Row joining her in Ishaan, she had little choice.

It was warmer than the last time Zarya had ridden on Rabin, and she closed her eyes, savoring the cool air against her warm cheeks. She hadn't realized how much she'd been sweating with nerves and the chase through the palace.

Nothing had gone as planned.

They swooped over the countryside, the Pathara Vala Mountains spreading across the northern horizon. Zarya squinted as she peered into their depths, imagining the range of mountains circling Andhera. She'd casually done some reading on the northern kingdom, discovering it was very remote, bordered by snow and trees and uncrossable mountain paths.

Zarya thought about this place that was a part of her more times than she could count. What if Abishek wasn't who Row claimed? What if Rabin was right about him? No one would replace the role Row had played in her life, but something about the man with whom she shared blood made something knot at the back of her throat.

After a few hours, Rabin lost altitude, and Zarya looked ahead to the walls of Ishaan, looming far in the distance. They'd crossed into Gi'ana and the miles of farmland and forest surrounding the city.

Rabin tipped forward, aiming for the earth before he landed with a gentle thump. Zarya and the others slid off his back before he dissolved into a puff of smoke, returning to his rakshasa form.

"We'll have to walk," he said. "I don't want to attract attention by flying too close."

"It's not a problem," Koura said while he stared up at the sky as if searching for meaning in the dimming stars. Zarya was exhausted but kept her complaints to herself as they trudged through the forest.

As they marched in single file down a narrow path, she kept an eye out for that black rot she'd encountered earlier. The voices and visions haunted her every time she closed her eyes. She thought of the flash that had signaled the presence of a demon, but surely if any were lingering around Ishaan, someone would have raised an alert by now?

Nevertheless, the guilt of harboring this secret nagged at her thoughts.

She couldn't disquiet the insistent voice suggesting that Abishek might be the only one who could offer the answers she sought. He did not fear the darkness. He embraced it.

Welcomed it. He was like her. Maybe he'd understand this strange thing happening to her. More importantly, maybe he would know what to do about it.

As they continued down the path, she made out the shadow of blackened leaves in the distance. If she hadn't been searching for it, it would have been easy to dismiss them as nothing but a trick of the light, but Zarya knew what she saw.

She stumbled over a root in her distraction, catching herself against a tree.

"Zarya?" came two voices—Row and Rabin—both of them approaching before they glared at one another.

"I'm fine," she said. "Just a little tired. It's been a long night."

"I can carry you," Rabin said, and Zarya held up a hand.

"Don't you dare. We're almost there."

She rallied herself and pushed off the tree, stomping along the path.

When they entered Ishaan, the city was already rising for the day. The smells of fresh baking wafted along the streets, and dozens of merchants were already setting up their wares for the market.

They skirted past the activity, making their way through the city, passing walls plastered with posters, all depicting the supposed likeness of Yasen and Zarya, offering even more money for their whereabouts. It spoke to the desperation of the Madans and their continued failure in rooting out the resistance.

Row stopped and studied the papers, rubbing his chin with a hand. "Is this supposed to be you and Yasen?"

Zarya looked around, ensuring no one was within earshot. "Will you be quiet?"

She grabbed him by the wrist and dragged him away. When

she looked over her shoulder, she saw Koura and Rabin now studying the pictures.

"I'll explain everything," she hissed before they turned to follow.

Zarya led them through Ishaan, her feet aching and her stomach rumbling with hunger, especially when she caught the scent of fried dough and fresh coffee from a nearby stand. Her mouth watered, but it wouldn't do to linger out here. Hopefully, Yasen had a pot already brewing.

"This way," she said, leading them down another street towards their flat.

When they entered, he was standing in the kitchen boiling water. He spun around as the door opened, blinking for a second before his face morphed from surprise into a scowl. "Zee! Where the fuck have you been!"

"Sorry," she said, clasping her hands together. "I didn't mean to worry you. I sent a note!"

"A *note*?!" he shouted as he approached. Sometimes, Zarya forgot how much bigger he was, but he towered over her in his worry and indignation. "All it said was *I'm fine. Back soon.* What was I supposed to interpret from that?"

She grimaced. "That I was fine and I'd be back soon?"

"You scared me half to death!"

She tipped her head and thrust out her bottom lip. "Aw, were you worried about me?"

His lip curled up, fire flashing in his stone-grey eyes. "*Yes.* I thought some monster had you. I thought you were swallowed into a pit. I thought you were—" He cut off before his eyes narrowed. Zarya looked over her shoulder to discover he was now glaring at Rabin. "Right. *You.* I was hoping she'd told you to fuck off."

Then, his gaze fell on Row and Koura, his brow furrowing further with confusion before he noted the state of their attire. They were all a wind-blown mess. Well, Zarya was. Rabin looked perfect. Koura didn't have any hair to mess. And Row always looked formidable no matter what.

"What on earth happened?" he demanded.

"Come on," Zarya said, "we'll explain everything."

They called down to the local restaurant for breakfast and shared what had happened in Dharati. Or Zarya, Row, and Koura explained. Any time Rabin opened his mouth, Yasen threw him a scathing glare, so he sat back, grumbling under his breath but otherwise remaining silent.

"Vikram's different, Yas," she said. "I don't know what's happened, but he's not the same man he was."

Yasen shook his head. "I wish I could have seen him."

She laid a hand on his arm. "He might need a friend."

Yasen shifted in his seat as if trying to work away something uncomfortable. "At some point, I'll go back. Right now, we're needed here. So, what did you find out?"

"I'm not sure yet."

Zarya pulled the spelled notebook out of her pocket and flipped it open. The pages crinkled softly as she scanned them while Row hovered over her, devouring each word.

The Jadugara were founded shortly after the Hanera Wars when thousands of the Ashvins' descendants were rounded up. The ruling factions were focused on eradicating the darkness, and anyone with ties to the twins had a target on their backs.

One young Aazheri hid away, escaping his fate, and went in search of others like him—namely those with six anchors. He founded a fledgling underground movement as a refuge for others with the darkness inside them. Eventually, they resurfaced as an organized group, hiding their dark magic and vowing to hunt down anyone with Ashvin blood in the name of Rahajhan. The rulers quickly came to rely on them, thankful to have the dirty work passed out of their hands.

Thus, they survived their own persecution while hiding in plain sight and dooming their own to a cage.

They quietly used their sixth anchor to create the ink and were responsible for the collars, further earning them the trust of Rahajhan's royals. The vanshaj were Aazheri—they always had been. Only the circumstances of their birth, and quite likely, being in the wrong place at the wrong time, landed them on the wrong side of everything.

The Jadugara began seeking out young male vanshaj with the sixth anchor to bolster their ranks. They'd devised some kind of technique to sense it within their blood and would remove the children from the mothers when they were born, claiming their babies had died. They then raised the boys within the Imarat, training them to become Jadugara.

Zarya could hear the echoing screams of the distraught mothers, crying for their lost children, having no idea they'd actually been stolen. As she read the tale out to the silent listeners, a tear slipped down her cheek that she brushed away with the back of her hand.

When she was done reading, everyone sat still, stewing in their thoughts. Row looked like he wanted to be sick. She hadn't managed to copy all the book's contents, but they'd already confirmed enough.

"What else does it say?" Yasen said a minute later, his voice soft as he leaned forward with his elbows on his knees.

Zarya flipped through the pages, looking for anything else that might prove useful.

"Fire. It says the most effective way to remove the collars is with fire."

She frowned at the page, wondering what that meant. Fire as in an anchor? Or regular old fire? Could it be that easy?

"This is..." Row said. "I had no idea."

"How has this remained hidden for a thousand years?" she asked.

"Everyone has been so scared for so long that they all refused to admit the sixth anchor still existed."

"But surely someone must have talked."

He shrugged. "It has obviously been a very closely guarded secret."

Row opened his mouth as though he were about to say something else and then snapped it shut with a shake of his head.

"Is something like this hereditary?" Yasen asked.

"It can be," Row answered. "But like all genetics, it's not a guarantee."

"So, does that mean her mother might have had it?"

Row shook his head. "If Asha did, I'm sure she would have..." He trailed off and rubbed a hand over his face. "Or maybe she wouldn't have told me. I can't say for sure at this point."

"My father does," Zarya said as everyone around the table went very still. "Rabin told me." She looked at Rabin who offered her a slight dip of his chin.

"Is this true?" Row demanded. "He never shared that with me."

Rabin shrugged. "It is true. And is further proof that he has no need of Zarya's magic. He will simply be proud his daughter bears his lineage."

Row's eyes narrowed, clearly still doubting his claims. He turned to face Zarya. "So, what do you want to do with this information?"

"I think we need to expose the Jadugara for the liars they are. And we need to figure out what it means when it says 'fire' can help remove the collar. It reacted violently with the ink during my testing."

"Zee," Yasen said. "Not your fire anchor. Your *nightfire*."

She blinked. "You think?"

He waved a hand at her. "Your talking necklace said it: she will be the one to free them all. This has to be connected."

Zarya wrapped her hand around the jewel. "I can't shoot nightfire at anyone. That would kill them."

"Then I guess you'd better start practicing how to control it," Row said, laying a hand on her shoulder.

"Control it. So I can use it *on* someone?"

She exchanged a look with Row and saw the apology in his expression. Like he didn't want her burdened with all of this, but it was clear it had already gone beyond anyone's choice. She was committed now, and there would be no turning back.

They continued talking for a while longer. Zarya asked for updates on Farida's condition and Operation Starbreak, but everything was the same as when she'd left. They could barely keep their eyes open after being awake all night, and eventually, they all fell silent.

"So, where's everyone sleeping?" Yasen asked. "We only have one extra bedroom."

"Koura and I can share for now," Row said. "We'll find alternate lodging as soon as possible. This place is a bit small for so many of us."

"What about him?" Yasen asked, glaring at Rabin. "Toss him into the dumpster out back where he belongs?"

"I'll stay with Zarya," Rabin snarled.

"No, you won't," she said. "You can take my room, and I'll stay with Yasen."

When Yasen opened his mouth to protest, Zarya shot him a pleading look, and he sighed. "Okay. Sure. Just don't touch my things."

She rolled her eyes as Rabin glared at Zarya across the table. He flexed his jaw momentarily before pushing himself up to stand.

"Fine," he growled, with such vehemence that she felt the tiniest quiver ricochet in the pit of her stomach.

THIRTY-FIVE

The gate squeaked as they entered the property from the back the following day. Yasen led the line, with Zarya behind him and Rabin, Row, and Koura bringing up the rear. After they'd all slept the day away, they'd met for a solemn dinner before returning to their beds and waking with the sun this morning.

The air was still and quiet, birds chirping in the distance and the last of the evening dew clinging to the flowers and leaves.

Yasen rapped on the back door in a series of sharp knocks.

They waited a moment before it popped open to reveal Rania blinking up at them. Zarya was surprised to see her outside of their flat and away from Farida's bedside. Her eyebrows drew together.

"What's this?" she asked sharply.

"We brought some friends," Yasen said.

She was about to protest when Yasen lifted a hand. "I assure you they can be trusted. And Koura may be able to help Farida."

Rania's gaze swept over Koura, who pressed a hand to his

chest and bowed. "I've been informed of her condition and would like to assist in whatever way I can."

Rania nodded as she opened the door wider. They entered the hallway to find Ajay waiting inside.

"Zarya, where have you been?" The worry in his voice was obvious, causing her another twist of guilt for running off without notice.

"I'll explain everything," she said. "I'd like to introduce you to some people."

"This is Row, and this is Koura."

She'd often mentioned both men to Ajay during her tales of stopping the blight.

Immediately, Ajay pressed his hands in front of his heart and bent at the waist. "It's an honor to meet you," Ajay said, his smile warm as he straightened and held out a hand. "Zarya has told me so much about you that I feel like I know you."

"All terrible things, I'm sure," Row said, and Ajay shook his head.

"Not at all. She admires you very much."

Zarya caught the tight look in Row's expression. They were still new to trusting each other, but she'd meant every word she'd said.

She might have had her differences with Row, but he'd also done all he could to protect her. It wasn't his fault he'd been saddled with her care, and if what Rabin claimed about Abishek was true, then her mother had deceived Row, too.

"And who's this?" Ajay asked, his attention turning to Rabin. She watched the two of them size one another up as Rabin glared and Ajay's gaze narrowed. Ajay had always known there was someone else in the picture, though she'd never revealed any details about him.

"This is Rabin," she said, waving a hand. "He's..." She stopped, having no idea how to define their relationship. They weren't friends. Or lovers. Though maybe neither of those things were strictly true. Especially the second one. "He also helped with the blight," she finished lamely.

She felt the heat of Rabin's glare at her less-than-authentic description but chose to ignore it.

"I see," Ajay said, lingering on Rabin for another moment before addressing the others. "And what brings you all to Ishaan?"

"That's what I want to explain," Zarya said. "Is Vikas here?"

As if saying his name summoned his entrance, Vikas came bounding down the stairs and broke into a smile.

"You're back!" he said. "We've missed you!"

"How have you been doing?" she asked. "I hear there's been no luck with the collars?"

"None at all," he said. "My friends and I haven't been able to convince a single person."

Zarya's heart sank again. Even if she *could* figure out how to use her nightfire to remove them faster, there would be no point unless someone came forward.

She puffed out a lock of hair from her eyes. "Well, then, we'd better tell you everything we've been up to."

They all filed into the living room, perching on chairs and divans around the space as they recalled their adventures in Dharati. When they were done, Zarya explained their beliefs regarding her nightfire and her concerns about turning it on anyone.

"So, where does that all leave us?" Ajay asked.

"I'm not sure. I'll need to do some experimenting and see if I can learn how to control it. There must be some aspect I'm missing."

Ajay rubbed his chin as he shared a look with Rania, a silent message passing between them.

"What exactly is your plan with all this?" Rabin asked, speaking for the first time since they'd arrived. "What are you hoping to accomplish?"

Ajay's eyes narrowed. "We're trying to free prisoners from their chains. I think that's obvious."

"Yes," Rabin answered in a dry voice that clearly did nothing to endear him to Ajay. "To what end? You need something definitive. Something the Madans can't undo to bring about a permanent change. They'll uncover what you're doing soon enough, and they will take every single one of them back. They have more money and resources than you can comprehend, and it will be nothing for them to simply collar these people again."

"So, what do you propose?" Ajay asked, his eyebrow arching and his voice dripping with derision. Zarya wondered if she'd have to throw herself between these two before the day was done. She could practically feel the sparks of hatred generating between them.

"Make a statement," Rabin answered simply. "You need to come at them with a powerful enough force that they'll have to listen."

Zarya watched as Ajay chewed the inside of his lip, his gaze again falling to Rania.

Rabin wasn't wrong. They could free a few vanshaj from their collars, but the moment they were discovered, the Madans would send every soldier in their army to hunt down every last one. They would never allow it to stand.

Still, Zarya could understand hearing someone who'd literally walked in the door moments ago, point that out might not be welcome. But then Rabin was never one to hold back on his thoughts.

The door to the back of the house banged open a moment later, and a young boy of no more than ten with a ring of tattooed stars around his neck came careening around the corner.

He clutched his thin chest, and it was obvious he'd been

crying, thanks to the tracks running through the dust on his cheeks.

"Nitin!" Vikas asked, standing up. "What is it?"

Zarya recognized him as Vikas's younger brother. The boy bent over, bracing his hands on his knees as he tried to catch his breath.

"They took them," he finally managed to gasp out.

"Took who?" Vikas asked.

"Mother and Father," he said, more fat tears spilling down his cheeks. "They claimed they had evidence you were part of the factory bombing and arrested them."

"Shit," Yasen breathed, echoing what they were all thinking.

"And not just them," Nitin continued. "They took others. Our neighbors. Our friends."

"How many?" Vikas asked, striding over to him and dropping to a knee as he clutched the boy's arms.

"I don't know. About a dozen."

Nitin sobbed and then wiped his nose with the back of his hand. "They said they're to be executed."

Staggering silence echoed through the room as those words sank in.

This was a message. A warning.

"Gods, what have I done," Vikas said, visibly trembling as he drew his sobbing brother into his arms.

"This isn't your fault," Zarya said. "They can't do this."

"Of course, they can," Ajay said. "And they're hoping this will draw out more of the Rising Phoenix."

"Well, it's working!" she said. "We can't let them die because of something *we* did."

"That's it," Rabin said. "Find out when they're to be executed. You need as many vanshaj freed from their collars as possible by then. I'm talking thousands. Tens of thousands. Then we storm the palace. We mount a revolution."

His very words made the air shiver with the promise of ruin and terrifying possibility.

"But we won't have enough time," Zarya said. "Even if they'd come, we'd need years to do that."

"Then you'd better find a way to use your nightfire to break them," he said, a challenge in his voice. There was no menace in it. No derision. Just the cold fact, and somehow, she knew that he believed she could. "And figure out how to convince the vanshaj you're working in their best interests."

She nodded as tension caught in her throat and tears pressed the backs of her eyes.

"We'll get a message to Apsara and Suvanna," Yasen said. "Maybe they can delay the execution and give us more time."

Zarya paced back and forth as a thousand bleak thoughts crawled through her head.

This was her *family*. These *awful* people who would do this. This was the blood that ran in her veins. She'd always known family was more than something you acquired at birth. Family wasn't always the people who bore you. And it certainly wasn't the ones who acted like vicious tyrants killing innocent souls in a bid to cling to their power.

She stopped pacing and stared about the room.

Nitin clung to Vikas, sobbing into his shoulder.

"Zarya," Vikas whispered.

"We won't let them die," she vowed. "I swear to you. I'll kill every Madan myself if I have to."

THIRTY-SIX

Over the next few days, Zarya spent all her time in the forest, trying to wrest control over her nightfire, ensuring she kept her distance from that menacing patch of black rot she'd been responsible for creating. She knew she couldn't keep ignoring it, but she also had too many other worries vying for her attention.

She had certain types of control over the magic. What she wanted was a trickle, and it resembled a hose, spearing out beams of magic. She'd only used it defensively when survival depended on maximum impact.

But she couldn't use this on a person. She'd kill them. She'd blow them apart. A fact that was evidenced by the remains of the decimated trees and bushes that formed a circle around the spot where Yasen and Zarya currently stood.

The night she'd used it in Dharati to suppress the demons, she'd avoided hurting anyone on the ground, but those had been different circumstances, and she couldn't trust that again without specifically understanding what she'd done.

"This isn't working," she said.

"You think?" Yasen asked as he bent down and picked up a small branch that had been reduced to a sad, charred twig.

Zarya stood with her hands on her hips, surveying the destruction. "What am I going to do? We need thousands, Rabin said. Tens of thousands. How am I supposed to do that?" Her voice started to rise, the pitch growing frantic.

"Hey, hey," Yasen said, striding over and wrapping his arms around her. She buried her face into his chest. "It's going to be fine. The weight of the world isn't on your shoulders. We're all going to help."

"But it is, Yas." She looked up at him. "For some reason, I was chosen to fulfill this task. To *free* them. If I don't do it, then who will?"

He opened his mouth and closed it. "I'm not sure."

"See?" she asked, pushing off him. "If I can't figure this out..."

Her heart twisted whenever she thought of Vikas's parents and the other innocent people locked up in the palace. They had families who needed them. And now they were being held for the things Zarya and the Rising Phoenix had done. This had always been a risk. They knew the Madans would make an example of someone, but facing the reality of those consequences was proving even harder than she'd imagined.

She prayed the prisoners weren't being mistreated, but it was a thin hope without much possibility.

"We'll get them out of there, Zee," Yasen said. "We will."

She nodded and tried again, firing another beam of nightfire at a distant tree as they watched it explode upon contact, the entire thing blowing into a shower of splinters that did little to convince her of anything.

As Zarya continued to struggle, everyone tried to help: Row, Ajay, even Rania traipsed out into the forest with her despite the fact Farida was still lying comatose in her bed.

However, Zarya had also brought Koura to Ishaan, and if anyone could help, it was him. He'd been spending many hours at her bedside, attempting to puzzle out the source of her ailment.

That meant Rania had ceased with the open hostility but still refused to speak to Zarya in much more than single syllables.

They received regular reports from Apsara and Suvanna inside the palace, who were keeping as close an eye on the prisoners as possible. Zarya's hopes they weren't being mistreated were somewhat mollified when they confirmed that while they weren't living in luxury, no one was being unnecessarily cruel. Perhaps it was the best they could hope for, given the circumstances.

It seemed the Madans were hesitating about what to do with their vanshaj prisoners. They'd assumed the Rising Phoenix would show themselves immediately upon their capture, and they were clearly struggling with what to do in the face of their defiance. As of yet, a date for the promised execution hadn't been set, but they were operating on a dwindling timeline, and the call could come at any moment.

Finally, after so many failed attempts, Rabin insisted on accompanying her, and she was frustrated enough with her lack of progress to join him in the forest. Until now, she had been doing everything to avoid being with him alone.

Row and Koura had no luck securing a nearby flat, and Rabin continued to stay alone in Zarya's room while she slept in Yasen's bed every night. She'd let herself get swept up in the moment when they'd been at Rabin's estate, but she was trying to keep a clear head.

It was proving almost impossible, of course. She wanted to be near him. And it was about more than her physical reaction to him. He made her feel... calm. Like the storm inside her settled whenever he was around. Their time at his home hadn't been just about sex—though that had been pretty good—but rather the undeniably deep connection they shared.

As she continued to keep her distance, she couldn't ignore the growing ache in her chest. They'd spent months apart, and though she'd put on a brave face, the truth was she'd been miserable without him. She didn't want to need him or admit that he cast her world in different colors—everything just a little brighter and richer.

Today, they stood in the middle of a clearing she'd used many times already. The artifacts of her failure—charred trees and leaves—surrounded them. Rabin attempted to talk her through her magic. He stood behind her, his hands on her shoulders, whispering in her ear.

She tried to ignore the shiver that rippled down her back and spread through her hips when his lips brushed her skin. She also tried to ignore that scent of fresh earth and sun-warmed grass that filtered into the chinks of her bones. And she definitely tried to ignore the way she wanted to lean against him and feel his hard chest and thighs against her back. To have his big hands wrap around her waist and maybe... travel lower.

"Zarya?" he asked after a moment. "Are you ready?"

She startled out of her fantasies and cleared her throat.

"Yes."

She held out her palm and focused a thin beam of nightfire into a tree. Immediately, she felt the difference in her control with Rabin standing behind her. Screwing up her concentration, she then directed the light to another tree, aiming for the center of its trunk. Slowly, she wove the beam through the clearing, wrapping it around each one as she spun in a slow circle.

"Good girl," Rabin rumbled, and she tried not to let *that* affect her, too. She was tempted to tell him to knock it off but didn't want to break her concentration. Directing her magic to another tree, she felt it swell under her fingers. A moment later, the trunk shattered, just like so many others, but when she looked around the clearing, she realized the trees around her target all stood unscathed. It wasn't perfect, but it was immense progress.

She screamed and jumped up.

"I did it! I did it!" Then she spun around and threw her arms around Rabin's neck as he lifted her up and swung her in a circle. "I did it!"

His hand cupped the back of her head as he leaned in and softly said, "I knew you could."

Another shiver traveled over her skin, and she became acutely aware of their proximity. As he set her back on her feet, she looked up, their faces so close she felt his breath against her lips. She wondered if he was planning to kiss her, and then was annoyed with herself for wishing it.

"Zarya," he whispered in a rough voice before he closed the distance, his mouth slanting over hers. She didn't fight it. She didn't try to resist. She probably should, but she couldn't. She was helpless to give in to her wants. She let herself melt into the sensation. The feeling was like drowning and coming alive all at once.

She moaned as he deepened the kiss, his hands sliding down to cup her from behind. His hips pressed into hers and she responded in kind, craving something to fill the building emptiness between her thighs. Her hands slid up his chest as he pulled her closer.

But that's when her brain finally caught up.

"Wait," she said, pulling away. "Wait. Stop."

Immediately, he released her, stepping back, though he didn't look happy about it. She smoothed down the front of her top and then her hair, attempting to wrest control of her raging hormones.

"Sorry. I got carried away." She avoided looking into his eyes, dodging the weight of his disappointment and confusion.

"Zarya. What are you doing? Why are you fighting me?"

She looked up, finally meeting his gaze, but what she saw was so much worse. It was heat and fire and the entire world reflected in the endless pools of those dark eyes. She could dissolve into that look and be content until the end of her days.

She shook her head. "I don't think this is a good idea. I know we had a nice time in your manor, but... I'm..."

He pressed his mouth together. "You just controlled your magic. It's because of the paramadhar connection."

She blew out a breath. "I think you're right," she admitted.

He stepped towards her, careful to keep a sliver of distance between them. She didn't retreat. In fact, she had to resist meeting him where he stood.

"We need to complete the Bandhan. If you have that much more control with just me touching you, think of what you could do."

She studied his face before her gaze wandered to the standing trees—the ones she'd destroyed and the ones that had *survived* her nightfire.

She sighed and ran a hand down her face, realizing he was probably right.

He was the key.

Not only to the riddle of her magic but maybe to everything she was hoping for.

THIRTY-SEVEN

The next morning, Zarya opened her eyes to find Yasen staring at her from the other side of the bed. He lay on his side with one hand propped up under his head.

"Morning, sunshine," he said.

She flinched, yanking the blanket up to her chin. "Why are you staring at me?"

"Did you know you snore?"

She made a sound of indignation. "I do not!"

"You do. It's like listening to a rhinoceros with a sinus cold."

She burst out laughing. "Shut up. It is not."

He laughed, too, and then said, "I'm staring because you've been avoiding me every time I bring up the topic of what you got up to during your little trip to see our nemesis, the dragon shifter. And now I'm not letting you out of my sight until you come clean."

She felt her cheeks heat. "I have no idea what you're talking about."

That earned her an eye roll. "Please. You ran out of here like your pants were on fire and disappeared for three days.

Why did you return with Rabin, and did you let him plow the field again?"

She snorted and shook her head. "You're ridiculous."

He grinned, and she blew out a breath before sharing everything. When she was done, Yasen offered her a skeptical raise of his eyebrow.

"And you believe him?"

"I think so," she said.

"So, why are you sleeping in here with me?"

She wrinkled her nose. "Because I'm still on the fence."

"About?"

"About trusting him. I *think* I believe him, but I also don't know if I should rely on my instincts. They haven't always been the most reliable."

He nodded. "And what are they telling you?"

"That he didn't hurt me on purpose, and though he messed up, I understand why he didn't initially admit the truth. Also, I think he tried, but then we got swept up in the battle for Dharati, and he never had another opportunity before it was over."

Yasen flopped back onto his pillow before turning his head. "I've always believed him to be honorable."

"I know. And that might be part of what's swaying me."

He shrugged, the movement rustling the sheets. "I also haven't seen him in decades, so he could be an entirely different person now."

"I know that, too. But do we ever really change the essence of who we are?"

He reached out a hand and wrapped it around hers. "I suppose not. Just be careful, okay?"

"Of course, I will be. Thanks, Yas."

She leaned over and pressed a kiss to his cheek just as a knock came at the door.

"Zarya," came Rabin's rough voice, threaded with authority. She rolled her eyes and slid out of bed.

"What?" she asked, opening the door. Wearing only shorts for sleeping and a thin, sleeveless top, she felt his tactile gaze travel over her body, causing an inconvenient flare between her thighs. She used the door to shield herself, not that it helped. At all.

She frowned. "What do you want? Why are you banging on my door so early?"

"We need to see the mystic today."

She scrunched her eyebrows together. "Who?"

"To perform the Bandhan."

"Rabin—" After his declaration in the forest yesterday, she knew he was right. But she also hadn't technically agreed to anything yet. Despite her best efforts, she'd spent a good part of last night tossing and turning, thinking about that kiss and kind of wishing she hadn't stopped, all while wondering if she was really considering binding herself to him forever.

"Zarya, you know we must."

Rabin regarded her with that signature intense look in his eyes, his expression serious. She dropped the door handle and rubbed her face with both hands. Binding herself to him would mean crossing a chasm she was trying to avoid. They could never be anything casual again. But this wasn't only about her feelings. This was about the vanshaj and everything they stood to lose if she failed at her task.

Rabin was in her life. Nothing would change that. A part of her—maybe a larger one than she wanted to admit—wanted that.

"We can do it in Ishaan?" she asked.

He dipped his chin. "Row has a contact."

"Today?" she asked, hoping he'd give her more time. But that was also a luxury none of them could afford.

Rabin planted his hand on the door and pressed it open. He

stepped into the room, towering over her like he was prone to do. "This is inevitable. Why delay? The longer we remain unbonded, the longer it will be until I can fully protect you."

She took in those words, still hesitating as she peered up. Her stomach did a little flip, and she cursed her body's involuntary reactions.

But she had to do this. For their cause. To fulfill her destiny. She'd been granted nightfire—possibly the only thing that could quickly break the collars—and then fate had also granted her with a protector *and* a way to control the magic. She'd always known he was a part of a pattern she couldn't see yet. But now it became clear. They were meant for this.

"Okay." Zarya ran a hand down her face. "Let me get dressed."

"I'll be waiting for you." He said it so sincerely and with such fiery passion that a secret spot in her stomach fluttered.

Their gazes held, and she understood that he didn't mean only right now.

She nodded. "Give me a few minutes."

When she closed the door and spun around, she found Yasen sitting up, arms folded and brow raised.

"What was that about?"

Pressing her back against the door, she blew out a long sigh. "Apparently, he's officially becoming my paramadhar today."

He opened his mouth and paused. "Are you sure about this?"

"Not really," she said, and Yasen frowned. "Okay, I'm lying."

"About?"

"The idea scares me, but it also kind of excites me... it's crazy that I want to be bonded to him, but I kind of do. He said it didn't have to be romantic. He said he would want to be my paramadhar no matter our relationship."

"And you believe him?"

"I think I do. If we're destined for one another, then don't I have to do this?"

"Maybe?"

She pushed off the door and started rifling through the pile of her clothing tossed on the chair. "Besides, after the way my magic behaved in the clearing, I'm sure this is the key to controlling my nightfire. He thinks so, too. This could be the edge we need to free the vanshaj once and for all."

Yasen tipped his head. "Are you sure you're not just looking for what you want to see?"

She stopped and turned to look at him. "I don't think I am."

He nodded. "Then I trust you to make good decisions, Zee. You're not that naive girl who escaped the swamp all those months ago."

Zarya gave him a rueful look. "I think a part of me will always be that girl, but I think I'm growing, too."

His answering smile was soft and maybe a little proud. "Do what you need to, Zee, and just know I'm here no matter what."

She felt tears build in her eyes as she crossed the room and threw her arms around his neck. He was warm and solid and was her family in a way that no one ever had been. "I love you, Yas."

He drew her in closer, hugging her around the waist. "Don't cry on me."

"I'm not," she said in a thick voice as a tear rolled down her cheek.

Yasen snorted. "You're so... emotional."

She laughed and wiped her tears before finally choosing a long black dress made of light fabric that fit over her bust, flowed to her ankles, and left her arms bare. She tied her hair up and swept on a bit of makeup, not at all hoping Rabin would think she looked nice.

When she was done, she headed into the living room to find

him perched on the edge of a chair, prepared to leap out of his skin.

"I'm ready," she said, spreading her arms. Row and Koura sat at the kitchen table nursing mugs of chai.

"For what?" Row asked.

"To visit the mystic," Rabin answered. "You said you'd tell us where to find them."

"Now? Isn't that a little sudden?" Row asked, clearly having all the same reservations.

"Now," Rabin said in a tone that invited no room for arguments. Row glared at Rabin and then turned to Zarya.

"I've agreed to it," she said, and when she saw he was about to protest, she lifted a hand before explaining how her magic had reacted with Rabin at her side. "I want this, and I'm hoping this can help me control my nightfire enough to help."

Row nodded slowly, his gaze full of distrust. "It might, but Zarya, this cannot be undone. Once you complete the Bandhan, there is no turning back. The only way to sever it is with *his* death." Row scanned Rabin up and down. "Not that I'd object to that."

Rabin said nothing, just arched a disdainful brow as though he was used to having his life threatened on a regular basis.

"I understand all that, Row," she said. "But I don't think I have a choice."

"Then let's go," Rabin said, standing up and stalking towards Zarya, his burning gaze raking her from head to toe, making her stomach tighten. "The decision has been made and it's really none of your business."

Rabin aimed the comment at Row, who hesitated for another moment before he scribbled something on a piece of paper and handed it over to Zarya. "As long as you're sure."

She reached out to accept it and answered, "As sure as I'll ever be."

* * *

Rabin followed Zarya out of the flat and into the bustling streets of Ishaan. No one had any reason to recognize him here, but he still felt exposed within these crowds. Being around too many people always made him anxious. He preferred quiet and solitude. The company of only those he trusted—though that circle was rather small.

Zarya walked ahead of him with purpose, clearly familiar with the city. She'd been here for months, and he couldn't help but notice the way she seemed to belong here, like these sights and smells and sounds had been imprinted into her by her mother's hand. He ran to catch up as she gave him a sidelong look.

"You're sure about this?" she asked. "Row is right. I could just kill you if I get tired of you."

Though she said it matter-of-factly, he detected the note of insincerity in her voice. She was fighting this with her mind, but her heart sought this ending, too.

"Zarya," he snagged her arm and stopped her as the crowd surged around them. "What do I have to do to prove to you that I'm yours, body and soul? That I want to protect you and be there with you through all of this?"

She narrowed her eyes. "But you don't fully agree with what I'm doing. You understand that this will only make my goals more possible."

"I agree with your cause, Zarya. I'm only worried about the consequences."

"I don't care about the consequences," she said, and it took every ounce of restraint to hold back the tirade he wanted to unleash. That she shouldn't play with her life so casually. That he'd be ruined if anything happened to her.

"I know that." He stepped in closer, brushing a strand of hair from her cheek. "And that's why I love you, Spitfire. You are fearless and brave and so damn strong. So if you insist on doing this, then let me be there with you." He meant that part. He did love that about her, but it also scared the shit out of him.

He watched her blink heavily, her lids sliding closed and then opening as he realized what he'd just said. *Love.* It had slipped out. This wasn't how he'd planned to say it, but it had been there pressing against the surface, ready to burst through the thin veneer where he'd been keeping it and couldn't contain it anymore.

There was no denying what he felt for her—what he'd *felt* from the moment he'd seen her in the dream forest all those months ago.

She cleared her throat and then spun around. "We should go." She was walking faster now, her shoulders stiff.

He watched her for a moment and then once again jogged to catch up. He was such a fool. When had he ever let his emotions get the best of him like this? But being around Zarya called into question everything he'd ever known about himself.

They continued to wind through the streets that grew more crowded as the hour passed. Finally, Zarya consulted the paper Row had handed them and pointed down a narrow alley.

"I think it's this way."

Rabin peered down the shadowy path and nodded, his guard always up. "I'll go first."

"Fine, tough guy." She waved him on and he heard her following as the cool shadows enveloped them. They passed several narrow doorways, some with iron numbers screwed into the surface and others with numbers inelegantly hacked into the wood.

"What's the address?" he asked.

"1043. I think. I always forget how terrible Row's handwriting is." She squinted and held the paper further away. "Is that a *Q*?"

They continued down the alley, counting the numbers they

passed. After another minute, they stopped before a plain wooden door.

"This appears to be right," she said, consulting the paper again and then knocked. They waited as someone shuffled on the other side, and the door popped open to reveal a stunning woman with deep brown skin and silver hair hanging down either side of her face. She appeared around Zarya's age, but the depth in her eyes suggested she was positively ancient.

Mystics were their own brand of magical being. Very rare and very mysterious. Some believed they were a distant relation to Aazheri, but they denied the connection, claiming their magic was entirely unique.

"Yes?" she asked, her gaze open but cautious.

"We're looking for a mystic," Zarya said, and the woman cocked her head, studying them both.

"Why?"

Zarya gestured between them. "We need you to perform a Bandhan."

The mystic blinked as if she needed a moment to absorb Zarya's words.

"Well, then, come in," she said. "I'm Thriti."

After closing the door behind them, she crossed the room. She wore a long black dress embroidered with mirrors along the hem, covering her from chin to wrist. She folded her thin arms before she assessed them both from head to toe. Zarya looked at him, but he nodded. He didn't sense anything amiss with the mystic, only a deep curiosity.

"You are masatara and paramadhar? Are you sure? You've entered the mind plane?" she asked.

They nodded. "We have," Zarya said. "Many times."

"Tell me about it."

Rabin listened as Zarya described the dream forest.

When she was done, Thriti looked at Rabin. "And you've also been able to control it?"

"I have." He bowed at the waist. The mystic radiated a sort of quiet power and authority he couldn't help but respect.

"That is very difficult for paramadhar."

"I had guidance from a powerful Aazheri."

She dipped her chin as if accepting that answer.

"And you both understand what this means? The limitations and consequences of this bond?"

"We do," he said solemnly.

"It's been lifetimes since I performed my last Bandhan," she said, studying them for another moment. "I almost believed that old magic had died out completely."

"What do you think it means if it's returned?" Zarya asked, and he tried not to let the hope in her voice bother him. She was still trying to find a way to convince herself this was right.

Thriti turned to her. "I can't say for sure, but when magic disappears or returns, it's always for a reason."

Zarya nodded. He watched her swallow and blink rapidly as if trying to hold in her tears. He kept his eyes on her as Thriti moved to a workbench, where she started shifting various pots and pans and began mixing ingredients together.

Zarya's gaze flicked to him, and he noted the glossy sheen in her eyes. What did those tears represent? She clung to so many layers of emotions and feelings that sometimes it was difficult to read her.

"Is there any chance we're not paramadhar and masatara?" Zarya asked, turning back to Thriti, who continued working. Rabin tried to ignore the painful twist in his chest again.

The mystic stopped and looked back. "It certainly sounds like it. But the marks will only take effect if you are, regardless."

"And if we aren't?" This time there was a thread of nervousness in her voice.

"Then you'll have a nice bit of decoration on your skin."

"Oh," Zarya said, and Rabin hoped that was disappointment he sensed this time.

"You'll need to choose an object or a symbol to connect you," she called over her shoulder as she ground something with a mortar and pestle. "It can be anything, but it's best if it's something personal."

They both paused as their gazes locked. He watched something flicker behind her eyes.

"A dragon," Zarya said a moment later. "What do you think?"

She gave him a raw look that rattled something loose in his chest before it slotted into the hole he carried beneath his ribs.

A dragon. Something that was important to them both.

"Just like the one you have?"

"Do you already have a marking?" Thriti asked, again looking over her shoulder.

He pulled up the side of his kurta to reveal the dragon tattooed on his skin.

She approached and touched it with cool fingers.

"This was done by a mystic with great skill."

Rabin nodded. "It was encouraged by someone important to me. The magic helps with my dragon transformation."

Thriti raised an eyebrow and held out a hand. "May I?"

Rabin nodded and pressed her fingers to the tattoo, her eyes fluttering closed as she explored the sinuous lines created by Abishek's royal mystic. After a few seconds, she nodded.

"Yes, I feel it," she said. "It's very powerful."

Thriti peered at him for perhaps a moment too long before she clapped her hands. "Well, the good news is that I can make use of this for the Bandhan, and you've just cut my job in half."

She turned to look at Zarya. "Where would you like it?"

"Does it matter?"

"Not really."

She looked at Rabin as if seeking help, and he crossed the room, placing one hand on her waist and tugging down the sleeve of her dress before he kissed the back of her shoulder.

"How about here?" he asked against her skin, feeling her shiver under his touch.

"Sure," she whispered. "That would work."

"Then lie on the bench face down," Thriti said, gesturing to the center of the room. "This will sting a bit. Take your arm out of your sleeve. I'll need clear access to the area."

She nodded and did as Thriti asked before lying on her stomach.

"You can grab that stool," she then said to Rabin. "This will take a while."

Rabin dragged it over and settled near Zarya's head. She stared at him while Thriti worked, wincing at the needle's first sharp prick.

"Does it hurt?" he asked.

"I'm fine." Then she reached towards him. "Take my hand. Please?"

His heart squeezed inside his chest as he held his hand out, and she slipped her warm fingers into his. He stared down at their linked fingers, thinking of everything that had brought them to this moment and that first mysterious call when he'd felt the pull to seek her out in his dreams.

He looked up to find her watching him, and something passed over her expression at that moment.

Something that felt like hope and the shining possibility of a future together. Like his entire world was changing and nothing would ever be the same again.

THIRTY-EIGHT

After a few more hours of pain, Thriti announced she was almost done. Zarya whimpered with relief. Her shoulder felt like it was on fire, and she wasn't sure how much more she could take.

Thriti explained that an enchanted marking caused more pain due to the infusion of a special substance that would allow magic to bind with it.

"Is that how they add the collars?" Zarya asked without really meaning to. She didn't have to explain what she was referring to as Thriti's eyes darkened.

"Yes. It is a similar process."

Zarya thought of the vanshaj babies screaming as they were branded with their collars. It was painful enough on her shoulder that she couldn't imagine what it would feel like on the delicate skin of their tiny throats. She swallowed down a surge of nausea. If she had any lingering reservations about the Bandhan, they were just wiped away. She was committed to this. To the rebellion. To everything that had brought her to Ishaan.

Her gaze drifted to her left.

And to Rabin, too.

"We're done with this part. Now I'll infuse the ink with the magic to seal the Bandhan," Thriti said a moment later. "It will hurt."

"More than this?" Zarya asked.

"Much more." She winced. "Sorry."

"It's okay. Just do it." Without thinking about it, Zarya turned to Rabin, seeking his strength. She saw something in his eyes: worry, fear, *love*.

He'd said it so casually like it had been something on his mind for a while. Had he meant that? She was sure it was a slip, but the moment it had left his mouth, she felt something shift, like a bend in the air. It was like a key turning on a lock she'd been keeping bolted up for fear of being hurt again.

Sitting with him in this room, she could feel the altering of her course. Maybe it was the magic around them. Maybe it was the knowledge they were binding themselves together. He was doing this willingly. Giving up his autonomy for her. And though she had endlessly worried it would feel unbalanced, she realized then that it would never be that way.

They were two parts of a whole. Not master and servant. That was just a technicality—two words for the magic that joined them. They were equal. As Rabin had said so many times, he was her destiny.

After today she could push him away all she wanted, but he could only ever go so far. Everyone was doubting him. Row. Yasen. And with good reason. But they didn't know him the way she did.

He loved her. One might say it was ridiculous. That they'd only known each other a short time, but they'd already been through so much together. They'd already crossed so many divides.

Love.

Maybe.

It was what she'd always wanted. The stories in her books

had been the only thing keeping her whole during her lonely life. And a man like Rabin... well, he was exactly as she'd always imagined. Actually, he was so much better.

He squeezed her hand tighter, and she wondered if he could sense what she was thinking. If he could feel a transformation slowly taking place, the shedding of her old skin to reveal another version of herself underneath, one that wanted to release the past and embrace the possibilities of their future.

"You too," Thriti said to Rabin. "Get your shirt off."

She gestured to him, and he reached behind his head, yanking off his kurta in one smooth movement, exposing warm brown flesh. Zarya traced the lines of his body with an admiring look.

"Can you stand?" Thriti asked Zarya. "It's best when you're touching. The more the better."

"Sure," Zarya said, swinging her legs off the bench with a wince. Her shoulder throbbed as Rabin helped her stand and drew her close.

"Arms around each other," Thriti ordered. Zarya slid her arms around his waist as he folded her against him. "Close. Close."

She felt Thriti's hand on her back as they shuffled together. "Now hold on."

Zarya looked up to meet Rabin's gaze as he squeezed her tight. He leaned down and pressed his mouth to the arch of her throat as Thriti began murmuring soft words. It felt like they were the only two people in this room as ribbons of silver light began to surround them, spinning in wide, lazy circles.

The light reflected in Rabin's dark eyes, illuminating the slice of his cheekbone and the angle of his jaw, bouncing off the golden flecks in his pupils. She reached up and tucked a piece of hair behind his ear before trailing a finger over his cheekbone.

She remembered during their first meeting when she'd thought he was the most beautiful man she'd ever seen. But that was nearly too banal a description. He was raw animal magnetism and coalescing shadows all bound together to create this storm cloud of bone and sinew that would pull her apart and put her back together over and over.

He clasped her hand in his and brought it between them as their foreheads tipped together.

Thriti continued to chant as she felt a cool touch of magic against her new marking. And then... agony. Searing, mind-numbing agony. She cried out as she tried to hold still, squeezing Rabin's hand so hard she worried it might shatter.

But he held on, his gaze never wavering as they stared at one another, lost in an abyss as deep and endless as midnight.

Another wash of pain had her gritting her teeth as she groaned.

Rabin pressed his mouth to her fingers, his jaw hard as he fought off twin waves of pain. "You can do this, Spitfire. I'm here with you."

She nodded as tears leaked from her eyes, sliding down her cheeks and under her chin.

"You're so fucking strong," he whispered as he brought his face closer, and anguish coursed over her in waves. His other hand found the back of her head. "Beautiful. Brave. Magnificent."

Another twist of pain had her whimpering, and then, it finally eased, draining out until all that was left was a dull throb. She drew in several long, deep breaths, waiting for the worst of the pain to drain away.

"Are you okay?" she asked him.

"Are you?"

She pressed her hands to his bare, warm skin, feeling the vibration of his heart pounding in his chest. "I'm fine."

"Take these," Thriti said, thrusting her hand under their noses with four small pills cradled in her palm. "Two each. This should help."

They nodded and accepted the medicine.

"Did it work?" she asked after she swallowed.

"You tell me," Thriti answered. "Can you feel anything? You should be able to sense each other now."

Zarya looked at Rabin again as she squeezed his hand, and then they nodded. She felt it like a second soul was living inside her. She imagined she could almost sense his feelings or thoughts like a phantom shadow.

"I feel it," she whispered, realizing she was now truly tied to this man forever.

"Excellent," Thriti said as she began to clean up. "It's been a while since I've done a Bandhan, but I've still got it."

"Thank you," Rabin said. "How much do we owe you?"

She rattled off a number, and Rabin handed over the coins before tugging his kurta over his head. Zarya slowly worked her arm back into her sleeve and rotated her shoulder to work out some of the tension. It still hurt, but it was nothing she couldn't handle.

They thanked Thriti and entered the narrow alleyway again, walking quietly with Zarya in front. She couldn't help but continue looking back at him. Where she'd been drawn to him like a moth to a flame before, now it was like a lion to its prey.

She stopped and turned around as he came up to her, looking down. The paramadhar wasn't supposed to be romantic in nature, but all she could sense was this all-consuming swell of emotion and desire building under her skin. She'd felt it before, but it was even more insistent now.

"Rabin," she whispered, and he must have felt the same because his eyes darkened to pools of ink. He wrapped a hand around the back of her head and tipped it for a kiss. His tongue drove into her mouth, and she looped her arms around his waist as he shoved her against a wall, flattening his body to hers. She felt the angles of his solid form lining up with her softer curves, along with the fact he was already growing hard.

She moaned, wishing, *wishing* they were alone right now. And that her apartment wasn't currently full of people.

But Rabin didn't seem to care. He shuffled her into another alley, this one concealed by shadows where it finished in a dead end. When they hit the far corner, he reached down and lifted her skirt to her hips and then, with his hands under her ass, hoisted her up, pressing her against the rough brick wall.

His fingers dug into her thighs, the tips only a hair away from where she ached for his touch.

"I need to fuck you right here, Spitfire. Unless you tell me to stop."

"No," she gasped as he thrust his cock between her legs. "Don't stop."

He reached between them, pushing aside the fabric of her underwear to find her wet center, his thick finger slipping in.

"Fucking soaked already, dirty girl," he said with a malicious grin. He pulled out and ran the tip along her seam before circling her clit. She moaned as her head fell against the wall.

His finger dipped into her again, pumping slowly, going deeper and deeper as her hips writhed against his hand. He added a second finger, stretching her with pain and pleasure.

Then he fumbled with his pants before she felt the wide head of his cock pressing into her entrance. Slowly, he inched into her, making small thrusts with his hips as she adjusted to his size, feeling like she was being split apart.

"That's it," he said with pride in his voice. "Take every inch. This needy pussy is mine."

"Oh gods," she gasped as he drove into the hilt, stroking every sensitive spot.

She clung to him tight as he thrust into her, her legs clamping around his waist. She forgot where they were. That anyone could come around the corner at any moment. The only thing that mattered was him and this coming together. This melding of their spirits.

"Zarya," he groaned into the curve of her neck as he thrust his hips harder and harder. "Fuck, Zarya. I love you. I've loved you from the moment I saw you." He thrust again, *hard* and with purpose, as though he were trying to imprint these words into the texture of her soul.

"Today we are bound, body and spirit, and I will do everything I can to be worthy of you." He gripped the back of her neck, staring into her eyes as he fucked her, slow and deep. "Tell me you feel something, Zarya. Even if it's not love yet. Just tell me you feel something more than just... this."

She exhaled a soft breath as she felt her release rising in her core. "Yes. I feel something," she gasped. "Of course I do."

He smirked, but the triumphant light in his eyes betrayed the somewhat understated reaction. "Then that's all I need right now."

He continued pounding into her, the sounds of their bodies slapping together echoing in the narrow alley. It was reckless and probably stupid to be doing this here, but it felt like everything about their relationship was a little bit impulsive and like they were stumbling over broken glass trying to avoid a thousand cuts, but the high—the *high* was like plunging off a cliff and screaming into the wind.

Rabin pumped his hips again, crushing his lips to hers as she came apart, crying into his mouth as he continued thrusting. A few moments later, she felt him thicken, and then he spilled into her with a moan that rattled through every bone in her body.

When he was spent, he collapsed against her. They stood still for a minute, her legs and arms clamped tightly around his waist as they waited for their limbs to stop shaking. Then he pulled up and rubbed a thumb along her bottom lip before he reluctantly pulled away and let her slide to the ground, her skirts falling around her ankles.

He'd said it. *I love you.*

Clearly and plainly. It was out in the open and was yet another thing they could never return from.

The words sat in the back of her throat, perched on the edge of whatever came next.

But she wasn't ready.

So she stepped closer and stretched onto her tiptoes, pressing her lips to his, hoping it conveyed everything she couldn't quite say out loud yet.

THIRTY-NINE

Zarya and Rabin immediately returned to the forest to test out the control of her magic. She wasn't surprised to discover that everything felt different.

They stood in the clearing while she managed to channel small, delicate threads of nightfire with Rabin at her side. He didn't even need to be touching her anymore.

She twisted them in the air, drawing loops and swirls, marveling at her control. This had been the answer. It almost seemed too easy. But she was probably getting ahead of herself. There were still many bridges to cross.

The tendrils of sparkling black light spun around the clearing as she once again contemplated the purpose that found her standing in this spot.

She will be the one to free them all.

But Rabin wasn't watching her magic. He was watching her. It was impossible not to wonder if he'd been destined for her in more ways than one. Had her mother known about him, too?

And what were the odds that the man who'd rescued him

was *her* father by blood? Maybe Rabin was right and his task *was* to see them reunited. This couldn't be only a coincidence.

"Try it on me," Rabin said, moving to stand in front of her. "Circle them around me. And don't argue about it being dangerous. I trust you."

She pressed her lips together and nodded. She did have to try, but for the first time since the idea of using her magic on the collars had arisen, she wasn't afraid. She *could* do this.

She twisted her fingers and sent out a thin tendril, snaking it around his ankles as it circled up his thighs and hips. She wound it around his chest and then his throat as she gently touched the tip against his skin.

"Does it hurt?" she asked, and he shook his head.

"It tingles a bit. That's all."

Then, an idea occurred to her.

"Let me see your tattoos," she said, and he didn't question her as he stripped off his shirt and waited with his arms held at his sides. Seeing him like this always made her a little breathless. It also reminded her of the narrow alley less than an hour ago as her cheeks heated and her stomach tightened with need.

After her feeble attempt to keep him at arm's length, she'd let him back in with all the resistance of a wet tissue.

And now that they were bound, there would be no way to distance herself anymore.

As her gaze traveled over him, he returned the favor, his eyes darkening as if he, too, was remembering the way he'd taken her against that wall without a care for who might see them.

She licked her lips and then walked over and placed a soft hand on his left pectoral before kissing him just below his collarbone, where she could reach without stretching onto her tiptoes.

"Spitfire," he growled. "What are you doing?"

She looked up and grinned. "Hold still. I want to test something."

* * *

Rabin did as Zarya asked while he watched her send another tendril of nightfire out, twisting it in the air. It was amazing how much control the Bandhan gave her. He wondered how close they would have to be for it to take effect.

Perhaps one of the most surprising things was that he could now feel her using it through a small tug behind his navel. He wondered if there was anything he could do but stand here, so he concentrated on helping her control the magic, trying to channel his focus into her.

Her nightfire touched the tattoo on his ribs, and she closed her eyes while he held completely still. He watched as she explored the lines of the dragon covering his ribs.

"Do you feel anything?" he asked, already surmising her plan.

Her fingers flexed against his chest where she still pressed her hand, and he resisted the urge to drag her against him. He could still hear the way she'd moaned when he'd fucked her in that alley. Gods, the way she felt coming around him was transcendent.

He'd told her he loved her. Maybe that was foolish, but why did he need to hold anything back? He'd made what he wanted clear; now he belonged to her, body and soul. She hadn't returned the sentiment, but he was sure he wasn't imagining what he'd seen in her expression. Both when they'd been with the mystic and after he'd revealed his heart. She was standing on the precipice, waiting to tip into the promise of everything he wanted to offer her.

"Do *you* feel anything?" she asked, looking up at him, and he shook his head.

"No. It feels like nothing."

"I can sense the vibrations of the molecules," she said. "Just like with the vanshaj collars. There are similarities between this marking and theirs like Thriti said."

"That's good?"

She smiled, and his heart cracked at the sight. It was the only light in his dark. "It's a great thing. I think I can do this."

He wrapped an arm around her waist and tipped her chin up. "I'm proud of you, Zarya."

"Even though you don't entirely agree with what I'm doing?"

"Aren't I here doing everything I can to help you?"

She nodded, but he knew she wasn't convinced. It wasn't that he didn't believe in the purpose of the Rising Phoenix. He did. It's why he'd never employed a vanshaj servant himself, but that was only a small act of defiance unlikely to ruffle feathers. What they were all talking about was so much more. So many people would die before this was over.

"You are, but I want you to do it for the right reasons."

"Which are?"

"Not just following me."

Rabin shook his head. "I'm not. It started out that way, but I understand what you're doing and agree with it. I'm just afraid of you getting hurt in the process."

She pulled away from him and clutched the pendant dangling around her neck. "I can't stop this. You know that. This is my duty, even if it weren't also the right thing to do. I was handed this responsibility, and I have to see it through."

"I know you do," he answered, meaning it.

"So you're with me? This is your destiny now, too. Maybe it always was."

"I already told you I'm with you, no matter what."

She nodded.

"Then we should return to the house," she said. "I have to see if this works."

FORTY

Zarya and Rabin opened the gate to the back of the house to find everything as quiet as usual. She knocked on the door, and it swung open to reveal Ajay, who greeted Zarya before his eyes narrowed at the sight of Rabin standing behind her.

"What's going on?" he asked, taking in Zarya's smile. "Do you have good news?"

She nodded and pushed past him with Rabin on her heels. Ajay closed the door, and Zarya swung around. "I controlled my nightfire. I think I can use it to break the collars."

Ajay's eyes widened. "Are you sure? How?"

"I think so." She went on to explain the process of the Bhandan.

"*He's* your paramadhar?"

"He is, and my magic is completely different now."

Vikas appeared around the corner. "Zarya?" he asked. "You did it?"

He looked thinner, his skin ashen and dark circles ringing his eyes. It was obvious how much the worry about his parents was weighing him down, and she hoped this news would make a difference.

"But I need to try it on a vanshaj collar to be sure."

Vikas spread his hands in a gesture of helplessness. "We're trying, but no one will listen."

She blew out a frustrated huff. "*How* do we convince them we only want to help?"

Her question went unanswered as Yasen barged through the back, his hair flying wild and his chest expanding with shortened breaths. Behind him came Suvanna and Apsara, both bearing grim expressions.

"The palace," he said, panting with his hands on his knees. He was so meticulous about his training that Zarya didn't think she'd ever seen him winded. He must have run very fast.

"What about it?" Vikas demanded, already picking up on the gravity of the situation.

"The prisoners," Suvanna said. "They're about to be executed."

"What?" Zarya said as her blood ran cold. "We have to stop it!"

She wasted no time and went tromping out the door.

"Zarya!" Rabin called, chasing after her. "What are you planning to do?"

"I don't know," she called over her shoulder. "But we have to do something."

She didn't wait to see if anyone followed, but she knew Rabin was right behind her as she wound her way through the streets, her skirt bunched in one hand, running as fast as her legs would carry her.

Eventually, the others caught up as they made their way into the heart of Ishaan. Using the twisting alleyways as a shortcut, it didn't take long before they rounded a corner and came to an abrupt halt.

The palace courtyard was packed full of people, standing elbow to elbow, shouting and screaming, as the entire mass writhed like a snake without a head. She jumped up and down, trying to snatch a glimpse above the crowd.

"I can't see anything," she said to Rabin. "Can you?" He was a giant. Surely that was useful for something. Not waiting for an answer, she charged ahead. Her feet carried her past the wide gates and into the courtyard. Against the wall, she spotted a drainpipe and hoisted herself onto one of the brackets for a better view.

"Zarya, you can't stop this," Rabin said as he held out his hand and helped prop her up a bit higher.

"I know," she said, taking in the incomprehensible sight spreading across her view.

The plaza was a sea of dark hair and colorful scarves, where hundreds of vanshaj stood shoulder to shoulder with the free citizens of Ishaan. Against the wall of the palace stood a raised platform where a dozen shaking men and women waited with slack nooses looped around their necks. She recognized Vikas and Nitin's parents as she wiped away the sweat building on her forehead. This couldn't be happening.

The royal family stood on a high balcony stretching across the palace's front facade, observing the chaos like they were all nothing but scuttling insects to be crushed under their boots. That same conflicted tug she always felt in their presence pulled deep in her chest. Her plans had gone entirely off course when she'd arrived in the city, and the family she'd so desperately wanted to meet now stood as her greatest enemies.

She watched her half-sister Dishani approach the edge of the balcony, placing a delicate hand on the railing as she surveyed the crowd with a detached, imperious tilt to her chin. On her other side stood Miraan, the second oldest and her closest advisor. He stood with his hands behind his back and his spine stiff, his expression completely blank. Kabir, the king consort, came up a moment later and whispered something in Dishani's ear that caused her to nod.

Zarya returned her attention to the prisoners before scanning the plaza.

"Rabin, what should we do?" she asked.

"I'm thinking." His jaw hardened as he looked out across the scene, calculated thoughts flitting over his expression. Yasen, Vikas, and Ajay now stood on her other side.

"Vikas," Zarya said, reaching out a hand. He took it, and she could feel how cold it was. He was shaking from head to toe, and she wondered if they should get him somewhere else and away from all of this.

"Any ideas?" she asked the others as her gaze wandered back to Dishani.

Zarya then noticed Apsara and Suvanna slip onto the balcony before Apsara approached the princess. She could tell by their hand gestures and body language that they were having a heated discussion. Apsara gestured to the prisoners and then swept an arm over the crowd as Dishani shook her head.

Vikas looked at Zarya, having also noticed the confrontation. Zarya held her breath, wondering if Apsara could convince the princess to cease this madness but then Dishani dismissed her with a wave of her hand. Zarya's shoulders sagged as Apsara peered out at the crowd, searching for them. When she found Zarya and the others, Apsara shook her head gently. There would be no stopping this.

The crowd continued pushing and shoving like waves rippling over the sea. The noise was deafening.

Dishani turned to face the plaza and raised a hand. Slowly, her signal filtered through the masses until everyone fell into an almost eerie silence.

Then the princess looked down at the platform and nodded to a group of waiting soldiers as she lowered her hand.

It snapped a spell she'd cast over the plaza as everyone began shouting and screaming even louder. The prisoners were shaking and crying, a few collapsing to their knees, inadvertently pulling their nooses tighter.

Zarya stopped thinking as the world around her dimmed to white noise, and her surroundings ground into slow motion. She leaped off her perch and dove into the crowd, shouting as she elbowed bodies out of her way. She heard Yasen and Rabin calling after her, but she ignored them. She had no idea what she was planning to do, but she had to do *something*.

"Zee!"

"Zarya, stop!"

She halted and spun around, glaring at Rabin and Yasen. "Just fucking help me!"

Rabin's eyes flashed before he pushed past her, pressing through the crowd using his much larger frame to clear a path while Zarya and Yasen followed closely behind.

But this was taking too long. They'd barely covered any distance and wouldn't reach the prisoners in time. What they needed was a distraction.

With the crowd jostling her from every side, she scanned the clear sky. Knowing this was beyond reckless, she lifted a hand and blasted out a stream of nightfire, striking the palace right above where the royal family sat.

She winced as the wall exploded to the sound of panic as the crowd's energy swelled, ballooning to dangerous proportions. It felt like the very atmosphere was on the verge of collapse. Rabin turned to look over his shoulder with a *what the fuck did you just do* expression on his face.

"Move! Now's our chance!"

Wasting no time, she flattened her hands on his back and *pushed*, using him like a battering ram. He resisted for only a second before they continued shoving through the crowd.

"Almost there!" she shouted as Rabin continued to bulldoze his way through the panicking throngs. She chanced a glance up at the royal family, wondering if she'd hurt anyone. She'd been careful to ensure it was only a *small* explosion. She didn't want to hurt Apsara or Suvanna, after all. They were covered in dust and were brushing themselves off but appeared no worse for wear.

With one eye on the royals, Zarya continued fighting her way to the front. She watched as Dishani recovered from her shock, one hand gripping the railing as she cast a suspicious gaze over the plaza, seeking out the culprit.

Zarya ducked her head, hoping her half-sister wouldn't notice them fighting their way to the prisoners.

Then Dishani turned and started shouting orders, her hands flying.

"Faster!" Zarya screamed before they finally burst through the edge of the crowd, coming to a stop in front of the platform so abruptly that she almost tripped. The guards slowly turned their heads.

For a split second, they all stared at one another.

Making use of their surprise, she grunted as she dashed up the platform, yanking the noose off the first prisoner.

"Zarya!" Rabin roared as she continued to the next, uncomfortably aware of how stupid this was. She couldn't save them like this.

Guards stormed up each end of the platform a moment later, closing in on both sides. She held out her hand over her head. "Stay back or I'll bring down this entire palace."

Again, she'd caught them off guard, but all it took was a second before they started laughing. Gritting her teeth, she fired out another blast, aiming for a high tower. It exploded in a spectacular shower of stone and marble. That set off another wave of panic as the crowd pulsed, the noise reaching a thunderous crescendo before it surged dangerously close to where Zarya stood.

The royal family was watching her now, a mixture of confusion and surprise on their faces. Yasen and Rabin valiantly battled dozens of soldiers as a gate opened at the side of the palace. Another stream of guards came pouring out, surrounding them on all sides. They were officially and woefully outnumbered.

Zarya, Yasen, and Rabin were seized, their arms wrenched behind their backs before they were all cuffed in iron. Zarya felt the tears of frustration pressing the back of her eyes as she was forced to her knees. She breathed in and out as a wave of sorrow threatened to consume her. She shouldn't have just run out here. She hadn't saved anyone, and now, they were trapped.

"Show me her face," came a deep voice, and then a rough hand gripped her hair, yanking her head up with enough force to make her gasp.

She came face to face with Miraan, her older half-brother.

He cocked a head as he raked her up and down, and Zarya couldn't understand what she read in the shadows of his dark eyes.

He stepped towards her before slowly sinking on his haunches as he studied her face. His cheeks went pale, and his eyes widened with the barest hint of surprise.

Then he reached out a hand. Zarya jerked, trying to move away, but he held it up in a gesture that implied he meant no harm. She blinked as Miraan touched the turquoise stone Zarya always wore around her neck, exhaling a soft, strangled breath.

"Mother," he whispered.

FORTY-ONE

Zarya, Rabin, and Yasen were hauled into the palace and forced to kneel on a hard marble floor in the center of a large circular room. Her vision blurred, making it difficult to focus on the colorful tiled mosaic of swirling patterns.

The room was bordered by rounded niches set with life-sized statues of stuffy-looking people in opulent clothing. The ceiling curved in a dome overhead, painted in gold. There was no other furniture or ornamentation, only a circle of queens-guards in their crisp white sherwanis standing at various points around the perimeter.

The sounds of chaos seeped through the windows as an angry tear slipped from the corner of her eye and down her cheek.

The pained look on Miraan's face had been unmistakable. After all these months of carefully avoiding the Madans and their attention, she'd flung herself right into their path and hadn't saved a single person in the process. How could she ever live with the fact she'd let Vikas and his family down so spectacularly?

In the silence of the room, Miraan watched them with a

severe expression. Her half-brother. He was even more handsome up close, with long dark lashes, a strong jaw covered with a trimmed beard, and a straight nose. With that confident posture, he was dashing in a navy sherwani and pants expertly tailored to his slender frame.

She dropped her head, unable to face the enormity of what she'd done. She tried to call on her magic, but it was dulled to almost nothing. An effect of the enchanted blue stone that surrounded them. Even if she could touch it, Miraan would stop her. He was powerful and had more experience. She'd been able to destroy the palace exterior, but that was only because she could still access her anchors while standing in the courtyard.

Sharp footsteps sounded from behind where they knelt. From the corner of her eye, Zarya watched someone circle around them.

"What is your name?" asked a crisp voice, and Zarya peered up, looking over at Rabin and Yasen before directing her gaze to the speaker.

Zarya's half-sister Dishani looked down at her, her arms folded over her chest. She wore a bright green sari decorated with silver beading, and her long hair was pulled into a thick braid, woven with pearls, that hung over her shoulder. Silver jhumka dangled from her ears, and more silver jewelry covered her throat and wrists. She dripped with authority and self-assurance.

"Me?" Zarya asked.

"Yes," Dishani answered with the slightest flare of her nose.

Zarya understood they were in a delicate position, but nothing good would come of the Madans knowing too much about them. "Uh. Why?"

The princess arched a dark eyebrow, her gaze simmering with bottomless anger. "You will do as I command."

Zarya hesitated. It wasn't like her name would mean

anything, but they all believed the prophecy, and it seemed imperative to hold on to any information she could. Dishani approached on sharp steps, her heels echoing around the room.

She grabbed Zarya's chin and wrenched her head up. Too surprised to move, Zarya grunted as her half-sister squeezed, her sharp nails digging into her skin.

"Do *not* touch her," Rabin snarled, but Dishani didn't so much as blink at the menace in his tone. Four guards immediately peeled themselves from the wall and surrounded him, their spears pointed at his chest.

"Who *are* you?" Dishani asked Zarya, clearly not interested in or intimidated by Rabin. "Why are you the spitting image of our mother, and why have you stolen her necklace?"

Zarya inhaled a deep breath, understanding she had no choice.

"I didn't steal anything. I'm... your half-sister."

Dishani glared at Zarya, her grip tightening.

"Was that you destroying our palace?" she asked.

"Maybe?"

Something dark flickered across Dishani's expression, her grip pinching to the point of pain. Zarya tried to jerk her head out of her sister's hold, but Dishani only held on tighter.

"Let go of me," she snapped.

"Why did you interrupt the execution?" she asked, ignoring Zarya's demand. "Are you with the resistance?"

Her jaw hardened and she pulled again, finally wrenching herself from Dishani's grasp. She worked her sore mouth, wishing she had use of her hands.

"Because you are monsters," she said, her voice dropping to a low growl. "Vile, horrible, heartless monsters."

A moment later, she also found herself with four silver spears aimed at her heart.

Dishani's expression remained cold, clearly unfazed by the

accusation. Instead, she asked, "What manner of magic was that?"

Zarya glared, willing steel into her posture. "Perhaps if you removed these cuffs, we could attempt a civilized discussion."

"You refuse to answer my questions?" The princess tipped her head, assessing Zarya with a sweep. When Zarya continued to glare, she added, "Throw them in the dungeons. We'll see if that loosens their tongues."

"Dishani," Miraan said. "Should we not treat her with a little more dignity? If she's who she claims—"

"She's a liar," Dishani answered with a dismissive wave of her hand.

"She has Mother's necklace."

"Anyone could have made a replica."

"*Look* at her."

Dishani pressed her mouth together, her gaze sliding to Zarya.

"You just saw what she *did*. You know what she is," he said.

Once again, the princess peered at Zarya, and she read so many things in the iron chill of her flat expression. The certainty she was now walking the thinnest of lines, balancing on a thread ready to snap. She'd attempted a futile rescue and, in the process, had permanently tipped the scales into something wild and unpredictable.

"Yes," Dishani said a moment later. "I saw *exactly* what she did."

* * *

Rabin didn't bother fighting as they were hauled to their feet and dragged through the palace. Once they were in the dungeon, they could devise an escape. He'd seen the way the princess had looked at Zarya—like she wanted to cut out her heart with a dull, rusty knife—and they had to get out of here and as far away from Gi'ana as possible.

The trouble would be convincing Zarya of that.

Rabin walked with his shoulders straight and his hands behind his back down a red-tiled hallway with red-painted walls hung with portraits in thick golden frames. It took several minutes before they approached a wide stone archway flanked by armed soldiers.

Zarya walked ahead of him, a guard on either side, while Yasen marched at the back. He wished he could reach out to her. It was hard to believe it had only been a few hours since they'd gone to see Thriti and bound themselves to one another.

They were tossed into a cell, and Rabin immediately felt the rest of his already muted magic drain away. After the door slammed with a clank, three guards took up their position at the end of the hall, keeping watch. It wasn't ideal, but at least they might converse without being overheard.

"What happened?" Zarya asked, flexing her fingers. "My magic was dulled before, but now it's gone."

"Enchanted bars," Rabin said, placing a finger on the metal and watching as it shimmered faintly at his touch. "An added precaution."

"Oh," Zarya said, and he watched as the realization of their situation dawned on her. He wanted to strangle her for throwing herself into danger like that.

"Zee, what the fuck were you thinking?" Yasen asked, echoing Rabin's thoughts as he peered at the tiny window at the top of the wall. He leaped up, grabbed the bars, and hoisted himself up to peer out.

"I was trying to save their lives." There was a touch of petulance in her voice.

"Yeah," he said, dropping back to the floor. "Great plan. This is exactly what we needed."

She glared before her shoulders dropped and she rubbed her hands down her face. "Fine. It wasn't my best moment."

Yasen snorted and sank to the floor, letting his head smack against the wall.

"We have to get out of Gi'ana now," Rabin said.

Zarya frowned. "I'm not going anywhere. We just found out how to"—she peered at the guards stationed down the hall and lowered her voice—"you know. Do the thing with the thing." She stroked a line across her throat with her finger.

"Zarya, did you not see the look on your sister's face?"

"Sure, she's angry," Zarya said. "But maybe we can talk things out."

Rabin shook his head. "There will be no talking things out. She wants you dead."

Zarya looked so taken aback he wanted to hug her and shake her at the same time. "Why would she want that?"

He grabbed her by the arm and dragged her into the farthest corner of their cell, joining Yasen, and spoke in a low voice so only they could hear.

"This prophecy has ruled this family for two centuries. They spent their lives existing in the shadow of a child that was never born."

"Right..." Zarya said.

"Except she *was* born, and now she's shown up to blow apart all of their lives."

"I don't want anything from them," she protested, and Rabin shook his head.

"It doesn't matter. Dishani is ambitious. Her coronation is finally around the corner. She is this close to getting the crown she's coveted her entire life, and now you're here to take it all away."

She stared up at him while he waited for his message to sink in.

"The queens of Gi'ana have always been chosen by who is

most powerful," he added, hoping that would help her grasp the precariousness of her situation.

She slowly nodded. "And I have nightfire. And she knows exactly what she saw out there."

"Yes. And it means *you* are the most powerful."

"So, she thinks I want her crown, and nothing will convince her that isn't true."

She looked to Yasen for confirmation.

"She did seem to take a particularly strong dislike to you," he said. "But that's sort of normal when people first meet you."

"Row explained all of this," Rabin said gently, knowing her well enough to understand she'd tried to shove it down, refusing to believe it could be true.

She sighed and bit her bottom lip, obviously trying not to cry.

"I thought he was exaggerating. I thought..." She ran a hand down her face. "Gods, I'm so stupid."

"You are not," Rabin replied, placing a finger under her chin. "You are brave and selfless, and you were trying to do the noble thing."

"Sometimes a little stupid," Yasen said, holding his fingers close together. "But your heart's in the right place."

She huffed out a laugh through her tears. "I don't want her crown. That's the last thing I want."

Rabin tucked a lock of hair behind her ear. "I know, but she won't believe that."

Her gaze met his, determination entering her expression. "So we have to get out of here."

"That's what I'm saying." Then for good measure, he added, "And probably kill her."

Zarya sighed loudly and massaged the bridge of her nose.

"Perfect. Just... fucking perfect."

FORTY-TWO

The trouble was there appeared to be no way out of this damn cell. The walls were thick stone, the bars made of enchanted iron. Several days passed with no signs of Dishani, Miraan, or anyone from the royal family. And the longer they waited, the more Zarya's nerves knotted with apprehension. She knew it couldn't be because the princess had forgotten about them.

She had to be planning something.

Their only visitors were the occasional guards who dropped off what was probably food, but tasted more like shredded paper boiled in gutter water.

Their only point of normalcy was the tiny window, which at least gave them a sense of time and the passing days.

As they waited, she couldn't stop thinking about the prisoners she'd failed to save in her foolishness. Logically, she knew there was nothing she could have really done to stop the execution, but she was still furious with herself. If she ever saw Vikas again, she'd beg his forgiveness and do whatever she could to make it up to him.

The sun had set hours ago, and they sat in a line against the wall with Zarya in the middle. Somehow, Yasen had fallen asleep upright with his head tipped back and his jaw open. Idly she wondered how he'd react if she dropped one of the many mice living down here into his mouth. He'd probably lose his mind and curse her until the end of time. The thought nearly made her smile.

Rabin on the other hand, couldn't seem to sit still. He was like a caged animal, his gaze darting around their cell and his leg bouncing impatiently. He'd pounded the walls, rattled the bars, and even tried to smash the window to no avail. Not that any of them would have fit through it, anyway.

Zarya sat with her knees up, her skirt draped over her legs, and her arms wrapped around her stomach. She felt disgusting, wearing these clothes for days on end, sleeping on this filthy ground. A bucket sat in the corner covered with a board that did little to suppress the scent of its contents. It was hard not to feel like the very essence of this place wasn't burrowing into her skin.

Her stomach groaned, and she massaged it, dreaming of piles of fluffy naan, creamy bowls of chicken tikka, and crispy fried pakora. She watched Rabin in the dim light, noting the fluttering reflection of his clenching and unclenching jaw.

Feeling her gaze, he looked over.

"You okay?" he asked.

She shrugged and dropped her head back before rubbing her forehead.

"I'll get us out of here soon, Spitfire," he said with a whispered promise. If they remained here much longer, she was sure he'd tear this palace apart brick by brick if he had to.

"I know," she answered with a soft smile that seemed to ease some of the tension from his frame.

He sat back, and finally, his limbs settled as his shoulder pressed against hers. She peered up at him, noting the crescent of moonlight reflecting in his eyes. A few days ago, he'd told her he loved her. Despite her reckless and impulsive behavior, he'd rushed in to help her. She'd never had someone just *believe* in her before.

Rubbing her shoulder and her new dragon tattoo, she imagined she could feel the tether binding them like delicate silk ribbons.

"Having second thoughts?" he asked.

"No," she said, shaking her head. "Not at all."

It was the truth. She'd had reservations, but the moment Thriti completed the Bandhan, she knew she'd made the right call. She'd been stumbling through fog for months, but now it had lifted with the certainty of this choice.

He blinked and then dipped his chin, his face nearly expressionless except for the slight brightening of the golden flecks in his eyes. He leaned down and she stretched up to meet his kiss. Their lips pressed softly together before the sound of steady, rapid footsteps drew their attention to the dark corridor outside their cell.

Zarya sat up as they exchanged wary looks. No one had ever come down to see them this late. Rabin crossed an arm over her body as they approached while shadows bounced against the walls, indicating someone was carrying a source of light.

Three figures emerged from the dark a moment later and Zarya had no idea what to make of them. Apsara and Suvanna stood on the other side of their bars, flanking the prince, Miraan, though he was no longer dressed in opulence, having traded his elegant attire for a simple black kurta and pants.

"What do you want?" Zarya asked.

"We're getting you out," Miraan answered, and she blinked. That was the last thing she expected. "Your friends have explained who you are and what you've been doing."

Her gaze bounced between Apsara and Suvanna and then back to Miraan. He was devoid of apparent emotion, his expression belying nothing. "And?"

"There will be time to explain later," Apsara said. "Do you trust us?"

"I trust *you*," Zarya replied as she eyed Miraan. He was Dishani's loyal advisor. Her enforcer. Why was he betraying her?

"Then we're asking you to trust this situation," Apsara said. "We only want to help."

Zarya turned to Rabin, who peered up at their supposed rescue team through a lowered brow.

She elbowed Yasen awake. He snorted as his head snapped up.

"What the—" His protests cut off when he realized they had visitors. "Oh. Hi?"

"They're getting us out of here," Zarya said. "Apparently."

Yasen yawned and ran a hand through his silver hair. "Well, that's very nice of them. Why?"

"They haven't shared that yet."

Yasen narrowed his eyes, already alert despite his nap.

"Come on," Apsara ordered. "We'll explain everything once we're safe."

"What about him?" Yasen asked, pointing to Miraan. "Isn't he the bad guy?"

Miraan glowered at Yasen, who lifted his hands in surrender. "Hey, you're the one who threw us in here."

"*I* did not," Miraan bit out as though the accusation deeply offended him.

"Whatever you say," Yasen grumbled as he heaved himself up.

"Please come," Apsara said. "I understand how this looks, but Miraan is on our side, and we will explain everything once we see you to safety."

Zarya shook her head. "He is?"

She also pushed herself up as Rabin did the same.

"What do you think?" Zarya asked Rabin. "You're the one with the instincts."

"I'm not sure," he answered, assessing Miraan from head to toe. "Seems plausible, and it's definitely better than rotting in this shithole any longer."

"Okay then," Zarya said, clapping her hands. "I guess we're letting you help us escape."

"Oh, thank you so much," Apsara said. "We're very grateful."

Miraan produced a key and opened the door before Apsara turned and waved for them to follow. Zarya went first, eyeing her brother as she passed, followed by Yasen and Rabin. Suvanna and the prince brought up the rear.

"Left," Miraan called to Apsara as they skulked through the dungeons and came upon a branching tunnel. Miraan used a ball of light to illuminate the shadows, and everyone held silent as they wound through a maze of dark pathways with the hush of his soft commands guiding their way.

As they walked for what felt like ages, Zarya had time to wonder what on earth was happening. She kept checking over her shoulder, catching glimpses of the prince. Why was he helping them, and how did Apsara and Suvanna get involved with him? Zarya traded a look with Yasen, and he must have read the questions on her face because he shrugged and shook his head.

Sure, the prince could have been leading them into some kind of trap, but what would be the point when they already had them locked up?

Zarya heard a rush of water in the distance as they continued snaking through the bowels of the castle.

"We're almost there," came Miraan's whisper through the dark. "Just past that corner."

They twisted around another bend, and sure enough, Zarya caught a distant sliver of moonlight through a narrow opening.

They emerged into a dense forest, and Zarya scanned her surroundings, reasoning they must be somewhere on the outskirts of Ishaan.

Six horses stood tethered to some nearby trees.

"You guys really planned this out," Yasen said, his tone filled with confusion.

"If my sister learns of my deception, there will be no escaping her wrath," Miraan answered. Again, his expression remained neutral, but Zarya thought she caught a tremble of fear in his voice.

"Yeah. She seemed friendly. You must be very close."

Miraan stared at Yasen for a beat before he shook his head. "Gods. You have no idea."

Yasen grinned before they made their way to the horses.

"Where are we going?" Zarya asked Apsara.

"Back to the city."

"Didn't we just break out of there?"

"Yes, but Operation Starbreak needs you, and we're entering through another route."

"We're not taking *him* there?" she said, pointing to Miraan. "You *told* him about the manor?"

"Zarya, please," Apsara said. "We shouldn't discuss this here. I swear to you he can be trusted."

Zarya gave her half-brother another skeptical look before she offered a curt, "Fine. But if you're wrong, then it's on your heads."

They made a wide loop around Ishaan, arriving on the far side of the palace. They'd have to navigate the network of back alleys to reach their hideout. When Miraan gave the signal, they hopped off their horses, concealing them in a thick patch of bushes.

"What will happen to them?" Zarya asked.

"Someone will retrieve them in the morning," Miraan said.

She still didn't understand what was happening but was

relieved to be free of that dungeon. It didn't *seem* like they were being led into a trap, but she kept a close eye on Miraan regardless. After exchanging a look with Rabin, he nodded. She couldn't hear him—the paramadhar mind connection required deeper concentration than she could manage right now—but somehow, she knew exactly what he was thinking.

Be on your guard. Be ready to run. What the fuck is going on?

Miraan then led them to a gate hidden by a tangle of vines and leaves. He used a tendril of fire magic inside the keyhole. It flared brightly for a moment before the gate swung open on silent hinges. Zarya would have to ask him about that trick later. Provided she didn't have to kill him first.

He pulled up his hood as they entered the city, quickly making their way down quiet paths. It didn't take long before she spied the familiar fence surrounding the manor house.

A light burned in the kitchen as they approached. Zarya knocked in their secret pattern, hoping someone was awake. When no one came, she tried again, louder this time. It took another minute before the door popped open to a sleepy-eyed Vikas.

"What's..." He shook his head. "Zarya? Yasen? You're here!"

He gestured towards them. "Come in. Come in. We thought you were goners."

"Well, thank you for your faith in us," Yasen said. "We were perfectly fine."

Zarya rushed up and threw her arms around Vikas. "I'm so sorry."

He pulled away. "For what?"

"I tried to help them, but..." Tears filled her eyes as she clung to his shirt.

For a moment he gave her a confused look. "No, Zarya—you *did* stop it. They called off the execution. They're still in the palace, but we have every reason to think they're still alive."

"Really?" she asked, hardly daring to believe it.

"Really. I owe you my thank you."

She exhaled a long breath. "You owe me nothing. I'm so relieved."

They hugged again before Vikas called up the stairs.

"Ajay! They're here!"

Thumps came from above, and a moment later, Ajay descended, looking rumpled and dragged from sleep. A moment later, Row also followed him down.

"What are you doing here?" Ajay asked. "We've been trying to find out what happened to you." He strode over and threw his arms around Zarya, wrapping her in a tight hug.

"We're okay," she said. "At least we are now."

Ajay pulled away and then hugged Yasen, who tolerated it for only a second.

"Get off me," he said, and Ajay smiled.

"I missed you, too."

Row embraced Zarya tightly, then shook hands with Apsara and Suvanna.

Everyone had yet to notice the last person hovering at the edges.

It was then Ajay and Vikas fell silent, peering at the hooded stranger.

"Who's that?" Vikas asked.

That was when Miraan stepped forward and pulled off his hood.

"You might call me an interested party."

FORTY-THREE

"Your Highness," Ajay said, immediately dropping his head and bowing as Vikas did the same. Ajay's worried glance darted to Zarya and she understood his fear. She still wasn't sure why they'd revealed their secret, illegal operation to the prince, either. "What are you doing here?"

Miraan returned their bows with his hands pressed to his heart. "That is a long story."

They all stared at him, waiting for him to continue. He cleared his throat, perhaps feeling a touch awkward under their intense scrutiny.

"Is there somewhere we could sit?" he asked, looking around the hall.

"I'm sorry. Where are my manners?" Ajay asked, stirring out of his shock. "Can we get you something to drink or eat, Your Highness?"

"Sure, we're starving," Yasen said. "We've barely eaten in days."

"I wasn't talking to you," Ajay said, and Yasen's expression turned into a mock pout.

"No, please," Miraan said. "Get them all something to eat. I sincerely apologize for the way you were treated in my home."

"Why don't we gather in the kitchen?" Ajay asked. "If it's not too simple for you? There's plenty of room for everyone, and we can talk."

"Good," Yasen said, not waiting for the prince's response as he strode ahead and began raiding the cupboards for anything he could get his hands on.

They all filed into the kitchen and took stools around the large island before he dumped a mound of food in the center. Zarya reached for a plate and started piling it high. She was filthy and could definitely have used a bath, but she was too curious and hungry to care right now.

"Please tell us what this is all about?" Row asked a moment later. "Does your family understand what you're doing? You're sure it's safe to be here?"

Miraan stared around the room for a long time before blinking and then turning to face Zarya. "May I ask you some questions first?"

She nodded. "I suppose, but I don't get what you're doing here or why we should be trusting you."

Miraan pressed a hand to his heart. "I would like to tell you everything."

Zarya sat up and nodded. "Okay. Then ask."

"Who are you? Are you truly our sister?"

Zarya reached for her glass and took a sip of her water. Her throat had suddenly gone very dry. Everyone waited quietly for her to set it back down. "I am. Well, your half-sister."

She looked at Row, and he dipped his chin, silently giving her permission to share the story about her upbringing, including his role.

"Your mother had a lover," she said, wincing at the words, hoping they didn't sting.

But Miraan showed no surprise. "Yes. Many, I believe. It is

not a secret that she never loved our father, and theirs was only a marriage of convenience."

"Did you know who any of them were?"

"Some," Miraan answered. "She wasn't always discreet about her affairs. Hers was a wild heart that belied taming. She and our father had an agreement. Neither one minded who they took to their beds. They were good friends, and they respected one another but never had romantic feelings."

Zarya scratched the side of her nose, wondering how to phrase this. "Were any of them... important people?"

Miraan shook his head. "I'm not sure what you mean."

"Like a king, perhaps?"

He blinked and it was the most outward display of emotion she'd seen from him yet. "A king?"

Zarya looked to Row again for guidance and strength. Some assurance. He nodded and laid a hand over hers.

"Tell him," he said softly. "He already knows you exist. The rest must now be revealed." She didn't miss the dark look Row shot at Rabin with those words.

"What king?" Miraan asked.

"Abishek," Zarya said.

The prince exhaled a sharp breath before his expression cleared. "Abishek," he repeated. "Yes. I remember him coming to Gi'ana frequently before she disappeared. But they weren't lovers as far as I'm aware." His gaze once again found Zarya. "How old are you?"

"I'm twenty," she answered as she watched him put the pieces together.

"Abishek is your father?"

She shrugged. "Apparently."

Miraan's eyebrows dipped slightly. It was the barest reaction, but she sensed this was his taciturn way of showing surprise. "But I've never heard of a child? Did you grow up in Andhera?"

She shook her head and once again sought Row's calming strength. "No. I grew up with the man who your mother loved." She gestured towards Row, and Miraan shook his head, obviously confused.

She then told him everything their mother had believed, including how she'd come to Gi'ana to meet her family.

When she was done, Miraan watched her with a penetrating look.

"And when you arrived, you discovered we are all monsters," he said, his voice still devoid of emotion.

She gave him a rueful smile. "Well, you didn't seem all that approachable."

He pressed his mouth together before he continued. "And so you joined the Rising Phoenix."

They all stiffened at those words. Suvanna and Apsara had assured them it would be okay to bring Miraan here, but what if they'd revealed everything to one of the only people who had the power to crush them?

Everyone around the table exchanged wary glances, Rabin's fists curling on the counter, his body vibrating like he was ready to pounce.

"Please," Miraan said. "I will not turn you in. I..."

"It's you. *You're* our mysterious benefactor," Ajay breathed a moment later, and Miraan swallowed as every eye turned to him. "Why didn't I see it? Who else would have those kinds of resources?"

Miraan paused and then dipped his chin. "When I first heard about the Rising Phoenix, I wished to be involved but could not come out publicly for obvious reasons. Other than getting her crown, my sister's ambitions include stamping out all forms of vanshaj support. She lives in terror of an uprising."

"You could try standing up to her," Yasen drawled as Miraan shot him a dark look.

"It is not that simple," he answered. "There would be little point. She would also toss me into a dungeon, and then I would be of no use to anyone. She trusts me and shares everything. I have used that to my advantage, impeding her actions without drawing attention to myself. When I learned of the resistance, I orchestrated a means to fund the cause." He looked around the room and towards the hallway. "And I am very pleased to see what that money has been able to do."

"All this time, a *royal* was helping us?" Vikas added, shaking with disbelief. He had more reasons to despise this prince than anyone in this room. "You have my family."

Miraan's stoic facade finally cracked as he rubbed a hand down his face and through his dark hair. "I'm so incredibly sorry. I've spent the last several months trying to stop the raids and delaying the execution for as long as humanly possible. And I won't stop now. I will do everything I can to get them out unharmed."

Vikas didn't reply, only nodded slightly.

"How did you find us?" Ajay asked.

"I have many resources to draw upon. More people support your cause than you understand and many are doing what they can to push back against Dishani in subtle ways."

"So subtle we can't see them?" Ajay asked with an arched brow.

Miraan tipped his head. "You are right. They could and should do more, but they also helped me find you, the people who *are* making a true difference."

He turned to address Zarya, Yasen, and Rabin. "Dishani had been hoping to draw out the resistance, but then we all saw Zarya and couldn't believe our eyes. You look so much like her, and we saw your magic, and then there was the necklace..." He shook his head. "How long have you known who you are?"

"I only found out a few months ago," Zarya said.

"What a difficult upbringing you must have had."

She smiled and cocked her head. "Sometimes I thought so,

but I was very well cared for in the end." She slid a glance to Row, who gave her a pleased smile.

"So, how did you all figure this out?" Yasen asked, gesturing to Suvanna and Apsara.

"We didn't realize Miraan was supportive of the resistance until the day of the execution," Apsara said. "He noticed Zarya and I exchange looks across the square and put it all together. Then he approached us."

"And you didn't think to tell us this?" Ajay asked. "They were captured days ago."

Apsara gestured to the prince with a wave of her hand. "He pleaded for us to keep his secret. At least for now."

"Why?"

Miraan answered. "The fewer people who know my role, the better. But when Apsara revealed what you've been doing and the progress you've made, I knew I had to get you out and see it for myself. Please tell me more about Operation Starbreak."

"You know about the collars?" Zarya asked as she noticed Vikas shift uncomfortably in his seat. Miraan might claim to be on their side, but she understood that Vikas would need more time and more proof to trust that claim.

"I do. Your nightfire." He stopped. "I can't believe the prophecy finally came true."

She held up her hands in a gesture of helplessness. "Yeah."

He pinned her with a serious look. "My sister wants you dead. I know of no other way to say this other than to be forthright. Her plan is to do away with you before the coronation so that no one can contest her position. You are a threat to her very essence. Remaining in Gi'ana may not be the best course of action."

Her gaze slid to Rabin. Miraan was confirming all the same things he'd told her. Things she hadn't wanted to believe.

"You are now a competitor for her crown, and she is merciless and ruthless," Miraan added.

"And you?" Zarya asked. "You're betraying her right now."

"I am," he answered simply.

"I don't want her crown."

Miraan shook his head. "It does not matter. Not only will she never believe that, if you are proven the strongest female heir, it is yours by right. Nothing can change that."

"So now what?" Yasen asked. "You're here? What are you planning to do?"

Miraan's gaze then fell on Vikas, who squirmed under his stare. "You are... were vanshaj?"

Though he seemed terrified to be addressed by the prince, he rallied his courage. "Yes, Your Highness. Zarya freed me."

"And you have magic?"

He nodded. "I do."

"Including the sixth anchor?"

Vikas's face turned pale before he croaked out, "Yes, Your Highness."

"And it is needed to break the collars?" he asked, now addressing Zarya.

"It's one way," she answered. "Along with my nightfire."

"And you two are the only ones?" he asked, looking between Zarya and Vikas.

"So far, yes," she said with a nod.

Miraan rolled his neck as if he was about to reveal something heavy. "Well, now you have one more," he said. "This secret has shaped the course of my entire life, always hanging over me. I have the sixth anchor, and if you will show me the way, I will do everything I can to help you."

Zarya's brows furrowed. Today certainly hadn't ended the way she'd expected.

"What are your plans?" Miraan asked after a moment. "In

the grand scheme, what do you hope to accomplish with all of this?"

"We want to see the vanshaj freed," Ajay said.

"But how? You break the collars, and then what?"

Zarya had been thinking about the question ever since Rabin had brought it up.

"Revolution," Rabin said, filling the silence with his deep voice. "I already told you, free as many as you can, and that's how we can make a difference."

"And then what?" Miraan asked.

"And then we storm the palace," Rabin said, his gaze sliding to the prince as if gauging his reaction. "We take back what was stolen from a people who never deserved their chains and demand reform. There are far more of us than there are of you."

Ajay shook his head. "How do we do that? These are simple people, not soldiers."

Rabin placed a fist on the counter. "With enough numbers, anything is possible."

"You really think that would work?" Zarya asked.

"We'd have Daragaab's number-one army commander on our side," Yasen said slowly. "If anyone could do this..."

"Daragaab?" Miraan asked as he blinked and scanned Rabin up and down with a piqued sense of interest. "Commander *Ravana*?"

He nodded with a sharp jerk of his chin.

"The same Commander Ravana who decimated Gi'ana so many times. Who stole our library? Who brought our army to its knees during the Khetara Wars?"

Rabin's answering smile was cold and vicious, spreading slowly across his face. "One and the same... Your Highness."

Miraan exhaled a puff of air and then looked around the room.

"Yes," he said. "Then maybe there is a chance we could win this."

FORTY-FOUR

Everyone continued talking well into the night before retiring to their sleeping quarters, agreeing to meet in the morning to continue discussing their plan. Row returned to the flat to check on Koura and see how he was faring with Farida, while Apsara and Suvanna returned to the palace, lest they arouse any suspicion with their absence when it was discovered that Zarya and the others had gone missing.

Miraan insisted no one would suspect him, nor would they miss him for a few nights. It wasn't uncommon for the prince to take off for days or sometimes weeks to attend to clandestine royal matters. He sent a note to his staff, letting them know he'd departed on such a journey and would return when he was through.

They set him up in one of the manor's empty bedrooms, and Ajay, Yasen, and Vikas all retired to their usual beds. Zarya and Rabin were the last ones up. She stood on the bottom step with her arm on the railing when he came up behind her.

Brushing her hair to the side, he whispered in her ear, "Would you like me to sleep somewhere else?"

She looked up at him and then shook her head. "No. I want you with me."

And that was it. He swept her up in his arms and carried her up the stairs as she directed him to her room. Still filthy from their nights in the dungeon, they spent a generous amount of time "cleaning up" in the shower and then fell into bed, exhausted and wrapped in one another's arms.

While her eyelids grew heavy just before she drifted into sleep, she couldn't help but think how right it felt to be here in this bed, cocooned in his warm skin and his comforting scent.

After getting some rest, they met again in the kitchen to discuss the problems and pitfalls plaguing every level of their plan.

"How do we convince the vanshaj to come?" Ajay asked Vikas, who sat across from him at the kitchen island. Ajay had woken early and picked up breakfast while Yasen made tea and coffee.

"I'm out of ideas," Vikas answered. "My friends and I have explained what Zarya did. We've shown them the collar is gone. We've shown them some of us have magic." He shook his head. "They're too scared. Magic caged them. Why should they trust it to free them?"

"We need to find a way to prove ourselves," Zarya said. "How do we mount a revolution without soldiers?"

Everyone fell into silence as they stirred spoons in their mugs and chewed quietly, lost in their thoughts.

When a soft knock at the back door broke through the quiet, everyone sat up. That wasn't their secret knock, and their gazes met with worried looks.

"I'll go see who it is," Vikas said, sliding off his chair and disappearing around the corner. Zarya also followed, tiptoeing behind him as if that might shield any of them from royal soldiers standing on the other side of the door.

Surely they wouldn't knock, though?

Vikas bent down to check the peephole while Zarya clutched the wall, holding her breath. He made a noise of delighted surprise and flung the door open.

On the other side stood two young vanshaj women, both looking extremely uncertain.

"Mina! Kajal! Come in," he bellowed, taking each of them by the arm and closing the door behind them.

He herded them down the hallway to where Zarya stood. When she stepped aside, they eyed her warily, and Vikas directed them into the kitchen.

Perhaps that wasn't the best move because as soon as one of them recognized the prince, she screeched and stumbled back, bumping into Vikas.

"Mina, it's okay," he said. "He's on our side. Please, I promise you are perfectly safe here." Vikas smiled at her, and after a moment, she slowly nodded.

"Okay," she whispered before Vikas turned to everyone.

"These are two of my best friends. This is Mina, and this is Kajal."

"We're so glad you're here," Zarya said, pressing a hand to her chest. "Have you come to remove your collars?"

Mina nodded. "I think so."

Zarya slowly approached. "I understand why you're nervous, but I promise we only want to help."

"We saw you trying to save them in the square," Kajal said. "My sister is also in the dungeons. It's why we've come."

The two women's expressions remained guarded, but at least they weren't running away.

"Maybe we should take them to the salon?" Zarya asked Vikas.

"Right," he answered. "Come this way."

When they didn't move, he grabbed each of them by the

wrists and towed them down the hall, keeping up a stream of encouraging chatter.

This was a chance to try her nightfire, but she would have to explain the risks first.

She spun around to address everyone left sitting in the kitchen. "Miraan, you come and see how it's done," she ordered. "Rabin, I need you, and the rest of you stay here. I don't want to overwhelm them."

Rabin's expression was smug as he lifted off the stool and passed her by, but not before saying, "I need you, too, Spitfire," in a low voice that did indecent things to her insides. She shook her head.

The three of them joined Vikas and his friends in the salon. Zarya sat down and explained everything, including her fears and what might happen, and then asked if they were comfortable with proceeding.

After some consideration, Kajal nodded. "It's all true? You can break it?"

"I can. We all can." She gestured between Vikas and Miraan.

"But he is a prince," Mina whispered. "He's the reason we're in this place." Her gaze flicked to Miraan as if fearing his ire, but the prince only dropped to a knee, one arm propped on his thigh.

"You are absolutely right," he said solemnly. "And you have every reason to distrust me, but I have realized how wrong I've been and now want to do everything I can to make amends. I understand that nothing I *ever* do will be enough to make up for the life you've been forced to live, but I will never stop trying."

Mina and Kajal traded looks as an unspoken message passed between them. It was hard not to be moved by the passion and sincerity in Miraan's voice.

"He's also responsible for this whole house and the fact that any of us are here with the means to help you," Zarya added, "if that helps ease some of your hesitation." She shot a glance at the prince. "And I wasn't expecting help from any of the Madans, either, but extreme circumstances sometimes produce the most unlikely allies."

She *hoped* he was sincere and that he wasn't simply a very good actor.

"Okay," Mina said. "We'll do it."

Zarya exhaled a relieved breath. "Okay, then—who wants to go first?" she asked gently.

"I do," Kajal said, raising her hand. "I want this gone."

Zarya dropped to her knees as well. "You're sure? You understand the risks?"

"I'm sure. Please. Just take it away."

Zarya nodded and then held out her hand for Rabin. He immediately settled next to her, clutching it. She wasn't sure if she needed to be touching him, but she wanted as much control as possible and thought this might help. Even if it had little effect on her magic, having him near made her feel safe and confident in other ways, too.

She looked up and he gave her a small nod. "You can do this," he said in a low voice. "I have every faith in you."

She squeezed his hand tighter, called up her nightfire, filtering out that thin tendril she'd been practicing, and reached for Kajal's collar.

The woman held so still that Zarya didn't think she was even breathing. That was probably for the best. Any sudden movements might throw her off.

Zarya touched Kajal's marking and ran through the usual steps to find the spaces between the magic and ink. This felt smoother and lighter, and she was sure she was on the right track.

With another small surge of magic, she broke through the enchantment, and the collar disappeared instantly, small puffs of black ink dissipating in the air. Zarya stared at the woman's throat, hardly daring to believe it. That had been so easy. So quick.

This changed everything. *This* gave them a fighting chance.

Kajal widened her eyes as she clutched her throat. "What happened?"

"What did you feel?"

"Only a tingling."

Zarya exhaled the single most relieved breath of her life. "It worked. It took only seconds, and it worked!" She began laughing. She'd done it. All those years locked away, all those nights wondering if she'd ever have a purpose, and this destiny had been awaiting her all along. This felt *right*. She looked at Rabin, and the small smile on his lips was so full of pride that she thought she might burst.

Kajal was crying as Mina and Vikas wrapped their arms around her, and they all laughed and wept.

"Okay, next," Zarya said, overcome with emotion and wiping her eyes, but Rabin laid a hand on her arm.

"Don't do it here," he said.

"What do you mean?"

His gaze moved around the room. "You need to show them." He swept an arm out towards the vanshaj district. "If Mina is willing, you must do this with witnesses where everyone can see no harm will come to her. A demonstration to convince everyone of what is possible."

He looked at Mina, who sat back with wide eyes as she regarded him warily.

"I understand this is asking a lot of you," he said in his rumbling voice. "You were very brave in coming here today, but this is for your people. This is a chance to change the course of a thousand years of wrongdoings committed against you and everyone like you. We are on the cusp of something so much bigger than any of us, and I'm asking you to be brave again. Perhaps braver than you've ever been in your entire life."

He laid a hand on Zarya's arm. "This woman is destined to free you. I know those words might not mean much on their own, but trust me when I say this is meant to be. You can be this change. We are all fighting a war, and you are its newest soldier. Will you have the courage to stand in front of everyone and be the catalyst for a brighter and better future? Everything rests on this moment, but I see so much strength in you, Mina. I see the opportunity you bring."

When he finished, everyone was silent. Zarya didn't think anyone could speak even if they wanted to. She understood then why he'd been such a formidable army commander.

Who could resist those words and that impassioned plea?

Who wouldn't fall to their knees and tear down mountains if he asked?

Mina looked at Vikas, who took her hand and squeezed it. "He's right. You can do this. We all believe in you, and it might be the only way to end this."

"Okay," Mina whispered, nodding quickly. "I will do it."

She turned to look at Zarya with a determined set to her jaw.

"Let's show them what's possible."

FORTY-FIVE

A short while later, Rabin led their entire group through the alleys of Ishaan, entering a busy square at the heart of the vanshaj district. Fruit and vegetable stands and other vendors surrounded the perimeter, most of them with long snaking lines as everyone gathered necessities for the week.

Rabin stopped and looked around, surveying the exit and entry points and the flow of people in and out of the square. They would have to do this carefully, but they'd chosen an area deep inside the district where no one but the vanshaj ventured —even the city watch mostly avoided the area. It acted as an unspoken boundary between them and everyone else.

Zarya came up next to him as she also studied the plaza. He would protect her, no matter what. This had all been his idea, and now he was responsible for everyone he'd lead into this task.

Yasen stood on his other side, and they easily fell into an old pattern as he awaited his commander's orders. They'd spent many years together operating like this, though their rank and duties hadn't allowed them the freedom to be anything more than leader and subordinate.

"Have someone at each exit point to keep an eye out for the city watch or royal soldiers," Rabin ordered. "You take the others and spread out. If there's anything amiss, give the signal."

"Yes, Commander," Yasen said and then turned on his heel, rounding up Ajay, Row, and even Miraan, who'd wrapped a scarf around his head to conceal his identity.

What Rabin wouldn't have given for a trained battalion, but they'd have to make do with their meager resources. Yasen was an excellent soldier. Rabin had been the one to train him, after all. And though Ajay hated his guts, Rabin wasn't too proud to recognize competence when he met it. With Row and the others also helping, perhaps they could pull this off.

Then Zarya, Mina, and Kajal all moved deeper into the square. Rabin and Vikas flanked their sides as they made their way to a raised fountain in the center. It stood dry and empty, the basin cracked, but the stairs would provide an elevated demonstration point.

As they ascended the steps, their presence started to draw a few curious glances. Their lack of star collars stood out in contrast to the people milling about. They waited for another minute as whispers began to filter through the crowd and every eye slowly drew their way.

Hundreds of vanshaj came to a stop, clutching their children or anything they were holding to their chests as they all checked in with one another, wondering if anyone understood what was happening.

They all appeared intent on fleeing at any moment until Vikas raised a hand and began speaking. "Everyone! Please. These people mean no harm. They are here to help. I know that many of you have heard me talk about the magic that can break the collars, and I understand you are afraid, but I beg you to listen."

Rabin nodded to Yasen, Ajay, Row, and Miraan as they spread out, manning the different streets leading into the plaza.

Vikas was still talking, encouraging everyone to move closer. A few brave souls took a few careful steps towards the center. As more advanced, more joined them, comforted by the safety of their numbers.

From the corner of his eye, Rabin noticed Yasen conversing with two members of the city watch, but he kept it to himself. Everyone was already on edge enough.

He held one eye on them as Yasen slowly maneuvered the watch away from the square, gesturing for Row to follow. They melted into the shadows, and a second later, both guards lay dead on the ground. Row waved a hand, and they both disappeared from view. It all happened in nearly the blink of an eye.

Satisfied the situation was under control, Rabin returned his attention to the plaza as everyone shuffled to the center. Soon they found themselves surrounded by hundreds of vanshaj peering up with hope and fear in their expressions. He felt the weight of this mission in a way he hadn't until now. These were living, breathing people who'd been punished for absolutely no reason. He understood why they had to do this. No matter what happened to any of them, they could no longer turn away.

"This is Zarya!" Vikas shouted. "She's been gifted with special magic that can break the collars. She removed mine and those of my friends. I have magic! Many of us have magic!" He then conjured a ball of flame, sending it into the air before it exploded in a shower of sparks.

Though Vikas had shown them all this before, it had fallen on unwilling ears. As Rabin stared over the crowd, he wasn't sure this time would be any different. Not without proof.

"But you want to see it with your own eyes," Vikas continued. "I understand that. You are right to distrust the Aazheri. You are right to be wary of their magic. The Jadugara have held us captive for centuries, but they have been lying to all of us. They have kept us prisoner only to save themselves, but today that changes." He pressed a hand to his heart. "On my life, I swear to you, everything changes today."

Vikas then backed up and then made room for Zarya and Mina.

They stepped forward, and Zarya reached out her hand towards Rabin. He took it, wrapping his fingers around hers as she looked up at him with a trusting expression. Gods, he loved her. It wasn't until a few days ago when he'd said it in that alley, that he realized how much. Saying those words had untapped a well of emotion he hadn't even known he was capable of feeling.

Abishek's warnings about keeping his distance from Zarya itched in the back of his thoughts, but he pushed them away. They were bound now, and nothing would change that. The king would be displeased when they returned to Andhera, but there was little he could do about it.

Rabin would never understand what he'd done to deserve this. Why the fates had chosen him to be hers, but he would thank them every day for the rest of his life.

"You can do this," he said to Zarya softly, and she nodded.

"With you, I can." Her voice was barely a whisper, but her words exploded against his chest, nearly knocking him sideways.

Then she turned towards Mina and performed the same spell as she had with Kajal, adding a little extra flourish for dramatic effect. The glittering black ribbon of her magic twisted in the air, spiraling over everyone's heads before it gently circled around Mina's throat. Zarya squeezed tighter and then the tattoo melted away almost instantly as the ink dissipated into puffs of dark smoke.

When she was done, she lowered her hand, and Mina stared wide-eyed with her fingers wrapped around her bare skin. Every single person standing in the plaza stood frozen as Zarya stepped towards Mina and began whispering in her ear.

Rabin heard her giving Mina instructions on how to find her magic, just like he'd taught her in the dream forest.

Mina pressed her lips together as she held up her palm and stared at it while Zarya continued to whisper encouragement.

And then, a tiny flickering flame appeared in Mina's hand, hovering above her palm. The delight on her face could have melted every heart within a thousand miles.

That's when Rabin felt the shift. This wasn't just a demonstration of magic. This was a sign that *anything* was possible. No matter what happened in the past, today, things would start to change, one way or another. They'd just opened a box of secrets that could *never* be closed.

He scanned the faces of the crowd, noting the wonder in their expressions and the tears building in their eyes. It had taken some convincing, but finally, they saw it. This was real. This was *possible*.

A moment later, the crowd exploded into screams, cheers, and excited chatter, the loud noise shaking the very ground where they stood. They hugged and jumped up and down, laughing and celebrating. Even Rabin's heart squeezed at the sight.

In the center of the square they all shared looks around their circle.

"You think that worked?" Zarya asked Vikas, who stared over the crowd with tears tracking down his cheek.

He nodded and grinned. "I think that worked."

FORTY-SIX

It was then the real work began.

The demonstration in the square had lit a fuse, kindling a fire that had been waiting to ignite. After all the years and months of planning, the setbacks and the futility of their actions, the Rising Phoenix finally had a direction and a purpose. An end goal with a possibility of success in their sights.

They discovered Mina also carried six anchors, and Zarya's hope grew with that knowledge. If they could keep moving forward, this endeavor might have a chance.

Everyone had their jobs. Suvanna and Apsara traveled between Operation Starbreak and the palace to keep an eye on the prisoners. They were also frequently active in the vanshaj district with Row, discreetly directing people to the manor via the city's alleyways.

Rabin was in charge of security and, along with Yasen and Ajay, began recruiting freed vanshaj and other members of the Rising Phoenix to patrol the streets to ensure no one came near the house, or if they did, they'd have fair warning.

Miraan also trekked between the manor and the palace, doing whatever he could to discover any useful information while funneling gold into procuring weapons for their growing army. This required a careful chain of orders that filtered down from him and through a twisting network of contacts so the purchases could never be traced to a single person.

If Dishani were to ever get wind of what he was doing, they'd lose him and his money. The fact they were generously funded was one of the only things working in their favor.

Miraan had returned a few days ago with news that construction of the ink factory had also resumed. They were also attempting to pass the proposed laws that would see many vanshaj banished to the Saaya. The incident during the execution had shaken another piece loose, rattling the careful hold the Madans had been clinging to for centuries.

They, too, must have felt the shift around them.

The air was charged with the promise of a different tomorrow, and the winds of change howled through the city streets with the whispers of rebellion.

The good news was it would take at least another month or two before the construction would be complete.

Zarya, Vikas, Miraan, and Mina's job consisted of using their magic to break the collars day in and day out. Thanks to their efforts, a stream of willing vanshaj now came and went all throughout the day. Zarya's magic was effortless, even when Rabin wasn't even in the house, and Vikas and Miraan were both becoming faster with every passing day. Mina was also catching up, and every once in a while, they'd encounter another vanshaj with a sixth anchor, who was immediately recruited to the cause.

Despite their progress, Zarya was constantly on edge, worried about discovery. More and more people were arriving daily, and hundreds of vanshaj were wandering around wearing false collars. No matter how hard they tried to hide it, *someone* could slip up.

They'd impressed the need for discretion on everyone, but

the more widespread their success, the more they risked exposure.

Still, all they could do was press on and hope.

Three weeks after the demonstration in the vanshaj district, they were finishing up for the night. The last few people of the day sat with the artists applying the temporary tattoos while Zarya and Vikas cleaned up.

She heard the back door open, and then Yasen and Miraan came around the corner. Their expressions suggested something dire had happened. Vikas and Zarya closed up the drawers they were tidying and then rounded the corner, where Yasen and Miraan waited.

"We have news," Miraan said.

"Let's just finish up here and then you can share," Zarya said. She didn't want anyone overhearing and panicking before they discussed how to deal with whatever disaster awaited them next.

"Sure," Yasen said before Zarya and Vikas helped finish off everyone for the day and then walked them to the back door. Rabin stood outside, peering into the shadows with a hand resting on the hilt of his sword.

They bid everyone goodnight and then Zarya gestured Rabin inside. After giving the order to another man guarding the entrance, he followed Zarya in.

They all gathered in the hallway as Miraan shared what he'd learned.

"They raided another part of the vanshaj district tonight," Miraan said as Zarya felt her blood turn cold. "It was violent, done purposely to instill fear, of course. When everyone awakes tomorrow, they'll see what's happened and understand they could be taken even when they least expect it."

Zarya's breath turned to lead as she listened.

"I went to see them," he continued. "Some bear the false collars and I worry how long they can hide them from the guards and my sister."

"We have to get them out of there immediately," Vikas said as Zarya laid a reassuring hand on his arm.

"That's not all," Miraan said. "They're keeping this quiet for now."

"What?" Rabin demanded when the prince hesitated.

"They're planning to stage another execution in two weeks' time. They'll conduct more raids to gather as many vanshaj as possible and then make a statement of their own."

Zarya clutched her stomach, sure she was about to be sick.

"Why in two weeks?" Rabin asked.

"That is when they expect the factory to be complete," Yasen said.

"Two weeks? But there's still so much to do! How can they possibly be finished by then?" Zarya asked.

"They've poured every resource into it," Miraan answered. "Spending more money than you can conceive. The Jadugara are threatening harsh consequences to the workers if they don't complete the project on time. They're doubling and tripling the shifts, working everyone around the clock. They want their position made clear. The Rising Phoenix will not stop them."

"So we'll use that as our standoff," Rabin said, already thinking six steps ahead. "We keep going. We continue breaking as many collars as we can over the next two weeks. We train as many as possible to defend themselves. Then we mount a raid on the palace."

"We don't have enough people," Zarya said. "You said tens of thousands. Plus, they need training."

"In an ideal world, but we don't have that luxury. We have to act. Once that factory is done, it will only bolster their position."

"So we'll work longer," she said.

"Zarya, all of you are running yourself to the point of exhaustion," Yasen argued.

"I'll be fine." She looked at Vikas, who nodded.

"Whatever it takes," he answered.

Her gaze met Rabin's, and she saw his worry, but he didn't try to argue with her. He already knew there would be no talking her out of it.

Zarya turned to Vikas. "We'll extend our hours. We have eight people helping us now. We'll extend the shifts. What do you think?"

Vikas nodded. "I'll ask whoever is willing."

"Then we get back to work," she said. "And hope it's enough."

For the next week, Operation Starbreak moved at full tilt, working through every hour of the day.

They devised a system of assigning groups to the house in batches. Each one spent about thirty minutes inside, having their collars broken and their temporary tattoos applied. Then they left one by one, and the next group was welcomed in. In this way, there were no lineups or clusters hanging around outside that might attract too much attention.

It wasn't a perfect system, but the Madans were distracted with their raids and the factory and were paying little attention to the operation happening under their noses.

Miraan also reported the royal soldiers were hunting for Zarya, but he'd done his best to steer them away from this area, offering up false tips delivered by his network of contacts that placed her anywhere between the Dakhani Sea and the Pathara Vala Mountains. She kept to the house, relying on others to run any necessary errands.

Thanks to Miraan's intelligence, they could also predict what areas the royal soldiers would hit each night and warn the residents. Of course, the royals would catch on to this coincidence soon enough, if they hadn't already, but the Rising Phoenix had to press any advantage they had.

Rabin had moved on from security, putting someone else in charge as he, Yasen, and Row started training their new recruits, now dubbed the Army of Ashes.

With a steady supply of weapons thanks to Miraan, they spent hours in the courtyard training freed vanshaj in the basics of fighting and the use of their magic. None of it was ideal and what they all wouldn't have given for months instead of days, but it would have to suffice.

Vikas kept up the stream of communication between Operation Starbreak and the council, making collaborative decisions to the greatest benefit of the movement.

It was a delicate house of cards with the potential to topple on every side, but all they could do was keep going, holding their breath.

While Zarya worked on a young woman one afternoon, Rabin came in and sat down next to her. "The factory is nearly complete. The Jadugara are using their magic," he said in a low voice. "They're sparing nothing to speed up its completion."

Zarya sent out a tendril of magic as the woman watched, her gaze flicking to Rabin as he spoke. Zarya nodded. They tried to keep bad news between them, hoping to alleviate everyone's worries. They all had enough on their minds.

"Will they finish early?" she asked.

He shook his head. "I don't think so, but they won't be much longer."

Zarya turned to the woman and affected her most reassuring smile. "You're all done. You can go see the artists now."

The woman hesitated for a moment, her gaze flicking between them.

"Thank you," she said before she stood.

"Come to me in the courtyard when you're done," Rabin said to her. "You look like you'd be good with a spear."

The woman paused again, jerked her chin, and threw her shoulders back. "Okay," she answered before heading for the room's opposite side.

They continued in the same way for the next week until there were only two more days before the proposed execution. Miraan had returned earlier, confirming the plan was still the same. The Madans would announce it that morning: the execution would be taking place in the palace square. They'd chosen to give little notice, hoping to catch the resistance off guard while also gathering as many witnesses as possible.

They, too, were walking a delicate line as their control slipped further and further.

When Zarya had finished the last person of the day and could barely sit in her seat any longer, she tidied her station and trudged up the stairs, her eyes on her feet, willing them up one by one.

She rounded the corner with a hand on the wall when she came to a stop.

Miraan had Yasen pressed to the wall, their mouths locked and their hands roaming all over each other. She opened her mouth in surprise before it morphed into a mischievous smile.

She *could* have quietly slunk away and pretended she'd seen nothing. But where would be the fun in that? Yasen would *never* walk away from an opportunity like this.

She crossed her arms and leaned against the wall with a smug look, wondering how long it would be until they noticed her standing there. She was pretty sure a royal parade could have wandered through here, and they wouldn't have noticed due to the way they were nearly eating each other's faces.

When Yasen tugged on the button of Miraan's pants and thrust his hand under his waistband, she decided she should probably make her presence known.

She cleared her throat as loudly as she could. That did the trick. They both went entirely still and turned towards her. Yasen with a grin and Miraan with a rabbit-caught-in-a-trap look on his face. She watched his cheeks heat and the tips of his ears turn pink. It was probably the first time she'd seen him be anything less than one hundred percent composed.

"Zarya... we uh... were just discussing..." he stammered.

"How far you can get your tongue down his throat?" she asked innocently, and he turned even redder.

"Yasen and I... you see... we..."

Zarya laughed. "It's okay, Miraan. You're both big boys. You can do whatever you like."

She glanced at Yasen, who was smiling in a way she'd never seen before. His eyes sparkled and his cheeks were flushed. "Do you mind?" he asked.

"You and I will be talking later," she said, and he gave her a salute.

"Yes, boss."

"Maybe find a room, hey?" she added before turning down the opposite hall in search of her own bed.

As she entered, she found Rabin half-dressed, sitting under the blanket reading a book.

"What are you smiling about?" he asked.

She slipped out of her dress and tossed it on a chair before undoing her braid and running a brush through her hair.

"I just caught someone making out in the hallway," she sing-songed.

"Who?" he asked.

"Oh, look at you," she said, pointing her brush at him. "My big tough warrior wants the gossip."

He laughed softly as she climbed on the bed and crawled up to him.

"I know you're dying to share, so don't put this on me," he answered in a dry voice.

She laughed, rolled onto her back, and tucked her arms behind her head. "Yasen and Miraan."

Rabin snorted as he flipped a page in his book.

"That's the only reaction I get?" she asked.

"I've already walked in on them twice. They can't keep their hands off each other."

"What?" she asked, her voice pitching high as she sat up. "How *dare* you not tell me?"

"It is not my place to spill a man's secrets," he said, his eyes still on his page.

"Yasen is my best friend, and you are my..."

He looked up at that.

"Your what?"

She shook her head. "My..." She stopped and frowned, scanning him up and down. "I don't have the right word for you. But you aren't supposed to keep secrets from me." She gestured between them. "We have a bond, remember?"

Suddenly, Rabin's eyes darkened. He tossed the book aside and grabbed her hand.

"Marry me, Zarya."

"What?" she sputtered, tugging her fingers out of his hold. He crawled up onto all fours and leaned over her.

"Before we storm the palace. We might die in there, but I want to die knowing that you were mine. Yes, we are paramadhar and masatara, but we are so much more."

He sat back and pulled her up, cupping the sides of her face with his hands.

"I love you. The more I'm with you, the *more* I love you. I want a name for us. I want to be the world to one another, and I want *everyone* to know it."

Zarya inhaled a shaky breath. How had their light and fun conversation turned to this? But the signs had been there for the past weeks. The way he looked at her. The way he rarely left her side. Every night, he told her that he loved her, and every night she went to sleep with those words lodged in her throat.

They kept bubbling to the surface, and she didn't know what was stopping her from saying them. Until now. When she looked at him, she *did* see the whole world. She couldn't have done any of this without him. He'd saved her over and over and never asked for anything in return. All he wanted was her heart, and he had it. He'd had it ever since that night she'd fallen asleep on a lonely beach and dreamed of a bigger life.

"I love you, Zarya," he said in that low, growly voice that spread through her chest, filling up the space behind her heart and the one between her thighs. He made her *feel* everything. With him, she was fearless and bold. Stronger than iron. Nothing could stand in her way. "I want to be yours in every way possible. I want you to be mine. Masatara. Friend. Lover. *Wife*."

He lowered his hands and stared at her, silently willing her to let go and stop being afraid of what she wanted.

"I love you, too," she finally whispered as her heart squeezed and her stomach swooped. "I love you, Rabin. Thank you for waiting for me."

His eyes lit up, those golden flecks growing brighter as he touched her cheek, sweeping aside a lock of her hair.

"I would have waited until the sun burned out of the sky, Spitfire. I thought I made that clear."

She smiled and nodded, tears prickling the backs of her eyes. "I love you," she whispered again, suddenly desperate to say those words over and over.

He wrapped an arm around her waist and hauled her against him, tipping her chin up.

"Then marry me. Tomorrow. We'll find somewhere quiet. Just the two of us."

"What about my father?" she asked. "Won't he be angry with you?"

Rabin shook his head. "It's our lives and our choice. I'm fine with it if you are."

"I owe him nothing."

"Then say yes," he implored.

She opened her mouth and paused. Were they really doing this?

He cupped the back of her head and slanted his mouth over hers. Her back arched into him, his warm chest pressing against hers as he devoured her with hungry kisses.

When he pulled away, she could feel a flush creeping over her cheeks.

"Okay," she whispered. "Let's get married."

FORTY-SEVEN

After the proposal, they'd been too tired to stay awake any longer. Rabin wrapped her in his arms, and she drifted off to sleep in the honeyed warmth of knowing this was the right choice.

Yes, they'd had their ups and downs, but they were beyond the mistakes either of them had made. What they had was so much bigger than that.

Zarya awoke early the next morning, knowing the first of today's vanshaj would be arriving soon. It was still dark, the sun just barely peeking over the horizon. She let Rabin sleep a bit longer. He looked too peaceful to wake up. He'd start his busy day soon enough.

She pulled on a clean salwar kameez of green cotton and brushed her hair into a high ponytail before scrubbing her face and her teeth. Dark circles hung under her eyes and her skin was pale from all the long hours they'd been working. She tapped her cheeks, hoping to generate some color, but what she needed was a quiet room and a week of uninterrupted sleep. Maybe she'd get a chance if they were successful the day after tomorrow.

She headed down the stairs to find Yasen already at the kitchen island with his elbows on the surface and a mug between his hands as he stared into nothing. His silver hair had been brushed and neatly braided, and he wore a grey kurta that clung to the swell of his biceps.

She leaned in the doorway and grinned, waiting for him to notice her.

After a moment, he looked over and frowned.

"Good morning," she said.

He looked away and took a sip from his mug. "If you think you'll embarrass me, you're about to be very disappointed."

She laughed and grabbed the pot of coffee on the counter, pouring herself a cup and sliding into the seat next to him. They sipped in companionable silence until Zarya couldn't take it anymore.

"Rabin said he's caught you twice already."

Yasen took another sip. "Apparently, Rabin can keep a secret better than you."

Zarya huffed and smacked her mug on the counter. "I can't *believe* you didn't tell me. He's my brother!"

"Half-brother," he answered with an arch of his brow. "And you didn't tell me about Rabin at first, either."

He gave her a pointed look, and she huffed.

"Fine. Keep your secrets."

They fell into silence again as Zarya blew on the top of her coffee, even though it wasn't very hot, and drank a long sip. Her leg bounced up and down on the rung of her stool as Yasen peered over and let out a sigh.

"Fine. Ask what you want. I can tell you're about to explode."

"Ahhhh!" Zarya said, placing down the mug and grabbing him by the arm. "Are you in love? I saw the looks you were giving each other. How did it happen? Is it serious?"

Yasen held up his hand. "Geez. Slow down."

Zarya leaned forward, resting her elbows on the surface and smiling up at him as he rolled his eyes.

"It's not serious," he said. "I don't do serious. I'm a soldier."

Her mouth formed into a pout. "You're not a soldier anymore, technically."

He shook his head. "It's the only thing I know how to do."

"Maybe you just haven't met the right man yet?"

Yasen pushed out a slow breath. "No. Miraan is nice, but don't foist your romantic fantasies on me. I'm just here for the hot sex."

Zarya wrinkled her nose. "Do I want to hear about my brother having sex?"

"Half-brother."

"He's more like a friend, though, I suppose."

Yasen gave her a pointed look. "Zee. Don't make more of this than it is. We're just having fun. He's a prince. It could never work."

She sat up and did her best to keep her bottom lip in check. "Fine. Do you like him, though?"

Yasen gave her a rueful smile. "Yeah, I like him. Despite the rest of that family, he seems like a good guy."

Zarya squealed and clapped her hands.

"Zee," Yasen warned.

She held her hands up in surrender. "I'm not saying anything. I'm just glad you found someone nice to spend time with."

Yasen rolled his eyes again as he poured himself another coffee.

"What about you and the dragon?" he asked. "You two seem pretty cozy lately. Everything okay since you completed the Bandhan?"

She nodded. "No regrets. We've worked through our issues, and I understand why he did what he did. I can trust him. Right?"

He nodded. "I think you can. He made a bad call, but the way he looks at you... that's all real. Even I can see that."

She couldn't help the little flip in her heart at those words. It *was* real. "Good. Because we're getting married today."

Yasen spit out his coffee. "What?"

She shrugged and winced. "We thought we'd make things official. We're in this weird middle place of being important to one another but having no way to describe the significance of our relationship."

"So? You don't get married because of that!"

She knew he was right. It was fast. But sometimes your heart just knew the true course, and she was trusting her instincts. "This mystical, destined purpose already connects us. Is marriage really so illogical? We're literally *bound* to one another."

Yasen placed his mug on the counter with a soft clink. "I... suppose not."

"I want us to be more than just 'destined' partners. He's more to me than that. And the Bandhan technically makes him my 'servant,' and that doesn't make sense, either. He's my equal."

"I suppose I get that," Yasen said. "You two don't really have a normal relationship." He scanned her up and down before searching her face. "And you do seem a lot happier lately. Even with all of this going on, it's obvious he's good for you."

She nodded. "I think so, too."

He gave a wry shake of his head. "And man, is he different around you."

"Good, different?"

"Very good," he answered.

"Thanks, Yas."

"So, when are we doing this?"

"We thought we'd find a cleric to marry us alone later today.

Do you think it would be okay to sneak away for a few hours? I know the others need us—"

Yasen slapped his hand on the counter, interrupting her.

"Yes, you're entitled to take a few hours off, and absolutely not. There is no way my second-best friend is getting married without me."

In the end, both Yasen and Miraan insisted on tagging along.

When Vikas found out what was happening, he demanded they all take the night off and enjoy themselves. He'd hold down the operation with Ajay, who warmly hugged Zarya despite his obvious distaste for Rabin. Maybe they'd come around to one another eventually.

Her half-brother insisted she couldn't get married without at least one blood relation present, and when it was decided that Yasen and Miraan were joining, Zarya knew she couldn't leave Row out.

She took him aside to explain when he arrived at the manor that morning.

"Zarya," Row said, his voice low with that chastising parental tone she was so familiar with.

"I know," she interrupted. "I already know all the things you'll say. And I know it seems reckless and fast and definitely a bit impulsive, but that's only because you're on the outside looking in.

"I believe him when he said he never meant to hurt me, and he loves me, and I love him."

He clasped his hands. "Yes, all of those things are true, but I feel I should mention Abishek would not support this."

"What do you mean? How did you know that?"

"I told you once that he felt strongly about Aazheri mating with other magical species due to the nullifying effects of the magic in their offspring. He believes it affects the purity of Aazheri power."

Zarya recalled the conversation they'd had in Dharati after Row's return when she'd been asking questions about her father.

"He forbade Rabin from having a romantic relationship with me," she confessed. "But that was due to the paramadhar bond."

Row considered that. "Perhaps it was down to both reasons. And you're choosing to defy him?"

"I owe him nothing. This is my life and all of that is nonsense. Should we ever decide to have children, we'll deal with that when it comes. As for Rabin, that is his choice to make."

They talked for a while longer as Row listed all his objections, and Zarya offered her counterarguments. In the end, she simply said, "I guess you don't have to like it, but I hope you will accept it. But I really would love for you to be there. It wouldn't feel right to experience such a huge thing in my life without you at my side. You're the only parent I've ever known, and if I don't say it enough, I love you, Row. I'm so grateful for you."

When she fell silent, she watched as Row blinked several times, a myriad of emotions she could only guess at passing over his expression.

He sighed and then leaned forward, bracing his elbows on his knees. "When you were little, you were already so headstrong. I remember when you were about eight or nine, I told you starflowers would only bloom at night, and you insisted that couldn't be true. So you set up a camp for days next to those damn flowers, trying to prove me wrong."

He chuckled at the memory as his soft gaze found hers.

"You were right," he said. "They did bloom during the day sometimes."

Zarya smiled, remembering her excitement, jumping up

and running back to the cottage to claim she'd known it all along.

"And maybe you're right about this, too."

She reached out a hand and squeezed his. "Will you come?"

He covered her hand with his. "I wouldn't miss it for the world, my girl."

She threw her arms around his neck as they hugged tightly. "I'm sorry I was so horrible to you," she said softly as he patted the back of her head.

"All is forgiven," he said. "What kind of father would I be if I didn't understand your need to learn who you were while perhaps being a little hard on the people who loved you the most? It's simply the natural order of things."

She pulled away. "I'm so lucky that my mother chose you to raise me."

He gave her a soft smile and then pressed a kiss to her temple. "I'm the lucky one, Zarya. I never expected to be a father, but you've brought me more joy than you can possibly understand."

Once they were done talking, Zarya returned to her flat to raid her closet for something suitable to wear. She didn't have anything that was right for a wedding, and she spared only a passing second of regret that she wouldn't get a stunning custom-made lehenga and all the usual fanfare with hundreds of people and mountains of food and hours of dancing.

Though she'd daydreamed about a wedding like that, she also understood it didn't suit this moment. She wanted and needed to marry Rabin *now* and this was enough. So she opted for a dressier lehenga she'd purchased when they'd first arrived.

It was elegantly simple in a soft dusty pink, beaded with silver. She then braided her hair and made up for the dress by going all out on her makeup with thick lines of kohl, deep pink lips, and long lashes.

As she admired the results in the mirror, she noticed Yasen

leaning with his arms crossed in the doorway and one ankle over the other.

"You look nice," he said, and she grinned. Rabin, Row, and Miraan had all gone ahead to meet with the cleric who would perform the ceremony while she and Yasen would follow behind.

She spun around and then dropped into a curtsy. "You think he'll like it?"

"He'd be a fool otherwise," he answered. "But he's obsessed with you. You have nothing to worry about."

Zarya walked over and stared at Yasen before placing a hand on his forearm. "Thank you for everything," she said. "I kind of dragged you to Ishaan with me, and I've been so grateful to have you at my side during all of this."

He smiled. "You didn't drag me anywhere, Zee. I wanted to come. Leaving Dharati was for me, too."

"I'm glad," she said. "You deserve the world."

They paused for a beat, and she wondered if she caught the barest hint of tears lining his eyes. He blinked and shook his head. "Quit getting sappy on me, Swamp Girl. Let's go or you'll be late for your wedding."

They both donned scarves to conceal their identities, and Yasen took her hand before winding their way through Ishaan's alleys. They reached a squat, nondescript building and entered through the back entrance.

Zarya and Yasen found a room that was little more than a box with two small windows at one end, a white marble floor, and painted white walls. There were no flowers and no rings and no fancy food. Row, Miraan, and Rabin all turned at the sound of their entrance, and Zarya couldn't take her eyes off the man who would soon become hers forever.

He wore a black sherwani borrowed from Miraan embroidered with deep purple thread, and his dark hair fell in midnight waves around his shoulders. Her breath stuck in her chest as she stared at him, and his gaze roamed over her from head to toe.

He held out his hand as her stomach did a little flip and her heart squeezed in her chest. Any lingering reservations or doubts she had—this was too fast, this was too reckless—evaporated in that moment. She glided towards him, taking his hand as he pulled her in close and wrapped an arm around her waist.

"Ready, Spitfire?" he asked.

"Ready," she whispered.

"You are breathtaking." He leaned down and kissed her. "I love you. I will protect you until the end of our days."

"I love you, too," she replied. "Thank you for coming into my life."

Then they turned to the cleric, who performed a quick ceremony without any bells or whistles. Maybe this made more sense. Their relationship was already extraordinary enough on its own.

When it was done, they turned to face their friends and family. Yasen and Row gave her extra-long hugs, and she did her best not to sob all over them.

Miraan had snuck in a case of very expensive sparkling wine, which they popped to the sound of cheers and congratulations as they drank straight from the bottles. They all snickered when Yasen dribbled some down his front, but he had the last laugh when he dumped half a bottle on Miraan.

The normally stoic prince burst into raucous laughter before they shared a sticky, wet kiss and the cleric threw them out, grumbling under his breath about finding a mop. Miraan assured him he'd pay for the trouble, but the cleric waved them off.

"Have a lovely life," he said to Zarya and Rabin, pressing his hands at his heart and dipping his head.

"We plan to," Zarya answered before grinning at Rabin. He pressed a finger to her jaw, and they kissed one more time before donning their scarves and cloaks and spilling into the streets where the sun had set.

Ishaan was alive with activity as Miraan guided them past bustling taverns and busy cafes and up the sweeping steps of the city's grandest hotel. Knowing a prince certainly had its advantages because he'd booked them a private room inside its lavish restaurant, where they were served overflowing courses of lamb biryani, dal bukhara, and bursting bites of litti chokha.

They toasted and drank and ate until they were stuffed.

From across the table, Zarya watched Yasen and Miraan talking, their heads bent close. As if sensing her gaze, Yasen looked over and Zarya smiled. He might claim things were casual with the prince, but she was sure there was something more. Yasen winked and held up his glass, and she got misty-eyed thinking about how much she loved him.

Miraan pushed away from the table and announced, "I've also secured you a room for the night. You won't have time for a honeymoon yet, but I hope this helps make up for it."

He held out a golden key and Zarya reached out to accept it. "Miraan, this is too much."

He waved her off. "It's not nearly enough. I'm not sure what the future holds for any of us, but I'd like to know you better if we get that chance."

"I'd like that too," she whispered, clutching the key to her chest.

"Now get out of here." He picked up his wine, clearly feeling a bit looser after downing several glasses. "We might all die tomorrow, so enjoy tonight to the fullest!"

They all cheered to that morbid reminder, but she smiled anyway, feeling like her heart would burst.

It hadn't been the wedding she'd imagined, but it was actually so much better. It had been intimate and warm and full of the most important people in her life.

Then everyone shooed Zarya and Rabin off before they

made their way upstairs to discover that not only had Miraan secured them a room, it was the best one in the entire hotel.

Sprawling over the top floor, it could have fit at least five of Zarya and Yasen's whole flat. Along the far wall, a set of wide arches opened to the outside, where they could see miles of forest and mountains in the distance. In the center of the room was a massive circular bed covered with gold sheets and pillows, along with ornately carved tables, divans, and the biggest marble bathroom Zarya had ever seen.

Miraan had arranged for more sparkling wine, and they poured two glasses before they stood on the balcony, enjoying the soft evening breeze.

"Thank you for marrying me," Rabin said before he took her hand and kissed the back of her fingers. "You've made me the happiest man alive."

"I love you," she said softly, watching the moonlight reflecting in his eyes and off the arch of his cheekbones.

They kissed slowly and deeply, languishing in the sensation and the tastes and smells of each other. He took the glass out of her hand and placed it on the table before he wrapped an arm around her waist and dragged her towards him.

"No more wine?"

"Have as much as you want," he said with a smirk as his hand slid down and cupped her ass. "But first, I want to spread you out on that bed and make love to my wife."

She grinned up at him. "Deal."

FORTY-EIGHT

Rabin scooped Zarya into his arms, loving the way she felt pressed against him. She squealed in delight and looped her arms around his neck. He'd never get enough of that joyous sound. She was the sunshine to his storm. The perfect ray of light piercing through the layers of his darkness. He hadn't realized how much he'd needed her until she'd blown into his life.

The decision to ask for her hand had been on his mind for weeks. Ever since they'd completed the Bandhan. It had brought them together in irrevocable ways, but it still hadn't felt like enough. It didn't encompass all the profound feelings he'd developed for this woman. He'd been alive long enough to understand there was nothing ordinary about their connection.

He strode across the room and tossed her on the bed, eliciting another happy scream.

Maybe, if he were being brutally honest with himself, a small part of him had proposed to defy Abishek's orders. He'd been seized with a sick sense of fear that someone would take her away. So he'd asked her to marry him, and now nothing could ever come between them.

"Take off your clothes," he ordered as he began opening the

line of buttons running the length of his sherwani. At first, she didn't move. She cocked her head and studied him as he shucked off his jacket and then unbuttoned his collar and then his shirt sleeves, rolling them up to his elbows.

He took a step, towering over her. "You promised me something that night in Premyiv," he growled.

"Did I?" She sat back on her hands as she looked up at him with those dark eyes that saw right into the center of his soul.

The corner of his mouth quirked up as he dropped to his knees and planted his elbows on the mattress. "That you'd show me how you use these fingers."

He lifted her hand and kissed the tips as a blush crept to her cheeks.

"Show me how you touch yourself, Zarya."

A row of ties ran up the side of her hip to fasten her skirt; he tugged on the first bow, feeling the satin ribbon give under his pull. Her breath hitched, and her mouth parted as he moved to the next, slowly undoing them one by one, exposing the smooth brown skin of her hip and the top of her thigh.

He ran his hand under the fabric and across her stomach, noting the flex of her muscle and the flush of her skin. He loved strong women—not just mentally, but the kind that could kick his ass. Pushing down the fabric, he exposed the waistband of her underwear and ran a finger along the lacey edge, watching goosebumps erupt.

"Take it off," he said, tugging on her skirt. She lifted her hips, and he slid it down, under her butt and legs, before tossing it aside.

She watched him with a mixture of excitement and lust in her eyes. His hands pressed on the inside of her thighs, spreading them wide. Her knees fell open and he stared at the bare scrap of fabric covering her pussy, noticing it was already wet. Fuck, he couldn't wait to taste her again, but first, he had other plans.

"Touch yourself," he ordered, and he watched the bob of her throat as she swallowed. He held out his hand for hers before guiding her down between her legs. "Show me," he rumbled as she ran a finger up the center of her underwear, exhaling a small gasp.

"Does it feel good?" he asked, and she nodded.

He licked his lips as he watched her fingers dance over her center while his hands opened her legs wider. His fingers crept closer until he reached the silk edges, digging his thumbs into her skin. She moaned as he watched her press harder, her center growing wetter with every sweep.

He grabbed her wrist and directed her hand under her waistband. When her fingers met hot flesh, she whimpered under his gaze. He watched them moving under the fabric, his cock already painfully hard.

He tugged aside her underwear so he could watch. "Fuck yourself with your fingers, Spitfire," he said, his cock straining against the fabric of his pants. He was growing warmer and warmer, but he didn't want to undress just yet. He wanted her naked under him, begging for him, craving him.

With his eyes never leaving the spot where her fingers dipped into her pussy, he reached around to undo the line of ribbons keeping her choli in place. When the last one opened, he slid it down her shoulders. She pulled her hand out long enough to free her arms before she resumed her movements.

"That's my girl," he rumbled as he leaned down and took her nipple between his teeth, biting down. She cried out as her back arched into him, her breasts pressing into his face. He licked the tip as he continued dragging his tongue down her body.

His gaze fixed on the thick vein running along the inside of her thigh, his mouth watering at the sight.

"You're going to come," he said, thumbing the vein, making

her shiver under his touch. "And I'm going to bite you. Understood?"

"Yes," she whispered, her eyes wide before he lowered his head and licked a trail up the inside of her leg. He groaned at the sweetness of her skin and the way her aroma overcame his senses.

"Don't stop," he said, wrapping a hand around her wrist as he guided her along her soaking wet pussy. He could smell it. Her desire. Her want. Her legs were already shaking as he scraped the sharp edge of a canine against her delicate skin.

He didn't give her a warning this time. With a sharp intake of breath, he sunk his teeth into her vein. He sucked hard, his mouth flooding with the earthy taste of her blood. It wasn't the way humans described it. Like copper. No, it was far more layered than that. The blood of an Aazheri literally tasted of magic. Like something fresh and crisp and electric.

And Zarya's blood was something entirely new to him. She tasted like flowers in spring and a soft breeze on a summer day. She tasted like honey and sugar and cream. Like cinnamon and pepper, but it was all layered with something darker, like coalescing shadows, everything twisting together to create something that was simply and unmistakably *her*.

His hand clamped above her knee as she continued touching herself, her finger roughly circling her clit as she moaned and her hips bucked. He continued sucking, drinking her in until she screamed, her orgasm ripping through her as her fingers dug into his hair and tugged hard enough for him to feel it to the roots.

He didn't care. She could do whatever she wanted as long as she let him do this every single day of their lives. When she stopped shaking, he slowly drew his teeth from her skin, carefully licking the two puncture wounds to seal them over.

He stretched up, licking his lips as he pulled her towards him and kissed her, his tongue driving into her mouth as he pushed her back on the bed. Crawling over her, he continued kissing her, luxuriating in the taste of her blood mixing with her mouth.

He kissed her until he could barely breathe and then lifted up, his eyes roaming down her body, taking in the sight of her big dark eyes and her full lips. The angle of her collarbone and the swell of her breasts. His eyes drifted lower over the plane of her taut stomach and down to her hips.

And then, he curled his fingers out before delicate vines crept across the bed and circled her ankles and wrists, twisting gently down her arms and legs as she watched.

"What are you doing?" she whispered as he unbuttoned his shirt and then his pants.

"Do you trust me, Spitfire?" he asked as he tossed away the last of his clothing.

"Of course," she breathed instantly, and he couldn't help but smile.

He filtered out another thread of magic as the vines pinned her to the mattress, leaving her helpless. Then he dragged a finger down the center of her throat and between her breasts as another creeping vine followed the same path.

She watched, her chest heaving in and out as the vine crept lower, tickling her skin down past her ribs and then her navel.

"Ready?" he asked, and she nodded.

"I think so."

He chuckled as the vine slid lower, the pointed tip touching her swollen clit. She cried out, her entire body seizing against her restraints as she moaned and writhed. He continued directing his magic over that sensitive spot, harder, softer, faster, slower as she begged and pleaded. For more. For release.

His hand smoothed up her thigh before he took himself in his hand, stroking himself with long thrusts as he directed the magical vine directly into her pussy. She gasped as it slid into her, and though he couldn't feel it, the way she arched into it had every nerve in his body burning with fire.

"You," Zarya managed to gasp in between her moans, and it took him a moment to understand she was asking for *him* to touch her. To fill her up.

He grinned and collapsed on all fours as her eyes met his. He directed the vine of magic into her with a few more gentle thrusts as he held her gaze and then pulled it away before pressing his cock to her entrance.

With her limbs still pinned in place, he eased into her, slowly at first, groaning at the exquisite bliss of her tight walls. Her heels scrambled against the bed as she continued urging him on. "Yes," she whispered. "Rabin, undo me."

And that finally tore the last shreds of his control. He slammed into her as they both whimpered, her heat enveloping his pulsing cock, making his vision blur. She was pure sensation and passion. He felt everything with her. More than he thought he *could* feel.

He thrust into her again, watching the spot where she took him, moving in and out.

"I love you," he rumbled as he filtered out a new vine of magic, dancing it on her sensitive clit and then thrust again as she came around him with a cry. He lost control, fucking her with abandon until he thickened and then spilled into her with a force that nearly turned him inside out.

When they both caught their breath, he pulled his magic away and she reached up to cup his face, bringing him down for a kiss. He would have done anything for her in that moment. Torn apart mountains and worlds. Climbed to the moon if she asked.

She was his purpose. His destiny.

As he took in the flush of her cheeks and the sparkle in her dark eyes that seemed to contain the entire universe in their endless depths, he felt like he finally understood himself for the very first time.

FORTY-NINE

Sunlight warmed Rabin's skin when he woke up the next morning. He rolled over to find Zarya breathing gently, her face soft in sleep. His *wife*.

He traced the lines of her face, dragging his finger over the curve of her cheek and the angle of her jaw. Every time with Zarya had been something magical, but after they'd said those vows to one another and promised themselves to each other forever, everything had shifted to another place, and he couldn't wait to spend the rest of his life at her side.

A knock at the door and a call of "room service" had her eyelids fluttering open. Miraan had truly thought of everything.

Rabin wasn't sure what to make of Zarya's half-brother. He seemed genuine in his desire to help, but Rabin usually had difficulty trusting people, and this prince was no exception.

Yasen certainly saw something in him. Rabin had overheard his conversation with Zarya when he'd claimed it was only casual, but Rabin had always been very good at reading people, and he didn't buy a word of Yasen's protests. He'd been around Yasen enough to know this was something special to him, too.

Reading people was one of a soldier's most underrated and

undervalued skills, and that's what had always made him good at his job.

"Let me get that," Rabin said, kissing her on the tip of her nose before he found a blanket to wrap around his lower half and opened the door to a member of the hotel staff dressed in a crisp black vest.

"Breakfast?" he asked, gesturing to the golden cart.

Rabin stood aside, and he pushed it into the room before revealing piles of eggs and paratha, along with bowls of fresh fruit yogurt, coconut cream, and pots of coffee and tea. Orange juice and sparkling wine completed the small feast.

"Is it to your liking?" he asked, and Rabin nodded. With a press of his hands at his heart, he tipped at the waist and then left. When the door closed, Rabin tossed the blanket back onto the bed, leaving him entirely nude, and then wheeled the cart closer, piling a plate high and handing it to Zarya.

"What are you thinking about?" Zarya asked after they ate in comfortable silence for a few minutes.

"I'm feeling bad you didn't get a big fancy wedding," he said, looking around the suite. "This room is beautiful, but you're a princess. You should have had something extravagant. Something bigger."

"Really?" she asked. "That's what's bothering you?"

"A little," he admitted. He didn't have much to offer her. It was only now that they'd passed the excitement of the proposal and the wedding that he realized it.

She shook her head. "I am not a princess. I'm a girl who grew up living in a simple cottage by the sea, and I will always be that girl, no matter what secrets drag me into the light."

He raised a skeptical eyebrow. She could keep denying it, but she had royal blood, and when Abishek met her, he would no doubt name her his heir. Zarya couldn't turn away from this part of her destiny, either. The marriage also meant Rabin was now fated to become king consort of Andhera, something he'd truly never imagined for himself.

"Our wedding was perfect," she said with such sincerity that he nearly believed it. "All the most important people in my life were there, and the only thing I really needed was you."

She popped a piece of mango into her mouth and then added, "But really if I'm a princess, shouldn't I have married a prince?"

It took him a moment to realize she was joking.

"Maybe I planned all along to trap you before some stuffy royal could get his hands on you."

She laughed at that. "You know how I *adore* stuffy royals."

Then she leaned over and lay a hand against his cheek.

"I'm so happy right now," she said, and despite everything in him warring not to believe her, he did. "I never imagined that I could be this happy. That I could meet someone like you to love. I didn't need a fancy wedding. I promise."

She kissed him and then pulled away, looking around the room with a forlorn expression. "Though I do wish we could stay here all day, we should get back to the house. We have work to do."

He grabbed her hand, returning her gaze to him. "When this is all over, I'm making up that shoddy excuse of a wedding to you," he said, and she smiled.

"That isn't necessary, but I'd never say no to presents. Maybe something diamond-shaped?" She pressed a finger to her lips with a curious expression.

Rabin took her hand and kissed her palm. "I'll buy you the biggest fucking diamond I can find. Even if I have to kill someone."

That won him a laugh. "I don't doubt you would."

Then she dragged herself out of bed, giving him an eyeful of her lush curves as she made her way to the bathroom. He groaned, also wishing they could spend the next three months in this bed.

She blew him a kiss and then gently closed the bathroom door.

Rabin rubbed his chest and let out a sigh, feeling strangely at peace.

* * *

Reluctantly, Zarya and Rabin dragged themselves out of bed and made their way back to the manor. Their magical bubble had to burst because too many people were relying on them.

With scarves covering their heads, they wound through the streets, nearly running straight into a group of Jadugara accosting a group of citizens. Ducking into an alley, Zarya stopped, peering around the corner to watch.

The Jadugara were questioning the people they had surrounded. Zarya could just make out their demands: they were asking who their parents were and where and when they'd been born. She narrowed her eyes as she watched a Jadugara take the wrist of a young man and grip it tightly. He then filtered out a thread of spirit magic, circling it around the younger man.

"What's he doing?" Rabin asked. He stood behind her, a hand on her hip and his body pressed to her back.

"I think he's testing for magic," Zarya said.

They both watched for another moment. "They're trying to catch anyone who might have escaped the collar?" he asked a moment later.

She nodded. "That would be my guess."

"We should go," Rabin said. "It's not safe for you out here."

Zarya nodded and watched for another moment before the Jadugara began harassing another group of passersby. They looked scared and worried and were behaving erratically, confirming the Rising Phoenix had wormed under their skin. It was a sign of the royals' increasing frustration. She hoped it was a positive omen.

When they returned to the house, it was already buzzing with the day's activity. Vikas was ordering Aazheri about as a new group of vanshaj entered for their procedure. Out in the courtyard, Yasen and Row were busy training soldiers.

From the window, Zarya and Rabin watched as Yasen corrected someone's handhold on their weapon. Zarya remembered watching him for the first time at Ambar Fort. He'd been such a patient and giving teacher, and it was obvious how much this role suited him.

The free vanshaj worked valiantly, and while some were naturals, plenty couldn't tell which foot was the left and which was the right. Rabin sighed and blew out a breath.

"If only we had more time," he said. "We'd need months to train a competent army, even if they already had experience."

Zarya followed the direction of his stare. He was obviously right. They didn't look particularly seasoned, but what they lacked in skill, they made up with heart. Every single one of them had a determined expression on their faces. This meant more to them than to anyone.

They passed through the house and into a room where dozens of people were busy scratching out notes on pieces of paper. "What's this?" Zarya asked.

"Something I dreamed up last night," Vikas answered. "They're copying the passage from *Age of Shadows* that shares the truth about the Jadugara. Ajay agreed it was a good idea, and we gathered as much paper as we could find."

"It's brilliant," Zarya said.

"How do you plan to distribute them?" Rabin asked.

"We thought we could hand them out to people in the square."

"Or I could fly over and rain them down over Ishaan," Rabin answered with a wicked gleam in his eyes.

Vikas grinned and nodded. "That would be perfect."

The door to the back of the house opened and they all went to investigate. Ajay entered, followed by Koura, and then... Farida stepped through the doorway with her arm wrapped around Rania.

"Farida!" Zarya cried, rushing towards her. Farida appeared pale and so much thinner, like a delicate twig in winter.

Zarya ground to a stop. "Is it okay if I hug you?" she asked, and Farida nodded with that kind smile she'd missed so much.

"Of course."

Zarya threw her arms around her. "I'm so sorry. I'm just so sorry."

"It's okay," Farida said. "Rania and Ajay have explained everything. I'm so proud of all of you."

Zarya pulled away. She stared at Farida's throat and her smooth, unblemished skin.

"You're okay?"

"Thanks to Koura," Farida answered, and he tipped his head. "A little tired and weak, but he promises I'll make a full recovery."

"Gods, I'm so relieved you're here," Zarya said. "You must meet Vikas."

Vikas approached with his hand out and a grin on his face. "I've heard so many wonderful things about you. I'm so glad to see you've recovered."

"I've heard the same," Farida said, causing Vikas's shoulders to straighten. "And despite Rania's protests, I wanted to come and see everything. Will you show me around?"

"Of course," Vikas said, looping his arm through Farida's as he took her through the manor, pointing out everything and answering all of her questions about Operation Starbreak.

Her pride in their work was evident, and for the next few

hours, she pitched in where she could while Rania hovered and fussed over her. Farida bore her attention with good nature, clearly humoring her after her near scare with death.

A somber mood settled over the house as the day waned and night fell.

Zarya and Vikas finished with the final group and started cleaning up as everyone else finished their chores and made for their homes. That left Zarya, Rabin, Ajay, Row, and Yasen as they closed the door on the final vanshaj they'd free before the sun rose tomorrow.

"This is it, then," Vikas said. "We're done."

"How many do we have?" Rabin asked.

Vikas consulted the ledger on the next table. "By my count, we're at just over three thousand."

Their gazes met around the room.

Thousands, Rabin had said. *Tens* of thousands. They weren't even close to that number but were also out of time.

"Is it enough?" Zarya asked.

"It might be. It's honestly more than I expected," Rabin said, blowing out a long breath. "We've done all we could. Trained them to the best of our ability. Now it's up to us and to each of them."

"Then may the gods favor us tomorrow," Ajay added, and they all shared a wary look before falling into their beds to dream of victory and the distinct possibility of their failure.

FIFTY

At the crack of dawn, Zarya awoke, sensing the energy in the air. Everyone understood what was at stake today, and either they would make a statement or many would die trying. As she lay in bed next to Rabin, she clutched her necklace, holding on to the stone, seeking strength from the message inside. This was her purpose. She was supposed to be doing this. That meant the gods had to be on their side. Right?

She looked over to find Rabin awake.

"Couldn't sleep, either?" he asked.

"Not really."

He reached out and wrapped a large hand around her forearm.

"Whatever happens today, don't leave my side. I can't protect you otherwise."

She opened her mouth to protest, but he squeezed harder. "I know you can take care of yourself, but this is my job." He paused. "And you are now my wife, and I will fight for you with every dying breath."

"Wife," she said with a small smile. "I'm not used to that yet."

He arched a brow. "And what do you think?"

She shrugged. "I kind of like the sound of it. *Husband.*"

She actually loved the sound of it, but his ego was already big enough.

"Good," he growled. "Because you'd better get used to it."

He rolled over and kissed her, his hard body pressing her into the mattress. He framed her face with his hands and devoured her mouth, their tongues meeting and their hips writhing. He pulled up, his dark eyes gleaming as he ran the tip of his tongue over a sharp canine, causing a liquid pit of desire to flutter in her stomach.

She sighed, knowing they would have to cut this short.

"What do you think will happen today?" she asked, trying to focus on their task. "Do you think the royal family will listen?"

He shook his head. "I think they will fight back with everything they have. No one wants to disrupt a situation that benefits them entirely. But we have numbers on our side. It's not as much as I hoped for, but it's still a significant amount. I think we can at least make a statement."

"I don't want anyone to get hurt," she whispered. "I won't be able to live with it."

"That isn't possible," he said. "War never comes without cost."

She nodded. She knew that. She couldn't help wishing there was another way, but centuries of oppression had proven that violence could only be met with force.

"Then let's go," she said. "And hope we aren't making a colossal mistake."

An hour later, Zarya stood amongst the crowd outside the palace, hemmed in by the walls and simmering atmosphere. A similar platform had once again been erected for the hanging, only it was much higher and surrounded by several rows of guards on every side.

Zarya peered through the masses, keeping her eyes down and her hood up, recognizing many vanshaj she'd freed from their collars. The fake markings around their necks weren't perfect—the artists had been forced to pick up their pace—but hopefully, they'd fool anyone who wasn't looking too closely. She caught a few smiles and nods directed her way.

With his years of battle experience, Rabin was leading today's charge, organizing different factions and doling out orders to be filtered throughout the vanshaj district and the rest of Ishaan at strategically determined points.

With this many people—and none of them trained soldiers —there were bound to be mistakes, but Rabin was mostly confident they could make up for some less-than-perfect technique with sheer brute force.

She hoped he was right.

The royal family perched on the balcony overlooking the square, including Miraan, who stood at the railing, seeking them out in the crowd. The execution wasn't only a message to the citizens of Gi'ana—Dishani also hoped it would draw Zarya into her clutches.

"So I'm waiting to give the signal until after the prisoners come out?" she confirmed with Rabin.

Yasen stood nearby, also with this hood up and his gaze fixed on Miraan. They'd briefly debated about Miraan returning to the palace, but the prince had argued it would be suspicious if he weren't present for such an important occasion. Plus he could help control things from the inside. Apsara and Suvanna also waited on the balcony for similar reasons while maintaining a careful distance from the prince.

"Yes," Rabin answered in a low voice. "I want everyone accounted for. It will be easier to get them to safety if they're already free of the dungeons."

"Right," she said.

"Let's move closer to the front," he urged, pressing on her lower back. He gestured to Yasen with his chin, who nodded before he followed. They eased their way through the crowd, which buzzed with nervous energy. Many of them didn't know how to behave, burdened with the secrets weighing on their consciousness. She hoped the royals wouldn't notice anything amiss.

They pushed their way almost to the edge, noting several Jadugara standing on the platform, staring over the square while dozens more stalked through the crowd, glaring at everyone leaping out of their way.

A boom of thunder echoed overhead just as the first drops of rain began to fall. She exchanged a worried glance with Rabin as they closed in. The plan was to rescue the prisoners, and when they were done, thousands of vanshaj would reveal their magic and their freedom before storming the palace, flooding the entrances, and overwhelming the guards. They'd lose access to their magic as soon as they passed into the halls, but that's exactly why Rabin had insisted on weapons training for everyone.

"Get up there," Rabin said, noting a small outcropping in the perimeter wall where she could stand above the crowd and send up the signal with a burst of fire in the sky.

The rain was starting to fall heavier, and the crowd appeared to grow increasingly nervous. Zarya hoped they'd bring the prisoners out soon. It felt like they were inside a balloon expanding with pressure, on the verge of exploding.

Her breath hitched with nervous apprehension when the door on the far side of the plaza slid open. Several soldiers emerged, leading a line of prisoners, each of them cuffed in iron around their wrists and ankles. Zarya recognized Vikas's parents looking thin and frail, and she shot a look at Dishani, wondering how she could be so cruel.

As the rain fell harder, the soldiers directed the prisoners up to the platform, their chains dragging over the wood as they were roughly arranged across its length. They began dropping nooses around the trembling prisoners' shoulders. Some looked at their feet while others searched the plaza, probably seeking out one last glimpse of their loved ones in the crowd.

Dishani watched it all without emotion, her face blank. Miraan stood next to her, his hands behind his back, playing the role of dutiful brother. A moment later, the Madan siblings looked to the crowd, their brows furrowing.

Zarya stretched up, trying to see what had caught their attention.

"What's going on?" Zarya whispered to Rabin as he shook his head.

"A commotion of some kind." He angled his body as if prepared to throw himself into the middle of whatever was happening.

And then Zarya heard the most devastating words she could have imagined. The one thing she hoped they'd get away with.

"His marking!" a Jadugara shouted, pointing to a young man who was covering his throat as if that might hide the damning evidence of what they'd all done. "It's been tampered with!"

A pause seemed to roll through the crowd as his voice rang out over their heads like a death knell. Zarya went still, frozen in shock, before the tension snapped, and the crowd swelled and shoved, growing louder to the sounds of screaming and shouting.

The Jadugara were already circling, seizing vanshaj at will.

"The signal!" Rabin called. "Zarya! Now!"

She looked at him. This wasn't at all what they'd planned, but she trusted he knew what he was doing. Nodding, she lifted a hand, shooting a column of fire towards the sky before it exploded into a shower of rainbow sparks.

She watched in horror as the crowd grew even more agitated, the taste of panic bubbling into the air. They'd lost control. She looked for Rabin, but he was no longer standing next to her. They'd been separated in the frenzy. A moment later, she spotted him wrestling against a crush of bodies, trying to get back to her.

Zarya dropped from her perch, shoved through the masses, and attempted to reach him, but he only seemed to be moving further away.

"Rabin!" she screamed as she was elbowed in the stomach and heaved into an unforgiving wall of bodies. Recovering, she continued fighting within a tangled mess of limbs. Screams pierced her ears, and she had no idea how they'd ever regain order or get their plans back on track.

A second later, she was seized by both arms and lifted off her feet by two massive royal soldiers. More of them surrounded her and were closing in.

"No!" she screamed, fighting and kicking, attempting to wrench from their hold.

"Rabin!" she screamed again as she reached for her magic, but it was already too late.

Something hard hit her on the back of the head before she went limp, and everything went black.

* * *

Rabin fought against the tide. Everything had gone to shit. The Jadugara were striking everyone down without mercy, magic flying in every direction. The vanshaj forgot every bit of their mediocre training in their panic. He'd known this was likely. It was nearly impossible to expect civilians without any battle training to keep it together when things went sideways.

Still. He'd hoped.

He'd been relying on the faint chance that Zarya's destiny

might somehow make this all work out. It had been a fool's wish. A true soldier didn't rely on chance.

He watched as she jumped from her perch, struggling to reach him. He fought in her direction, trying not to hurt anyone, but was shoved left and right in the press of bodies.

He wasn't used to this feeling of utter helplessness and he hated it.

That's when he saw two guards seize Zarya by each arm. She fought like a wildcat as more closed in around her, momentarily cutting her off from his view. *Fuck.*

"Zarya!" he roared as he continued to battle a human tide. "Zarya!"

Then he watched in horror as a soldier knocked her on the head before she went limp.

"Zarya!" He would *destroy* that asshole. Fucking tear him limb from limb. Every single one of them would *suffer* at his hands.

"Move!" Rabin shouted, shoving harder, no longer caring who got in his way. A guard heaved Zarya up on a shoulder, her arms and legs dangling as they carried her off. Rabin tried to follow, but he couldn't untangle himself from the press of limbs and panic, almost as if fate was *trying* to keep him away.

He pushed through the crowd with another thrust, closing the distance as he stumbled against the crush.

The soldiers reached the palace, the lead guards slipping through a door.

"Zarya," he screamed as he lunged. The others quickly stepped inside as he ran, just as the door slammed in his face. He rammed his entire body into it, backing up and then ramming it again, but it was solid wood, banded with iron, and offered no give. He speared a beam of copper light at the handle, but it dissipated against it. More fucking magic working against him.

"What happened?" Yasen yelled over the cacophony, coming up beside him.

"They took her." Rabin backed up, scanning the palace, his mind recalculating as he quickly took stock of every window and exit.

"Shit! What do we do?"

"Come with me," Rabin said, spinning on his heel and stalking away.

FIFTY-ONE

Zarya awoke to a pounding in her head, her vision blurring and smearing against grey light. She lay face down on a hard surface, and if she listened carefully, she could hear the muffled din that signaled thousands of panicking voices.

She groaned and attempted to move, only to find someone had tied her hands behind her back. She wiggled numb fingers and twisted her wrists against the bite of rope.

Blinking heavily, she waited for her sight to clear before she took in her surroundings. The floor was marble, inlaid with colorful patterned tiles, and a long row of windows curved around the room in a gentle arc. She watched rain pelt the surface, tracks sliding down the glass.

The sky swirled with angry, grey clouds and a clap of thunder mingled with screams and shouts and the clash of steel against steel, shattering glass, and the roar of explosions.

Her chest tightened. Everything they'd been planning had gone completely wrong. This wasn't a protest, it had become a riot. A boiling pot that had been bubbling for a thousand years, finally spilling over to consume everything in its path.

They knew success had always been a thin hope. Everything they'd done had been pieced together with tattered thread and a whispered prayer. She just hadn't expected things to go quite *this* poorly.

The sharp click of footsteps drew her attention and she shifted, whimpering as a sharp stab of pain flashed over her scalp.

She looked up to find her half-sister standing over her.

"You are responsible for this?" she asked.

Zarya grunted, refusing to answer as she glared up at Dishani. A swift kick to her stomach had her crying out. She gasped for air as she curled into herself, partly from pain but also from the shock that her own flesh and blood would treat her with such naked viciousness.

"Answer me!" Dishani hissed. "You think you can show up here, take my crown, and upset *my* queendom. Who the hell do you think you are?" Her voice reached a fever pitch, echoing off the marble floors and ceiling, ringing in Zarya's ears. She coughed, gagging as she writhed on the floor.

"Answer me!"

Zarya sucked in deep breaths, any words she might conjure lodged in her chest.

Dishani circled her with slow steps as Zarya tried to scoot around, attempting to keep her sister in her line of sight. She was like a fish trapped on the beach, out of its environment, gasping for air on the scorching sand with no rescue in sight.

"*Who* are you?" Dishani asked again as she continued walking with her hands clasped at her waist, her pointed shoes kicking up the hem of her skirt. "Why do you wear *my* mother's necklace? *Why* do you possess nightfire?"

"She was my mother, too," Zarya finally choked out.

"Liar!" Dishani screamed.

Zarya shook her head as tears of frustration leaked from the corner of her eyes. "I'm not lying. You know I'm not."

Her sister crouched on her heels, her teeth bared and her

gaze sparking with fire. "Understand this, you little *worm*—you will never use that power ever again. I will kill everyone who knows. You will *not* get away with this."

Zarya struggled against her restraints as she met her sister's glare. She would not be cowed by this spineless princess.

"You came to Ishaan to incite this *rebellion* against me? I want the names of every member of the Rising Phoenix. I want to know where you operate from. I want to know every one of your plans."

"I will tell you nothing," Zarya said.

Dishani raised an eyebrow, her gaze turning from fiery rage to ice-cold pellets. She lifted a hand and sent out a tendril of magic. Zarya tried to get a sense of what was about to happen, noting the ribbon of spirit twisting with earth as it wrapped around her body and tightened.

Zarya screamed as acid lashes of pain ricocheted down her spine, her back arching and her feet scrambling against the smooth tiles. She screamed and screamed as her voice cracked, but Dishani never relented. Zarya felt like her organs were being squeezed, her bones crushed, and her skull compressed until her vision began to smear at the corners, the world tipping out from under her.

After what felt like an eternity, it stopped. Zarya panted heavily, a line of sweat dripping down her cheek and down the side of her throat.

"I will tell you *nothing*," Zarya valiantly gasped out once more. "Torture me all you want."

"Oh, we will see about that," Dishani said softly.

The venom in her sister's voice was the most chilling thing Zarya had ever heard.

FIFTY-TWO

"Where are you going?" Yasen called after Rabin as they shoved through the seething crowd out of the plaza and into the streets, where they found a little more breathing room.

Even if it was still a sight of chaos.

All their somewhat tenuous plans had fallen apart. But they hadn't lost everything yet.

The rain pelted them from above, rendering the world into grey, which felt ominously appropriate.

"We finish the plan," Rabin said, his fist curled and his frame hunched. "That's what she would want."

"And then what?" Yasen asked, jogging after him.

Rabin came to a stop and peered over his shoulder, heavy, angry breaths swirling in his chest. "And then I'm going to tear apart this fucking palace to find her."

Yasen nodded, and Rabin turned and continued walking until he found an open plaza.

"You have the papers?" Rabin asked, and Yasen nodded. They'd planned to distribute them once the prisoners had been freed, but this would have to do. "Then get on."

Without further warning, Rabin dissolved into a puff of

smoke, transforming into his dragon. Everyone within the area began screaming and running away. Rabin shook his head as his wings flapped, crushing the silver astrolabe at the center of the plaza. He lifted his head to the sky as cool rainwater sluiced over his scales.

Yasen ran and leaped onto his back before Rabin's wings flapped. He took a step, followed by another, and then launched himself into the sky. They soared over the city, circling over the palace courtyard, where the seething mass of bodies churned like waves.

He roared, drawing everyone's attention up. Maybe this would help snap everyone from their panic. Then he felt Yasen moving before thousands of pieces of paper floated over the air, littering Ishaan with the truth.

More screams rose up as thunder crashed overhead and lightning flashed across the sky.

The pages fluttered on the breeze like ashes scattering off a burning stake.

And from this day on, nothing in Rahajhan would ever be the same.

* * *

Zarya screamed. The sound ripped out of her in a breath of wretched agony. Dishani stood over her, glowering as she assaulted Zarya over and over again.

Pain. More and more of it as magic circled her limbs, sinking into her skin. They'd been at this for what felt like hours as the sky continued to rage and the world shrieked from every side. Desperately, she tried to reach Rabin, calling to him through her mind. But whether it was due to her dulled magic or something else, he remained frustratingly beyond her sight.

In the haze of her torment, she caught a fleeting glimpse of snow falling from the sky. Not snow. The pages they'd copied from *Age of Ashes* revealing the truth to the world. The vanshaj were Aazheri, and the Jadugara were built upon a smoldering heap of lies.

Zarya started laughing, verging on delirious as Dishani stopped, clearly confused by her behavior.

"What are you laughing at?" Dishani demanded and Zarya shook her head.

Her throat was raw, scraped dry by her screams. She could barely answer even if she wanted.

No matter what happened now, no matter what Dishani chose to do, the world would know the truth, and there would be no going back.

A door slammed, followed by hurried footsteps. Zarya watched as someone handed Dishani a damp piece of paper. Flurried whispers circled around the room as Dishani scanned the page. Zarya knew exactly what she was reading, and she began laughing again.

The sound drew Dishani's attention as her nostrils flared. She crumpled the page in her fist, crushing it into a soggy ball. She hurled it to the ground, but the effect was lost as it slapped the tile and settled in a wet lump.

Slowly, Dishani approached, and Zarya looked up to see the rage in the princess's face.

The deep-seated loathing. The anger. The *fear*.

Things hadn't gone according to plan. Zarya would die under her sister's hand, but she'd accomplished what she'd been sent into this world to do.

She'd been the catalyst. The striking point. The first step on a long road to redemption and retribution. Though she wouldn't get the chance to witness the outcome, at least she'd been there to give people hope.

To show them anything was possible.

That good *could* win over evil.

Dishani held out a hand, closing it into a tight fist, and then... pain.

White noise and black static and an endless spiraling tunnel flashing with muted color and tiny pulses of wretched, mind-numbing agony.

Zarya screamed again, the sound echoing against the back-drop of a revolution that had been brewing for a thousand long, bloody years.

FIFTY-THREE

Rabin picked up a chair and threw it across the room before he resumed his pacing. It had been over twenty-four hours since Zarya had been taken, and he was ready to climb out of his skin.

He'd tried to reach her inside the mind plane, but she'd refused his calls.

Or rather, she *couldn't* answer, sending him into a violent spiral.

He currently stood in the salon with several members of the Rising Phoenix.

"Where is she?!" he roared.

After Yasen had finished tossing the damning story of the Jadugara over Ishaan, they'd landed in the square as everyone scrambled to get away, fleeing to the sound of screams.

Rabin had started picking up guards and tossing them against the walls of the palace like rag dolls, reveling in the sick crunch of bone and skin meeting marble. It helped calm the seething churn in his gut. It also allowed Yasen to jump down and free the prisoners, untying their ropes and ushering them out of the square to safety.

Though Rabin had wanted to find *her*, he understood Zarya would have demanded everyone else be rescued first.

Methodically, Rabin picked off the remaining soldiers one by one as a few brave souls attempted to stand their ground. Eventually, they gave up, either escaping into the palace or the streets. Then he'd turned his attention to the palace. Their plans had collapsed under the weight of their mistakes. Instead of thousands of vanshaj tearing it apart brick by brick, they'd spread into the corners of Ishaan in a disorganized mess.

But the smell of smoke and the scent of ash in the air suggested they hadn't been idle. The royals had retreated inside, armed on every side, and now sat safely behind thick enchanted walls as the city crumbled bit by excruciating bit.

Rabin had bared his teeth, staring at the windows where guards stood watching him with dozens of crossbows aimed at his heart.

He'd wanted to rip the palace apart and find her, but he also knew that would be pointless. She could be anywhere inside the sprawling building, and there was no telling what they might do if he muscled his way in. As it was, he was walking a thin line. He had to think logically, something he'd always been a master of, but Zarya had been taken and it was testing every one of his carefully constructed defenses.

Inhaling a deep breath, he'd calmed himself enough to transform into his rakshasa form. Yasen had convinced him to wait for a message from Miraan and learn where they were keeping Zarya before they went in to take her back.

Now inside the manor, his rage wouldn't be contained.

"Where is she? Where is my *wife!*" Rabin roared as he picked up another chair, prepared to send this one through the window.

Row stepped in front of him with his hands raised. "We'll find her," he said. "This isn't helping anything."

Rabin's nostrils flared as he turned and hurled the chair at the wall, watching it smash apart. "It's helping me," he snarled before he began pacing again. He would kill every single Madan. Tear them limb from limb with a smile on his fucking face.

"I'm going," he said, stopping. "I can't wait here. I'll find her."

"Rabindranath, please," Row begged. "Let's find out where they're keeping her first."

The door banged open, and Suvanna entered.

"Where is she!" Rabin demanded, storming up until she was backed against the wall. It must have been a measure of his pathetic state that she didn't immediately shove him off.

"She's in the solarium," she said. "Dishani is currently torturing her for information about the Rising Phoenix."

A growl tore from Rabin's throat. "Torturing. Her."

"Yes." An uncharacteristic softness entered her eyes. "Miraan tried to intervene... but she's lost her mind..."

"Where is the solarium?" Yasen asked.

"The top of the palace."

"You mean the circular tower?" Rabin demanded. "With all the windows around it?"

"That's the one," Suvanna answered with a nod.

Rabin's mouth curled up at the corner. "Perfect."

"What are you planning?" Yasen demanded as he followed on Rabin's heels through the unruly streets of Ishaan.

"What do you think?" Rabin snapped over his shoulder, not slowing his pace. Head down and teeth clenched, he shoved his way through the packed sidewalks, not caring who he crushed. He was a man on the most important mission of his life, and he would die before he failed.

"Rabin! You can't just barge in there!" Yasen shouted as he

followed, trying to keep beside him through the churning crowds. Ishaan was collapsing around them, glass and debris littering the streets, and smoke filling the air, thanks to dozens of burning buildings.

He stopped so abruptly that Yasen crashed into his back before Rabin spun around. "Who the *fuck* is going to stop me?"

Yasen opened his mouth and then closed it. "I mean, that's a good point."

Rabin growled low in his throat as he continued marching. He turned a corner, revealing a less populated path. He needed somewhere open. He'd never liked dense, packed cities, but he'd never felt so much like a noose was tightening around his neck.

"You're planning to do the dragon thing?" Yasen asked.

"Yes. The dragon thing." He called over his shoulder, "I've waited out here long enough. Don't bother stopping me."

"So we're just barging in there," Yasen said, still loping along next to him.

"Not 'we'. I'm going alone," Rabin snarled. He'd been forced to rely on everyone during this botched mission, but the only one he had ever been able to count on was himself. He would do this on his own.

Yasen stopped walking.

"I love her, too!" he called.

That halted Rabin in his tracks.

He turned to face Yasen, who stood with his hands spread. "Let me help you."

Rabin sucked in a sharp breath and then nodded. He took two steps and clapped a hand on Yasen's shoulder. "And I haven't thanked you for taking care of her."

Yasen offered him a wry smile. "Well, someone had to after *you* royally fucked up."

Rabin huffed out a near laugh. "I promise I'll spend the rest of our lives making it up to her."

Then he turned around and continued walking, stopping in

the middle of a sparsely populated square, deciding this would have to do.

Spinning around, he turned to face Yasen. "Starting right now."

FIFTY-FOUR

Zarya writhed in agony on the hard floor. She wasn't sure how long she'd been lying here hungry, cold, tired, and *suffering*. It felt like a hundred years, but it might have been only minutes. She had no sense of time or place. She thought she remembered the sun setting and rising, but it was impossible to tell.

Dishani remained at her side most of the time, or maybe it just seemed that way because Zarya kept slipping into unconsciousness. Her sister's questions cycled between demanding information about the Rising Phoenix and Zarya herself.

Who are the members? Where do they meet? Who are you really? Why are you here?

But Zarya held out. She wouldn't give Dishani a single scrap of leverage against the resistance, and anything Zarya claimed about herself was met with dismissal and doubt.

During a brief respite, Zarya lay panting on the floor, sucking in air, trying to catch her breath as every muscle and bone in her body ached like she'd been stretched and scored from the inside out. She tried to reach for Rabin yet again, but was met with only a wall of nothing.

A circle of guards lined the room, some facing the windows

and some facing her with stony expressions. Sunlight filtered through the tall glass. She had just enough presence of mind to realize the rain had stopped.

She licked her dry, cracked lips, tasting blood and wishing for a drop of water. How far would Dishani go? Would she kill Zarya? Without her in the picture, Dishani's crown would remain uncontested, and she was still alive only because Dishani wanted information about the Rising Phoenix.

Which was another reason Zarya couldn't give in to her demands. Rabin would be looking for her. She just had to hold out long enough.

She scanned the room from her place on the floor, noting her sister had left. But she would return soon. Zarya groaned, hoping a guard would take pity on her and offer some water, but they stared straight ahead, pretending she wasn't there.

What had happened to the others? Where was Yasen? What had happened to the vanshaj? She heard no sounds of fighting inside the palace, suggesting their planned coup had failed. Her eyes fluttered closed as a wave of exhaustion nearly pulled her under. She'd cry if she had the strength.

She squeezed her eyes tighter at the sound of the door opening, listening for Dishani's slow, hard steps. How long had she been gone? Was it time for another round?

She sensed someone dropping in front of her and did her best not to whimper. What fresh hell did the princess have planned now?

"Zarya," came a soft whisper, and her eyes peeled open to find Miraan kneeling in her blurred vision. In his hand, he held a canteen of water. After unscrewing the lid, he held it to her mouth. She was too weak to sit up, and he tipped it gently, patiently waiting for her to take small sips as a cold trickle dribbled down her chin.

"We don't have long before someone tells my sister I'm here," Miraan said. "I'm only getting away with this because of who I am. But help is coming, Zarya. They're coming." He said the last words so softly she wasn't even sure she'd heard them. She looked up to meet his gaze, noticing he also had that line between his eyebrows that formed when he was worried. Just like Zarya. Just like that image she'd seen of Asha in Row's bedroom all those months ago.

She wanted to say something to him about family and how she'd first come to Gi'ana with so much hope. She wanted to tell him how much she'd always wanted a brother or a sister.

"I'm sorry," he said, running a thumb over the arch of her eyebrow as if he understood what she was thinking. "I'm sorry that we weren't what you wished for."

She felt her eyes fill with tears as she slowly shook her head.

The door opened again, and Zarya whimpered.

"What are you doing?" Dishani asked, her steps ringing against the marble. "You're *helping* her?"

Miraan stood and faced his sister, the canteen clutched in one hand and the other gesturing to Zarya. "What am *I* doing? How can you treat her this way?"

Dishani's eyes narrowed. "She deserves this."

Miraan exhaled a short breath that sounded like a mixture of disbelief and disappointment. "She's our *sister*. Mother would be so ashamed of you right now."

Dishani took a step towards her brother. "Don't presume to tell me what Mother would want. She *abandoned* us."

"She didn't have a choice!" Miraan shouted.

"You don't know that!"

"She would never have willingly left us!"

Dishani leaned back, her mouth pressing into a thin line before hissing, "No, but she *would* have a secret child and try to ensure I never got my crown."

"You're wrong," Miraan said. "That wasn't what she did."

"How could you know that?"

Miraan hesitated and then looked down at Zarya before he dropped to his haunches.

"Can I tell her?" he asked, and Zarya hesitated for a second before giving the slightest nod. She knew the information would make no difference to Dishani. She had already proven what kind of woman she was, but maybe, just maybe, she'd realize that Zarya had never come here to take anything from her.

"Tell me what?" Dishani demanded. "What is going on? Do you... *know* her?"

"I know her. And I know everything about her," he answered, peering up.

Confusion crossed Dishani's face. "Know what? How?"

Miraan inhaled a deep breath. "I'm the one who freed her and the others from the dungeon."

Zarya felt what those words had just cost both of them as the drag of steel signaled every guard around the room drawing their swords. Miraan stood as her only ally in this place, and now he'd just revealed the side he'd been playing all along.

"You betrayed me?" Dishani snarled, taking a threatening step towards him.

"You have become something ugly. You are not the sister I grew up with. Who I admired once. You've made all your insecurities everyone else's problem."

A crack filled the air as Dishani slapped Miraan so hard his head whipped to the side. Zarya watched as he blinked heavily several times before he turned to face the princess.

"I *knew* you were attempting to usurp me!" Dishani screamed and then kicked Zarya in the stomach with a sharp toe. Already bruised from so many earlier blows, it layered fresh pain over the agony already searing her bones. Zarya groaned as she curled into a ball.

"Stop that!" Miraan said. "Mother *loved* her. She sent her away to protect her. She did it to shield her from her father, but perhaps she was also protecting her from you. Maybe Mother knew what a disgraceful queen you'd eventually become!"

"*Her* father?" Dishani seethed, and for the first time since Zarya had the displeasure of meeting her half-sister, something wavered in her confidence.

Miraan then shared the story of Zarya's life and her upbringing as Dishani listened, open-mouthed. When the prince finished speaking, Dishani studied Zarya with an expression she couldn't interpret.

"These are lies," Dishani said a moment later, but she seemed to be clinging to those words. If she continued denying them, then they couldn't be true.

"No," Zarya croaked. "It's true. Return my necklace."

Dishani hesitated.

"Please," Zarya said. "I will prove it to you."

"Dishani, do it," Miraan said. "It will prove everything I'm saying is real."

The princess's mouth opened and then closed. It was obvious she didn't want to cooperate. It was obvious she wanted to throw them both from this tower and watch their bodies crack on the stones below.

"If there is an ounce of decency left in you, then listen to me," Miraan said.

Dishani swallowed, slowly reached into her skirt pocket, and pulled out Zarya's chain, the dangling turquoise stone flashing in the light.

"Channel spirit into it," Zarya croaked. Row suspected only Zarya would be able to make the stone speak, but she was hoping someone of her mother's blood would be enough.

Dishani gave her a skeptical look but did as she asked and wrapped a delicate thread of golden light around the necklace.

When her mother's voice floated out of the stone, Zarya breathed a sigh of relief.

The words she'd listened to so many times circled around

them, making the air shift. She remembered that night on Ranpur Island when she'd first discovered the prophecy, and her entire world had changed. She felt that same change again.

After the stone went silent, Dishani stared at her as her hand lowered to her side.

"The one to free them all," she said hollowly.

"I'm not here to take your crown," Zarya whispered. "That was never what I wanted."

Dishani blinked, her brows furrowing. "No, but you want to free the vanshaj. Destroy this city and this queendom. Perhaps all of Rahajhan. One way or another, you *will* take my crown."

Despair collapsed in Zarya's chest. Even if she didn't want the crown, she *had* attempted to upset the order of everything.

"You can't keep them caged any longer," Zarya whispered. "Your rule was built on the suffering of others. You never deserved this."

"How dare you!" Dishani hissed. She took a step, preparing to deliver another blow to Zarya's stomach when Miraan grabbed her by the arm and tugged her so hard she stumbled.

"Stop this!" he shouted. "Stop tormenting her and *listen*. Do something better with your power. Leave her alone. Free the vanshaj. Stop this madness!"

"You..." Dishani said, looking Miraan up and down. "I trusted you."

"I've been funding the Rising Phoenix," he said, his voice dropping to a cold whisper. "For *years*. I carry tainted dark magic and helped free *thousands* of them." He pointed towards the window. "And I would do it again and again."

Dishani blinked as her face turned pale. She didn't move for several seconds as she absorbed the enormity of what he'd just confessed.

Then she snapped. "Guards!" she screamed. "Arrest him for treason!"

The queensguard stirred into action, and Miraan was seized

by each arm as he was surrounded on every side. They were both lost.

Dishani held the power in this city, and they never stood a chance.

Zarya was never leaving this place.

She *would* die here at her own sister's hand.

She sobbed as she thought about the life she'd never get to enjoy with Rabin.

At everything she'd just lost.

Every time she took a step towards her future, someone came in to sweep it all away.

She curled further into herself, tears coating her cheeks.

And that's when a dark shadow fell over the room.

FIFTY-FIVE

Rabin soared over the city with Yasen clinging to his back, his focus trained on the enchanted blue palace in the distance.

From this vantage, he noted a giant plume of smoke billowing across the sky, realizing it was the ink factory. In spite of everything, Rabin smiled to himself. This had always been his plan B. One he'd shared only with Vikas. They would hit the royal family through a different artery if things went off course.

The palace raid had failed, but everything wasn't lost.

Circling over the factory, he let out a roar of triumph before turning and aiming for the solarium tower, banking left as he made a wide loop. He could make out soldiers guarding the perimeter, all of them facing inward.

He swept around, doubling back, trying to get a sense of Zarya's position. His dragon eyesight was superior to even that of his rakshasa form, and he made out the edges of a group huddled in the center of the room.

Miraan was on his knees with his hands tied behind his back while Zarya lay on the floor, her hair spilling over the tiles as her vile sister stood over them both. He brushed close enough that his wing grazed the window, scraping along the surface. Everyone looked up, the guards finally taking note of the danger lurking outside.

They began tracking his movements as he circled again, drawing in closer. Then he tipped his head up, stretched his jaw, and roared so loud it shook the very clouds in the sky.

Yasen bellowed out a triumphant whoop.

"Let's get our girl!" he screamed, and then Rabin dove, bracing himself for the impact before he hit the glass. The windows shattered around him into a thousand fragments, scattering like dandelion seeds on the wind.

He felt a brief press on his back as Yasen leaped off and landed in a crouch. The guards were already rushing towards him as Rabin's massive form skidded over the smooth marble, coming to a stop directly over Zarya.

He swung his head, circling it around the room and exhaling a burst of pure blue fire.

* * *

Zarya watched as the massive shadow blocked out the sun. She didn't fear what swooped past the window because she knew. He'd come for her. He would tear apart the world to find her. Of course he would.

Another pass of shadow darkened the windows, and she heard the scrape of a wing grazing the glass along with everyone's surprised whispers.

Then came the crash—glass exploding, people shouting, Dishani's scream as Rabin crouched over Zarya, exactly like a dragon protecting his hoard.

Blue fire and the boiling rage of his vengeance.

She drifted in and out as she felt the air shift, and then he was back in his rakshasa form as he circled around her, fighting off the guards and keeping her safe and protected.

She saw Yasen out of the corner of her eye, fighting furiously with all his cunning and strength. Yasen, who'd followed her across the continent without a word of complaint. Yasen, who deserved every bit of happiness the world might give him.

She caught his eye and he nodded. In his eyes, she read his silent message.

We're getting you out of here, Zee. Hang on.

She returned his nod and didn't even try to stop her tears.

It took Zarya a moment to realize someone was screaming in high-pitched, wretched agony. She rallied her strength and pushed herself up to discover it was coming from Dishani.

She was screaming in pain. In horror because she was now a truly gruesome sight. The left side of her face and her arm were charred and bubbling, and her sari was melting into her skin.

Zarya covered her mouth as bile surged up her throat, sure she was about to be sick.

"Stop them!" Dishani screamed with her remaining strength, but it came out garbled before she collapsed to the floor.

Then Zarya felt a pair of strong arms lift her. Rabin cradled her against his warm body, and she curled into him, absorbing the comfort of his presence.

"Take her," she heard him say as she was passed into another pair of arms. "Keep her safe."

"I've got you, Zee," Yasen murmured as he pressed his lips to her forehead. "She can't hurt you anymore."

Then they were moving.

She was propped onto Rabin's back behind Miraan before Yasen sandwiched her from the other side. Together they kept her from sliding off as she veered on the edge of consciousness.

She heard the continued clash of weapons and tried to open her eyes, but it was all a blur.

And then... she felt the flap of Rabin's wings, followed by a blast of cool air.

They launched into the sky, soaring over the world before everything went dark.

FIFTY-SIX

Zarya drifted in and out of consciousness as the cold wind tore at her hair and clothing. She felt Yasen's warm arms circle her as she leaned back, tipping her head against his shoulder. Rabin circled in a wide arc, flapping his wings steadily.

When she felt him dip, losing altitude, she had no idea how much time had passed. They landed on the ground with a gentle thump. Her limbs hung loose and pliant like someone had pulled out her bones as she was guided off Rabin's back by careful hands.

Then she felt herself transferred into his arms as she inhaled his fresh, earthy scent.

"Rab—" she tried to say as he hugged her closer.

"Shh," he said softly. "You're safe now."

Then he started walking as a dark haze settled over her vision, her mind sluggish like her head had been stuffed with cotton.

She heard voices and doors opening and closing before she was laid on a soft bed.

Briefly, her unfocused gaze took in a small dark room she didn't recognize before she once again drifted off.

. . .

When she awoke, it was to the welcoming, warm smell of food and a roaring fire. She blinked, noting the small window above her and the frost glazing the panes. The walls were constructed of wide planks of honeyed wood, and she was covered with a dark blue blanket woven of the softest wool.

Rabin sat next to the bed in a plush armchair, his hands clasped and his head angled against his shoulder in sleep. His hair was wild, his clothes covered in blood, and a crusted scar marred his cheek. She stared at him, hardly daring to believe he was here. Some part of her thought she'd never see him again.

But he'd come. No one would ever keep them apart.

A glass of water sat on the bedside, and she reached for it, groaning when her joints and muscles seized. Rabin's eyes flew open, his head snapping up.

Zarya paused, her hand in midair, as she noted the dark ferocity in his expression. Then he blinked, and it cleared. Immediately, he was up.

"Zarya," he breathed as he fell to one knee. She wrapped her arms around him and dropped her face into the curve of his neck. "I was so fucking scared." His big hand cupped the back of her head as they held one another, breathing in each other's scent.

She thought she'd used up every tear she'd ever had, but now they resurfaced, burning in her throat and eyes.

These were the soothing tears of relief, not ones of terror and failure. He squeezed her tighter, enough that she felt it in the deep ache of her bones, but she didn't care.

"You can't get rid of me that easily," she whispered.

"I'll kill her," he said in a voice that shivered through the room. "I'll make her suffer and then I will kill her."

"You hurt her."

He exhaled a sharp breath. "It isn't nearly enough."

She pulled up and looked at him.

It would take some time for Zarya to sort through her feelings for her sister. Dishani had crossed every line, and Zarya knew it was foolish and naive to still hope something good was buried somewhere inside her. The princess had been scared, backed into a corner. She'd been faced with her greatest fears when Zarya had dropped into her life.

Maybe it had been her fault. Maybe so much of this could have been avoided if she'd just gone to them when she'd first arrived in Ishaan and explained who she was.

"Tell me everything that happened?" Zarya asked, just as a knock came at the door.

It swung open and she sobbed at the sight of Yasen and his soft smile.

"Zee," he whispered before he dropped next to Rabin on the floor. She reached for his hand and squeezed it.

"You both came for me," she said in a raw voice.

"I'd follow you anywhere," Yasen replied, and she nodded.

"I know. I would follow you, too, Yas."

He returned the squeeze of her hand, pressing his forehead to the back as he inhaled a deep breath.

They explained everything briefly while she sipped on her water before lying back on her pillow. She wasn't sure if she'd ever been more tired in her life, and sitting up was a struggle.

Another knock interrupted their conversation and Miraan appeared at the door with a tray balanced in his hands. She couldn't believe how relieved she was to see him, too.

"Do you want something to eat?" he asked, holding it up with a hopeful expression. Yasen had already explained how much guilt her half-brother was feeling for everything she'd suffered under Dishani's hand.

"Miraan," Zarya said. "Come in. It's so good to see you."

He entered and placed the tray on the nightstand. On it sat a bowl of soup, some bread, and a plate of fruit. Her stomach rumbled, and she reached for the bread, tearing off a piece with her teeth.

"I'm so sorry," he said, pressing a hand to his chest. He'd lost that polished air, his hair hanging loosely, and his clothing rumpled. "For everything she did. I knew she was ambitious, but I've never seen her like that. She became a monster."

"It's not your fault," Zarya said. "There is nothing to forgive. You tried to help."

"Not quickly enough," he answered, and she shook her head.

"Please don't blame yourself."

Miraan nodded, though she could tell he wasn't convinced.

"You should rest," Rabin said. "After you eat something."

There was no room for argument in his voice, so she allowed him to spoon-feed her soup until he was satisfied. Eventually, Yasen and Miraan drifted away, and Rabin took off his boots and his bloody clothing before climbing into the bed and wrapping her in his arms.

She buried her face in his chest, inhaling his presence.

"Where are we?" she asked.

"On the edge of the Saaya."

She exhaled a soft, surprised breath. They'd traveled further than she thought, but she was too tired to give it much thought right now.

"I love you," she whispered.

"I love you, too, Spitfire. Now get some rest."

Then the last thing she remembered was the press of his lips to the top of her head before she slipped into a deep sleep.

Over the next few days, Rabin, Yasen, and Miraan helped nurse her back to health. At first, she slept a lot, waiting for the worst of the bruising to subside, slowly regaining her strength.

They were lodging inside a remote inn on the northern

border of Gi'ana, used by travelers crossing the Saaya. It sat empty except for themselves and the friendly couple who ran the place.

During her recovery, reports from Ishaan filed in.

"What's the latest?" Rabin asked Miraan one afternoon when Zarya was feeling a little more herself. She sat on the bed, leaning against the wall with Rabin at her side. Yasen and Miraan occupied two chairs facing them.

"She's still alive," Miraan confirmed. "She's been seriously injured, but she has access to the best healers in Gi'ana and should eventually recover." He looked up at Zarya. "And when she does, she will be more furious and determined to kill both of us than ever. You are her greatest threat, and I betrayed her. She won't allow us to live."

Zarya swallowed a tangled knot in her throat.

"The ink factory is in ruins," Miraan continued. "They'll have to start rebuilding yet again. The riots continue throughout the city and chaos rules. With my sister out of commission, I do fear for what will happen next. My father has little interest in ruling and my other siblings have no experience managing the queendom."

"What about the others?" Zarya asked. "Is everyone okay?"

"I received a message from Vikas," Yasen said. "Ajay and all the others made it back unharmed. Suvanna and Apsara are living at the manor now and have abandoned the palace." Seeing the question on Zarya's face, he added, "Row is fine, too. He hopes you're okay and that he can see you soon."

"When can we go back?" Zarya asked. "We have to check on everyone. We have to finish what we started."

That's when Rabin, Yasen, and Miraan all shared a look.

"What?" Zarya demanded. "What aren't you telling me?"

"We don't think it would be smart to return to Ishaan yet," Rabin said. "Did you reveal anything about the Rising Phoenix to Dishani?"

Zarya shook her head. "No, I don't think so."

"Then Vikas and the others will have to operate without you for a while."

She shook her head. "But the city is in chaos! We can't just leave them to it."

"Zarya," Rabin said. "We will go back. But I think we should let Dishani think you and your brother have left Ishaan for now."

She huffed out a breath. She understood his point but hated that it had come to this. "I don't want to abandon them," she replied, her voice small and uncertain.

"We're not," he promised. "We will finish this. But we can't do anything if you're dead."

"So, where are we hiding?" Yasen asked. "We shouldn't remain here much longer."

They shared a look and Rabin slid off the bed, falling to his knees and taking her hand. "Let's go to Andhera. Your father will shield us from anything Dishani can throw at us."

Zarya stared at Rabin as her stomach dropped.

Andhera. Her father.

"And it's not so great a distance that we can't easily return when the time is right," he urged. "Consider it."

Zarya shook her head. "I'm not sure."

"I swear you will be safe. I won't let anything happen to you."

She checked in with Yasen, who gave her a look that suggested he would do what she thought was best.

"Maybe. I need to think about it."

Zarya's boots crunched over the snow as she crested a ridge offering her a sprawling view of the Saaya and, beyond that, the dark Pathara Vala Mountains looming in the distance, their peaks so high they were lost to the clouds.

She shivered as the wind tore through her thick woolen cloak, and she pulled her fur collar tighter. Already her cheeks and the tip of her nose were growing numb, but she relished this sensation. After her brush with death, it felt like being reborn as the fresh, icy air filled her lungs.

It was time to leave. She was mostly recovered but for some minor bruising and some aches and pains. There wasn't any reason she couldn't travel.

But indecision delayed them.

Their options were few.

Anywhere they might run, someone would find them.

Except perhaps... north.

They'd be protected behind Raja Abishek's walls even if their location was uncovered.

She peered into the distance, over the miles of forest stretching as far as an ocean. It was hard to comprehend how vast it was.

He was out there. And if Rabin was to be believed, he was waiting for her.

Her father. The man who might be able to answer questions about her magic she couldn't bring herself to ask anyone else.

The wind whipped strands of hair across her cheeks as she stared ahead.

A few minutes later, the crunch of snow sounded behind her.

She didn't need to turn around to know who it would be.

Rabin stood beside her, also dressed in a cloak, fur blanketing his shoulders.

She looked over at him, remembering the night in the forest when he appeared to her like her own warrior god. The wind tossed his hair as he slowly met her gaze.

"What are you doing out here?" he asked.

"Just thinking." She turned to face the horizon once again.

Together, they stood side by side, comfortable in their silence.

"You're sure it's safe?" she asked, keeping her eyes trained on the distance.

"No less so than returning to Ishaan."

She almost smiled. Of course, he wouldn't sugarcoat this.

"If I'm wrong, then I'll spend every breath in my body keeping you safe, Zarya."

She nodded as she pulled her arms tighter against a gusting wind. "I know that."

Finally, she looked at him, studying the outline of his profile against the snowy landscape.

He turned to her and she nodded.

"Then take me to Andhera," she whispered. "Take me to my father."

A LETTER FROM NISHA

Dear Reader,

I want to say a huge thank you for choosing to read *Storm of Ink and Blood*. If you enjoyed it and want to keep up to date with all my latest releases, just sign up at the following link. Your email address will never be shared, and you can unsubscribe at any time.

www.secondskybooks.com/nisha-j-tuli

If you loved *Storm of Ink and Blood*, please consider leaving a review on your favorite platform. And if you'd like to get in touch, I love hearing from readers! You can join my Facebook reader group, send me an email on my website, or message me on Instagram.

Love,

Nisha

KEEP IN TOUCH WITH NISHA

www.nishajtuli.com

facebook.com/NishaJT

instagram.com/nishajtwrites

tiktok.com/@nishajtwrites

PUBLISHING TEAM

Turning a manuscript into a book requires the efforts of many people. The publishing team at Bookouture would like to acknowledge everyone who contributed to this publication.

Audio
Alba Proko
Melissa Tran
Sinead O'Connor

Commercial
Lauren Morrissette
Hannah Richmond
Imogen Allport

Cover design
Andrew Davis

Data and analysis
Mark Alder
Mohamed Bussuri

Editorial
Jack Renninson
Melissa Tran

Copyeditor
Angela Snowden

Proofreader
Catherine Lenderi

Marketing
Alex Crow
Melanie Price
Occy Carr
Cíara Rosney
Martyna Młynarska

Operations and distribution
Marina Valles
Stephanie Straub
Joe Morris

Production
Hannah Snetsinger
Mandy Kullar
Jen Shannon
Ria Clare

Publicity
Kim Nash
Noelle Holten
Jess Readett
Sarah Hardy

Rights and contracts
Peta Nightingale
Richard King
Saidah Graham

Printed in the USA
CPSIA information can be obtained
at www.ICGtesting.com
LVHW091752101024
793452LV00002B/173